Praise for #1 *New York Times* bestselling author
Robyn Carr

"A remarkable storyteller."
—*Library Journal*

"Strong conflict, humor and well-written characters
are Carr's calling cards."
—*RT Book Reviews*

"This is one author who proves a Carr can fly."
—*Book Reviewer* on *Blue Skies*

**Praise for *USA TODAY* bestselling author
Christine Rimmer**

"Appealing characters, comfortable pacing and plenty
of passion demonstrate just why Christine Rimmer is
such a fan favorite."
—*RT Book Reviews*

"What distinguishes this story is the level of
psychological insight displayed by [Ms. Rimmer]
and the lovely way she dramatizes the characters'
discovery that they are more like each other than they
know…. [The] characters enjoy a relationship that is
as deliciously physical as it is deeply emotional."
—*The Romance Reader* on *A Hero for Sophie Jones*

ROBYN CARR

is a RITA® Award-winning, #1 *New York Times* bestselling author of more than forty novels, including the critically acclaimed Virgin River series. Robyn and her husband live in Las Vegas, Nevada. You can visit Robyn Carr's website at www.robyncarr.com.

CHRISTINE RIMMER

came to her profession the long way around. Before settling down to write about the magic of romance, she'd been everything from an actress to a salesclerk to a waitress. Now that she's finally found work that suits her perfectly, she insists she never had a problem keeping a job—she was merely gaining "life experience" for her future as a novelist. Christine is grateful not only for the joy she finds in writing, but for what waits when the day's work is through: a man she loves who loves her right back, and the privilege of watching their children grow and change day to day. She lives with her family in Oregon. Visit Christine at www.christinerimmer.com.

#1 *New York Times* Bestselling Author

ROBYN CARR

Informed Risk

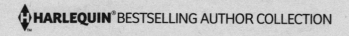

HARLEQUIN®BESTSELLING AUTHOR COLLECTION

If you purchased this book without a cover you should be aware that this book is stolen property. It was reported as "unsold and destroyed" to the publisher, and neither the author nor the publisher has received any payment for this "stripped book."

Recycling programs for this product may not exist in your area.

ISBN-13: 978-0-373-18075-2

INFORMED RISK
Copyright © 2013 by Harlequin Books S.A.

The publisher acknowledges the copyright holders of the individual works as follows:

INFORMED RISK
Copyright © 1989 by Robyn Carr

A HERO FOR SOPHIE JONES
Copyright © 1998 by Christine Rimmer

All rights reserved. Except for use in any review, the reproduction or utilization of this work in whole or in part in any form by any electronic, mechanical or other means, now known or hereafter invented, including xerography, photocopying and recording, or in any information storage or retrieval system, is forbidden without the written permission of the publisher, Harlequin Enterprises Limited, 225 Duncan Mill Road, Don Mills, Ontario M3B 3K9, Canada.

This is a work of fiction. Names, characters, places and incidents are either the product of the author's imagination or are used fictitiously, and any resemblance to actual persons, living or dead, business establishments, events or locales is entirely coincidental.

This edition published by arrangement with Harlequin Books S.A.

For questions and comments about the quality of this book, please contact us at CustomerService@Harlequin.com.

® and TM are trademarks of Harlequin Enterprises Limited or its corporate affiliates. Trademarks indicated with ® are registered in the United States Patent and Trademark Office, the Canadian Trade Marks Office and in other countries.

Printed in U.S.A.

HARLEQUIN®
www.Harlequin.com

CONTENTS

Dear Reader,

Firefighter Mike Cavanaugh has rescued plenty of people without getting all tangled up in their personal lives, but when he meets Christine Palmer, homeless young single mother with two little kids and a cranky dog, everything about his life and work changes with the beat of a heart.

I love firefighters. I've always loved firefighters as much as I admire and respect them. They're our everyday heroes, the men and women who daily put their lives on the line, doing the people's work to keep their communities safe. It's been quite a while since I originally wrote this story, but my opinion of the men and women who daily save lives and bring comfort to those in need has only grown stronger, more esteemed. Their techniques and procedures may have improved over the years, but their values and commitments are those same powerful driving forces that created Mike Cavanaugh for *Informed Risk*.

This reissue marks the third time *Informed Risk* and the story of courage, faith, love and intrepid spirit comes to you. Mike Cavanaugh is the same relentless hero; Christine Palmer the proud and brave young woman who captures his heart.

Welcome back! The encore is as much fun as the first run!

Robyn Carr

INFORMED RISK

#1 *New York Times* Bestselling Author

Robyn Carr

For Beth Gibson, with affection.

Chapter 1

Chris heard a loud thump. The furnace had turned on; soon warmth would begin to flow through the rickety little house. She wrinkled her nose, then remembered that heaters always smelled of burning dust and soot the first day they operated. She returned her fingers to the laptop keys, and her concentration to the last chapter of her story about a twelve-year-old boy named Jake. After seven rewrites, Jake was finally about to enjoy some resolution to the previous 122 pages of pubescent tribulation he'd suffered in his first year of junior high school.

This was her fourth attempt at a young adult novel, and Chris knew she was getting closer. Of earlier attempts editors had used such words as *brisk, lively, smooth*. Also words such as *awkward, unresolved, clumsy in places*.

She stopped typing and wrinkled her nose again. Should it smell *that* bad? She had asked the landlord if the furnace should be serviced or cleaned before she set the thermostat, but he'd assured her it was fine. Of course, he said everything was fine, and this old rat-trap was anything but. To be fair, she had never actually seen a rat, but she *had* swept up plenty of suspicious little pebbles, which she assumed were mouse turds. The traps she set, however, remained—thank you, God—abandoned.

She and the children had made do with oven heat until now, waiting as long as possible before turning on central heat. Utility bills were hard on a Christmas budget, and, when you got right down to it, hers was hardly a budget. But the temperature might drop to freezing tonight, and sleeping bags alone wouldn't keep the kids warm.

She looked at the kitchen clock. Nearly midnight. Her eyes were scratchy, but tonight she was determined to finish the last chapter. To be published...finally? Much of this great push, she had to admit, was for Jake himself, a great kid who deserved a resolution that was not awkward or clumsy in places. As did she.

As for publishing, the responses she collected had been consistently more encouraging, asking her to send future work. "Write what you know," a writing instructor had advised. Chris certainly knew what it was like to be twelve, to be struggling for self-reliance while simultaneously fighting feelings of incompetence. She knew this dilemma even better at twenty-seven.

The shrill siren of the smoke detector interrupted her musings. The sound wrapped strangling fingers around her heart and squeezed. Stunned, she looked up from the gridlock of library books, photocopied magazine articles and her laptop on the kitchen table. Through the kitchen door, her wide eyes quickly scanned the little living room with its two beanbag chairs, old television, clutter of secondhand toys and card table littered with the remnants of the macaroni-and-cheese dinner she had given the kids hours earlier.

And there, from the floor vents in the living room, poured smoke.

She bolted from the chair, fairly leaped to turn off the thermostat and raced into her kids' room. She grabbed one in each arm—five-year-old Carrie and three-year-old Kyle.

"There's a fire in the house," she said, hustling them through the thick smoke and toward the door. "We have to get outside, quick." As she rushed past the smoking vents, she prayed the situation wasn't as grim as it looked. Maybe it was only dirt? Soot? Dead bugs? But she didn't pause in her flight out the front door.

Only when they were safely outside did she stop to take stock of her predicament. The neighborhood was dark. Even in broad daylight it left something to be desired; at night it seemed almost threatening. There was not so much as a yard light shining. Her seven-year-old Honda sat on the street, and she opened the car door, nearly threw the kids inside and reached into the back seat for a blanket. "Wrap up in this, Carrie. Wrap Kyle up, too. Come on, that's a girl. I have to get someone to call the fire department. Don't get out of the car. Don't. Do you hear?"

Kyle started to whimper, rubbing his eyes. Carrie pulled the blanket around her little brother and nodded to her mother. Then she began to comfort Kyle with little crooning, motherly sounds of "'s'okay...'s'okay...."

Chris slammed the car door shut and ran to the house next door. Like her own house, it was small, ramshackle and in need of a paint job. She rang the bell and pounded on the front door. After a minute or two she gave up, ran to the house across the street and began ringing and pounding and yelling. She was panicked. How long do you wait for someone to get up? She jumped from one foot to the other, cursing her decision to cancel her cell phone because it cost too much money. No light came on at this house, either. "Come on, c'mon! Anybody home?" The porch light across the street went on, where she had begun. "Damn," she muttered, turning away from the door to run. The porch light behind her came on. "Jeez," she hissed, doubling back.

A sleepy, unshaven and angry-looking man opened the door. He was holding his robe closed over boxer shorts. That was when Chris remembered she was wearing only an extralarge T-shirt, moccasins and her undies. Purple silk undies, to be precise. That was it.

"Call the fire department," she begged her unsavory-looking neighbor. "The furnace is on fire. My kids are in my car. Hurry. Hurry!"

She turned and ran back to her car. She opened the door. "Are you okay?" They looked like two little birds peeking out from under the blanket.

"Mommy, what about Cheeks?" Carrie asked.

"Cheeks is in the backyard, sweetie. He's okay." She lifted her head to listen. "He's barking. Hear him?"

Carrie nodded, and her yellow curls bounced. "Can Cheeks come in the car with us?"

"I'll get him in a minute. You stay right here. Promise?" Again Carrie nodded. "I'll be right back. The fire truck is on its way. Pretty soon you'll hear the siren."

"Will our house burn down?"

"Burn down?" Kyle echoed.

"It'll be okay. Stay here now. I'll be right back."

Chris knew it was stupid to go back into a burning building; people died that way. But under these circumstances, she rationalized, it wasn't entirely stupid. First of all, she had seen only smoke, no other evidence of a bona fide fire. Second, the house was so tiny that the kitchen table, where her laptop and all her research lay, couldn't be more than ten steps inside the front door, which she intended to leave open in the event she had to make a fast getaway. Third, she wasn't going inside unless it looked relatively safe.

She heard the distant trill of the siren. The station was only about a mile away. She would be quick. And the smoke was not terrible, not blinding or choking. She had a plan.

She filled her lungs with clean air and bolted toward the kitchen. Even if the whole house burned to a cinder, the refrigerator would remain intact, like the bathtub in a tornado, right? Since she couldn't possibly gather up all her materials and her laptop and get them out of the house in one trip, she opened the refrigerator door and started heaving papers into it. It wasn't even supposed to be a long book. How had she ended up with so much stuff? And the books—the sourcebooks and expensive reference volumes—went in next. One marked Sacramento Public Library landed in the butter dish, but she didn't have time for neatness. She yanked out a half gallon of two-percent milk to make room for a pile of photocopied pages—the sirens were getting closer—

and replaced a jug of apple juice with the large, old dictionary she had gotten at a garage sale. The sirens seemed to be winding down.

Suddenly Chris started feeling woozy. The laptop, she thought dimly. Could she carry it out? But things started to blur. She looked toward the vents. That sucker, she thought remotely, was really smokin'....

The first fire engine stopped behind an old green Honda, and the men sprang off. The truck with ladders and hydraulics was right behind. As his men pulled a hose to a hydrant, Captain Mike Cavanaugh glanced at the burning house and approached the man in boxer shorts and a ratty bathrobe who stood on the curb. The furnace, he'd been told. He saw heat waves come off the roof. A furnace fire could have started in the basement, but in these old houses without fire-stops there could be an attic fire already. The ladder company would go up. Over his shoulder he called, "Take the peanut line in to fog it, and we'll open up the top." Then he turned to the bathrobed man. "Anyone in the house?"

"It ain't my house. Some woman's house. She's only lived there a couple of months. Them's her kids, there."

"Did you call it in?"

"Yeah, she was pounding on my door, said her furnace was on fire and her kids was in the car."

Mike felt someone tugging on his coat, and looked down. The face that stared up at him jarred him, almost cut through him. A little blond girl with the face of an angel, a face something inside him seemed to remember. She wore pajamas with feet, and beside her was a similarly attired little boy, one hand dragging a blanket and one hand holding on to his sister's pajamas.

"Our mother's in the house," she said. "She told us to stay in the car."

"Then you'd better get back in the car," he said. "I'll get your mother." He spoke gently, but he broke into a run, pulling at the mouthpiece of his air pack so he could cover his face. "There's a woman in there," he informed a firefighter nearby. "Number 56 will initiate rescue. Take over incident command." The man, Jim Eble, turned to pass the word.

"Women," Mike muttered. Women invariably thought there was something worth saving in a fire. Usually a purse or some jewelry, but sometimes they were goofy enough to go back after a pair of shoes, or a robe.

Even these thoughts left him totally unprepared for what he found just steps inside the front door: a small woman, her thick, wavy hair in a fat ponytail, wearing only slippers, an oversize T-shirt and purple—yes, purple—silk underwear. He knew about the underwear because she was actually bending over, digging in the refrigerator, in a house cloudy with smoke.

He tapped her on the shoulder. "What are you, hungry?" Through his mask it came out something like "Bflust uurrr doooo, flungee?"

When she turned toward him he instantly recognized the ashen pallor and the glassy eyes. She coughed, her knees buckled, and he put his hands on her waist. She folded over his shoulder like a duffel bag. He supposed she might toss her cookies down his back; it wouldn't be the first time.

He pointed that purple silk rump toward the front door. It was right beside his ear, creating an indelible impression even in the midst of chaos.

Once he got her outside, he put her down by the rear of the engine and pulled down his mask. "Anyone else in the house?" he barked.

"Cheeks…is in…" she wheezed and choked "…the backyard."

"Cheeks?" he asked.

"Dog…wirehaired terrier," she managed. She gagged and fell against Jim, who held her shoulders and backed her up to the tailboard of the engine so she could sit down.

"I'll get the dog," Mike said to his friend. "Furnace is in the basement. We'll have to go down. Right smack in the middle of the house. That's not a new roof." He headed toward the backyard.

"Here," said Jim, pushing a mask toward Chris. "You'll feel a little better after some oxygen."

Chris decided this fireman was much gentler than the one who'd deposited her on the sidewalk. But his voice seemed to become smaller and more distant as her head whirled and her stomach flipped. She abruptly leaned away from him and lost her dinner and several cups of coffee in the street. Bracing a hand on the tailboard, she heaved and shuddered. The man handed her a bunch of gauze four-by-fours to wipe her mouth. "Sometimes you feel a lot better after that." He touched her back. "It'll be okay now. Take it easy."

Chris, mortified, accepted the wipes and mopped her nose and mouth, meanwhile dying of all kinds of embarrassment. A large green trash bag miraculously appeared and covered the mess. All of this, she assumed, must be standard business at a fire.

"Is our mother sick?" Carrie asked in a small voice.

"Mama?" came Kyle's echo.

The fireman hunkered down and smiled into their little faces. "Naw, not really. She smelled too much smoke, and it made her sick to her stomach. She feels better now. Dontcha, Mom?"

She straightened up, eyes closed, and nodded. She couldn't speak yet, but she felt her pea-green face turning red. The irony was not lost on her that her house was burning down, and all she felt was shame because she was wearing practically nothing and had thrown up in the street.

"Our mother is going to be upset if her book burns up," Carrie told the fireman.

"Well, now, we can always get another book, can't we? But it sure would be hard to find another mommy as special as this one. That's why we *never* go back into a house where there's a fire."

"Our mother is *typing* her book, and it takes a very long time and is very hard to do," Carrie informed him rather indignantly.

As the fireman glanced at Chris, she stretched her T-shirt down over her thighs. She was recovering now. "Never mind that, Carrie. The fireman is right—I should not have gone back into the house. It was very dangerous and very stupid." She looked up at the fireman. "I don't suppose you have a drink of water?"

"Well," he said, standing and looking around, "water is pretty hard to come by."

She noticed three different hoses reaching across the lawn toward her smoking house and shook her head.

"I'll ask a neighbor," he said, moving away.

A minute or two later he returned with a paper cup. After she had taken a few swallows she noticed that he was holding a blanket toward her. "Thanks," she said, trading the water for the cover. "If I'd known you were coming, I would have dressed."

"No problem," he said. "Besides, you don't have to be embarrassed by those legs," he added as he turned away. The blanket, thankfully, reached her ankles.

"Whoa!" came a baritone shout, followed by a crashing sound.

Part of the roof where men had been poking opened up, and flames leaped out. Two firefighters came shooting out the front door of the house, then two others dragged a larger hose in. They were everywhere—inside, outside, on the roof.

It was amazing, Chris thought. Just a few minutes ago she'd only seen a little smoke. Now there was a great deal more than smoke; red-orange flames were eating up the little house.

Out of the darkness the tall fireman who had saved her life approached them with a silver ball of fur that went *grrrr* in his arms. He handed Cheeks to Chris. Cheeks, very particular about who carried him around, snarled and yapped in transit. He was cranky.

Carrie and Kyle pressed closer to Chris, and her arms wrapped around them reassuringly, enfolding them in a circle of safety she herself didn't quite feel. As she drew Kyle up onto the tailboard and hugged Carrie closer with her other arm, she saw that all the neighbors she had never met were up, watching her house burn down.

"Maybe we should have a block party," she muttered, kissing one child's head, then the other, then getting a dog's tongue right across her lips and nose. *"Phlettt."* She grimaced.

"Do we have a second alarm?" one fireman asked another.

"Yep." Just that fast another huge rig rounded the corner, bringing the total to four. They had not heard the sirens, Chris assumed, because of the general pandemonium immediately around them: shouting, engines, radios, gushing water and the hissing, creaking, crackling sound of everything she owned in the world turning to ash.

This new fire truck blinked its headlights like a great behemoth, and soon its ladder and basket rose like a stiff arm over the tops of the eucalyptus trees. A hose that was threaded upward began to pour water down on the little house.

Fire fighting had turned to demolition, from Chris's point of view. She flinched at the sound of crashing glass and splintering wood as windows and doors were smashed in. She looked back to the mounting traffic. Police cars blocked the street, and an ambulance had arrived. Chris and her kids and dog sat quietly on the bumper of engine 56.

Tears ran down her cheeks. There it all went. And there hadn't been very much. Five weeks until Christmas. She was twenty-seven years old, and this was the third time in seven years that she'd stood by, helpless, hopeless, while everything she had, everything she thought she *was,* disappeared—this time, before her very eyes. First, when her parents both died in a small plane crash. She had been twenty, and an only child. Then, when Steve walked out on her without so much as a goodbye after having used up her every emotion and every penny of what her parents had left her. Now this.

"Mommy, where are we going to sleep?"

"I...uh...we'll work that out, baby. Don't worry."

"Mommy? Did our sleeping bags burn up? How can we sleep without our sleeping bags?"

"Now, Carrie," Chris said, her voice breaking despite her effort to fake strength, "don't we always m-manage?"

The house was fifty-six years old and, because of the landlord's minimal maintenance, badly run-down. It didn't take much time for it to look like one big black clump. Chris sat watching, stunned, for less than two hours. She wasn't even aware of being cold.

The last fire truck to arrive left first. The neighbors went to bed without asking if there was anything she needed. Hell, they went back into their houses without *introducing* themselves. A policeman took a brief statement from her: the furnace came on after she set the thermostat, then it made smoke. Not much to tell. He gave her a card that had phone numbers for Victims' Services and the Red Cross and headed back toward his car. The disappointed ambulance was long gone. Kyle snored softly, his blond head against her chest, the fireman's blanket that she wore wrapped around him and Cheeks. Carrie leaned against her, wrapped in her own blanket, watching in fascination and fear. She was silent but wide-eyed. It was after 2:00 a.m., Chris estimated, when she found herself sitting on the bumper of engine 56 with no earthly idea of what she was going to do next.

The fireman who had saved her life stood in front of her. He seemed even taller now that her house was a mere cinder. His hair, thick and brown and curly, was now sweaty and matted to his scalp. Dirt and perspiration streaked his face. His eyes were deeply set and brooding under thick brows, but there was a sympathetic turn to his mouth.

"If you take this fire engine out from under me, I have absolutely no idea where I'll sit."

"You don't know any of the neighbors?"

She shook her head. If she attempted to say a word about how all the neighbors had just gone off, she might cry.

"Is there someone you can call?"

She shrugged. Was there? She wasn't sure about that.

"You can go to the police station and make some calls. Or we can wake up a neighbor so you can use their phone. Or you could come to the firehouse and—"

"The firehouse," she requested abruptly. "Please." She couldn't face a police station tonight. Or her ex-neighbors. At that moment, looking up at the man who had carried her out of a burning house and even managed to rescue Cheeks, she had the uncanny feeling that he was all she could depend on.

"Got any family around here? A husband? Ex-husband?"

"Oh, there's an ex-husband…somewhere," she said.

"Don't I know you?" he asked.

She frowned.

"Iverson's," he said. "The grocery store."

Of course, she thought. Before tonight, that was the only thing she had known about the local firemen. They shopped for their groceries together, finicky and cohesive, in much the way women went to restaurant rest rooms together. Chris was a checkout clerk at Iverson's grocery store, and it had always amused her to see the truck pull into the parking lot and five or six big, strapping men wander in to do their shopping for dinner. "Yes. Sure."

"Well, you must have some friends around here, then."

How that followed, she was unsure. Did being a clerk in a grocery store ensure friendship? She had only moved to Sacramento from Los Angeles in late August, just in time for Carrie to start school. She had a few friends at work, but their phone numbers, which she'd rarely had time to use anyway, were in that big ash heap. And she couldn't call anyone in L.A. She'd live in a tent in the park before she'd go back there.

"I'll think of someone on the way to the firehouse," she emphasized. "There are probably fewer criminals there than at the police station." She looked down at her slippered feet. "I'm not dressed to fend off criminals tonight. How long can I use the blanket?"

For the first time Mike remembered the purple panties and was glad it was dark. His cheeks felt warm. *He* felt warm. It was a vaguely familiar feeling, and he liked it. "Until you're done with it, I guess. You can get some things from the Red Cross. I'll get the officer to drive you to the firehouse. We can't take you on the engine."

"What about my house?" she asked.

"Well," he said, looking over his shoulder, "what house?"

"Won't it be looted or something?"

"Lady, there isn't a whole lot left to loot. You have any valuables that might have survived the fire?"

"Yeah," she said, squeezing her kids. "Right here."

He grinned at her approvingly; it was a great, spontaneous smile of crowded, ever-so-slightly protruding, superwhite teeth. A smile that did not hold pity but humanity. And one deep dimple—left side. "You got the best of it, then." He started to turn away.

"The refrigerator," she said, making him turn back. "Did the refrigerator go?"

"Well, it'll never run again."

"I don't care about the refrigerator itself," she said, her voice gaining strength. "I put my laptop in there. And research papers. There's a book on the computer. It's the very last thing of any value I—" She stopped before her voice broke and she began to blubber. She hugged her children tighter. Inside she felt like a little girl herself, a defenseless, abandoned, pitiful orphan. *Won't someone do something, please. Why, oh, God, why does my luck get worse and worse, and just when I think I might make it, it goes wrong and I don't even know what I did to deserve this and, oh, my God, my kids, my poor kids.*

"Is that what you were doing?" he asked her.

She looked up at him. Brown eyes? No, green. And crinkled at the corners.

"What…what did you think I was doing?" she asked.

He reached into the engine cab for an industrial-sized flashlight. "I had absolutely no idea. I'll go see if the fridge made it."

She stood suddenly, struggling to hold on to Kyle and Cheeks. "Well, be careful."

The hoses were being put away, and the shortwave radios were having distant and eerie conversations with one another.

He came back. He had it. A laptop she'd salvaged from her former life. He showed it to her, smiling. It wasn't even singed. "It's got butter on it. And something red. Ketchup, I think."

"I don't believe it," she breathed.

"Well, I hope it's good. It almost cost you way more than it could possibly be worth. Don't you know better than to go into a burning—"

"The sleeping bags? Toys? Clothes?"

He shook his head, exasperated. "Really, there wasn't time to save anything in there. We tried, but… Come on, let's get you into the squad car. These old houses, jeez."

Chris walked ahead of him in the direction of the police car. She carried Kyle and Cheeks while Carrie held on to Chris's blanket, trailing behind. The fireman followed with the laptop. "I've known women to go back for their purses, but I couldn't imagine what you were doing in the refrigerator! They'll never believe this one. You're lucky, all right."

"I'm not feeling all *that* lucky."

"Well, you ought to. That old house went up like kindling."

Taking her precious laptop, Chris managed to get into the police car without saying anything more, and they followed the fire engine to the station. The policeman carried Kyle inside, but Chris was stuck with Cheeks because of his obnoxious attitude. She struggled to hold the terrier and her laptop.

Inside the station she was taken into a little living room that boasted two couches, several chairs, a desk, a telephone and television and even a Ping-Pong table. This must be where they lounged between fires.

The big fireman, out of his coat now, suspenders holding up his huge canvas pants, a tight T-shirt stretched over his enormous chest and shoulders, was standing in the living room as if he were the welcoming committee.

Carrie tugged on his pants. "Our mother types on her book every night because she is trying to be a book writer and not work at the grocery store anymore."

"Oh?" the fireman said.

"And it's worth a very lot," Carrie informed him proudly.

Chapter 2

After the other firemen were finished, Mike Cavanaugh took his turn in the upstairs shower to wash away the acrid odor of smoke that clung to his hair and skin. While he lathered his hair he thought of his mother, who lived nearby. She would have heard the sirens and might be lying awake, wondering if her firstborn was all right. Mike knew this because his father had told him; his mother had never admitted it. He could give her a call, his father had suggested, making Mike suspect it wasn't only his mother who worried. But, hell, he was thirty-six years old. He was not going to call his mother after every middle-of-the-night alarm so she could fall back to sleep without worrying. Besides, it would start a bad pattern. If he obliged, sometimes his phone call would come fifteen minutes after the sirens, occasionally it would be hours. Calling would become worse than never calling. Sooner or later she would have to get used to this. He had been a firefighter for more than twelve years.

He did, however, check in with his parents during the daytime. And he had bought them a multiband radio scanner so they could listen to the radio calls. He wasn't as stubborn as he pretended.

It had been 3:00 a.m. when he left the woman—Christine Palmer, he'd learned when they finally had a moment to exchange names—and her kids in the rec room. He'd given her a couple of pillows and blankets to tuck her little ones in on the couches, and some extra clothing for herself—the smallest sweatpants and sweatshirt that could be found. He'd told her which line to use to make her calls. He'd told her to go ahead and close her eyes for a while if she could; the men would be getting up for breakfast and a shift change in a couple of hours—around 6:00 a.m. She could have someone pick her up in the morning so as not to upset the kids' sleep any further.

Upstairs in the sleeping quarters there had been some grumbling. It was not customary to bring homeless fire victims to the firehouse. It was very rare, in fact. Jim had said it might set a bad precedent. Hal had said the kids might be noisy and rob them of what little sleep they had left. Stu had said he suspected it was that little purple tushie Mike had carried out of the house that had prompted this innovative move. Mike had said, "Go to sleep, girls, and try not to get on my nerves." Mike was in charge tonight.

He couldn't stop thinking about her, however. It wasn't the purple silk butt, even though that did cross his mind from time to time. It was the way she seemed unusually alone with those two little kids. He thought he'd picked up a defiant loneliness in her eyes. Blue eyes, he remembered. When she thrust out her chin it gave her otherwise soft face a sort of challenge. It was peculiar, especially during a catastrophe as exciting to the average man or woman as a house fire, not to have people rally around the victims. Even in neighborhoods where folks were not well acquainted or friendly, it was odd not to have someone break out of the crowd and ask all the right questions, take the family in, call a church or a victims' aid organization. The Salvation Army. But Christine Palmer seemed to hold them all at bay with her look of utter isolation.

Mike could have called the Salvation Army himself. Or the Red Cross. He'd taken a shower instead. His first reaction had been to distance himself from this little family; their aloneness made *him* feel vulnerable. But he felt them pulling him like a magnet. Now he decided to go downstairs and see if she was awake. He wouldn't bother her if the lights were out. Or if her eyes were closed. He was just too curious to go to sleep.

Christine Palmer was a curiosity—an attractive enough one, to be sure—but it was that precocious little blond bombshell who'd gotten right under his skin. He had had a daughter once. And a wife. They had been dead for ten years. Joanie had been only twenty-three and Shelly three when a car accident stole them away and left holes in Mike's soul. He had felt a charge, like a shot of electricity, when that Shirley Temple reincarnate tugged on his coat. What a kid. He felt a giddy lightness; then a familiar, unwelcome ache.

When his foot touched the bottom step he heard a predictable *grrrr.* Then he heard "Shut up, Cheeks."

So he knew she was awake. Mike stood in the doorway of the rec room and saw that Cheeks was sleeping on the end of the little boy's couch, right on the kid's feet. He liked that, that the dog guarded the kids. He felt as though these kids needed that. They slept soundly; the boy snored softly. Christine Palmer sat at the desk nearby, her feet drawn up and her arms wrapped around her knees. An old phone book was open in front of her, and her back was to him.

The terrier stiffened his front legs, showed his teeth and growled seriously. She turned to see Mike standing there, surprise briefly widening her red-rimmed eyes. Then she turned away quickly and blew her nose as though it was humiliating to be caught crying after your whole world had burned up. "Shut up, Cheeks," she commanded sternly. "Down." The terrier obliged, but he watched.

"Has he ever actually bitten anyone?" Mike asked, working hard at sounding friendly and nonthreatening.

"No," she said, wiping her eyes before swiveling the chair around to face him.

She had pulled sweat socks up to her knees over the sweatpants, probably to take up some slack; she was drowning in the smallest sweats they could find. Small boned, but with a wiry toughness that showed. She was a very pretty woman. Her blue eyes were fierce, her thick, light brown hair willfully wavy, springing loose around her face. If they hadn't just been through a fire and if he hadn't caught her crying he would wonder if contacts gave her eyes that intense, penetrating color.

"Cheeks is only crabby," she said. "He's not dangerous. But I don't mind if strangers are wary around my kids."

"Why'd you name him Cheeks?"

"His mustache. When we first got him, Carrie grabbed him by that hair around his mouth and said, 'Mommy, look at his cheeks,' and it stuck." She shrugged and tried to smile. The rims of her lips were pink, and her nose was watery. "This is very embarrassing," she said, becoming still more fluid.

"Look, it was a bad fire. Of course you're upset."

"No...no, not that. I...I have no one to call. See, I'm new in Sacramento. I only moved here at the end of August, just before Carrie started school. I got a job at Iverson's about a month, no, six weeks ago. I only know a few people. I don't know anyone's phone number except Mr. Iverson's at the store. I have a babysitter for Kyle and for Carrie after school, but she doesn't have—" She stopped. *Anything* was the next word. The babysitter, Juanita Jimeniz, was the mother of another grocery-store clerk; the Jimenizes were practically destitute themselves. There were more family members living under one roof than there appeared to be beds. No help there.

"I could give you a lift to the bank after my shift change if you—"

"My checking account has $12.92 in it."

"Where'd you come from, then?" he asked, moving to sit on one of the chairs near the desk. Cheeks growled, watching. Mike wasn't convinced he wouldn't bite.

"Los Angeles."

"Well, that's not so far away. Maybe someone there could send you a few bucks? Or invite you back down till you get, you know, reestablished?" He felt his heavy brows draw together, and he tried unsuccessfully to smooth out the frown. His mother had warned him that he looked mean, threatening, whenever he got that brooding look, his heavy brows nearly connecting over the bridge of his nose. But his forehead took on contemplative lines now because he was confused.

Something about Christine Palmer did not sit well. She appeared indigent, yet he'd shuffled a goodly number of indigent families off to Victims Aid, and she didn't fit. People totally without resources, without family, friends, money, without memberships in churches, clubs or unions, did not usually rush into burning buildings to save the books they were writing. Strange. What's missing from this picture? he asked himself.

"L.A. was also...pretty temporary," she said.

Her hesitation and her downcast eyes made Mike think she was lying.

"Mrs. Palmer, are you in some kind of trouble?"

Her head snapped back. "Yeah. My house just burned down, my car keys are in there somewhere, I have no money—oh, I *had* forty-two dollars and some cents in my purse for groceries for the rest of the week till payday, but I imagine that's gone, too. And I lied about L.A. I was there for more than three years. I had already borrowed as much as my former friends were willing to—" She stopped abruptly, took a deep breath and quieted herself. "There was no farewell party, all right? I didn't actually do anything wrong, I just...had a run of bad luck. An unpleasant divorce. My ex is a... scoundrel. It gets rough sometimes."

"Oh," Mike said, pretending to understand. "Make any calls to the Red Cross? Victims' Services?"

She nodded. "And two crisis counseling centers, four shelters and a church group that's helping illegal aliens.

Do you know what? My house burned down on the first freezing night in Sacramento. Everyone, it seems, has come in off the streets."

"No luck?"

She shrugged. "I have two more numbers here. The Opportunity Hotel and a place called Totem Park. Do you suppose you have to sleep outside in Totem Park?"

"I know so," he said, frowning. "Here, let me try the hotel," he offered, pulling the phone across the desk. She turned the pad on which she had written the number toward him. He glanced at the sleeping kids as he waited for an answer on the line. Their shiny yellow heads were clean, their pajamas the warm and tidy kind. They were obviously well cared for, with healthy skin and teeth. Bright, alert eyes, when they were awake.

This particular shelter, called a hotel because they took a few dollars from people who either overstayed or could afford it, was possibly the sleaziest place in the city, Mike knew. Some people actually preferred the street to places like this; protection from the other homeless was difficult to provide. Even though she didn't have anything to steal, Christine Palmer didn't look tough enough to fend off an assault. He glanced at the kids again; the ringing continued on the line. The shelter was filthy, nasty. He wondered if there were rats.

Finally there was an answer. "Hi, this is Captain Mike Cavanaugh, Sacramento Fire Department. We're trying to place a homeless family—woman and two small kids. Any room down there?"

The man on the line said yes.

"Oh, too bad. Thanks anyway," Mike said, making his decision and hanging up quickly.

"I'll call Mr. Iverson in the morning, when the store

opens. He's a pretty decent guy. Maybe he'll advance me some pay or something."

"Are you *completely* orphaned?" He didn't mean to sound incredulous, but he came from a large family himself and had trouble picturing a life without relatives. Cavanaugh. Irish Catholic. Six kids.

"My parents are dead; I'm an only child. There's this unmarried aunt back in Chicago, where I grew up, but she probably hates my guts. We parted on very unfriendly terms a long while back." She gave a short, bitter laugh. "Actually, it was all my fault. But I'm sure if I grovel and beg and apologize enough, Aunt Florence will invite me and the kids back home. Chicago. Ugh. I hate the idea of crawling back to Chicago, all ashamed and sorry." She slapped the laptop on the desk. "I was going to go back, you know. Patch things up with Aunt Flo, who is the only family I have in the world besides the kids. But later, hopefully with my tail straight up and not tucked between my legs." Her voice quieted. "I'm not a bad writer. Some people have liked my work."

"'It's worth a very lot,'" he said, quoting the little girl.

"Oh, to her," Chris said, her voice becoming sentimental, almost sweet. "Carrie's my biggest fan. Also the greatest kid in the whole world. Never lost faith in me—not once." A large tear spilled over.

"No one, huh?" he asked her.

"I'm sure I'll think of something in the morning. I've been called resourceful. Gutsy, even. Probably nice ways of saying I'm contrary and not easy to get along with."

He laughed. She wasn't nearly as hysterical as she

could be, under the circumstances. Nor as scared. And he could relate; he wasn't always easy to get along with, either. "Just so you get along," he said.

"One way or the other."

"Well, this doesn't look good," he supplied.

"No, but them's the breaks, huh? I'll think of something. I hope."

According to six o'clock news stories, Mike considered, this was how it happened: some perfectly nice, smart, clean, decent individual hit a cultural snag—illness, divorce, unemployment. Fire. Then, with no money for rent deposits, utilities turn-on, child care or retraining, he or she was suddenly living out of a car. After about three weeks of living out of a car, no one would hire them. Then, if they did land a job by some miracle, they couldn't work it because there was nowhere to shower, leave the kids or do the laundry. A mean social cycle. No money, no job. No job, no money. The forgotten people who were once accountants or engineers.

The press indicated the homeless situation was getting worse every year. The reported living conditions were terrifying. Hopeless and vile. The one common link among these people seemed to be aloneness, lack of family. Mike had family. Boy, did he.

"You know what?" he began. "Maybe we could help you get a news spot. A little—"

"What?"

"You know, get channel five to do a spot on the fire and your circumstances."

"What are you talking about?"

"Donations to a post-office box or bank or—"

"*Be* on the news?"

"Yeah, because your house—"

"Oh, *please*. Please don't do that. I'd die!"

"Well, it's nothing to be ashamed of. It's not like it was your fault, you know."

"No. No. That would be awful!"

Okay, he thought, she's hiding. From the ex? She didn't look like a bank robber or kid— Kidnapper? He wondered if the ex had gotten custody. Yeah, he decided. That was probably it. Well, maybe. Whatever, she was hiding something. He wondered how much.

"Tell you what. I live alone. You could use my place for a couple of days. It's a roof."

"What?" she said, almost laughing. "Come on, that's not your usual policy. In fact, judging from some of the looks we've gotten, I'd say you don't have a whole lot of fire victims in your rec room, either."

"It's not usual," he admitted. He shook his head. He had surprised himself as much as her with the offer. But Christmas was coming, and the kids were clean, cute, precocious. She had some secrets, but he was sure they weren't the dangerous kind. Bad luck, she had said. Most of all, they had no one. No one. Well, what the heck, he was someone.

"Fact is, none of this has been policy. The only other time we brought a fire victim here in the middle of the night, it was a relative of a firefighter. Upstairs they think I've gone soft in the head."

"We'd better get out of here."

"Naw, no problem. Here's the deal, Christine. Can I call you Christine? Chrissie?"

"How about Chris."

He nodded. "Well, here it is, Chris. I'm a little soft in the head. You seem to be having some rotten luck, and I don't have to know what happened to you, but that little girl of yours reminds me of my little girl. She was a lot like that one," he said, jerking his head toward the sofa. "Blond, opinionated, had an IQ of about four thousand. She died in a car accident with her mother about ten years ago. She was only three. And hell, it's almost Christmas."

Chris stared at him. She had only lost a house and everything she owned. Suddenly it didn't seem like much.

"So," he said, watching her watch him. "I don't spend all that much time at my house. I sleep here when I'm on duty, I have a cabin I like to use when I have a few days off in a row, and I have family all over Sacramento. It's a pretty good-sized place, I guess. Three bedrooms. You could make a few calls, get some things like insurance paperwork started. You might say a few things to that landlord about the furnace, and he might settle with you real quick, but there could be a lawsuit in it. You didn't hear that from me, okay? And then, before you grovel to your old-maid aunt, you'd have a little edge. There don't seem to be many alternatives." He shrugged. "It would be too bad to have to take those kids to one of those crappy shelters. Most of them are pretty awful."

"Your house," she said, her voice barely a whisper. She looked at him a little differently. She judged his size and musculature.

"My parents live just around the corner, and I could stay with them when I'm not here. I might be soft in the head, but I'm pretty safe. Anyway—" he smiled "—you have *him*," he said, glancing at Cheeks.

"Gee, that's…really generous of you," she said, but she said it cautiously, suspiciously. Mike wondered if she had been abused by the ex. He wondered *how* abused.

"It's a pretty well-known fact that firefighters have a weakness for little kids. It's up to you. I live alone, but I have this house. I didn't even want it, to tell you the truth, but my family started hounding me about doing something with my money—real estate, you know. Sometimes you have to do something just so that everyone in your very nosy family will get off your back. So they talk you into buying something, investing. Then they stop worrying and start calling you moneybags." He chuckled to himself. "In my family, everyone minds everyone's business but their own. It's an Irish tradition."

"What will your very nosy family say if you take in this completely unknown, whacked-out, poverty-stricken divorcée with two kids and a dog?"

"Oh, I don't know. They'll probably shake their heads and say, 'It figures.' They gave up on me a long time ago; I'm the one they always shake their heads over. They call me ornery. Probably just a nice way of saying I'm not easy to get along with," he said, and grinned that big grin again.

"You?"

"Yeah. Don't I seem ornery?"

She tilted her head and looked at him. He smiled confidently through her appraisal. "No," she said after a moment. Gentle. Generous. Never ornery. "But they know you better than I do."

"They have their reasons, I suppose." Reason number one, they couldn't get him remarried after Joanie and Shelly were gone. Not a one of them—not three brothers and their wives, not two sisters and all the friends they had in Sacramento. Tough, he told them. He had never liked dating, and he kept his few liaisons to himself; they had never come to much, anyway. Though he missed Joanie and Shelly, he no longer minded being alone. He had gone through school with Joanie, married her when he was twenty and she was eighteen. And he had known he was going to do that the first time he kissed her.

He had liked being a husband and father. And he wasn't anymore.

What he also liked was to hunt, a reclusive sport. He liked the department's baseball team, the gym, the little one-room house in the mountains and sitting in front of a television set with his dad and brothers when they couldn't get tickets to a game. He liked to read, and he liked to putter under his car. He was solitary but not antisocial. Sometimes he needed sex, someone to make love with, but he didn't like doing it with strangers and there hadn't been very many women over the years who'd become friends. It had been quite a while, in fact. He was a little disappointed in himself for that, but he had become a man who put his energy into a lot of physical things and thereby coped with a primary physical need left unmet. The longer he waited, the less urgent he felt.

He was a quiet, private, sometimes lonely man who had no one to spend his money on except his mom and dad, his brothers and sisters and their spouses and kids. Uncle Mike. He knew what he was becoming—the odd uncle, gentle with some, crotchety with others. Difficult and sometimes short-tempered. Like Cheeks.

"What do you think? Got any better ideas?"

"I…uh…it's hard for me to take…you know, charity. I don't know if…"

He tilted his head toward the sleeping kids. "They won't know the difference. You oughta see some of those shelters. You've got a job, so pay me a little rent if you want, later, when you get it together. Or maybe you could do a few things around the house? Like cleaning or laundry?" He tried not to draw his eyebrows meanly over his nose, which happened whenever he lied. His house was immaculate, and his mother did his laundry. She insisted.

"What if I'm a crook or something? What if I hot-wire my old Honda, clean out your house and haul your TV and stereo off to Mexico?" She was weakening.

Mike laughed. "They'd never let you across the border with that dog." Cheeks growled on cue. "God, he's a piece of work. If he bites me, he's out. Does he, um, make any mistakes?"

"No," she said, smiling. "He's really a very good dog, just crabby. And the kids are pretty good, too." And there it was. Without her saying anything more, he knew it was decided. She and the kids would move in tomorrow.

In the morning, while Jim scrambled eggs for the whole crew, Carrie tugged on Mike's sweatpants. He looked down into her pretty blue eyes. "Our mother says we're going to stay at your house for a little while, because our house is burned."

"Do you think you'll mind?" he asked her.

"No," she said. She smiled at him. "Do you want us to?"

"I invited you, didn't I?"

"We always pick up our toys and our dirty clothes," she informed him. "Kyle is just learning, but he's learning very good."

"I'm sure you're very neat," Mike said. "But I'm a little bit sloppy."

Carrie's expression changed suddenly. She looked over her shoulder toward her little brother, who was sitting on the couch with his thumb in his mouth. Then she looked back up at Mike's face. "Our toys burned up," she said, her expression stoic.

"Oh, didn't I tell you? I must've forgotten. I have toys. They're at my mother's house, but she'll let you borrow them. If you promise to pick them up, of course."

She smiled suddenly, and her eyes became very like her mother's. "We'll pick them up. We're learning very good."

Cheeks growled.

"Can you make him stop doing that?" Mike asked her.

"If he gets used to you, he stops it. You must not hit him. It will make him mean."

"He already sounds mean."

"Yes," she said, smiling a wild young smile that was tangy with innocence and made Mike feel warm all over. "But he only *sounds* it," she added with a giggle.

He wanted to crush her in his big arms. He became afraid of himself, his hard and trembling shell, his gushy innards. He was an uncle who had cuddled many nieces and nephews since he'd lost his own child, but he suddenly, desperately, wished to hold a child who *needed* to be held.

He picked her up, gently. His loneliness, his aching desire for a family of his own, pressed against the backs of his eyes. What was he doing with this child in his arms? A long time ago he'd stopped trying to replace what he'd lost. After ten years, he'd built a strong enough wall that he didn't have to face what he had lost. But holding this little girl shook loose the bricks he had used to build his wall.

Everything they had was gone, and it hadn't been much to start with. Yet these people were not the destitute ones.

Chapter 3

Mike opened the front door for them but did not go in to show them around. He and Chris had talked on the way over. He said he had a lot to get done on his days off, and she had important decisions to make, phone calls to place. Calls that Mike suggested might be easier if he wasn't there to listen.

"You go ahead and look around," he told her. "You won't have any trouble recognizing the two extra bedrooms. The one with the desk and the couch, well, the couch folds out into a bed. And keep the kids out of the garage, okay? There are power tools out there. I'll be back around lunchtime."

"Look, I feel kind of funny, going in alone and everything. There's no reason you should trust me, you know. I mean, it's not too late to—"

"Is there anything you're looking for besides a way to take care of your kids?" he countered.

"No," she answered.

"That's what I figured. Just make your calls. I'm going to stop by the house you rented. If I found an ash that might have been a purse, would your car keys be in it? Maybe a crispy cell phone?"

"Yes, keys. No phone—too expensive." She smiled. "Hey, that would be great. Really, I don't know how to thank you for all this."

"Don't worry about that. I don't usually do things I don't want to do. It just isn't that big a deal."

"It is," she said, peeking into the house. "It's a very, very big deal."

"Naw." He shrugged. "The place just about stands vacant. I'll see you in a few hours, then. And listen, I'm going to be pretty tied up for a couple of days, so I hope you can handle all your reorganizing without my help." As if it had just occurred to him, he added, "Since I'm going to stay with my folks, take…uh…the master bedroom, if you want."

Then he vanished. Chris cautiously placed Cheeks on the floor inside the front door. As she and the children stood watching, he ran down the stairs from the foyer into the carpeted living room. "Please, God," she said, "don't let him pee." He scooted around the floor like a windup toy, his whiskers flush against the rug, zooming a pattern of certainty that no other dog had marked the place. He paused for a long while at the coffee table leg. "I'll kill you," Chris warned. The terrier looked over his shoulder at her, then zoomed on.

As Cheeks sniffed and scooted around downstairs, Chris and the kids peeked up the short flight of steps leading to the bedrooms. The three of them were all a little frightened of the fireman's house. It was quiet, new, immaculate, not theirs. Chris finally stepped across the hardwood entry onto the thick gray carpet that flowed down the steps.

The living room was decorated in masculine colors of blue, gray, dark purple and brown. Walnut accent tables held a few decorator items—coasters, a scented candle, coffee-table books. A fireplace with a great granite hearth took up most of one wall. Even the logs in the tray beside it looked impossibly clean.

The kids stared at the entertainment center as if it were a rocket ship. Stereo, DVD player, large HD television, DVDs, speakers, knobs by the dozen, dials, all enclosed in glass. Spotless, smearless, dust-less glass. And paintings—prints, actually. Could he have chosen the prints? Also behind glass. Two McKnights. McKnight was known for his happy, homey, bright settings of rooms devoid of people. No hazy pastels, but sharp-featured living-room scenes crowded with things, not people, paintings of rooms that seemed to celebrate themselves with vibrant aloneness. Like Mike?

"My God," she muttered, "I might have to feed you kids in the bathtub."

"He said he was a little sloppy," Carrie told her, "but I think he's learning very good."

"Yeah," Chris replied absently. "Don't touch anything. See that coaster there, on the coffee table?" She pointed. "That brown thing that you put your glass on so you don't leave a mark on the table?" They nodded. "That's the only thing in this room that I can afford to replace."

"Are we going to put our glass on it to not leave a spot?" Carrie asked.

"No," she said. "You're not going to eat or drink anything in the living room." She looked around fretfully. "I'm going to keep a bottle of Windex strapped to my belt."

"I never eated in the bathtub," Carrie said.

"Ate. And I'm kidding. Maybe."

She felt a lump in her throat and turned them around before they could look with envy at the living room any longer. "Come on, let's see if we can find where we're going to sleep."

Upstairs was not the showplace the downstairs was, but it, too, was immaculate. The bedrooms were large and airy and practically unfurnished. The only furniture in one was a set of twin beds, with not so much as a lamp or cardboard box in addition. The other room had a love seat, which, upon inspection, Chris found was the hide-a-bed. And there was a desk where Mike paid his bills. The desk had a glass top. Underneath the glass were a few pictures. One was a picture of a woman and child, and by the woman's hairstyle, Chris guessed it was *them*. She stared at it a long time, the ones he had lost. Her heart began to split into a bleeding wound. Poor guy. How could you lose that much? It was incomprehensible. She had buried her parents before becoming a mother. She had since decided that the overwhelming pain of that still could not approach what a parent must feel when burying a child. Her throat began to close.

"Is that me with the lady?" Carrie asked.

"No," she said, her voice soft and reverent. "No, honey. That's Mr. Cavanaugh's little girl and his wife.

They died a long, long time ago. Way before you were even born."

"Does he miss them, then?"

"Yes, of course. This is his private stuff, all right?" Private feelings. "I don't think we should ask him questions about it. Okay?" Chris crouched so she could look into Carrie's eyes. Her own wanted to water, but she tried not to cry over borrowed heartache. "In fact, I don't think we should even mention we saw the picture, okay? Please?"

"Okay. Can we watch TV?"

"Sure," she said, straightening. "If I can figure it out. Come on. Back downstairs, where you may sit on the floor and touch nothing."

"I thought you said we could touch that brown thing?"

Chris was not in awe of Mike's moderate, tasteful wealth, even if her children might be. She was in awe of *him*. There was stuff to steal here. How was he so sure she wouldn't? How did he know she'd be careful? How could he do this, trust her like this? He knew nothing about her, nothing at all. Except that she was alone and had nothing. She felt a trifle insecure about using his discriminately chosen, carefully placed things, but her chief insecurity was that she didn't deserve this charitable act.

Chris had grown up in a house that would make Mike's place look like the maid's quarters. The fireman's house, in fact, was much like the place she and Steve shared the first year they were married. The kids wouldn't remember anything so comfortable, however. The comparison to what they *did* know made her shudder, and the tightness in her throat grew into a lump of self-pity as she took the children downstairs to deposit them in front of the television while she made some calls.

Mr. Iverson excused her from her job for a few days and agreed to give her a hundred-dollar advance on her salary, which he would deduct from her pay over an extended period of time. She gave him the phone number where she could be reached and called the babysitter. Juanita asked her if there was anything she needed. In spite of the fact that they needed everything, she said nothing. Juanita, good-hearted and hardworking, had too little to share. At Carrie's school, the secretary offered the names of places that might offer help. Chris didn't mention she had already tried most of them, but simply informed her that Carrie would not be back for a while. Actually, she didn't know where Carrie would go to school next, and she was grateful it was only kindergarten.

The call to the landlord was another story. Not a story of compassion, either.

"Well, Mrs. Blakely, when do you think Mr. Blakely will be able to return my call?"

"I'm sure I don't know, Mrs. Palmer. He's a little upset about the house, you know. We don't know how that happened."

Chris laughed hollowly. "It happened because the furnace was old, in poor repair and hadn't been serviced in a good many years."

"Ah, I see. You, of course, have the arson report?"

"Arson report?"

"Could you possibly have been…smoking?"

"I don't smoke! Hey, listen, I've got two little kids, and we could've all been killed! We didn't even get the car keys out of that old house, it went up so fast! Would you like to take down this number, please?"

"I'm sure we don't need your number, dear, as long as the police know where you can be found."

"What?"

"Well, we don't want to make any accusations, naturally, before the investigation is complete, but I'll take your word that you won't leave the area."

Chris was stunned for a moment. Then, thanks to the finesse she had learned too late from her missing ex-husband—who she hoped was at that very moment being subjected to some incredible torture that would leave vicious scars—she let out a knowing sigh.

"Mrs. Blakely," she said smoothly, "my lawyer suggested that I find out when your husband will be available for a settlement meeting. We should probably talk before any further medical tests are run on my children so that you'll be fully and fairly apprised of all possible expenses and punitive suits that could be forthcoming."

"Tests? What kind of tests?"

"Smoke inhalation. Possible internal injuries. Possible brain damage. And, of course, stress, trauma, emotional—"

"What is that number?"

She recited Mike's phone number.

Click.

Chris's husband had been a con man. A wheeler-dealer. A schemer. A crook, a louse, a liar. But she couldn't prove it. The sad truth was that she knew where every freckle on his body was located, she would be able to pinpoint his very individual male musk in a stadium holding twenty thousand people, but she had not known what he did for a living. Or what he did with her money. The word *incomprehensible* popped into her mind again, associated with catastrophic loss and the fact that she knew nothing at all about a man she had been married to for four years. Because she had been inside-out-in-love and feeble with idealism and ignorance.

While her children watched a nature program on a cable network, Chris brooded about her past. It was checkered indeed. Poor Aunt Florence.

Chris's grandfather had started a furniture business as a young man; he had started his family as a much older man. By the time Chris's father was twenty-two and married, Grandfather was nearly ready to retire. His company, Palmer House, was respected and very successful. Chris was born into a family that included her young parents, her elderly grandparents, her father's younger sister and piles of money.

When Chris was small, her aunt, Florence, spoiled her, played with her, babysat her and bought her lacy undergarments and expensive shoes to match every dress. When Chris was older they went on trips together—to Hong Kong, London, Tibet. They bought everything of leather, gold, silver and jade that they could carry or ship home. When Chris was eighteen Flo made a down payment on a car for her. A Jaguar.

What she remembered most vividly, however, and missed most painfully, were the letters and phone calls. While Chris was at Princeton, she emailed and called Flo daily. And Aunt Florence replied—consistently. Chris, studying literature, couldn't believe that her job for four whole years would be reading all the greatest books ever written. She was a straight-A student. She loved books, always had, especially Regency and Victorian romances, from Austen to Brontë. And she loved the inexpensive love stories you could buy at Walmart for $6.99. So did Aunt Florence; they agreed that everyone deserved a six-ninety-nine happy ending. They often discussed the books the way other women discussed their favorite soaps.

They had been so close, the best of friends, confidantes.

Florence had never married—the "old-maid" aunt. Except that Aunt Florence was only fourteen years older than Chris. More like an older sister than an aunt, actually. Five-year-old Chris had sobbed for hours the day Flo left for college; she sat by the front bay window all afternoon awaiting Flo's first weekend home. Flo was brilliant, sophisticated, fashionable and rich. She was also bossy, fiercely independent, ambitious and stubborn as a mule. Devoted, sometimes controlling. Loads of fun or a pain in the butt, depending. Such was the deal for an aunt and niece who were more like siblings. Flo couldn't help it that she was the elder.

Chris, her parents and Aunt Florence had always lived on the same street. Flo had kept the old Palmer family home on the upper river drive after her parents—first her father, at the age of seventy-two, then her mother, at sixty-four—died. Flo was only twenty-one then, and Chris vaguely remembered an argument over Flo's living alone in the big house when she could just as easily move in with Randolph's family. Flo, predictably, won.

Chris's mom, Arlene, whom Chris still ached for, was the nurturer of them all. Chris longed to revisit the smells from her early childhood: her father's cologne, her mother's cooking and baking, Flo's furs. Arlene had married Randolph and, she joked, Florence. And indeed, Arlene was like a wife to both of them, representing both Randolph and Flo at charity functions. A society wife—philanthropic, on a number of boards—and caretaker in one. Randolph and Florence had inherited the family business and worked at it. Arlene hadn't "worked" technically, except that no one ever worked harder at taking care of a family. And that was all the family there was. The Palmers of Chicago. Randolph, Arlene, Florence…and Christine.

Then it happened. Arlene and Randolph. Dead. They were in their forties—too *soon*. Chris came home from Princeton to help Aunt Flo bury them, to pack up what they wore and wiped their noses with. It had been black and horrid. She didn't go back to school. What for? For *literature?*

She met Steve at a nightclub. Steve Zanuck—they called him Stever. Hotshot, arrogant, sexy Stever. He was a few years older than she, and Aunt Florence became instantly bitchy, as if she were jealous of him. As if she didn't want Chris to be in love. Flo believed he might be no damn good, as she so tactfully put it. Chris, who needed love, assumed that her grieving aunt had turned mean and selfish. Steve had said that Florence was clinging and manipulative. The pot was definitely speaking of the kettle. So Chris slept with him, married him and sued her Aunt Florence, the executor of her parents' estate, for control of her trust. What had happened? Had she been having an out-of-body experience? Had he drugged her? With sex and flattery. She was so vulnerable and alone she was just a big dope. She had somehow managed to stay asleep for four whole years. Dear God, what an imbecile she'd been.

Trying to emerge from that nightmare had produced some growth and even a little dream or two, like writing, but also immeasurable loneliness. At one time she had had more friends than there seemed time for. The past few years, though, had been largely solitary. Trying to make it on her own, to develop independence and self-reliance, had led to a fundamental absence of people in her life.

She looked at the back of her children's blond heads; they stared up at the television, transfixed by luxury. Kyle's toe stuck out of a hole in the foot of his pajamas. And that was all he had now. So, to prevent their being hurt or further deprived, she might have to call Aunt Flo. For them.

She had hoped, somehow, that she could reverse her circumstances. She could never recover her entire lost legacy, but she could be at least a self-supporting single mother, couldn't she? And so here she was, lying in this bed she had made, because she had to take responsibility for her own mistakes. And because, when Flo was proved right about Stever, her sensitive remark had been, "Well, you just couldn't listen to me, could you? You had to let that slimeball run through everything Randy left for you before you could even figure it out! Will you *ever* learn?"

Probably I will learn, Chris thought. *Probably I have.*

That was why calling Flo was on the very dead-last bottom of her list of possibilities. She loved Flo, she missed her desperately, but she didn't expect her aunt to be very nice about this.

Of course, she deserved Flo's anger, her scorn, but...
Perhaps Flo would forgive her? Be somewhat kind?

Perhaps she would hang up, like the landlord's wife.
Or say, "Chris who?"

"Hi, Ma," Mike yelled as he walked through the living room toward the kitchen. "Ma?"

"Yes, yes, yes," she called back from the kitchen. "I'm up to my elbows in dough. Come in. Come in." She pulled her hands out and turned to look up at him. She frowned. "You look hungry. But good."

He laughed and kissed her forehead. "I weigh one-ninety-five, and I'm not hungry." He took a cookie from the cookie jar. "Not real hungry, anyway."

"You must have had a quiet night," she said softly, quickly looking away from him and back to her kneading. "No bags under the eyes."

"Not so much as a peep," he replied, leaning against the cabinet, watching her back. She glanced over her shoulder, and he smiled. Then his shoulders shook. They both knew she had been awake, stayed awake, and they both liked that to some degree. "Where's Dad?" he asked. But she didn't have to answer. The toilet flushed, the bathroom door opened, and Mike's father, a short, muscular and thick, bald-headed Irishman carrying a newspaper, wearing his eyeglasses on his nose and his leather slippers on his feet, came down the hall into the kitchen. His name was also Michael.

"I thought I heard lies being told," he said. "Mikie, my boy, 'not a peep' went by the house at about the witchin' hour, round ninety-five miles an hour, followed by the second bell."

"Oh?" Mike's mother said without turning around. "I didn't hear it. I sleep like the beloved dead."

"We went down Forty-second Street, as a matter of fact, four blocks east," Mike said. "House burned down—one of those little ones over on Belvedere."

"Everyone okay?" his mother asked, turning around. "And the firemen?"

"Everyone is fine, but as a matter of fact, that's the reason I stopped by. Last night's fire. Ma, I've gone and done the craziest damn thing; they just might lock me up for a lunatic. The woman who was burned out is a young divorcée with two cute little kids, just three and five years old. They had nowhere to go, and I loaned them my place. Can I sleep over here tonight? Maybe a couple of nights? Until they get settled?"

"Your house?" she asked. She decided to take her hands out of the dough altogether and wash them. "You gave this family your house?"

"No, Ma, no, I didn't give it to them. I offered them a place to stay until they can make some plans. See, she's pretty young, I'd say about Margie's age, under thirty. And she has no family except the kids. It's so close to Christmas, and the shelters are—" He stopped. His parents were looking at him as though he'd slipped a gear. At any moment he expected his mother to feel his brow.

He didn't know how to explain how it made him feel to think of those kids in one of those crappy shelters. *Or* how it made him feel to think of them in *his* house. Something peculiar and personal had already attached him to them. Maybe he wouldn't have done it if the woman, Chris, had been totally unappealing. He briefly considered her appeal; not a bad-looking woman, and feisty. He had gotten snagged on their helplessness, on them, all three of them, even that stupid dog. No way would they get that dog into one of the shelters, and the kids needed the dog. He had no idea what was happening to him.

"Crammed," he finally said. "The shelters are crammed full."

"They could stay here," his mother said.

"No, Ma, no. My place is fine."

"This divorcée? She's pretty?"

"Ma, she's a little short on houses right now, and I'm hardly ever there. Anyway, I'm sure it'll only be for a few days. Oh," he said, looking at his dad, "do you have an hour or so you can spare? I need a hand; her car is still over at her house. There's been an inspection and cleanup crew going through the mess, and they found her purse and keys. Maybe you could drive my car so I can ferry hers back to my place?"

"Sure," he said slowly, looking over his glasses at his son, maybe considering putting him in a rest home until he became stable again.

"Okay, then."

"Okay, then," his parents replied in unison.

"Anything we can do to help?" his mother asked. "How are they for clothes? Do they need clothes?"

"Well, since you asked, you know that box of toys and coloring books and things you keep here for when the kids come over? I think her kids would love to borrow it. What do you say?"

"And some bread, maybe? Rolls?"

"No, Ma." He laughed. "There's plenty of food. Just some toys for the kids."

"Clothes, then?"

"No, really…"

"So what do they have for clothes, then?" she asked.

"Mattie, never mind," said Big Mike, who was far smaller than his son, whom they called Little Mike. Big Mike stopped his wife as though she was getting personal. Mattie—short for Mathilda—and Michael Cavanaugh looked with deep concern at their eldest son, who stood nearly six foot two and was about as wide as a refrigerator.

"Don't worry, Ma," he said, touching the end of her nose with a finger. "They aren't naked. There are no naked women and children running around my house. I can stay the night here? No problem?"

"Sure, Mike, sure. Let me give you some rolls to take to her. I'll roll a few, and you tell her to let them rise and have them for her dinner. Do you take dinner here, or there, with her?"

Mike thought his mother stressed *her.* After all, his sisters, Margie and Maureen, had brought home plenty of good Catholic women who were not divorced with kids. "She'd love some rolls, Ma. That's nice. I'll bring Big Mike back in about an hour, okay? Then I'm going to go back to my place to make sure that anything kids can get hurt on is locked up—the tools and all that. I'll have dinner here. I'll be back around five. I won't put you out, huh?"

"You never put us out," she said, patting his cheek. Actually, she slapped his cheek, but she did so affectionately.

An hour later, when the car exchange had been accomplished, Big Mike walked into his house. Mattie came out of the kitchen, wiping her hands on a dish towel. "So?" she asked her husband.

"There is a dog, too," Big Mike said. "A woman, pretty, two kids, both, like he said, cute, and a little dog with no manners."

He walked past his wife to his favorite chair and picked up the newspaper, which he had already read twice. Big Mike had been retired for a year and still had not done any of the projects he had been saving for retirement. "Do you think the dog will hurt his carpet?" Mattie asked.

Big Mike sank into his chair. He shook the paper. It always read better after a good shake. He looked at his wife of almost forty years over his glasses.

"Mattie, four times you saw your boys fall in love and get married. Two times you took our little girls to the bridal shop and took me to the cleaners before you let me take them down the aisle. Why do you act like you don't know nothing about your own kids? That dog could make Tootsie Rolls on Little Mike's head and he don't care. You pay attention then, Mattie," he said, shaking his paper again. "Little Mike's gonna keep even the dog. And it's a terrible dog. His name is Creeps."

"Rolls?" Chris asked.

"Listen, just count your blessings that she didn't come over here to dust you, dress you and feed you with her own hands. All I had to say was you've been burned out, and my mother almost adopted you all, sight unseen."

"That would be nice," she said. "Your dad looked, well, I don't know…reticent. Hesitant." Suspicious.

"Suspicious." At least he said it. "I've never done anything like this before. At least he didn't frisk you."

He went back into the garage, brought in two more bags of groceries and put them down.

"Why would he want to frisk me?"

"Well, my mom and sisters have been parading nice Catholic old maids past me for ten years without any luck at all. And then I go and invite you and your kids to move into my house," he said with a laugh. "When I told them what I'd done, the first thing my mother said was, 'So, is she pretty, this woman?'" Mike decided Chris could find out how his mother felt about divorcées later, or maybe never. "I told you, they shake their heads over me. I'm sort of a special project. Since Joanie died, anyway."

He left again, brought in two more bags. "You want me to put this stuff away?" she asked.

"Please," he said, getting still more.

"Gee," she said, "this is because we're here. You shouldn't have done that. I feel—"

"Hungry, probably. The rolls have to rise. Put them in the sunlight—there, on the windowsill."

He brought in more bags. Eight. He felt very big across the chest, bringing so much food into his house. Taking care of people, really. It was not like giving things to his siblings or folks, who all tolerated it very patiently, even gratefully, but, no kidding around, they didn't *need* his giving. They could get by fine without his gifts, his interference. What he gave his family was extra, not essential, like this. Today was the first time since he'd lost his family that he'd stocked so much; it filled him right up.

Next he brought in different kinds of bags. Then the box of toys, which he took into the living room for the kids. In the kitchen Chris was trying to figure out the cupboards. "I can't really tell where things go, Mike. You don't have a lot of food here."

"I almost never eat here. My mom would die of grief if she couldn't feed people all the time. I go over there almost every night. Here, I keep chips, beer, coffee, pop, cereal and eggs. And toilet paper. I don't even get a newspaper." He took out his wallet, unfolded some bills. "I ran into your landlord, and he told me to give you this to tide you over. I bought a couple of things for the kids, so you don't have to take them shopping in their pajamas. I would have picked up something for you, but I didn't know...you know..."

She looked at him in disappointment. "Mr. Blakely?"

"That his name?"

"That's not true, Mike. You didn't run into him."

He didn't seem to mind being caught in a lie. "You sure?"

"I talked to his wife. They're thinking of suing me. They aren't going to be generous about this."

"Suing *you?*"

"It would seem. I'm going to have to fight them."

"The son of a bitch. Here," he said, holding out the money. "You can pay me back out of your settlement. You ought to fry the bastard."

She smiled but hesitated to take the money. "Thanks. Why didn't you just say it was yours straight out?"

"I was afraid you wouldn't take it. You suffer too much, Chrissie. It's almost like you want to."

"No," she said, feeling a slight shiver at the sound of the nickname. Her dad had always called her Chrissie. "No, it's just that I have an extraordinary amount of bad luck for someone who doesn't take drugs or pick up hitchhikers. And I don't want to take so much from you that I feel guilty."

His face lit up. "I didn't know you were Catholic."

"I'm not," she said, confused.

"Oh. You mean other religions borrow guilt when they don't have enough, too?"

"Come on," she said, taking the money.

"I think these will fit the kids," he said, picking up the department-store bags. "I didn't even want to take a chance guessing your size…. You'll be okay in that sweat suit, huh? It isn't high fashion, but it isn't pajamas."

"People shop at Iverson's in worse than this. Why are you doing all this?" she asked him, a gentle inquiry.

"I don't really know," he said, the enormous honesty of it causing his dimple to flatten. He didn't break eye contact with her, even though he knew the heavy brows were probably making him look dangerous. "But I am. I want to. Just let it go. Okay? Please."

"Mike, I appreciate this. It's very generous and kind of you, but—"

"In the closet in the room with the desk, there's a printer. You can connect your laptop. You'll have to buy paper. And there's a wireless connection—just jump on. And here's a house key, since you'll be coming and going."

"Mike," she said slowly, "do you have some crazy fantasy about all of this? About these poor, destitute little kids and you're the big strong fireman who—"

"Don't," he said, holding up his hands and looking as though something had just poked him. "Don't, okay? Don't start all that. My family has been dead a long, long time—I don't have a lot of fantasies anymore. It's almost Christmas, for Pete's sake. I'm not trying to make you feel too grateful or too guilty. I don't have any big plan here. It's just sort of happening. They're good kids—they're too young for bad luck. Just get things back together. I don't expect anything. Let it be."

"Well," she said, "it's a lot to do…for a complete stranger."

"Did you find everything? Bedrooms? Bathrooms? Towels? Need to know where anything is?"

"No. You have a wonderful house."

"Well, you have your keys and some clothes for the kids. Go get something for yourself, have a good supper, take a bubble bath or something. Relax. There's some liquor in the dining-room cabinet, if you drink. So the heat's off for a while, okay? Your run of bad luck has been replaced by a little good luck, huh? And, Chris? I wouldn't hurt your feelings for the world, but you smell sort of like a ruined brisket."

Chapter 4

In one bag from the department store were three pairs of jeans, three shirts, pajamas, underwear and socks and a pair of tennis shoes, close enough to the right size, for Kyle. Pants, shirts, undies and tennies for Carrie were in a second bag, these in pink, lavender and white. All the price tags were removed, as was done with presents. "How did you feel, Mike, buying these things for the children?" she had wanted to ask him. But even had he stayed while she went through the bags, she would have lacked the nerve.

She suspected, or imagined maybe, that he would say it felt like something he had needed to do for a long, long time. She remembered how he had looked after the fire, his features rigid from hard work, wet with sweat and smeared with dirt. He had seemed so physical, rugged, dominant, yet there had been this tenderness all along. His kindness and humanity had glowed like a light in his soft green eyes. It was as though he did things from the heart, not necessarily prudent or logical things. What was prudent about running into burning buildings to save lives?

She had been pulled out of a fire; there was hardly any position more vulnerable than that. He had pulled her out, taken her in. There was hardly anything more masterful.

He had so quickly, so bravely told her about his missing family—not flippantly, not melodramatically— openly. Raw with honesty but no longer stinging with pain. An uncomplicated man who could speak in simple terms; he gave shelter, just like that. Because he was hardly there anyway, because the kids were too young for bad luck and because the shelters were awful…and because he'd had a daughter once. This gave her comfort and hope; her own pain was still fresh, and she looked forward to a time when she could calmly discuss all that had happened as the distant past rather than a current event.

"Here's the deal, Chris, your daughter reminds me of my daughter…."

He had locked up his tools in the garage with new padlocks before leaving again. To keep the children safe. He asked if she would mind leaving him notes on the refrigerator, taping up her schedule so he would know if she was out for errands, working, whatever. He didn't mean to pry, but he would have to stop by for his things now and then, and he didn't want them to be tripping over each other or getting in each other's way, surprising or embarrassing each other. And he gave her his mother's phone number, plus his cell number, which he wouldn't be able to answer when out on a call. It seemed to Chris as though she was being given everything, including space and privacy, when he should probably be asking her for references.

She had told him as little as possible about herself, secretive because her life story was so complex and astonishing. Mysterious Chris, so alone with her kids and their mean little dog. Him she had sized up within a day.

His eyes were a little sad, which was easily accounted for. He didn't have a mustache now, but in a photo she had found while looking for the TV remote he had a thick brown mustache. He had been photographed in a T-shirt that read SACTO #54; he'd been younger, his cheeks shallower, his eyes wider, not yet experienced and crinkled. He'd been prettier, not more handsome. That was the man, she imagined, that Joanie had fallen in love with. A strong, lean, hopeful youth.

She liked his older looks. He had cozied; his manliness, the strength of maturity, even his sadness, gave him a depth a woman would be tempted to sink into for comfort, for pleasure. Every plane on his face reflected seasoning, seasoning by pain and sorrow but also by compassion and abundant love. When Mike Cavanaugh had offered to provide for her and her kids, and then did so, the gesture had settled over her like a warm blanket. He seemed sure, capable, sturdy. Here was a man, she thought, who wouldn't collapse when leaned on. He was a complete stranger to her, but she felt perfectly safe. She hoped she would not become drugged by the feeling.

She had felt safe at other times in her life. She had felt the security of an only child; then suddenly she was an orphan. She had depended on her aunt's uncondi-

tional love, then felt betrayed by Flo's rage. And then—
three strikes and you're out—she had felt safe because
she'd had a bunch of money and a husband she loved
and a baby and what could go wrong?

She had obliquely asked Mike if he were trying to
compensate for his losses. And he had said, "Don't,
okay? Just don't. Just let it be, okay?" And then that
little breathy way he had of saying, "Please?"

There was more, Chris knew. She felt a familiar pull.
She was attracted to his power, his arms, his tanned
face and curly hair, his bright, imperfect smile. The
dimple. It had been such a long time since her body
spoke to her of needs that she was shaken by this sudden, spontaneous awareness. And she sensed his feelings were not very different. Oh, this was supposed to
be for the kids, but he looked at her in a way that made
her think he was trying not to look at her in *that* way.
She couldn't help but wonder what his motives were.
Maybe he wanted a woman. Or a family. He couldn't replace what he'd lost, but he could try to recapture some
of those emotions he had experienced when they were
alive. The feelings of usefulness, companionship. This
he could do by providing shelter. The thing he didn't
know was that he was exercising a need to provide on
a woman who had a terror of dependency.

"It's a roof," he had said. She would try to remember
what it was. And she would remind him, if necessary.

Chris scribbled a note. "Gone to shop, post office,
Iverson's, babysitter's and burned-down house. Be home
all evening. Thanx. Chris."

She hiked up the sweatpants, pulled down the sweatshirt and was grateful her moccasin slippers had rubber soles. On her modest shopping spree she bought

two pairs of blue jeans, shirts, some underwear and tennis shoes. She had purchased the barest minimum, and all on sale, but still the money Mike had given her was nearly depleted.

She stopped to pick up a new smock from Iverson's Grocery so she could get back to work. Her boss and co-workers offered sympathy and help, which touched her deeply but did that other thing, too: made her feel even worse. What right had she, after all, to such concern, such sympathy? She had been an heiress, for God's sake, and she had bungled it. She felt like an impostor. She longed for her mother, as she often did. Her mother would understand.

She dropped by Juanita Jimeniz's house to explain her time off and to plan a new babysitting schedule for when she could get back to work. Then she went to the old house, which was roped off to keep the neighborhood children out. Her own children stayed in the car. The house was hopelessly destroyed, but some of the books that had been shoved in the refrigerator had survived. She took them back to Mike's house but left them in the garage to air out.

She fixed herself and the kids a simple, cheap dinner; she didn't want to use up too much of the food Mike had bought. She would repay him, in any case. Then she soaked off the burned-brisket smell and washed her hair with Ivory—she had been too cheap to buy shampoo. She borrowed very little of what belonged to Mike and was not fooled by the appearance of new, unsqueezed toothpaste in the bathroom he probably never used. In fact, there were many new, unopened items in that bathroom, while he had a bathroom off the master bedroom full of half-used things. She didn't think he had much call for Jergen's Lotion or baby powder, yet it was available for her.

She scrubbed the kids, gave them ice cream, snuggled them for a while. She tucked them in early. Then she lounged, indulging in a weak bourbon and water. She wore her jeans because she wouldn't spend her limited funds on sleepwear. The soft, deep sofa was decadent; the movie channel was as entertaining as a producer's screening room. And she waited.

For Mike. Because she had left the note, she wondered if he would stop by. To see how she was holding up? To see if she needed anything? To see if she had ripped off the TV? To see if the kids were okay?

But he didn't come by. He might not even have been there to read the note.

Her next day's note said: "Out for errands, home by six. Will be here all evening. Thanks for everything. Best, C."

But again there was no evidence that he had come home. And the phone didn't ring while she was there. It felt very odd. Being in his house was somehow intimate, as if he surrounded her and was everywhere she looked but still was far away and hard to reach. Like Santa Claus. Or God.

She looked for something to read and found a small library in the master bedroom, which she entered guiltily. She was afraid to intrude, to invade. His books, in a bookcase by the bed, were almost all men's adventure and spy novels. Cussler, le Carré, Ludlum, Follett, Shaw. Some horror by Stephen King. The book that was open on the bedside table was the latest thriller on the bestseller list. The books gave her a good feeling about him; he read by choice and for fun, entertainment, to imagine, to widen his vision. She wrote for similar reasons. Then she went to the study, where she made her bed from the couch. She opened the closet there. "Well, what do you know," she said out loud.

The printer sat on top of a small bookcase that held some very different titles. Collections of Dickens, London, Melville, Tolstoy, even Austen. There was an old copy of *The Jungle Book,* a children's edition of *Tom Sawyer,* and other classics. There were hardcovers and paperbacks. *The Little Prince,* and *Illusions,* by Richard Bach. Did he read them, or were they here for another reason? Had they been his wife's? She finally picked up a copy of *Moby Dick* and, caressing it, went downstairs to luxuriate in the living room again. And to wait.

For him. What kind of guy can do this? she asked herself again. Give a complete stranger, who's obviously in a mess, a key to his house? And be so unworried? It was pretty hard not to like this guy. She liked his house, his generosity, his soft spot for a couple of unlucky kids. The thing that bothered her the most was that she couldn't quite tell if she liked him as a friend... or a man.

Then it was Friday, her third day in Mike's house. She knew she shouldn't complicate things. But she wanted to know about the man who owned interesting books and clothed and fed them because it was "just happening." Her note said: "Will be at the library today until 2:00 p.m. Appointment downtown with landlord at 2:30. Do you like tacos? We'll eat at 5:30–6:00 or so. Join us if you can. C."

She was back at the house by four. On the bottom of her note were some pencil scratchings. "I'll bring beer. M."

She showered and washed her hair. She was eager for his presence, for his approval and his concern. She would promise not to take up his space for long, and maybe she would learn a little more about the man who locked the tool cupboards to keep the children safe, the man who kept classics in one room and new fiction in another. The man who would bring beer, even though there was already beer in the refrigerator. He had been here, but his presence had flowed through without leaving a mark. Had he been here every day? Waiting for just such an invitation?

No way could he flow through her life without leaving a mark; already, she would never be able to forget him. He had touched them all in a permanent way. The way life can be forever changed by the smallest act. A man gives a quarter for a cup of coffee, but instead of coffee the recipient makes a phone call for a job and ends up being president of the company, makes millions, tells the story in the *New York Times*.

When he arrived he rang the bell. Carrie let him in, and Cheeks growled.

"Hello, Mr. Cabinaugh," Carrie said. "Mommy, Mr. Cabinaugh is here for tacos. Our mother is being very careful with your house, Mr. Cabinaugh."

"Carrie, you can call me Mike," he said, picking her up. She was light as a feather. A six-pack in a brown paper bag was under his other arm. "Are you feeling better?"

"Was I sick?" she asked him.

"No, but your house burned down."

"Oh, that wasn't our house, we were *renting* it. We had a 'partment before. Are you feeling better?"

He smiled broadly. "Was I sick?" He liked the games precocious children played.

"No, but our mother says we've taken your house."

He laughed, delighted. His laugh rumbled through the house, and Cheeks nearly lost his composure, seriously growling. "I loaned it to you because I wanted to. Have you told *him* yet that this is *my* house?"

"Maybe if you give him part of your taco, he'll start to like you."

"No way. He can like me or not, I don't care."

"Maybe he'll bite you if you don't share," she said.

He looked at her in such shock that her giggle exploded. Both her hands came together in a clap; she'd teased him good.

"He won't bite you really," she said.

Mike wished that adults could look at one another the way children looked at people. A child's look was so unashamed, so blatantly invasive. They wanted to *see* you. They looked hard. Without flinching or feeling self-conscious, looking you square in the face to see what you were made of, what you were about. And they didn't care a bit that you saw them looking. If adults could do that, friendship wouldn't take so long.

"Maybe we should have a fire tonight," he said. "It's cold and rainy outside."

"Our mother says the fireplace is brand-new."

"It's been used. Come on," he said, even though he carried her into the kitchen where the sound of meat sizzling indicated Chris was working.

Tacos were not fancy by anyone's standards, but Mike thought the kitchen smelled wonderfully homey; she might as well have been baking bread. And she might as well have been wearing an evening gown; she cleaned up real good. But it was only a pair of jeans. His eyes went right to her small, shapely rear, although when she turned around to greet him he shifted his gaze guiltily to her face. She smiled and said hello, and he began to color because he had sex on his mind and was afraid she would know. It had been a while since he'd had that reaction. He hardly knew this woman, but he couldn't wait. He was somewhat ashamed, somewhat relieved. He had hoped that part of him wasn't all used up. He also hoped he wasn't going to be terribly disappointed when he didn't get things his way, which he suspected he wouldn't. He handed her the bag. "Smells good. Can we have a fire? The screen is safe, and I'll watch the kids."

"That would be good. I don't want them to be afraid of safe fires."

He cocked his head to look at her, impressed. "I thought you might be more nervous about it...after losing everything."

"I have them," she said, smiling. "The other stuff wasn't that valuable."

Kyle was sitting on the counter by the sink, and Mike grabbed him with his free hand. Holding a kid on each hip, he hauled them off to the living room to get the fire started while Chris fixed tacos.

She heard him talking to her children, and she peeked around the corner to see what was going on.

"We're going to stack the logs very carefully, like this, so they won't fall. What would happen if a log fell off the grate while it was on fire? That's right, it might fall right out of the fireplace and onto the rug. Uh-huh, we have to put some paper underneath, here, like this, to start the fire easier. Yep, the wood would burn without the paper, but the paper makes it hotter quicker. Paper burns very easily. Now, Kyle, is that very hot? Yes, you must not go closer than this. The screen will be very hot, too, while the fire is burning. There, isn't that warm and pretty?"

Chris handed him a cold beer. "Thanks," he said.

"About ten minutes for tacos."

"The kids want a drink, too, don't you?" Both kids stared at him hopefully. "Chocolate milk?" Their eyes became wider, more hopeful.

"Uh, Mike, they should come into the kitchen...."

"They can't see the fire in the kitchen." He saw Carrie and Kyle holding back gurgles of desire.

"What if someone spills?" Chris persisted.

"So? We want chocolate milk by the fire. Don't we?" He looked at one, then the other, and they nodded very carefully. Carrie's tongue was poking out of her mouth, and her eyes beseeched her mother's sense of adventure.

"All right," she said. She heard them laugh, all three of them. When she was safely in the kitchen stirring chocolate into glasses of milk, a smile ran through her body. He was spoiling them, giving in. Thank you, God. He was gentle and giving and fun, and they would remember him forever. Chris had been worried about the total absence of male role models for them, but she had lacked the time, energy or courage for even the most innocent of relationships with men. Also, she had thought it necessary to keep them safe from her poor judgment. She had really messed up when she picked Steve. This was good; they needed a decent man to think about, to remember. As did she.

She brought them their drinks, a beer for herself. "I

turned the meat off for now. It looks like we're going to have a cocktail hour here," she said.

"Good," he said, passing the milks. "Relax. Enjoy yourself."

She sucked in her breath and flinched as her younger child sloshed his drink to his mouth. Before long Kyle's indelible mark would be on the fireman's rug.

"I said, relax. I could throw a cup of chocolate on the carpet right now just to get it over with if it'll help you calm down. Don't be so nervous."

"It's just that everything is so nice. Practically new."

Mike knew, as he had known the very night her house burned down, that although she seemed to own almost nothing of any value, she was not a person who had done without all her life. She didn't come from poor people. He didn't know how he knew, but he did. *He* had come from poor, blue-collar Irish Catholics transplanted from the East Coast. His mother had fried round steak on special occasions; his father had said, "Chewy? Good for your teeth." The way Chris talked, or walked, or held her head, or something, he knew she had grown up differently. "It's new because it's hardly been used, Chrissie. That isn't necessarily good." That won him a grateful smile. "What did the landlord say?"

"He said he'd get back to me."

"What?" That made Mike a little angry.

"Actually, he offered me a few hundred dollars— my original deposit. But he wanted me to sign a paper that promised we were uninjured and wouldn't seek a larger settlement. I wouldn't sign it. I told him that I lost several thousand dollars' worth of stuff—none of it new, but none of it stuff that we could spare. It's not as though it was my fault, really, although I should have had some insurance. I would have expected him to be a bit more compassionate."

"Son of a bitch. Sorry," he said, glancing at the kids. "Now it'll only go harder on him. Sue him."

"I'm not really the suing kind," she said, and thought about adding, *anymore.* "But I will try to get a little more money out of him."

"A bunch of money. The fact is, you could've all been killed."

"I know," she said, shuddering. "I've given a lot of thought to that."

She had condemned herself for the risk she had exposed Carrie and Kyle to, living on pride as she was, struggling to be independent. Renting a cheap, crummy house in a questionable neighborhood when Aunt Flo would have taken them in—probably after a mere tongue-lashing and Chris's promise never to disobey again. Her kids could have more, be safer. It only meant admitting that she had been a fool, a senseless fool, and she had already been punished plenty for that.

But having more had never been the issue. Even though she had grown up rich, she didn't miss luxury all that much. She wanted to recover, not beg forgiveness. She wanted to make herself safe, not sink into someone else's provisions. She wanted to call Flo and ask if they could make up, *not* call Flo and ask for plane fare. She didn't want to be completely beaten, a total victim. She had been teetering on the edge before, ready to pick up the phone and call Chicago collect, but she always managed to steal one more day of independence. Pride. Her father's gift to her. Fierce and unyielding. And sometimes quite tiring.

"I haven't called my aunt yet," she said apologetically.

"No hurry on that," he said. "Did you find the printer?"

"Yes. And books—wonderful books."

"My brother," Mike said. "I'm the oldest one in the family and wasn't interested in college. I just wanted money and a man's work—my father's son, all right. The other kids are all hotshot brainy types. Tommy— he's about twenty-nine, I guess—is a professor. Big-shot professor. And a coach. Every time he was working on a book with his class, he wouldn't shut up about it. You'd think he was gossiping about the neighbors, he was so wound up and chatty. He'd always give me a copy." He laughed at himself. "I never let on that I read them, but I read them. Hell, with Tommy carrying on for weeks, it's like taking the class."

"I had a little college myself," she said. "Two years. I studied literature."

"Then you know," he said, as if there were a club for the few people who cared enough to discuss the little-known secrets about things that happened inside books, a small group who entered these classic stories, lived in them briefly but were forever changed, deeply touched.

During tacos they talked about Chris's writing, even though she usually tended to be secretive about that, too. She was slightly embarrassed about her novice status and the enormity of her ambitions. She wanted to be the next J.K. Rowling. Her love of books had begun these dreams, but it was the way creating a story of her own could take over her life, consume her thoughts, charge her with energy, that kept her enthusiasm so high. It took her away from her petty, surface concerns, while at the same time making her probe more deeply into her inner self than was possible to imagine.

She especially liked stories for kids; there was something magical about them, and she identified so closely with the emotional impact of their experiences.

"I don't think everyone remembers details from their childhood the way I do," she offered in partial explanation. "I remember what I was *wearing* the day Barbara Ann Cruise pushed me out of the lunch line; I remember the exact feeling of being third-to-the-last picked for the soccer team. It might as well have been last to be that unpopular. And the first boy-girl party, sixth grade. I *know* I was the only one not invited, and I was so miserable and hurt that my mother let me sleep with her. I remember those feelings so exactly that it's almost scary."

And, she explained, she loved kids in general. Loved what they had to build on, endure, traverse, overcome, become. Had she finished her degree, likely she would have chosen a field in which she would be working with children—probably teaching at the elementary level.

She was amazed at how she went on and on, how natural it felt, and how nice it was to have someone encourage her to continue.

"Do you want more children?" he asked her.

"I'd like to concentrate on doing all right with these two. I've got no real job skills, but I'm a good writer. Eventually I want to stay home with the kids and write for a living. Writing for kids is the only thing I've ever done that feels right."

Carrie and Kyle asked to be excused and ran off to play quietly.

"How about if you remarry?" he prodded.

"No chance of that," she said emphatically. "My ex went on a business trip and never came back. Before Kyle was even born. Now my future is in these two hands," she said, holding up her palms.

"Never say never; gets you into trouble."

"I'll be fine. I land on my feet. When times get real tough, I work overtime, or I clean houses. If I clean for people who are away working, I bring the kids along. And with that schedule, I can write. As long as I take care of the kids and do enough writing so that I feel I haven't given up every little dream I ever had, then I'm as happy as I expect to be." She watched his face. "Maybe I won't write great books," she said. "I'll write a few good books if I work very, very hard—books like the kind you have in your bedroom, books that entertain, that help people imagine, get away and expand a little. The kind you have in your study, people are born to write."

He smiled a small smile.

"I didn't sleep in your bed," she said.

"I know," he replied quietly.

They shifted their eyes away. She wondered how he knew, wanted to ask, but had too much fun with the fantasy. Had he rigged something? Left a pencil on the bed? Positioned the bedspread just so?

He had glanced away because he was embarrassed by how he knew. When she was gone, doing errands, he had lifted the pillows from his bed, hoping to smell her on one of them, disappointed when he had not. He had thought about the pillow on the hide-a-bed but had restrained himself.

He was relieved when the children chose that moment to interrupt. They all played a game of Candyland in front of the fire and watched a thirty-minute Muppets rerun on TV. Mike scratched Cheeks behind the ears, inadvertently creating a slapstick routine with the terrier. Every time he reached toward the dog, Cheeks snarled blackly, then allowed the scratch anyway. The game made the children laugh with uncontrolled passion.

At eight o'clock Mike turned off the television. The fire was dying down. He turned on the light behind his recliner, pulled the kids onto his lap, and opened a big Richard Scarry picture book. He began to read.

At eight-thirty Kyle was asleep on Mike's chest with his thumb in his mouth. But Mike was still reading. His shoes were off; his voice was growing slower and scratchier. Chris stood and hovered over them. "Come on, Carrie. Bedtime. I'll help you."

"Not yet, Mommy. I want to fall asleep here, like Kyle did."

"It would be better if you brushed your teeth and fell asleep in your bed," Mike said gently, kissing her forehead.

"Okay," she said, "but first finish the story."

"I'll read to you again next time. Let Mommy put you to bed."

Chris lifted Carrie out of the recliner. "Let me get Carrie settled, then I'll come back for Kyle."

"Okay," he said. He didn't offer to carry Kyle. He wanted to be left alone with him for a few minutes, alone in the dim evening with a child in his arms. Mike embraced the little boy tightly. He inhaled the smell of his hair, the redolence of child. Tangy. Sharp. Kyle snored when his thumb came out of his mouth. Mike put it back in. Childhood was so short.

Too soon, Chris took him away. Mike felt a choking sensation in his throat and something binding his chest. He reached behind him to turn off the lamp. The living room was bathed in firelight, glowing but dark. When Chris returned to the living room she said, "There," in that way a mother does when her duties are done, even though she's still on call. Joanie had said it that way when she finally tucked rambunctious Shelly into bed; that kid wanted to go all night.

Then Chris sat on the sofa and looked at him. He knew he was caught in the shadows and that she might see the tear that had slipped down his cheek. He decided he wouldn't wipe it away because then she would know for sure. He wasn't ashamed of emotions like these, but crying was so intimate, and he didn't want to invite her in any further yet. He wasn't all that sure this was something she could share. She must have known, however, because she gave him a few moments of respectful silence while he suppressed his emotions. She did, after all, know of his losses.

"Did you read *Out of Africa?*" he finally asked her.

"Years ago. Way before anyone considered a movie."

"Me, too. It was Holden Caulfield's favorite book, remember? I read *The Catcher in the Rye* with my little brother Tommy's class. Then I read *Out of Africa*. This part wasn't in the movie, anyway. There's a place in the book where she tells about the veldt-sores you can get in Africa. If you're not careful, the sores will heal on the outside, but inside they get worse; they get infected and runny and full of poison. The only way you can get rid of them is to open them up, dig them out at the roots, leave them open on top until they get the proper scabs and scars."

He brushed off his cheek.

"You don't just get them in Africa," Chris said.

"Don't call your aunt yet," he said. "Please."

"It might be better if I called her right away."

"Please," he said again.

"Look—"

"There's plenty of room here. There's no hurry."

"But—"

"You need a place for them. For you. For now."

"It's not mine, though. It's hard to—"

"You wouldn't exactly be taking charity, Chrissie. This works as well for me as for you."

"Mike, what's happening here?"

"Stay awhile. Just awhile. I gotta get a scab on this, so I can scar. I'm way behind. I didn't do it on purpose, but I waited too long."

"Oh, jeez," she said through a sigh.

"Maybe I can grout the veldt-sores. If I can't, it's not your fault."

"What if staying here only makes new ones?" she asked him.

"No. I don't see that happening."

"Just what the heck *is* happening?"

"Nothing bad, I don't think. Big Mike calls things like this 'unconscious plans'—when you do something that looks to the whole world like it's crazy as hell and totally coincidental and you don't think it ran through your brain for one second first, but unconsciously you knew all along you were going to do it. Like I wasn't looking to help out anyone, for a family to move in here—there have been lots of burned-out families over the years—and I didn't know I was going to offer you a place to stay even when the shelters were full, and I sure as hell didn't know I'd ask you to hang around longer than you have to, but—" He stopped and shrugged. "But Ma says Big Mike is full of it."

A huff of air escaped Chris—it was almost laughter.

"I don't talk about my feelings very well," he apologized.

"You're doing fine."

"If things had been different, if I'd met you at the zoo, I'd just do something normal, like ask you out to dinner or offer to take you and the kids to a movie."

"You would?"

"But it isn't that way. You got burned out. You need a place to stay. Feels like it oughta be this way, like this is the natural order. That's all. I haven't brought a lot of food into this house before. I don't have to be quiet when I get up early. No one messes anything up; it's pretty quiet all the time. And it has one or two advantages for you and the kids, too."

"But—"

"Not just the kids," he added in such a way that she thought he felt he should be completely honest.

"Oh."

"I'm not making a pass," he said.

"This is crazy," she said, leaning an elbow on her knee and cupping her chin in her hand.

"Yeah, the whole world is crazy. Your ex left you when you were pregnant. Your only family hates you. Your house burned down. And some lunatic wants you to hang around awhile because…"

She waited for him to finish. When he didn't, she prompted, "Because why?"

"Because, why not?"

"Look," she said, taken aback a bit. What kind of

reason was "why not?" "You've been very generous, you seem like a nice guy, but really, Mike, I don't know you, and you don't know me, and—"

"This is crazy, Chrissie, but I'm not. I'm pretty safe. I mean, I pulled you out of a burning house, for Pete's sake. You want some references? Want to meet my mother?"

"I just want to know what you're after."

"An extension. Of tonight. It was a fun night, huh?" He grinned, proud of himself.

He had a contagious smile that made you smile back even when you didn't have a smile ready. It *had* been a nice evening. She had even had the fleeting thought that she liked him, desired him, felt comfortable and secure for the first time in a very long time. What she had *not* had was the slightest notion of this kind of invitation.

"And that's all?"

"That's all I have the guts to ask for."

"You're making me nervous," she said.

"Don't overthink it. Men say more daring things than that in singles' bars, right?" Again he grinned. He knew. She knew. He knew she knew he knew. "Won't hurt anything if we're friends."

"How long?" she asked him.

"How about Christmas? It isn't very far away. It could be fun, huh? For the kids, anyway. Maybe for me and you, too."

"Christmas?" she asked doubtfully.

"Shelters and places like that, well, they're some-times…pretty dangerous. Dirty, a lot of unsavory types hanging around…people get hurt. It wouldn't be a good idea. Really. If you don't like the idea of staying here, you should call your old-maid aunt who hates your guts.

I think it would be lousy for you to go to Chicago because then we wouldn't find out if we like each other—
all of us, I mean—but all things considered, it would be
no fun at all to visit you at one of those awful shelters."

"Christmas?"

"It might be nice for the kids to know where they're
going to be for a while. To have something to look forward to."

"I find this a little scary," she admitted.

"No scarier than sleeping in your car."

"True. But—" She couldn't think of any buts. Even
though she hadn't expected him to ask her to stay, she
had known almost instantly why he had done so. Because he missed his family, because he wanted his home
to be less lonely, because Carrie reminded him of his
daughter…because he was attracted to Chris.

"But you understand." He looked at her with easy,
unbrooding eyes, relaxed, trusting eyes. She'd have to
be nuts herself not to understand that they'd started
something. "Don't you?"

"Are you going back to your mom and dad's?" she
asked.

"Yeah," he said, sitting forward and reaching for
his shoes.

"You don't have to." He stopped. "If you'd prefer,
I understand, but it's your house." She curled her feet
under herself. "If what you're looking for is some noise,
it'll break loose at about seven."

He leaned back, leaving his shoes where they were.
"Thanks. Sure you don't mind?"

She shook her head. "I'd just like you to remember
that this is temporary."

"I know."

"Don't get yourself all caught up in it."

Too late. "I won't."

"I appreciate the generosity."

"I appreciate it, too. Your part, I mean. I understand why this would make you a little nervous. You probably don't trust men."

"Not a lot, no."

"Well, that's understandable. It'll be all right."

"Roommates. This is really astonishing."

"Probably nothing like this ever happened before," he said.

"Never."

"That hide-a-bed is okay? Comfortable?" He lifted one eyebrow.

"Perfectly," she said.

"I could take it. Or—"

"Don't even think it," she said.

This time his eyes sparkled with the grin. He was feeling a lot better. "Come on, Chrissie. You can't make me not *think* it."

She threw a couch pillow at him. And, in spite of herself, she laughed at him. Or at herself—it was hard to tell which. After all, she'd been thinking the same thing almost since she met him. It just scared her, that was all. But not enough to run for her life.

It was the middle of the night, and Mattie Cavanaugh was sitting up on the edge of her bed. She reached toward the bedside table.

"If you touch that phone," Big Mike said, "I will break your arm."

"Shouldn't we know he wasn't in a bad accident?" she asked.

"No, and I don't care if you don't sleep for a month. You leave the boy alone. He had a hard time of it. Some things his mama can't take care of."

"But we don't know this woman, this *divorcée*."

"Both arms," Big Mike said. "I'll break both arms."

"I hope he's all right, is all. I hope he's all right."

"He ain't been all right for ten years now. Lie down. Come on, here," he said, pulling her back into his arms. "If we're going to be awake thinking about what Little Mike's doing, maybe we should fool around, eh?"

"Fool around? How can I fool around with some old man when all I can think about is my son, maybe lying in a ditch somewhere?"

Big Mike laughed and kissed Mattie's cheek. "That isn't what you're thinking about, Mattie Cavanaugh. The priest is gonna get an earful at confession, eh? Nosy old woman. Come here. Closer." He was quiet for a long time. "It ain't the woman worries me so much as that dog, Creeps. That dog's gonna maybe take Little Mike's toe off."

Chapter 5

Chris had pulled out the sofa bed at 10:00 p.m. She left her door ajar to listen for the kids, although they always slept soundly. She had left the desk lamp on, propped *Moby Dick* on her knees and trained her eyes on the page. But not a word of it soaked into her brain.

She could hear the sound of the television downstairs. Also, she heard him make two trips into the kitchen and slam the refrigerator door once. She heard water in the sink, lights clicking on and off and, finally, at eleven, the squeaking of the stairs. *What in the world have I gotten myself into?* she asked herself.

She heard his shower running. She had never heard of a man showering before bed. Unless… Just what was he cleaning up for? She heard a blow dryer. So his wet hair wouldn't soak the pillow? His mattress creaked softly, his light clicked off, and before very long she heard the purr of a soft snore that hit an occasional snag and tripped into a brief snort. Her shoulders began to ache from the tension of listening.

Chris's imagination always worked best late at night. For someone who was struggling to make it alone, she was the last person who *should* be alone. Night noises always grew into monsters; melodramas unfolded in her mind at the slightest provocation. Once the sun came up she was remarkably sane. It was, however, nearly midnight before she began to realize that as long as she could hear him snoring, he wasn't tiptoeing down the hall toward her sofa bed. What kind of guy wanted to have kids—someone else's kids—in his house? No, no, surely not *that* kind of guy! He seemed like a nice, normal fella—pretty good-looking, too. Just what unusual habits had prevented his remarriage?

At one she put down the book, of which she had read four paragraphs, and turned off the light. She got out of bed and peeked down the hall. He had pulled his door too, but it was ajar a few inches, which was why she could hear him snoring. She got back into bed, but her neck was stiff and her nerves were taut. What if he *was* crazy? If she and the children suddenly disappeared, would Mr. Iverson, or Mike Cavanaugh's Irish mother, demand an investigation?

At about two, rather bored with the rapist, pedophile, murderer fantasies, she began to indulge another kind. He was a nice guy, a decent and friendly man who'd had his share of troubles but had not been destroyed by them. Only wounded. Chris had not had to listen to him long before she could actually feel his desire to heal himself. He had accomplished a feat that Chris still felt was slightly out of her reach—he was managing on his own—but it hadn't made him whole. He hadn't asked that much of her, she reflected, and a small part of her was even relieved to not be the only needy one.

She wanted to drift off to sleep, but his presence down the hall overwhelmed her. It was so long since she had shared her space with anyone but the kids. All she could think about was him—what he wanted from her and what he'd done with the past ten years. Why hadn't he found a fire victim with two little kids five years ago? Would his "unconscious plan" have fallen into place with someone else in similar circumstances?

At three Chris tried putting her pillow at the foot of the bed. Steve had never read to Carrie. He'd rarely held her. He wasn't at the hospital when she was born, and he only visited twice; he said he was in the middle of a deal. He didn't care what they named their daughter; Carrie was fine, he said. A person's name for a whole life...fine. After he had been missing for quite some time her lawyer finally found him in Dallas, living, she was told, very modestly. Struggling. Staying with acquaintances, friends. Driving a borrowed car. Wearing last year's clothes.

"What about my money?" she had asked the lawyer.

"He doesn't seem to have it anymore."

"But it was *mine!*" she had exclaimed.

"Did you have a prenuptial agreement, Chris? An account number somewhere? Anything? We could sue him, but you should be aware of the cost, and the consequences of losing...or of finding out there's nothing left anyway. So, Chris, did you do *anything* to protect yourself?" the lawyer had asked her.

The lawyer had then asked Steve if he would contest the divorce.

"Absolutely not," had been his answer. "Chris deserves better than me," the lawyer reported Steve as saying.

What a generous bastard he was.

"And the custody of the two children?"

"Two?" he had countered.

"Since you don't want to sue him for support," the lawyer had said to Chris, "I imagine it doesn't matter that he questions the paternity of the second child."

Oh, hell no, why would a little thing like that matter?

She turned her head. Her pillow had become somewhat damp from remembering. If she hadn't been used the first time around—lulled away from her home, tricked into betraying her own family, abandoned and humiliated—then maybe she would walk down that hall and curl up against that strength and power and comfort, just as her kids had. Because they weren't the only ones who needed to feel some of that. And they weren't the only ones who missed having a man around. Life was very big. Everyone needed a top and a bottom, a right and a left, a masculine and a feminine, a full circle that connects. Wouldn't it be nice, she thought, if she hadn't been so thoroughly educated in the perils of trust?

At three-thirty she noticed that Mike wasn't snoring, but she had decided he wasn't dangerous a couple of hours earlier, so she wasn't worried that he was sneaking down the hall. She hadn't stayed only because it was safe and comfortable for the kids, and she hadn't been afraid of him for one minute, not really. After those few hours of wild sleeplessness she had finally remembered that the only person she was frightened of was herself.

She fell into a jerking sleep, every muscle taut from insomnia, her brain throbbing from vacillating between the idea of reintroducing sex into her barren life and running away with her kids before she became tempted.

Morning had been around awhile when Chris awoke. She heard her kids talking quietly, and she sat up with a start. Her back was sore, and her head ached. An insomnia hangover. By the time she had fallen asleep she must have been in a double pretzel position. She rubbed her eyes; they were swollen from crying. She tried to smooth her wavy hair and reached for her jeans to pull them on. Then she heard *his* voice. He was up taking care of her kids. This was going too far.

Distracted, she failed to glance into the bathroom mirror to see how the night had worn on her. She immediately began looking for the kids. She could hear their voices coming from his bedroom. She stood at the door, listening.

"Do you shave your legs, too?" she heard Carrie ask him.

"Women shave their legs. Not men."

"Why?"

"No telling. Want shaving cream on your legs?"

"Yes. Then you'll shave them?"

"Nope, we're just practicing today. You have to be older."

"Kyle? Carrie?" Chris called, not entering his bedroom. "What are you doing in there?"

"Mommy, come and see us shaving."

"Shabing. Vrooom," Kyle added.

She thought about it for a second. "Mike? Can I come in?"

"Well," he said, dragging the word out, "I don't know if you should, but—"

She shot into the room. What had she expected? That he would be naked? She shook her head at them. Carrie sat on the closed toilet seat with shaving cream on her legs; Kyle sat on the sink beside where Mike stood shaving. They had their own bladeless razors to scrape shaving cream off themselves, and slop it into the sink. They smiled at her, all three of them. Mike met her eyes in the mirror.

"What are you kids doing?" she asked, looking at the biggest kid of all.

"Got anything you want shaved?" he asked. He turned around to face her, and his brows drew together a little. "Didn't you sleep well?"

She peeked around his shoulder to look in the mirror. Ugh. It must have been a worse night than she remembered. How did you apologize for waking up ugly?

"I've never slept on that bed," he remarked, turning back to the sink. "Is it terrible? Maybe I should take it. Or try the couch downstairs. Or maybe one of the kids, being pretty light, would be able to—"

"It wasn't the bed," she said, feeling stupid. "It was one of those nights, you know, when you're being chased all night long and wake up exhausted." And then she made a decision that the next time she heard rapists and murderers in the night, they were just going to have to get her in her sleep; she wasn't waiting for them anymore. It wasn't the first time she had resolved this, but maybe from now on she could make it stick.

"Chased? As in nightmares?"

Kyle had scraped off all his shaving cream and was ready for more. He grabbed the can and gave it a squirt. Bad aim. It snaked toward Mike's ear. Chris grimaced. Then she laughed.

"Not exactly nightmares," she said, reaching for a towel and wiping Kyle's face. "No more," she told her son. "You're done." She wiped Carrie's legs. "More like a vivid imagination."

"You overthink everything," he told her, starting to shave the other side of his face.

"Want some breakfast, Carrie?" she asked.

"We had pancakes already. Clown pancakes."

"Oh. Okay. Go watch TV."

He wiped his face clean. He turned around. "So, what chased you all night?"

"Just your basic neurotic fantasies."

"You want a lock for your door? Think you'd sleep better?"

"How'd you know?" she asked, amazed that he had seen through her that quickly, that easily.

"Well, to worry about things that *have* happened is one thing, but to worry about things that *might* happen…well, you seem to specialize in that. But you have a long way to go to catch up with Mattie."

"Mattie?"

"My mom. Guilt and worry. She's got a Ph.D. Dr. Ma."

"Well, gee, we're strangers, you know. All you have to do is read the newspapers to—"

"Chrissie," he said solemnly, touching her nose and leaving a little spot of shaving cream. "We're not strangers anymore. And we almost never were." She looked into his green eyes. "Chrissie, Chrissie, maybe you have good reason to be careful. Me, too. But honest, there isn't any reason not to get a good night's sleep. Take it easy. I like you guys. I'll take good care of you."

"I don't want to be taken care of," she said, though

not very vehemently. It was, in fact, something she still wanted very badly sometimes, something she hadn't grown out of naturally before her parents were suddenly killed. But she'd spent four years remembering that such wants were immature, grounded in ignorance *and* double-edged. Let someone take care of you, and they might just take care of you.

"Fine," he said, smiling. "So, wanna chat awhile? Or can I take a shower?"

"But you took a shower last—" He smiled more deeply. "I think I'll go eat something," she said, turning away.

"I have the day off," he called after her. "Wanna rent a movie for the kids or something? I left two clown pancakes for you in the kitchen. There's coffee, too. Chrissie? Chrissie?"

She leaned against the wall outside his bedroom door, arms crossed over her chest. She didn't answer him. She wanted to eat the clown pancakes. Rent a movie. She wanted all of it. *Oh, please, God, don't let me wake up for a while. Please.*

There were a lot of things besides men and sex that Chris had given up. She had simply been too busy to notice. Leisure time had been the first thing out the door behind Steve. Things like walking around the mall, or sitting at a picnic table tossing birdseed to ducks. Things like sitting down to a meal *with* her kids rather than cooking something for them while she ate out of a pan over the sink. And friendship—having someone reach for your hand or give you a hug at precisely the right moment. These were the kinds of simple things that made life satisfying.

"I didn't think I was smart enough for college," Mike told her when they were walking around the mall. "I missed that gene the other kids got, the one that made them ambitious and convinced they were smart enough. I worked construction for a couple of years out of high school. Then I drove a truck until I got hired at the department. Like I said, I always just wanted physical work and a solid paycheck. That's all."

"But what kind of gene does it take to never doubt, not for one second, that you're going to get out of that burning building?" she asked him.

"I doubted it once or twice," he said.

"Too scary."

"Wanna know what's scary? Fear itself. I've seen two guys, in my twelve years, get scared. Too scared of the fire to do it anymore. They all of a sudden couldn't go in. Whew."

I can relate, she thought.

"That's why I try not to think too much."

"If you don't think about it, it won't happen?"

"Sort of. Ever read any of those books, you know, the how-to-get-through-anything, or how-to-love-someone-who-loves-someone-else, or—"

"Pop psychology?" she supplied.

"Yeah. Well, I went through about fifteen of them in the two years after Joanie and Shelly. *Love Yourself First. Grief Management. Living Alone Happily.* Think, think, think."

"Didn't they help?"

"Yeah. They gave me something to do while I was letting time tick away. I'd be right here, right now, doing exactly what I'm doing if I hadn't read a word. In fact, most of the ones I read about grief said you just have to admit your feelings and feel them. Hell, I couldn't *help* that."

She laughed sympathetically.

"How many of those books have you been through?" he asked her.

"Oh, twenty or a hundred."

"And did it ever turn out that your husband hadn't walked out after all? Did you ever slam the cover shut after the last page and find your life any different?"

"You're an analyst's nightmare," she suggested.

In the park, tossing birdseed to the ducks, she told him a little about herself and her divorce, though she remained cautious of the exact circumstances.

"He said he was going to a business meeting in San Diego," she explained. "Then the phone started ringing—people were looking for him. He didn't call. I was afraid he was dead. I called his office. They hadn't heard from him, his secretary said. I called the police; he wasn't missing long enough. I started dialing every hotel in San Diego. It was horrible. It was two weeks, then four. I started to find out how little I knew about him and his life away from me. I realized I was pregnant, and even though I had a little money and could pay some of the bills, I didn't know how to go about finding this joker.

"When I started calling some business acquaintances I'd heard him mention, I found out he'd done a lot of lying. The big wheeler-dealer was a con artist, and he'd skipped town. Literally." She decided not to mention that she herself had been conned.

"What did he do for a living?"

"He said he was a lawyer. I'm even starting to doubt that."

"And you never found him?"

"Once I had myself convinced I wasn't a widow but an abandoned wife, I hired a lawyer. The lawyer found him in another state. Do you know what I asked the lawyer to do for me? I asked him to ask Steve if he would please come home, for the children." She turned her head and looked at him. Tears filled her eyes. "He said, 'Children?' He didn't even know about Kyle."

That was when he reached for her hand. He gave it a squeeze and did her the courtesy of saying nothing.

"After he walked out on me when I had a one-year-old and was pregnant, I asked him to come home. Can you beat that?"

"'Course you did, Chrissie. Whenever something bad happens, the very first thing you want is for it not to have happened."

"The kids don't even know him."

"Kids. They're always the lucky ones, huh?"

He put his arm around her shoulder. Carrie and Kyle hopped around while ducks chased them for birdseed.

"What I've been trying to figure out for the past four years is how I could have been that stupid. I believed everything he told me. I trusted him completely, even though he did all these things that should have signaled me he was a liar. Not being where he was supposed to be, not getting home when he was expected, not following through on any of his promises, not showing any real affection. He was so good-looking and entertaining and funny that I, big dope that I was, went right into a coma and didn't wake up until he left me."

Mike squeezed her shoulders. "I don't mean to butt in, Chrissie, but aren't you blaming the wrong person?"

"I don't ever want to be that stupid again, know what

I mean? Hey!" she said when he pinched her upper arm. "What was that for?"

"Just making sure you're wide-awake," he said, grinning.

Later that evening, after the kids had gone to bed, they stayed in the living room, Mike in his recliner and Chrissie curled up on the couch. He had made them each an Irish coffee. And they talked. About what he'd done with the past ten years. About his women.

"My mom thinks I've been celibate for ten years. That's fair, since I think she has. She's always worried I'm alone too much, but she has to know where I am every second, so I can't really be alone *with* someone, right?"

There had been only a few women in his life over the years. Sometimes he knew right away it wasn't going anywhere, and he'd end it after a couple of dates. No one-night stands; he'd never understood how people could do that. Men did it all the time, he knew, but it didn't appeal to him. There was a guy, Stu, he worked with, for example, who seemed to be hot to trot every minute. A married guy, no less.

Then a few years back there had been two women at once; he dated them both on and off for a whole year. One was a flight attendant who was out of town a lot, and with his twenty-four-hour shifts at the department, it was hard for them to connect. They seemed to get bored with trying. The other one he liked pretty well, but he knew she was on the rebound. She'd broken up with a guy she had really been in love with, then ended her affair with Mike when the guy came back. "My sister Maureen found out about me seeing two women at once and gave me a book about fear of intimacy. She's the family counselor. I told her to shove it."

"Well, that was a nice thing to tell her."

Then there had been the woman in Tahoe. An artist. She threw pots, painted, sculpted, did incredible and beautiful things, things no one would ever think of doing, and lived in a small adobe house furnished by her own hands. She had made the rugs, furniture, wall hangings…everything but the toilet.

"When I first met her I thought I'd died and gone to heaven. She's a little older than me—she's over forty. After a year of driving to Tahoe every time I got a few days free, if she had a few days free, too—she traveled and taught, gave workshops and all that—I started to figure out there was something missing. I *admired* her. *Envied* her. That talent, skill. Those ideas. Like a pioneer. I couldn't wait to get to her place and see what she'd done. I was actually surprised to realize I didn't love her. I *liked* her a lot—still do.

"She's one of the neatest people in the world. But you know what was missing? She needed absolutely nothing from me. There were things I could give her, like friendship, or like, you know, the physical stuff. But she never suffered without it, either. The last time I was in Tahoe and gave her a call for the first time in almost a year, she said, 'Mike!' real excited-like. 'You're back! Come on over!' Then I realized she had never once, in over two years, called me in Sacramento. A real free spirit. She needed herself, period. Amazing."

"I think that's where I want to be," Chris said.

"Would that be good? I don't know. What if everyone was like that, really? Totally without needing other people?"

"There might be a lot of people who were in places they *wanted* to be, not trapped in places because of need," she suggested. "Need weakens you."

"Lip service," he scoffed. "You say that because you had a bad experience needing somebody you shouldn't have trusted. But you were pretty young."

"Well, yeah, but—"

"I'm not talking about that trapped kind of needing; that's no good. I've never been trapped by anything, but I know it would be no good. I'm talking about give-and-take. Like, I could get by just fine without my family butting into my business every single minute, but there's not a one of them I could give up. Plus, I complain, but if they didn't butt in, I'd probably feel ignored. Do you know what I'm talking about?" he asked seriously, his brow furrowing. "If nobody needs you, then when you're gone, you just slip through the cracks and disappear, and everything stays the same. You've had a whole life, and you've made no impact."

"But your Tahoe friend has," Chris argued. "Her art!"

He drained his Irish coffee. "*I* don't have any art."

"You've saved lives in fires! That's impact!"

He got out of his recliner. "People I've rescued don't call me Sundays and say, 'Come and watch the game.' They won't know I've gone when I go. I'm just doing my job, and that's not the same thing, is it? I sort of felt as if I was just doing my job with the artist—that she didn't need me for anything and wouldn't know I was gone if I was." He flipped on the TV. "Wanna see who's on Letterman?"

"Sure," she said, after a moment. "But did you need her, the artist?" she couldn't help asking.

"Yeah. I guess. I think that's why it ended as undramatically as it did; she didn't need me back. No connection."

No wonder he'd told his sister to shove it when she gave him the book. He wasn't as afraid of intimacy as he was of never having it again. That real, vulnerable intimacy of needing another person. And having that person need you back.

Chris couldn't dispute its worth. She had two little people depending on her, really needing her, and often that was what kept her going, kept her from self-pity. But, she wanted balance—to be able to lean on someone who wouldn't betray her or control her or collapse under the weight of her need. She knew, unfortunately, how unlikely it was she would find such a person. Thus, she was on her own.

Maybe Mike wasn't afraid of needing because he hadn't been let down. He'd been tricked by fate. There was a difference.

Many times she had asked herself, if Steve had been honest, loving, devoted and dependable but had died, would her loss and pain have been terrifically different? She never answered herself, because the answer seemed almost as shameful as what had happened to her.

"More Irish?" he asked.

"Yes, please." *Maybe it should be a double,* she thought.

Chris worked three six-hour shifts at the grocery store during the week before Thanksgiving. Mike worked two twenty-four-hour shifts. That left a lot of time to be filled with chores, cooking and watching movies or television. They shared the cooking, but Mike had her beat by miles; firefighters were great cooks, she had learned. There was time to talk—not only the kind of talking that's done when all is quiet and dim, but also the kind of casual talking you do while one of you is sweeping the kitchen floor and one is loading the dishwasher.

"What about that book of yours?" he asked her while she was folding some clothes. "Shouldn't you be working on that book?"

"I have sort of missed Jake—he's the twelve-year-old I've been writing about. He's had a rough year—seventh grade."

"Well, why don't you work on Jake while I make dinner. It's my turn, right?"

They had done it, as he'd said. They'd stopped the clock. She hadn't worried about the burned-down house or the kids or anything. She slept well; the sound of his snoring had become as comforting as the purr of a well-tuned engine. She threw his shorts in with her dirty clothes. He washed her old Honda when he washed his Suburban. He brought doughnuts home with him in the morning when his shift was relieved. She brought ice cream after work.

Chris turned off her brain. She refused to analyze. She scorned common sense. She was briefly, blissfully content. The dog ate Mike's socks, the kids spilled on the floor, there was warmth and an extra hand to wipe off a chocolaty mouth, to hold a tissue and say, "Blow." And in the eyes, the smile, the occasional touch of a hand, there was a pleasant tug-of-war of sexual possibility.

Chris knew that the past seven years of her life constituted a trash heap of problems that should be sorted out, organized, settled and resolved. No way she could make that mess go away. She should contact her estranged Aunt Flo; she should reaffirm her goals and sense of direction.

But she waited. She couldn't bear to upset the applecart, couldn't bring herself to spit in the eye of good luck. In fact, if real life would be so kind as to not intrude for a few short weeks, she had the potential to be disgustingly happy.

Chapter 6

There was nothing to prepare Chris for the Cavanaugh family. After having met Mike's father, she had been afraid to meet his mother. The prospect of meeting them *all* simply terrified her. But she couldn't think of how to refuse. She was scheduled to work until two o'clock on Thanksgiving day, and Mike suggested that, since he was not working, he would babysit until she was finished, and then they would have turkey dinner with the Cavanaugh clan.

Clan, indeed. What would they ask her? she wondered. Would they ask if she slept with him? Should she say no politely? Or indignantly? Or disappointedly. Would they ask her how long, precisely, she would be staying with him? Should she say: "Look, Mike is a good and generous man, and he needs my little family for a while, to complete his grief, as I need his strength and friendship, and you must not interfere"? Or should she say, "Until December 26"?

"So this is Chrissie," said Christopher Cavanaugh, the brother closest in age to Mike. "Glad you could come over. Well, you don't look too badly singed. Everything going okay since the big burnout?"

"We're getting it together, I guess," she said, weak-kneed and shaking inside.

"My wife, Stacy. Stacy, here's Chrissie. Palmer, isn't it? My partner's name is Palmer. Rusty Palmer. You know any other Palmers in Sacramento?"

She didn't.

Christopher Cavanaugh was an orthodontist. His wife, Stacy, managed his office. They had three children, the oldest in braces. Next came Matthew, about thirty-two. Wife, Maxine. Three kids, aged four, six and eight. And then Maureen, whom they sometimes called Mo, and her non-Irish, non-Catholic husband, Clyde. Maureen, a nurse, was in uniform because hospitals, like grocery stores and fire departments, did not close for holidays. She was a petite, feminine version of Mike: curly brown hair, bright green eyes, that notable, crooked Cavanaugh smile that seemed so perpetually full of fun. Then came Tommy, the professor-coach, his wife, Sue, and their two little kids. And finally Margaret, the twenty-six-year-old baby of the family, who was a graphic artist, and her husband, Rick, and her huge stomach, which would soon provide Cavanaugh grandchild number eleven.

Ten children. Fourteen adults. Mattie, on her feet the whole time, getting some trouble from the daughters-in-law about how hard she worked. They called her Mother, but her own children, to the last, called her Ma.

It was an experience in itself, hearing an orthodontist say, "Ma, hey, Ma—we have any beer to go with this ball game?" And the kids called her Gram, like a metric measurement, nothing so precious or pretentious as Mimi or Grandmother. Everyone called their dad and grandfather Big Mike, and of course they called the bigger Mike, Little Mike.

Chris should not have bothered to worry about what they would ask her. They talked so much, all of them, that they could easily have ignored her presence, except that they included her quite naturally.

"The *prints?*" Margie howled. "Did Little Mike pretend he had something to do with the McKnights? What a hoot! He didn't even buy the coasters! I did the house. He wouldn't let me upstairs, though. I bet he doesn't even have a shower curtain."

"I have a shower curtain, brat."

"Oh, yeah? What color?"

"Never mind the color. You don't need to know the color. I'm not helpless."

"I bet it's brown. Or green. Come on, is it green?"

"It's red," he supplied.

Margie laughed and held her big belly. "Red? In a blue bathroom?"

"It looks good. It looks fine. Tell her, Chris. Doesn't it look fine?"

Chris had a vision of them—six of them born within ten years—growing up here, in this four-bedroom, one-bathroom house, fighting or laughing, yelling all the time, the way their kids were doing.

Mattie managed them all. She placed them where she thought they would be most comfortable. She set up a card table and put children with coloring books

there, at the end of the living room where her boys—
her men—watched the game, so that arguments over
crayons could blend with shouts over a touchdown. The
women stayed around the dining room and kitchen,
talking about their houses, their kids, their work. That
was where Chris felt she belonged, yet didn't belong.
The bigger kids were in the garage-converted-to-a-
family-room with games. The family room had been
added, Chris learned, after the first three of Mattie and
Big Mike's kids had left home.

Carrie had been intimidated at first. She held back,
but Maureen swept her in with her five- and three-
year-old. Soon Carrie was playing hard, behaving like
a normal child rather than a whiz kid. And Kyle talked.
Carrie was too busy to speak to him, so he spoke to the
others, snatched toys away and alternately offered them,
negotiating his terms. Here, among so many Cavanaughs, no one looked askance at the things children did,
whether sweet or mean.

The small house became hot, close, with so many
bodies that Chris felt at once trapped yet never more
alive. They touched, this family, hardly ever speaking
without hands on one another. Even the men. Except,
perhaps, Big Mike, who sank into the role of patriarch,
letting them come to him. The children came readily
and often. "Big Mike, will you get this apart?" "Big
Mike, what color is this color? Is this color red or *rose?*"
They climbed on him, asked of him, sought comfort
from him. He attempted to look a little aloof, a little
bored, but he wiped four noses with his own old hankie.

Chris, who had been afraid they would be suspicious of her, saw Big Mike draw Carrie in, and she
had to look away before she wept with longing. Car-

rie, who had watched all the other children take their minor accomplishments and miseries to their Big Mike, had approached him holding a picture torn from a coloring book. She stared at him; he had a newspaper in his lap, which seemed natural for him, even with his entire, huge family around him. As if he might read it, hide behind it, while they carried on their intimate family relations.

"Does Big Mike mean Grandpa?" Carrie asked him.

"Around here," he said, looking at her over his glasses.

"I don't have any Grandpa. Or any Big Mike."

He stared at her for a long, gloomy second. Then he said, "You'd better come up on my lap, then."

She went very easily, as if she had climbed onto that lap many times before. Together they looked at the picture she had colored. As if she was one of them. With so many, there were no favorites. Or they were all favorites.

It took three tables for the Thanksgiving meal: the dining-room table, fully extended, pockmarked and burned from many such dinners; the kitchen table for the smallest children, where their spills would create fewer problems; and two card tables in the family room for the not-so-small children. Christopher and Little Mike took sides against Tommy and Clyde in an argument over unions. Rick and Margie tried to convince Big Mike about some investments that would yield him more from his retirement, even if there was a risk. It was perfectly clear that Big Mike had no concept of what they were suggesting, would not change anything about his retirement but loved their frustrated interference.

Watching them, Chris ached. She wanted to share

with them the way they shared with one another—
advice, arguments, concern, love. It was a family so
tight, so enmeshed, so interdependent—original Cavanaughs and in-laws alike—that there was barely enough
autonomy here to fit a gasp of surprise into. But no one
seemed to mind. Not at all.

She wondered how they had done it, how so many
people could achieve this kind of intimacy. But their
closeness, so involved and intense, seemed to be a thing
they simply had, not a thing they strived for. It was too
effortless to be contrived.

Through snatches of conversation and questions
freely answered she had figured out who was responsible for whom. Christopher had gone to college on
a football scholarship. Dental school had been made
possible through loans Little Mike, probably a young
widower by then, had cosigned. Matt had borrowed for
college with brothers cosigning, then Christopher had
paid for nursing school for Maureen. Tommy had gone
to school on Little Mike's and Christopher's money,
and Big Mike and Mattie were able to manage for Margie. They had all done it together. Whoever had, gave.
Whoever needed, took.

On the buffet were the pictures. A few studio por-
traits, six wedding couples in tuxedos and lace—yes,
Joanie and Mike, too—but mostly school photos in
their traditional tacky cardboard frames. And there
was Joanie and Shelly, the same picture Mike had on
his desktop, only larger. The young mother, the little
blond angel.

All things considered, she thought, the Cavanaugh
family had held together pretty well, lost little compared to what they had. The Palmers had been a fam-

ily of four, after all, and had lost two, leaving the two survivors estranged. Half gone, half broken. Still, Chris felt a twinge of despair over Mike's losses.

Mike. He seemed to need little. Chris had been surrounded by ambitious people: her father, her scheming husband, her aunt Flo. Her mother alone had loved her gently. For a man to be content with simple things—some work, some play, some family, some privacy and some companionship—seemed to Chris to be of the highest virtue. He did not seem to long for easy money so much as comfort he had earned. Nothing too fancy, nothing too complex, nothing too frivolous.

The Cavanaughs had no idea how different she was, had no idea of her secluded, privileged childhood. She had gone to Tibet when she was fourteen, for heaven's sake. She had had none of what they had and probably much of what they longed for. Despite the differences, though, they did not allow her to remain an outsider. They drew her in, delighted to have an audience.

"So, the big shot, Chris, says to me, 'If you go down the clothes chute, I'll go, too. I've already done it three times,' he says. And he says, 'Come on, Tommy, you're skinny, you won't get stuck. Chicken?' And of course I didn't get stuck, but the big shot, who had never—I mean *never* done it himself, got stuck. And I had to go to the church, where Ma was doing volunteer work with the League women, and get her and bring her home to try and unstick him from the clothes chute."

"Yeah, sure. As I remember, *you* called *me* the chicken and said you'd tell about the names I'd carved in the dresser top, under the doily...."

"And how do you s'pose he got out? You think Ma got him out, Chrissie?" Tommy went on. "Oh, no, nothing so nice and neat as that. Ma had a fit, and I thought she was going to die of a heart attack, because the big shot had turned his head inside the clothes chute and couldn't turn it back."

"I called the police," Mattie said. "What could I do but call the police?"

"You shoulda called the undertaker," Big Mike said.

"Almost had to after you got home," Little Mike said.

They had to tear out the wall to get Chris out of the clothes chute. When Big Mike got home and the wall had been torn out, it was almost murder. But that was nothing compared to the time Little Mike was kissing his girl—Joanie, probably—in the front seat of his car in her driveway, thought he had his foot on the brake when it was on the gas and plowed through her dad's garage door and into his car.

The banter continued throughout the meal, through cakes and pies and ice cream and coffee, engulfing Chris, making her laugh, making her forget herself.

Preparing to leave the Cavanaugh house, however, stirred up her original anxieties. In this intimate, nosy family where everyone minded everyone's business but their own, wouldn't someone mention the new house-keeping arrangement Little Mike had introduced into his life? She fairly shivered with nerves as she cloaked her children for the trip back to Mike's house.

"Goodbye, God bless you, go to Mass. Are you going to Mass?" Mattie quizzed her brood as they departed from the Thanksgiving gathering.

"Yes, Ma," each of them said. Even Mike.

Chris wondered what Mattie was going to say to her. Go to Mass, perhaps? Are you Catholic? Where, exactly, do you sleep?

"You come again sometime, Chrissie," Mattie said. "And the kids. Don't make them be too good, now. They're good enough, those kids."

"I won't. I mean, yes, they are. Thank you. Very much. It was lots of fun."

Big Mike said to Carrie, "Take care of that dog, now. You make Creeps behave himself."

"Cheeks." She giggled. "I keep telling you his name is Cheeks."

"I know, I know. Creeps. Good name for that dog."

During the quiet drive back to Mike's house, with the kids nodding off in the backseat, Chris knew what was going to happen later. She wanted him. She wanted to be part of something again.

She put her good-enough, happy, exhausted children into the twin beds in the fireman's house. They went to sleep instantly, but she waited a moment to be certain. She tried to warn herself about the danger of getting more deeply involved with this man, but she was drunk on family, on hope and life and pleasure. Lonely, weary, needy. A little afraid, but not afraid enough. All her alarms were malfunctioning; she could not summon the least ping of warning. She couldn't remember a time in her life, even way back when she had had a family of her own, that she had felt this secure. Mike's embrace was so wide. Had he known, she wondered, that by taking her to where he had come from, she would find the surety and peace of mind she needed to touch him, hold him, invite him in?

Downstairs, the house was quiet. A light was still on in the kitchen, but Mike was sitting in the living room, on the couch, in the dark. Waiting. He had known. Or hoped.

It would be a holiday from real life for them both, Chris decided. For just a little while there would be no tangled, complicated pasts for either of them. Nor need they consider their uncertain futures.

She went to the couch, knelt beside him, put her arms around his neck, kissed his lips. She meant for it to be light, preliminary, but he had little patience. He was a man, as he had said, who didn't think for a long time about things but simply did them when they were right.

"Oh, God, oh, Chrissie."

The arms that pulled her close were so caring. Powerful, caring, needing arms; this was the embrace she had wanted to fall into, to disappear within, where she would feel forever loved. His mouth, hard in wanting, covered hers with such heat that she felt wild inside.

"Mike," she whispered against his open mouth. "Mike."

They couldn't simply kiss for a while first, Chris realized, as if on a date. She lived in his house; she had come to him and put her arms around his neck. It was not a seduction and could not be misconstrued as one. It was surrender. Until now they had both reined in their desires, knowing it without speaking of it, until they were ready for all of each other. She would not have played with his delicate restraint; she wouldn't lean toward him, inviting, until she was prepared to take him into her body, and this unspoken fact was understood by them both. That was why his hands were fast and greedy under her blouse, her bra.

"I want to touch you," he said. "Every part of you. Every part."

His hands on her were desperate yet considerate as he squeezed her small breasts. He held her waist, his thumbs and fingers almost meeting. He pulled her onto his lap, across him, and her hands worked on his shirt, tugging open buttons, as frantic as his hands but less careful.

One of his big hands went under her, between her legs, his palm flush against her, pushing, rubbing. She wished she had come to him naked, saving time. Beneath her thighs and buttocks she felt him grow; she ached so deeply, wanted so much to be full of him, full of passion and love.

He lifted her. He carried her. She had never before been carried to bed. With her arms around him she kissed his neck, licking in the taste of him, floating in his arms up the stairs. As they approached his bedroom she lifted her head, glancing anxiously toward the bedroom where the children slept.

"Mike?" she whispered.

"We'll close the door," he said, entering and doing so.

They tumbled onto the bed together, their hands moving wildly over each other, struggling with clothing, desperate to get it out of the way.

"Do you want me to use something?" he asked her.

"Can you?"

"Yes," he said. "Sure." But he didn't stop kissing her or pulling at her clothing. He tugged at her jeans, her underwear, burying his head in her breasts, her belly, kissing, licking. She found the hard knot of his erection and unfolded him, rubbing him through his underwear, then beneath. He moaned. Then her jeans were gone, her legs kicking them away. Her panties flew off in pursuit. She tugged down his shorts, and he sprang out into her hand, large and hot and impatient. She folded her hands around him. She opened herself.

Mike rolled away a little, jerking open the drawer by the bed, retrieving a hard-to-open cellophane packet. "I can't wait. I can't wait, Chris."

"Me, either," she admitted, taking it from him and using her teeth to open it. "Is this ten years old?"

"Four days. Ahhh."

"You knew?"

"I don't think about things too much," he said, rising above her, sheathed, waiting.

"Don't think now," she whispered.

He pressed himself in, slowly, very slowly. Then, lowering his head slightly, he tongued her nipple. She locked her fingers together behind his head, holding him to her, and it happened. That fast. That wildly fast. Almost without motion, almost without any movement at all. She felt a pulsing heat and could not tell his from hers. Five minutes, maybe less. The moment they came together, tightly fitted to each other, wham. Incredible.

"That," she said when she caught her breath, "is almost embarrassing."

"Yeah? Well, what did you expect? A warm-up game?"

"Warm-up game?" She laughed.

"To tell the truth, I'm lucky I got up the stairs."

"You bought rubbers," she said, her tone accusing when it should have been grateful.

"Yeah," he said. "The eternal optimist."

"All along, you knew we would? You wanted to on that first night you invited me to your house?"

"Nope. Oh, wanted to, yeah, just about right away, but I didn't offer you the house because of that. And I didn't buy the condoms because I wanted to or because I knew we would. I bought them because things are complicated enough. And because if we got it into our heads we were going to, I didn't want you to say no at the last minute because there wasn't anything. So, what a Boy Scout, huh?"

"Yeah," she said, snuggling into the crook of his arm, not really wanting to discuss complications and what-ifs tonight. She had started to think responsible behavior was a thing of the past. Then Mike. "Thanks. I don't need any more problems."

"Who does? So, what do you need, Chrissie? Tell Little Mike."

"Ohhhh," she moaned, a laugh trailing on the end. "Little Mike...now maybe."

That was the sex and the brief conversation afterward. Then came the lovemaking, which was, like Mike, generous and serious and very physical. As with all things he did, he used earnestness and strength. He had power and control but was so soft and loving that Chris couldn't tell whether she was giving or taking.

She hadn't ever thought of herself as a little woman before this night. His hands turned her so deftly, so artistically, that she felt small, lightweight, almost fluid. And cared for, always cared for, as this man she had come to think of as quiet, a man of few words, spoke to her, comfortable with words that usually embarrassed people. "Like that?" he whispered to her. "Here?" "Now?" Or in giving her instructions. "Yes, here. Like this. Please, here."

He took his time. She, to her surprise, did not have nearly the stamina or patience he had. When she frantically begged, desperately squirmed, tried to stop his playing around and pull him into her, she could feel the smile on his lips against hers, and he said, "Okay, baby, okay. This is for you, and you owe me one."

His manner and tone were as sincere and good-natured in bed as at any other time in his day-to-day living. He seemed not to notice how skilled he was. She was astounded by his talent; she had not guessed at his abandon, the shameless fun he had making love. It intrigued her, for she had little experience and had never considered that men had such a good time with sex. It had seemed to her that men were driven by some need that, once fulfilled, was forgotten. She had not thought of men as giving of their bodies, until Mike. Mike was the only man she had ever known who was so completely sure of his feelings that, as a lover, he trusted himself and her completely.

Chris had thought of lovemaking as give-and-take; one gave, one took, alternating perhaps. With this man she was a participant. He pushed her up, up, up, ruthless in his determination to push her over the edge, relentless in his stubborn wish to blind her with pleasure, and then he held her tenderly in her shuddering release. And again. Sometimes there was a little request for himself. He had, after all, earned that much. "Come up, here, like this. Yes, just like this. For me, my way. *Oh, God.*"

Deep in the night, while she lay on her back beside him, he on his side with one large hand spread flat against her stomach, he whispered, "I love you, Chris."

She was silent. She bit her lip in the blackness but turned her face toward him. She had never felt so much love in her life as she had today, yet the words wouldn't come. Not even now.

He turned, fell onto his back, removed his hand. In

the silent darkness, still humid with the past hours, he sighed deeply, with hurt.

"Mike…"

"Never mind. No big deal."

"I'm afraid to say—"

"What you feel? Come on. I didn't *ask* you for anything!"

"Didn't you?"

"No! Saying what you feel doesn't mean you're promising anything."

"I love you, too," she said, her voice small and terrified. "It's just that—"

"Shh," he said, calmer now. "It wouldn't be a good time to talk. Anyway, I already know what it 'just is.'"

She was awakened in the morning by the sound of Mike's moving around in the bedroom. She opened her eyes, and, as if he felt her awareness, he turned toward her. He had showered and shaved, and he was putting on his pants and fireman's T-shirt. He smiled at her, and she saw that his joy had survived the hurt of her reluctant words.

He came to sit on the edge of the bed. "I have to go to work," he said.

"I know."

"Stay here and sleep. The kids are okay—I checked them. Want a T-shirt?"

"Yes, please."

He fished one from a dresser drawer, held it for her when she sat up to put it on. He playfully pulled her hair, wild and woolly, through the neck, then kissed her lightly on the lips. "You taste like a good night of it."

"I feel like I fell down the stairs."

He laughed, proud of himself.

"Mike, yesterday was wonderful. The whole day. And night. Your family is…well, they're just plain in-credible."

"My *family?*"

"And you." She smiled.

"Thanks. Anytime."

"I think I should call my Aunt Florence. Let her know I'm all right. That the kids are all right. I haven't even contacted her in years. You understand."

"Family is family." He shrugged. "You gotta be good to 'em. You can't let family slip away. She deserves to know you're okay."

"Yeah, she does. Don't worry."

"One thing? Don't surprise me. Please."

His eyes were begging her, his brows furrowed over his nose. She thought about the long-ago phone call tell-ing her that her parents were dead. She thought about the call Mike might have gotten. She remembered her shock and dismay when Steve had not come home. For the past several years she had put so much energy into deciding whether or not this person or that could be trusted, she seldom wondered whether she, herself, was trustworthy.

She summoned courage. She bravely faced the fact that she had crossed a certain line with him. Not ig-norantly, perhaps foolishly—time would tell—but not unknowingly. Even if she remained afraid to trust, she must prove trustworthy. Must. If she wanted to be able to live with herself.

She touched his eyebrows with her fingertips, trying to smooth them out. "I won't do that to you. I'll make plans and talk to you. You won't come home and find me gone. I promise."

"That's all I ask."

Chapter 7

She could not help making the comparison. If Mike knew her thoughts, he would say she was overthinking it. But the last time Chris had made love, Kyle had been conceived. Sexy old Stever, the last of the red-hot lovers, devil-take-the-hindmost man of the world…had not really liked sex all that much. They had not made love often; he was busy and preoccupied. He had been talented, not sensitive. Expressive and creative, not tender. Chris had been drugged by his sexual skill, for he could satisfy her quickly and efficiently, but the satisfaction was fleeting; she always felt unfinished. There was a lot left undone. Orgasm and fulfillment, she now realized, were not the same thing. Maybe that was why she hadn't really missed that part of her life. Maybe it simply hadn't been that great. Perhaps her body had felt Steve had not really loved her long before her mind knew it.

She got out of Mike's bed before her children awakened. She went down to the kitchen, poured herself a cup of the coffee he had made and stepped out onto the patio in T-shirt and bare feet. And breathed. Down to her toes. Feeling wild with life, positively smug with gratification. She thought about the differences between then and now, the differences between Chicago and Los Angeles and Sacramento. The sun was brighter here, the air crackling clean, cool, clear. If she looked over the fence she would see the mountains. Los Angeles, on the other hand, would be balmy and thick with humidity and smog, sort of like a dirty piece of crystal. She would be happy never to see Los Angeles again. Chicago would be dank, dirty, old. Like a woman planning to start her diet on Monday, Chris decided she couldn't face Chicago before spring. Today—and maybe for one day only, but maybe for a week, or a month, or many months, who knew?—she felt she was where she ought to be. That was almost a first, at least since she had buried her parents.

Feeling she belonged prompted other comparisons, as well. Though she suspected she was not extremely clear-headed—she was, after all, nearly limping with pleasure—she remembered how wrong she had felt during the years of grappling with Steve and Aunt Flo. Clearly she hadn't felt right about what Steve talked her into doing; not only had she cried a lot, but she had frantically sought alternatives to suing her aunt, options other than completely estranging herself from Flo. Nor had Flo's suggestions given her a feeling of warmth and safety; she had ached at the thought of giving up Steve, only to be managed by Flo.

She had had to choose. Between her only family and the only man she had ever loved. And the move to L.A. had been so painful and scary that she cleaved tighter to her man, her husband, in loneliness and fear. It had felt so wrong that she had struggled even harder to make it feel right. She had had to slam the door on her own feelings, her instincts. Now, barefoot on the fireman's patio after a wonderful night, she realized that when something was right, it just was. You couldn't make it so.

Then she heard the sirens. All her life she had ignored sirens, unless they made her pull off to the side of the road. Now, because Mike rode the engine, she took sirens far more personally. She had never realized there were so many emergencies in a quiet, residential part of town. Four times she heard that trill, that scream. Because the big firefighter had crept into her body and heart, she sucked in her breath in fear when she heard the sirens.

The nurturer in her wanted to keep Mike out of harm's way. In that and other ways she was like her mother. She had been certain nothing could satisfy her as much as to live the kind of life Arlene Palmer had lived. That was what had prompted her to fall in love with Steve; she had wanted someone to whom she was so intimately connected that his life became her life, and together they would create more life. That tendency helped make her a good mother; it also made her miss the aunt who was now her only family, even though Flo could be an ordeal in herself.

And then, of course, there was what she had done

last night with Mike, which made her shiver in after-shocks this morning.... She nested well.

And all of this made her hate the sirens. Mike went into burning buildings. Still, he was experienced, right? He'd been a firefighter for more than a decade. A fire-man had not been killed in a fire in Sacramento in years. Years?

She went back into the house and turned on the TV to check the local news. There wasn't any—at least none pertaining to fires. Not satisfied that there wouldn't be, however, she played the local radio station while she got ready for work.

She had only been at her cash register for thirty min-utes when it happened. The event that overturned all the safe, peaceful, nesting feelings she had decided to indulge for the past week, especially the past twenty-four hours. Chris had been in a better mood than usual, joking with the customers, bagging groceries quickly, clicking those old buttons like a demon. Then she pulled one of those gossipy rags past the cash register between a box of Tampax and a pound of hamburger, rang up the price and saw the tabloid cover. Her face stared back at her.

Missing Heiress Speaks from the Grave.

No! She picked it up, stricken. The customer held a credit card out to her. Chris threw the tabloid after the other groceries. Please, God, no. She rang up the total, and the customer, unaware that Chris's life had just flashed before her eyes, authorized the payment. Chris stood frozen, panicked, paralyzed. Just when she started to think things were going to be okay, she tripped over some major event. Like smoke pouring out of the vents. Like this.

On automatic pilot she bagged the groceries, then checked two more shoppers through her aisle. At the first lull, she spoke across the partition to Candy, a college student who worked weekends and holidays. "I have to take a quick break. I'm closing for a minute, but I'll be right back."

She locked her register and grabbed a copy of the scandal sheet. Her face stared out between equally poor pictures of celebrities she couldn't name. Good Lord. In the worst of times life had not seemed as grotesque as this. She raced to the bathroom, closed the door and read.

"You should never be surprised," Aunt Florence had once said, "at what you read about yourself in the newspaper if you have a lot of money. Or fame. Or whatever." Chris wanted no part of money or fame; she had simply wished to disappear and re-create herself. But it looked as if she were stuck with her past.

In Chicago, where the Palmer family had been considered among the upper crust of local society, their names had occasionally appeared in the society column. They had had a minor scandal once, too—a manager of one of their stores sued Randolph for wrongful firing—but it hadn't come to much. And of course Chris had had a debutante's ball, there had been the death of her parents, and then her horrid suit against her aunt and the estate. But that had been the extent of press coverage on the Palmers.

Now, however, someone had written a book about her and Steve Zanuck. Steve, her ex-husband, was apparently dead. As was his wife, Mrs. Zanuck. Months ago a luxury yacht headed for some Caribbean island had left Miami and never been seen again. Recently a piece of the vessel with the name of the boat on it had been found. The authorities suspected an onboard explosion.

Chris was not that Mrs. Zanuck; yet, she realized, not everyone knew that.

According to the article, Aunt Florence was not certain whether or not it was her who perished. *"The last time Florence Palmer talked to her niece was four years ago, when Christine Palmer Zanuck, then a Los Angeles resident, was discussing divorcing Zanuck."*

Chris had married Steve in Chicago. A small ceremony with only a few friends. Florence had grudgingly gone along with this; she was even a little relieved that they didn't want a big wedding, since she didn't expect this "fling" to last. Chris had been twenty. And absolutely dumb with passion.

She had gotten pregnant instantly. Was pregnant, in fact, when she turned twenty-one and Steve insisted that the hundred grand per year she received from her trust fund would simply not do. Not when there were millions, at least, to be had, and he was an attorney, for goodness' sake! They had very politely asked Aunt Florence to fork it over, please, so that they could get on with their lives. She had said no.

It had taken a while for Chris to be completely convinced by her charismatic, con-artist husband that it would be logical to sue the executor of the estate, the trustee, for that money. And it had taken two years for them to win the lawsuit. Chris had already had precious little Carrie when she was given 3.75 million. And they moved to Los Angeles, where Steve was going into business.

The high life, then. What had she been high on? She lived in a palatial house on the side of a hill and went to many parties and opening nights. They went on cruises—Steve more often than she because she wanted to make a home with her child. Steve invested in films and other things and, according to his secretary, had a legal practice. Oh, Chris had seen the office and staff on occasion, but Steve didn't like to discuss business with her. And she, big dummy that she was, had plopped her entire fortune into a joint account. She trusted him. Why wouldn't she? In her grief and loneliness, he was all she had.

She began to suspect him of having an affair that year, for his attention toward her, his desire to keep her perpetually happy, had started to flag. Affair? That would have been easy by comparison. So she asked him to set up a trust for Carrie, and he said, "Sure, babe, we'll get that taken care of pretty soon." He was very busy with clients; he had a lot of socializing to do. She became pregnant with Kyle. Steve had to leave town on business. The phone calls began to pour in. Where was Mr. Zanuck? Bills had to be paid. The mortgage was due. The office had been closed. The secretary had vanished. The film company he claimed to be investing in had never heard of him.

Too ashamed to ask Flo for help, Chris had not known what to do besides call a lawyer. The long and short of it turned out to be that, during the first three years of marriage, the degenerate monster had lived on the hundred grand a year from her trust, and during the last year he had been busy either losing, spending or stealing her money. She had never been entirely sure whether he had converted it, moving it out of her name and into his, or whether he had actually *lost* it. But it was gone. Out of all that money she could only lay her hands on one account of around thirty thousand dollars. Was this an oversight? Or had he left her a few bucks purposely so she could take care of herself while getting a divorce? The rest was really and truly gone.

Kyle was born, and when she came home from the hospital, her house was locked against her. For the next two years she rented one tiny apartment or another, working as a receptionist, housekeeper or waitress, living mostly on the goodwill and generosity of friends she had made since moving to L.A. But those friends had been lied to, if not swindled by, Steve Zanuck, too, and, burned, they drifted away from her. The attorney stuck by her for a while, believing he was eventually going to get a big hunk of dough out of either Steve or Aunt Florence. Instead, he got most of the thirty thousand.

Steve Zanuck never reappeared in Chris's life. Though he was found, the money wasn't. Chris was left exhausted, afraid, weak. Once she understood what had been done to her, she committed the unpardonable sin in her lawyer's eyes. She wanted the divorce, period. The jerk she had married didn't even know or care that he had a son. She wanted to be Chris Palmer again. She refused to ask Flo to bail her out, refused to have Steve Zanuck prosecuted, refused to hire detectives to track down the money. "Let me out," she had said.

Though she couldn't ask Aunt Flo for help—not after what she had done to her—she did call her right after Kyle was born. "Yes, Flo, I'm all right, I guess," she had said. "And you were right. I married a real scumbag."

"Are you coming home?" her aunt had asked, her voice tight.

"Maybe when I can get myself together a little bit. I just had another baby."

"When are you coming?"

"I don't know. As soon as I can."

"Are you going to divorce that bastard?"

"Yes," she had said, and cried. Cried her heart out. And for what? For grief; he was gone, and she wanted him back. For fear; she was alone, all alone, unless you counted Flo, who was very angry. For shame; this was her fault, really. And maybe for love; though he made a mockery of that, she *had* loved him. "I am. I will. And...I'm sorry."

"I should think so."

She had hung up on Flo then, not answering the phone when her aunt rang back.

She should have gone home right then. She should have taken the little money that was left, gotten on a plane and told Flo to do whatever she wanted to do. Hire the lawyers, lock Steve up, have him knocked off, anything. The broken bird should have flown back under Flo's wing. Her aunt might have been angry, bossy, outraged, but she loved Chris. It wasn't Flo's fault that she didn't know how to give the unconditional, selfless kind of love and caring that Arlene had found so natural; that didn't mean it wasn't real love. And Flo would have forgiven her, eventually. But Chris had screwed up so badly and wanted so desperately to salvage something, she had only made it worse.

Every day since Kyle was born, for three long years, she had lived day-to-day, barely able to afford anything, but had not called on Flo for help. She had tried to find a way to rectify her mistake, to pull herself out of it. She wasn't sure she even knew why. Pride, maybe. Guilt and humiliation, probably. Also, a deep wish not to have Flo take care of her, which meant Flo would run her life.

Now this article. Someone had written a book about her, and within the book were dozens of little-known facts about her husband. It said that Christine Palmer was one of possibly four women he'd married. Wives with money. Wives who had disappeared. They didn't disappear, Chris wanted to say, they only ran out of money and became clerks and housekeepers. She ought to buy a copy of the book, find out what that weasel had done with her money.

But first she had to talk to Mr. Iverson. And Florence.

"You mean I gave you a hundred bucks and you're worth millions?" Mr. Iverson said. He held the paper in his hand. She sat across from him. He had an office, sort of. Two walls in the shipping area in the back of the store. A cluttered desk. A computer.

"Read a little farther," she said. "I was ripped off. I married this jerk who took me for my inheritance, and I am now a destitute grocery clerk with two fatherless children. That's who you gave the hundred bucks to."

He read farther. "Says here you're probably dead."

"Well, I suppose that's the *current* Mrs. Zanuck."

"Jeez. Who wrote this book?"

"I haven't a clue."

"Maybe you ought to read it."

"I was thinking that myself." She watched while his eyes roamed the page. "Look, I'm really sorry about this, Mr. Iverson, but I didn't exactly do it on purpose, you know? I'm going to have to get in touch with my aunt—I can't have her thinking I'm dead. I'm probably going to have to go home. Chicago." She swallowed hard.

"You want some time off? Jeez, you don't want to work here. You're an heiress, for crying out loud. What are you going to do? What about my hundred bucks?"

"Oh. That. Look, don't worry about that, okay? Here," she said, digging into her purse frantically, trying to pay her debts and retain her dignity. She stopped suddenly. This was what she'd been doing for more than three years. Trying to assure people that she wasn't a no-good, taking-you-for-a-ride con artist. She slowed down. People had helped her, had always said don't worry about it, but in the end they worried they might not get their loans back. They were, in fact, more suspicious of her when they found out she'd come from money than when they believed her to be poor, pitiful and down on her luck. It was as though she had no business being so stupid if she was so rich.

Well, they were probably right about that.

She pulled sixty-three dollars out of her purse. "Okay, here's sixty. And I worked the other day—six hours. Take that, too. And I'll ask Aunt Florence to send me something. But is that enough?"

"There's taxes."

She sighed and gave him the three dollars she had left. "Let me know if I owe you," she said quietly.

"How do I reach you?"

He instantly thought she'd run out. Would Mike see the paper? Would *he* think she'd run out? Would he *want* her to run out, now that she was someone else? People got crazy when they found out there was more to you than what was on the surface. And here was this terrifically nasty article, plus a book. Mr. Iverson was looking at her as if she were Patty Hearst.

"You can reach me at the same number," she said even more quietly. "I'll let you know if it changes."

She picked up the kids at the babysitter's and went back to Mike's. She told Juanita not to expect them unless she called but didn't quite say goodbye. She never had, she realized. To anyone. Anywhere. She always acted as though she was just going down the block to buy a candy bar and would be right back. And if she didn't do that to people, they did it to her. She was going to have to stop that. At once. Stop running, stop pretending that she would have this fixed in a minute. It was now officially bigger than she was. She would have to either fold her hand or learn to blame the right person. She didn't *do* this. It was done to her. Help.

That was her thought as she placed the call. She was thinking hard about it, about her promise to Mike, when she dialed direct rather than collect. She wanted to negotiate with Aunt Flo, if possible.

But when she heard Flo's voice, when she felt the tie that bound them tighten around her heart, she forgot negotiations. What she said, through her suddenly rasping tears, was, "Oh, God, Flo, I'm sorry. I'm so sorry! I never meant to hurt you like I have. Never!"

"Chris! Chris, where *are* you? Are you all right?"

"I'm all right. I'm in shock. I just read about myself in the paper, and I'm in total shock. I didn't know I was missing, didn't know I was the subject of a book, didn't know that Steve— I'm in California," she said, not mentioning Sacramento.

"California? We tracked him as far as Texas."

"Oh, I've been alone for years, Flo. Years."

"Where in California? I have been looking for you *forever!*"

"Flo, I didn't know that…honest. I thought you were still mad, which you have every right to be. I wasn't hiding, I was trying— Listen, listen, one thing at a time. I'm not going to hang up in the middle, I promise. But first, is he dead? Is he really dead?"

"Oh, who knows? Who cares? Three years, Chris! Good God, how could you? Even after all we'd been through, you had to have known that I…" Flo's voice caught and drifted away. Chris couldn't quite imagine her aunt crying. Flo could be angry, wildly happy, or her usual—completely composed. But cry? Make her pillow wet and wake up ugly, like Chris did? Was she in pain?

Chris, the nurturer, tried to comfort. "Oh, Flo, I kept trying to get it together, to salvage something. He wiped me out, naturally. And I have two little kids. Carrie is five now, and Kyle is three. I've been working, trying to get on my feet so when I did go home I wouldn't feel like such slime. I was wrong. I should have called you. But I…just couldn't get up the nerve."

"What about Steve? When was the last time you saw him? Did he leave you anything? Anything at all?"

"I haven't seen him since before Kyle was born. He ran out on me, left me holding the bag. I don't know what he did next. I hired a lawyer who tracked him down, finally, in Dallas. I got the divorce. I never got anything back. Except my name. I got my name back."

"Your name? Palmer?"

"Yes," she said through her tears.

"I guess that explains why I couldn't find Christine Zanuck."

I screwed that up, too, she thought. *Figures.*

"Come home," Flo said. "I'll send the money. I'll wire it. I'll come and get you. We can deal with this. We can—"

"Wait. Hold it a second, Flo. I'm coming. I'm coming home, I promise, but—"

"But? You said that before. You said 'as soon as I can,' and weeks went by. Then I couldn't find you. Then—"

"No, no. No, I won't do that to you again. No, Flo, but listen. It's a little complicated."

There was silence, then a short laugh. "How is it that doesn't surprise me?"

Chris started to cry again. "I'm like a bad penny. Why do I do this to people? I never meant to hurt anyone. Never."

"All right, all right, calm down, Chris. Try not to be childish. This isn't the worst thing, God knows. At least you're all right. First, give me the number where you are—the real number. Please don't lie to me."

Chris grabbed for a tissue to blow her nose. "No, I won't lie to you." She sniffed again and recited the numbers. "Now look, Flo, listen, I want to come home, I mean it, but I'm not ready yet. I can't just pick up and run. I won't. For the moment, the kids are more comfortable than they've ever been. I don't want to jerk them out of here. They're—"

"Out of where?" Flo interrupted.

"I'm living with a man. He's been very good to us. I can't run out on him."

"Who is this man, for goodness' sake?"

"His name is Mike. Mike Cavanaugh. It's real complicated."

"I bet. So bring him, too. Who cares? Or I'll come there. Chris, after all this—"

"Let me try to explain." She took a deep breath. "I moved from Los Angeles to Sacramento in August. I rented a house and got a job. The house caught fire and burned to the ground. Mike Cavanaugh was the fireman who carried me out of the house, and he let the kids and me move in here with him until we could get resettled. Since then it's gotten kind of, well, kind of—"

"Oh, God."

"He's a wonderful, generous man. He's calm. Sensible. He's good to the kids, and they adore him. It's the very first time a man has— He's been very good to me, too. I'm not going to stay here forever, but I promised him that I'd stay for a little while. See, he lost his wife and daughter in a car accident about ten years ago, and he's been all alone since then. And here I was, all alone with my kids, and we—"

"God Almighty."

"This is important, Flo. For both of us. It's as if we're both in some kind of recovery. This is the most comfort and safety I've felt since before Mom and Daddy were killed. It's not necessarily permanent—we don't have any long-term commitment, but—"

"Chris, listen to me. Here's what you do. Tell this nice man you appreciate everything he's done and you'll stay in touch with him when you get to Chicago. Tell him—"

It was all coming back to her. *Chris, here's what you do.... Chris, you don't study only literature, you have to have a few business courses. Chris, you don't just marry the first man you—* "Are you listening to me? Tell him you'll call him every night, all right? Visit him. Let him visit you! You've been *missing* for three years, and I am your only family! He'll understand. Do you hear me?"

Chris started crying again. "I'm not telling him that," she said. "I don't want to."

"Chris, now listen to me...."

"Flo, please, don't. Stop making my decisions for me!" She blew her nose again. Carrie found her, in the kitchen, pacing with the phone in her hand, crying her eyes out. Carrie tugged on her jeans. "Flo, listen, I haven't made this mess on purpose, but ever since Mom and Daddy died I've been bouncing between people who want me to do things *their* way, to take sides, to choose. Like now."

"Chris, you're getting—"

"Just this morning I told Mike I was going to call you so you'd know where I was and that we're all right. He thought that was good, but he asked me not to surprise him, you know, like run out on him without any warning. Don't you understand, Flo? His wife and baby— they were *gone,* without warning! And I know how that feels because Steve... Oh, please, try to understand. He saved my life. And I...I told him I was going to stay a while. Just a while. I can't keep doing this, Flo. I love you. I want to see you desperately. I want to make up for hurting you so much. I just don't want to hurt him, too. I'm sorry."

And she hung up. She blew her nose. "Mommy?" Carrie asked, her little chin wrinkling. Carrie would cry if Chris was crying; children didn't need to know the reasons.

Damn. She had hoped to find Flo tractable, reasonable. She had wanted Flo to be glad to hear from her, relieved to know she was safe and happy, period. She had wanted Flo's humor, generosity and spirit, not her commands. She *needed* Flo; Flo was her only link to her roots. She even liked Flo's take-charge manner on occasion; it sure came in handy in foreign airports. But that was where she wanted Flo to stop. She didn't want Flo to keep taking charge of *her*.

The phone rang. Chris laughed through her tears. "Hello."

"Dear God. You really are there. I don't know why I try. You are the worst brat."

"I really wanted to talk to you, you know. But I want to talk when you start listening and stop ordering that *I* listen to *you*." She was amazed at the strength in her voice. Yes, this was why she hadn't called before. Yes, she was sorry she'd hurt her aunt so deeply, frightened her so much. And she did love her, but she wasn't going to be pushed around anymore. By anyone. "I shouldn't have hung up, but I was upset. I would have called back. Do you want to talk awhile now? If you can listen and I can keep calm?"

"Please tell me exactly where you are. Tell me I can fly out there and see that you're all right, that you're alive and well, not living with some lunatic. Or some jerk like that Zanuck masterpiece. Please. I deserve some peace of mind, after all."

"Sure. But, Flo, you're going to have to hold back a little. I want to see you very much, but you're not going to keep telling me what to do. I'm going to make my own mistakes and pay for them myself."

"That," said Flo, "is the understatement of the year."

"Will you give me a couple of days, please?" Chris asked patiently. "Before you come? So I can get Mike ready for this? So I can explain what kind of mess I've made?"

"Two days?"

"Yes. And, Flo, you're going to have to understand that I have business to finish here. I might be ready in a day or in a couple of—"

Flo sighed heavily. "You want my promise that I'm going to leave you and the children with this—this fireman?"

"Flo, do you know anything about that book? *The Missing Heiress?*"

"I just read it."

"Is any of it true?"

There was a moment of silence. "Only the really bad parts."

Mike was hoping to run into Chris at the grocery store when he and the guys went shopping for dinner, and he couldn't hide his astonishment when he inquired about Chris's whereabouts and the clerk said she was gone. Quit. Poof.

Well, he thought, maybe Aunt Flo had come through, wired money. Then, back in the rig, Jim handed him the newspaper. "Isn't that your Christine Palmer?" he asked gently.

My Christine Palmer? So I had thought, briefly.

Back at the station Mike took the paper into the bathroom with him. He read it. Christine Palmer Zanuck, heiress to a multimillion-dollar furniture empire, possibly dead—one of four women Steve Zanuck had married and swindled. The Palmer fortune, excepting Chris's inheritance, was still sound and in the possession of Florence Palmer, who did not know where her niece was but had been actively hunting for her for three years. Even after the horrible ordeal of their lawsuit, Aunt Florence longed only to know that her niece was alive and well.

He left the bathroom.

They had two alarms in a row. One turned out to be nothing—a smoking stove. The other was a burning car, no injuries. He kept quiet, doing his job, straining his muscles, his mind elsewhere.

"Well," Jim said. "That her?"

"I guess so. Yeah, must be."

"She still at your place?"

"She didn't say she was leaving."

"You seen her lately?"

"Yeah, I saw her. Before I came to work." Jim probably knew, Mike figured, that he'd left her in his bed. The other firefighter knew how early they reported for their shift. It was pretty unlikely that Mike had gone from his parents' house to his house for coffee at 6:00 a.m.

"Think she's still there?"

"Well, I suppose so. I'm not afraid she's going to rip off the television, if that's what you mean. Especially now."

"Want to call? Take a couple of hours of personal time to run home?"

Want to? Oh, did he want to. So bad he could hardly stand it. But if he rushed home to check on her, what did that say about *him?* That he had not known what he was doing when he asked her to stay with no strings. That he could talk about love and trust but couldn't act on it. "Nope," he said. "She's a big girl." It was her life.

He lifted weights that afternoon. He thought it through. Long and slow.

He believed in people. He believed in love—in saying it, showing it, trusting people. And when he loved, he loved hard, totally and with faith.

He had known right off that Joanie was the one for him. The second time he'd felt that way was with Chris. With Chris he hadn't felt giddy the way he had with the flight attendant, desperate the way he had with the woman on the rebound, or entrenched the way he had with the artist. He had felt secure and strong and exact. So he had done what he had done—given everything he had. He didn't hold back a little, save a little, like for a rainy day, in case he had been mistaken. Nope. He'd plunged in with everything he had—every tear, every passion, every possession, every hope.

Kind of stupid to think you'd be more relieved to find out she'd kidnapped her own kids than to find out she was rich. _Stinking_ rich.

He didn't want to push his own needs on to anyone. He didn't want Chris to save him, exactly. He just wanted her to tell him the truth or refuse to answer. That simple, two choices. Don't say it if you don't feel it. When he had asked her to stay awhile and she had said okay, even though she'd been afraid of what it would mean, what it would become, it had meant she'd stayed because she wanted to. And when she said, "I love you," it meant she did. Oh, he knew she was reluctant to say that, and he knew why. Maybe he shouldn't have pushed her, but he had, and she'd said it. Simple. She didn't say she would stay forever, he didn't ask her to, and unless something happened to change her mind, she would probably go. But not without saying goodbye.

No alarms through the night, but he didn't sleep. He almost picked up the phone to call her about fifty times. But she had the number. He'd *told* her to call if she needed him. You can't be any plainer than that.

Long and slow, he thought about it. By morning he thought he knew what he felt. He wanted to take care of her, protect her and love her because it felt good. He wanted to have some time with her and those two little kids because if he could remember what it felt like to be loved and depended on as a man, a provider, a lover, maybe he could get on with his life. Finally. He wanted to hold her without holding her down.

He didn't hang around the station for breakfast. He drank a quick cup of coffee and went home. The old Honda was in the driveway, but he didn't breathe a sigh of relief—not yet. If Aunt Flo had recited the numbers on her American Express card, there might be a note on the refrigerator telling him to sell the car for his trouble. *Please, God, no. Please, God, all I ever wanted was the straight line.*

He unlocked the door. They might still be asleep; it wasn't even seven.

But Chris unfolded herself from the couch, already dressed. Her eyes didn't look a whole lot better than his. She picked up the tabloid that lay on the coffee table and carried it toward him, her lips parted as she was about to speak. She was going to tell him the whole thing. But he didn't want to hear it right now. He didn't care about anything now. She was there.

"Come here," he said, opening his arms, so relieved he was afraid he was going to shout. "Come here and fall on me. I didn't sleep all night."

"Me, either," she said, and a sniffle came. "There's so much to tell you."

"You're here. Tell me later. There's lots of time."

"You saw this, then?"

"Oh, yeah. Kind of hard to miss. And they told me you quit Iverson's."

"But you didn't call here?"

"You said you wouldn't surprise me. I had to believe you."

"How could you believe me? Especially after all this?"

"You maybe left a few things out, but you haven't lied to me. I would know."

"Oh, Mike. Oh, hold me. Please."

Which he was glad to do. Ah, that was relief. To believe and find that you were right. "Any of it true?" he asked.

"Some of it," she said. "Like the part about me being dead. That part's probably true. I'm probably just watching this film in purgatory."

He laughed at her. He squeezed her tighter. "Naw. If purgatory felt this good, there wouldn't be any Catholics."

Chapter 8

Firefighters do not think in rainbow shades of many possibilities but in simple light and dark. Hot and cold. Perhaps good and evil. Chris began to understand that Mike Cavanaugh lived in a yes-or-no world that he laboriously kept neat and uncomplicated. It began to make perfect sense to her, the way he thought, even if she didn't think that way herself.

Firefighters don't stand around the outside of a burning building and draw straws to see who goes in, who climbs up on the roof, or who drives the rig. Everyone has a job; he does it. They are decisive, with practiced instincts about safety and danger. They do dangerous things that no one else would dare, but they know it and they know how. They are men and women of skill and strength. They *never* overthink things.

On the Saturday morning after the tabloid story

broke, they curled up on the sofa with cups of hot coffee, talking until the kids woke up. He heard the whole long story about Chris's marriage, lawsuit, divorce and Aunt Flo's desire to come to Sacramento if Chris would not go immediately to Chicago.

"I told her I was staying here for a while, that the children are safe and comfortable here. She doesn't understand, of course, because the kids would be safe and comfortable in her house, but—"

"Did you tell her why you were staying?" he asked.

"Because the kids—"

"Did you tell her you love me?"

She looked at him for a long time. "In the past," she explained, "I haven't used the best judgment based on that emotion. My instincts, which I'm only just beginning to trust, say we're safe here. It isn't very logical, and it probably isn't fair to you, but if you still want us to stay a little while—"

He was either acting on instincts that told him he was safe, or he was using his skill and expertise to enter a danger zone. "I want you to stay."

"Aunt Flo wants to fly out, see me, make sure I'm all right. She's a pretty forceful person, Aunt Flo, and—"

"Chris, if you want to be here and I want you here, old Aunt Flo will just have to live with it. All that other stuff, about your instincts and your judgment, well, I think you ought to take your time with that."

"Well, she'll come here, then. Monday."

He shrugged. "I can't blame her. She's family. She's worried about you. We'll manage."

"My family, Mike, is nothing like your family."

"That's a relief," he said with a laugh. "I have the weekend off," he said. "Why don't we take the kids to the cabin? It's nice and cold in the mountains. It's snow-ing. It's quiet. Monday, huh?"

But no more running away or disappearing. That was another thing about firemen. Maybe they didn't borrow trouble, but they liked to face the fire, not have it hiding in a basement or behind a closed door. Some-times it came at them from above or behind or beneath. When they walked or crawled into a smoky, stinging, blinding problem, they liked to know where it was. So he suggested to Chris that she call Aunt Flo and tell her that she was going to the cabin, that she would be away from the phone, and give Mrs. Cavanaugh's phone number in case there was any emergency. And find out when, on Monday, Aunt Florence should be picked up at the airport.

Then they drove for two and a half hours to the mountains, to a place called Pembroke Pines, just north of Lake Tahoe. At Mike's cabin in the woods they could talk and play and worry in peace.

Mike swung Kyle up onto the back of the mare. "Hold on here," he told him, placing the boy's hands on the saddle horn. "Hold on, now."

Chris held the reins of Carrie's horse. Mike's nearest neighbors, the Christiansons, had loaned him the horses. Mike and Chris walked together, leading the small, gen-tle mares on which the children were perched. Cheeks trailed along, barking and snarling. They trudged down a sloppy dirt road in the Saturday afternoon sunshine, talking more like old friends than new lovers.

"Big Mike once saw that movie, *It's a Wonderful Life*. My dad gets an idea about something and makes it into a whole philosophy. Hurray for Hollywood, huh?"

"I liked the movie, too," Chris said.

"So that was how he handled us. Every single problem, from the fumbled pass during high school football to death and despair. 'So, Little Mike, what one thing would you go back and change, huh? What one thing that *you* could do would make it all turn out different?' And I would say, 'Well, I woulda studied for the test, that's what.' 'There you go,' he'd say."

"I should have paid more attention to the movie," Chris said.

"So, Chrissie, what one thing would you go back and change?"

"Ah! What wouldn't I change!"

"Your lousy ex? Wouldn't have married him, huh?"

"Starting there…"

"No Carrie and no Kyle. See, that's how this little game works. You go ahead and change something in your past, and you remove a big hunk of your future. That's the trick. You have to be real careful what pains you're going to trade for what pleasures. This is not as simple as it sounds."

"So what about you? What did Big Mike tell you?"

Mike laughed. "Oh, he had me so mad I thought I might deck him. Big Mike hasn't always been a little old man, you know. Even ten years ago I couldn't beat him arm wrestling. Yeah, he put me on the spot with Joanie's death. 'So what would you change? Never having met her? Never having married her? Never having Shelly…for even a little while?' For a long time I believed that would have been easier, better. Then I decided that if I could change anything, maybe I would have gotten up at night and changed the baby's diapers more. Or maybe I would have fought with Joanie about money just a little bit less. Maybe I wouldn't have asked her to join the Catholic church just so Ma would relax about the whole thing. But I don't know. I try to think, would that have made losing them feel any different? Easier? Harder?"

"And what about this?" she asked, taking his hand. "Starting to wish you hadn't been on duty that night my house burned down?"

"Oh, heck no. No, I really needed this. It shook things into place. I'm thirty-six. I had a bad deal, and I gotta get past that. I hadn't been with a woman in a long time. And before that I'd been with some without really being with them, you know?"

"Terrible waste," she said.

"In case you're interested, I feel like a big dope about it now. I was afraid of what I wanted from life. I want a lot, Chrissie. I want a family again."

"Whoa, boy," she said, shivering.

"You get worried when people tell you what they want, don't you?"

"If I think they want it from me, I do."

"No, that isn't it, I bet. You want it, too, and it scares you half to death. That's just what was happening to me. For ten years. I wanted a family again, but what if I tried to get one, got it and lost it again? After about ten years you decide to either play the hand you're dealt or stay out of the game."

"So," she said, "you're getting back in the game?"

"Me? I shouldn't have tried so hard to be alone. So, now that I remember, I'm not giving up on it again."

"I don't think you should."

"You're my first choice," he said, grinning at her. But he did not ask her to make him any promises. "Just having you around has been real good for me. It's like waking up."

"But will it always be good?"

"Chrissie, you'd make a great Catholic, no kidding. You borrow more trouble than Ma does. Never thought I'd meet a woman who could compete with Ma for worry and guilt."

The cabin, one open room with a large hearth and shallow loft, was equipped only with the necessities. But while the wind blew outside, the fire was hot. All four of them had to use sleeping bags in the central room. The loft wasn't a good place for the kids to be alone, in case they woke up in the night and began to wander. And downstairs alone, with a fire that had to burn all night, was an even worse idea.

"Why didn't you tell me the whole thing right off?" he asked her late in the night while the kids slept nearby.

"Because it's so shocking," she said. "People find the whole thing just plain incomprehensible. I told a couple of friends I met after Steve was gone, trying it out. The first thing they can't understand is why I didn't go after Steve, have him at least put in jail. People think you can do that, no sweat. You can't. He'd lost community property—proving he did it on purpose or stole it might have been impossible. Next, they wondered, if I had this rich aunt, why I didn't just call her right away. Say, 'Send a few bucks, you can afford it.' But a few bucks wasn't the thing I needed most. Pretty soon people look at you strangely, like you've made it all up. I began to feel weird, like a fraud or something, so I stopped telling anyone, which made me a real impostor. I might have had acquaintances but fewer and fewer real friends. With real friends you share personal things about your life. And my life was becoming more and more impossible to believe."

"But you decided to call Aunt Flo. Before the newspaper story," he pointed out.

"I wanted to call her because of the Cavanaughs. I had family once—very different from yours in a lot of ways, but tight, close, intimate family. Once Flo and I were very, very dear to each other—we were like best friends, in a way. There had been lots of other friends in my life, too—friends from high school and college— but I lost touch with some once I married Steve and moved, and the rest after the divorce because I was so embarrassed about how stupid I had been. When things settle down, I should probably try to get in touch with some of them.

"But first I have to deal with Flo. We didn't start to butt heads until my parents died and she took over as my parent. She began telling me what to do, what to feel, I guess because she felt responsible for me. Probably half the reason I married Steve in the first place was because Flo told me I couldn't.

"But I'm not really like you were. I'm not afraid of what I want. I'm more afraid I want all the wrong things. I'm afraid that I really and truly lack judgment. That I am really and truly incompetent."

"All you lack is confidence. It'll come back. Give it time."

"We're not talking about climbing back on a horse here, Mike. We're talking about lives and futures. Mine. Theirs."

"Ours."

"Don't," she said.

"You can hurt yourself more than one way, Chrissie. You can hurt yourself by making a wrong choice and loving some creep who just wants to use you, or you can hurt yourself by not loving someone who would be good for you."

Loving or not loving, she thought, was something she seemed to have no control over. But she had to try to have control over her *life*. "I'm not too worried about what's going to happen to me," she told him, "because I'm going to take my time and not rush into anything. But I would hate myself forever if I somehow hurt you... or them." She glanced at her children.

"One of the first things I noticed, Chrissie, is that you take good care of them. You're a good mother. That doesn't sound incompetent to me. I think," he said, pausing to kiss her nose, "you can be trusted with human life. I'm not worried about what you'll do to me."

"When Aunt Florence comes, Mike, would you like me to go stay with her at the hotel, or stay with you?"

"I would like you to stay where you want to be. But remember that your aunt has been through a lot, Chrissie, and you have to be careful with her. She's your family, and you gotta be careful with your family. You be nice to her, be gentle. But you can also tell her that you're a grown-up woman, a mother yourself, and you have to be where you have to be."

"She said almost the same thing about you."

"Oh?"

"She said, 'Oh, Chris, you just tell that nice man that you're very grateful for everything and that you'll call him, even visit.'"

Mike frowned his dangerous frown. "Well," he said

with a shrug, "even if Aunt Florence turns out to be a real bitch, we can handle it."

Yeah, Mike could probably handle just about anything, she decided as she tried to fall asleep.

She had always been attracted to independence and mastery. Her father, her lousy ex-husband, even Aunt Flo. Mike was like them all in many ways.

The next morning Mike wandered off, returning with firewood. Later, Chris heard a noise behind the cabin and found him repairing the pump. He puttered quietly, but when there was something to talk about, he opened up. It was all right when they didn't talk, too. One of the things that Chris learned was the kind of quiet she could have with intimacy. She had never had that in her marriage.

Mike took the kids for a nice long walk after breakfast while Chris cleaned up the dishes and rolled sleeping bags. They held on to his hands and toddled off, asking a million questions as they went out the door.

This was why she didn't leave. Not because she had any illusions about happily ever after, but because she was briefly visiting with her desires, the ones she was afraid were stupid and impossible.

For a short time she could indulge the fantasy of having a man for herself and for her kids. A man with enough love and caring to embrace a family. That was what she had thought she saw in Steve, but what she had seen was a lot of energy, not a lot of love. She had been too young and filled with grief to know it.

She had given her kids plenty of love and nurturing, even though she had been bereft herself, but they had lacked some vital things. A happy mother, for starters.

She worried about that a lot; what had they learned from her loneliness? Were there hidden emotional scars that would hinder them later, making it tough for them to form critical relationships? Would they not know how to make a family of their own because in their formative years all they had seen was their mother's tired, frustrated struggle? The absence of a father figure? Deprived of the sight of adults touching each other, showing easy and natural affection that came of love? What about a smile on their mother's face because a good man had made love to her?

There was no kidding herself, after making love with Mike she had felt different—relieved, soothed, fulfilled. And when a woman felt good, she mothered better. Did they pick up on these things?

And Mike provided. It wasn't just the things he provided, like cable TV or the new jackets, boots and mittens they had needed to go to the mountains. It was also the zone of calmness, sanity. His trust and confidence. She could see that they sat differently on his big lap, more secure because of his size and self-possession. They had hungered for a father, and for now they had a big fireman to show them what it might be like.

She wanted a life like the one they were pretending. To cook while he worked and to surprise him with something special. Or to not cook and have him complain. She wanted to be there to talk about the fires with him and take a casserole to Mattie and Big Mike's. She wanted to take her kids to the park, be a room mother, buy a chair she didn't need and argue over the expense, complain about the way he never wiped out the sink, and make love regularly. Then she wanted to work on her books and maybe have another baby. And be up through the night and nag that he took her for granted and have him say he was sorry and never would again.

She wanted a stupid, happy 1950s marriage that was fraught with give-and-take and pleasure and trouble, and sensible women did not want that anymore! Especially women who had jumped into that bonfire and been badly burned. She did not make any sense to herself.

He hadn't asked her to stay forever. She hoped he wouldn't too soon, but she knew he was sneaking up on that. She felt it. The fact that she would be tempted only made it worse. But she couldn't stand to think about leaving him, either. She was in love with him. And she knew it. If only she could have a little time to think.

But Flo was coming. *Better think fast, Chris.*

Late on Sunday night, when they were back in Sacramento and getting into bed, he asked her, "What time are you picking her up?"

"Noon."

"Bringing her here?"

"No, I made a reservation at the Red Lion."

"I'll be at work. Till Tuesday morning."

"The kids and I will spend the afternoon and evening with her, but we're coming back here, if that's all right."

"Stop acting like I'm going to change my mind. Old Aunt Flo doesn't worry me nearly as much as she worries you."

"That's because you don't know her."

"What's she going to do? Punch me out? Come on, relax. You call me if you need me. If she tries to kidnap you or something, we'll take care of Aunt Flo."

"Make love to me," she said. "Please. And don't make love to me like it's the last time."

"Is it? Is there any chance it's the last time? If it is, don't lie to me, that's all I ask. Just tell me the truth."

"I don't want it to be," she said, but tears came to her eyes. "I swear, I don't want it to be."

"That's good enough for me."

The Sacramento airport was small, tight and busy. Chris parked her car as close to the terminal as she could, but it was still quite a walk. She held hands with Carrie and Kyle. They were solemn, though they didn't exactly know why. They had been told about Aunt Flo, Mama's aunt from Chicago whom they had never seen before, whom Mommy hadn't seen in five years...since court. She didn't tell them that part.

Chris was so nervous about the reunion that she didn't even indulge in people-watching. She simply found them seats right outside security and waited. And waited.

The plane was late, but Flo got off quickly. She would have flown first-class. Naturally.

And there she was, more stunning and powerful than Chris remembered. She was five foot eight and still wore heels. She was dressed in a mauve suede suit and a low-cut lacy blouse. She wore boots—probably eel-skin. Her coat, slung over her arm, had a white mink collar. Flo wore as many dead animals as she pleased. Her diamond stud earrings glittered behind her short auburn hair. She was gorgeous, aristocratic. Forty-one years old. Good old Aunt Flo. *Be nice to her now.*

Chris saw her aunt spot them: she in her blue jeans, T-shirt, ski jacket and tennis shoes, no makeup, her hair pulled back into an unsophisticated ponytail; and two little kids who wore practically new but nonetheless rumpled clothes. Not a designer label among them.

The two women rushed toward each other and embraced. Chris was reduced instantly to tears. It was like meeting her past, her longed-for, frightening, grievous, essential past.

"Chris!"

"Flo! Oh, Flo!"

A camera bulb flashed.

"Oh, hell!" Chris gasped.

"Ms. Palmer, how long have you waited for this reunion?" "When did you first discover the whereabouts of your niece?" "Who died on that yacht, Ms. Palmer?" "Where will you be staying?" "Was any of the fortune recovered, Mrs. Zanuck?"

Chris grabbed her kids, one with each hand. She took only two steps before she looped an arm around Kyle's waist, lifted him onto her hip and headed down the concourse. Flo trotted after them.

"My God, Flo!"

"You think I invited them?"

"How did they know you were coming?"

"How the hell should I know? They know everything. Ever since that damn book came out!"

"Can't you get rid of them?"

"How, exactly? Let's just get out of here. Where's the car?"

"It's in the parking lot! Did you think I pulled the limo up to the curb?"

"You had to wear jeans? And those...shoes?"

"What do you think? That my designer is all tied up? Jeez, my house burned down! Anyway, who cares what I'm wearing? I didn't know it was going to be a damn press conference."

"Stop swearing. They'll hear you swearing."

"*You're* swearing."

"My luggage. Oh, forget the luggage. I'll send someone for it later."

"What if *they* get it?"

"Oh, they can't get my luggage. Later," she said to a reporter. There were only about six, but it seemed like six hundred. "I just want to spend some time with my niece. I'll give you a statement later."

"You will not!" Chris said.

"Just come on, all right?"

They were followed to the parking lot. They were half running, dragging Carrie along.

"Get a shot of the car! Get a shot of them getting into the car. Man, will you look at that car!"

They were not followed from the airport, but by the time they had Flo settled in her suite—after warning the manager about reporters, having someone sent to the airport for the luggage, and making various other arrangements for Flo's comfort—Chris was exhausted. And disgusted. She began to remember the photographers at the courthouse. When she won, she had had tears in her eyes, sensing if not admitting her betrayal. But Steve had been whispering in her ear, "Don't cry, for God's sake. Smile. Tell them you have no hard feelings, that you love your aunt, you know. Come on, we won."

We. There had never been any *we*.

Flo hadn't cried. "There should be no question of my motives or my relationship with my niece. I only attempted to protect her future as was spelled out in my brother's will. She didn't sue *me,* after all. I happen to think that it's a mistake for her to contest her father's wishes, but the court has made its decision, and we'll certainly abide by it." To Chris, later, Flo had said, "I am too angry to even talk to you. You just don't know how foolish you are."

In Flo's suite, Kyle bounced on the big round bed and Carrie carefully manipulated the buttons on the television. Flo spoke on the phone, ordering room service. Chris slouched in the chair.

"Well, they're sending up some sandwiches and sodas for the kids, salads for us, and I ordered a bottle of wine. We should toast this occasion, hmm? Then I think we should go shopping. I'm renting a car, and—"

"Tell me about the stupid book."

"Well," Flo said, sitting down gracefully, sliding into the chair and crossing her long, beautiful legs, "the 'stupid' book is exactly that. It is contrived almost solely from old newspaper articles and gossip and isn't nearly as revealing as it claims to be. I'm sure a great deal of it is made up. And I think it's been thrown together and rushed to print in the few months since that yacht has been missing. All of the pictures are previously published photos, and—"

"Pictures?"

"Oh, yes. How they got a baby picture of you is beyond me. Stole it, probably."

"Who did this? And why?"

"The author's name, Stephanie Carlisle, is a pseudonym. This is her third such exposé. She writes a decorator column for a Miami newspaper. The Miami paper ran a small piece about a missing yacht, a missing woman and an investigation of a man by the name of Steven Zanuck, the name under which the missing yacht was chartered. And I think I can tell you how this all started. That weasel's third wife, not his fourth, was the daughter of a Texas millionaire. Naturally. Her father began investigating him, not liking in the least who his daughter had fallen for. I think it's pretty certain that Steve took her off to Miami when things were getting a little hot in Dallas. We think, for example, that he might have married her before he was divorced from you. And we also suspect that he didn't divorce his first wife at all—a woman he married when he was only twenty-one and living in San Francisco. Precocious little devil."

"What? Who was that?"

"Sondra Pederson, daughter of a rich Swedish shipper. But that one wasn't as messy as the other ones. He managed to get a bunch of money before Daddy flew from Sweden to San Francisco and simply collected his brokenhearted daughter. She's alive and well and living with her family in Stockholm. That hasn't been mentioned, however. It would probably hurt book sales."

"Jeez. It figures."

"He wasn't a lawyer. No record of his ever having attending law school or taking the bar exam."

"Why didn't we know any of this sooner? When I was stupidly trying to win my fortune?"

"Believe me, if I had been able to find one thing on him, I would have used it. He checked out. There was a Steven Zanuck who passed the bar after graduating from law school in New York. There was even a yearbook picture that resembled your husband. He was pretty good at this little scam. And, although I thought he was a weasel and a creep, I didn't know the worst of it. It was that Texan, Charles Beck, who dug up the real dirt. And I think it's possible his family paid the biggest price."

"You think they're really dead, then? Steve and his—"

"Fred."

"Fred?"

"His name wasn't really Steve Zanuck. In San Francisco his name was William Wandell, and in Texas he was Steven Wright. He kept a place and a small business under the name Zanuck for a while, kind of living a dual identity. It probably had something to do with monies he had received as Zanuck. His real name is Fred Johnson. And the real Steve Zanuck, a nice young tax attorney with a practice in Missouri, isn't real happy about all this, either."

"*Fred?*"

"Terrific, huh? Well, I always knew he was no damn good. Just couldn't prove it. I hired detectives and lawyers, and they didn't figure him out, either. Real slick, this lizard. I ought to sue them. Incompetents."

"Is all this in the book?"

"This business about his aliases is our little secret so far. We're going to have to do something about that hair." Flo reached across the small table and plucked at Chris's hair. Chris withdrew. "You know you shouldn't wear your hair all the same length."

Chris put her forehead in her hand, leaning her elbow on the small round table. "Fred," she moaned. "This is simply impossible."

"It'll blow over. There's a little money, I think. The Texan found some money, but maybe it's not in this country. I wonder what the scum was saving up for?"

"Does he have a lot of children, too?"

Flo glanced at Kyle, bouncing, and Carrie, sitting entranced in front of the big TV. Her features softened. She looked back at Chris. "Not that I know of," she said gently. "You should have called me so much sooner."

"I know. I know." But then I wouldn't have been pulled out of that fire, she thought. She almost told Flo about the philosophy behind *It's a Wonderful Life,* but she held her tongue. Sophisticated Flo, who'd climbed to a mountaintop in Tibet to learn about meditation from the masters, would have a tough time swallowing something as effective as playing the hand you're dealt. "Well, I figured you were pretty mad, Flo. I was trying to make it on my own, I guess. I've been working, taking care of the kids and writing."

"Writing? What?"

"Never mind that. Not my life story, I promise. I was trying to take care of myself, trying to figure out what I really wanted to do. I'm getting a little tired of feeling stupid. I just wanted to make it on my own for a while. I thought I'd done enough damage. I wasn't planning to *never* call you."

"Well, you should have called me. I was worried sick. Now, when are you coming back home?"

Chris began telling her story. She tried to explain how for the first time in so long she felt free but coddled at the same time. This wonderful man and his lovely family had embraced her, and though they didn't have many luxuries, within their tender assembly there was such a rich intimacy, such love.

Room service arrived. They set up the kids at the table, and Flo brought the wine to the sitting room where Chris was telling her tale, knowing she sounded like a romantic fool. Yet another chapter in Chris's novel of misguided fortunes, fantasies and foibles. Flo poured wine and sat listening, pulling a long, slender cigarette from her snakeskin case, inhaling, the smoke curling up past her perfectly enameled nails, past her rose-colored lips, over her artistically fashioned copper hair. Listening to this story of love and woe.

"I always wanted to have a family," Chris said. "A family like my family was. Even before Mom and Daddy died, I always figured that whatever I ended up doing, I'd be doing it in a home with a husband and children."

"Well, you have children," Flo said.

"I should have listened to you. I shouldn't have married Steve—I know that. But I did, I have them, and in Mike's home and in his family the kids have a sense of belonging. For the first time. I can see a change in them already—they feel more loved, more secure, at ease."

Flo did not comment.

Chris told of parks, ducks, movies, stories read. "Imagine Carrie not knowing that men don't shave their legs! And they love his cabin, the horses they rode. The cousins at Mattie and Big Mike's."

"I can't come up with cousins," Flo said, "but the horses shouldn't be a big problem."

"It's more than horses and cabins and movies. As for me," Chris said, "I had been lonelier than I realized. I had let myself become friendless. I hardly even noticed that I had lost touch with old friends who probably would have stood by me. Then, meeting the Cavanaughs, I saw the potential to have family and friends again." She smiled almost sheepishly. "They liked me. Right off. Without knowing a thing about me.

"And Mike," she went on. "Logically I knew that all men aren't men like Steve…Fred. But I had stopped believing it was possible for someone to care for me, no matter whether I was rich, poor, smart or dumb. This guy just opened up his heart and his home, no questions asked. It had nothing whatever to do with my bloodline or checkbook balance. I can't tell you how it feels to have this man not give a damn about all that."

Flo stamped out the cigarette. She sipped the wine.

Then, Chris tried to explain, he had needs, too. He wasn't asking her for anything, really, but because his life had not been a picnic, this unit they had formed, the four of them, was helping him, too. He was finally getting in touch with what he had lost, what he could have, and was thinking in terms of having a real life again—one filled with love, people, give-and-take. Before Chris and her kids, Mike had cut himself off, afraid to feel, afraid to be involved.

"The long and short of it is, I'm simply not ready to leave him. That doesn't mean I'm planning to stay forever—I haven't made commitments—but the four of us, well, we're comfortable with one another when none of us has been completely comfortable for years. We're recuperating from past hurts. It might not sound very practical, but it's a good feeling to be needed.

"I love you, Flo. I know I haven't been very good family, the way things have gone. First the lawsuit, then disappearing like that. I'm sure you've been at the end of your rope with me, and I want to patch things up. I want to have our old relationship back. I want to be friends again. You're the most important person in my life, my only family. But I'm not going to do everything you tell me, and I'm not going to leave Mike's house until I'm ready. Until we're healthier. All four of us."

Her eyes were locked tightly on Chris's. Chris realized Flo probably thought her niece still had a screw loose, as though she had moved from one absurd situation to the next. But for the first time in seven years Chris felt sane. And—another first—she felt tough enough to deal with Flo. She lifted her chin, waiting.

"Well," Flo said, as composed as ever, lifting the wineglass, "how long do you think this is going to take?"

Mike had finally talked about it. He had told Jim some of this incredible tale. He had come right out and said it, that though he probably sounded like a lunatic, he had fallen for this goofy woman and her kids. And it was true, like the story in the paper said, she had been pretty well kicked around by that jerk she had married, but she hadn't known it was all a scam from the start. Young, you know, grieving over her dead parents, no one but her old-maid Aunt Flo, and then along comes this good-looking, fast-talking lawyer, and bam! Before you know it the whole family falls apart over money. Figures, huh? Money and sex, the biggest problems in America.

And yes, he had said, he'd told her to stay for as long as she wanted. He hoped it would be for a long time because he liked it; it was good to take someone to his mom and dad's, not go alone. They loved the cabin, all of them. Especially the kids. For a few years now he'd been thinking of building a room on. Maybe this spring he'd get started.

These complications from her past? Well, he had

said, who didn't have a past, huh? His past, for example, wasn't very tidy, all things considered. She had to try to reconcile with her aunt, keep her family together somehow. She hadn't taken any of her aunt's money, of course, only her own. She didn't need money right now, but everyone needs family. So he had encouraged her to be as patient and kind with old Aunt Flo as she possibly could. This would all work itself out.

The afternoon paper arrived. Mike had been playing Ping-Pong with a couple of the guys. Jim walked in and stopped the game, spreading the paper on the game table. At least it wasn't the front page. The headline said *REUNION*. The airport scene. Blue-jeaned Chris was being embraced by a tall, fashionable woman who looked to be about Mike's age. She wore jewelry everywhere, *big* jewelry. She carried a fur coat and a briefcase.

"Old Aunt Flo," Jim supplied.

"Holy shit," Mike said. Then he picked up the paper and took it into the bathroom.

Chapter 9

Mike entered his house quietly. He peeked in at the sleeping kids. Cheeks, the great watchdog, asleep on the end of Kyle's bed, didn't even greet him. Cheeks was exhausted from spending the entire night eating a pair of Mike's socks. He was sleeping with the remnants still under his chin.

When Mike found Chris in his bed, still asleep, he felt his chest swell with pride. He felt as though he were in possession, as if he had won. He didn't mean to feel that way, but he did. He wondered how many more mornings he'd leave his shift wondering what he'd find at home. He sat down on the edge of the bed, gently, and kissed her. "Hey, sleepyhead," he whispered.

She moved a little, moaning. "You had fires," she sleepily informed him. "I can't sleep through those sirens."

"I can't sleep through them, either." He laughed. "I'm going to have to sleep today though—I'm bushed. I saw Aunt Flo."

"You saw her?" Chris asked, coming awake, sitting up. "Where?"

"In the paper. Your picture was in the paper."

"Oh, yeah, I should have thought of that. There were reporters at the airport, but we ditched them. Was the story awful?"

"There wasn't much of a story, no quotes or anything."

"That's a relief. They didn't make anything up."

"Any particular reason you didn't tell me that Flo wasn't some crotchety old bat?"

"Is *that* what you thought?" she asked with a laugh. "Well, don't worry, I won't tell her. No, Flo is everything every woman dreams of being. Intelligent. Sophisticated. Independent. Beautiful. Rich. Successful." And a few other things, she thought, like belligerent, possessive, domineering.

"How old is she?"

"Oh, about forty. Maybe forty-one."

"Jeez. I had no idea. I was expecting this little old lady, like from *Arsenic and Old Lace,* just a rich old biddy who couldn't understand true love because her libido had dried up."

Chris laughed again.

"How was it? The reunion?"

"There were three things we had to get out of the way—first, how ashamed and sorry I am for having sued her, abandoned her and worried her half to death. Second, this business about my ex-husband and that stupid book. And finally, how I'm not getting on a plane with her this afternoon. Then we had a lot of fun reminiscing. I've missed her so much. We had such fun together when I was growing up. My mom would say that she had married Randolph and Flo. We were a famous foursome. And Flo was always there, spoiling me, pumping me up, taking my side. Auntie Flo," she said sentimentally, shaking her head. There had been affection, such hilarity, such joy in their relationship—so much lost since the death of her parents and the lawsuit. Chris longed to have it back. "My best friend while I was growing up. She's more like an older sister than an aunt."

"So. Not this afternoon, huh?"

She kissed him, quick and cute, on the lips. She wrinkled her nose. "You stink. Awful. Smoke?"

"And a bunch of other things. I would have showered at the station, but we had a shift relief in the middle of a fire."

"What other things?"

"God knows. Sweat. Mud. Good old Jim ought to take an emesis basin into a fire with him, for starters."

"A what?"

"You know, that curved little pan they give you in the hospital when you have to throw up. It's amazing—everything hits your turnouts, but you still come away smelling like all of it. Jim shot me with the hose to clean me off, but I still need a scrub, huh?"

"Oooo. I guess I thought only the victims threw up."

"Bet you also thought only the victims swallowed a lot of smoke, huh? I'll take a quick shower."

"Were they bad fires?"

"One was at a paint store. Those are almost the worst—chemicals and all. That one will be on the news—horrible mess. It took hours in the middle of the night, but it was just about over by the time I left. The other two were pretty good fires."

"Good fires?"

"Manageable fires, no injuries, easily contained."

"Do you like fires?"

"I like to put water on fires."

She watched while he stripped off his shirt and pants, heading for the shower in only his briefs. She remembered the young fireman in the photo she had found, the leaner, trimmer man. But though he was thicker now, he was firm and graceful. He walked with such purpose, even without clothes on.

"Mike, have you ever gotten hurt in a fire?"

He shrugged. "Not bad."

"This is really dangerous, what you do. You could be killed."

"Don't overthink it. I know what I'm doing or I wouldn't do it." He yanked down the briefs.

"*Overthink* it? What about firefighters' families? What must they go through every time they hear the siren? What if you—"

He stood in the bathroom doorway, hands on his hips, not in the least distracted by his nudity. "Chrissie, being born is dangerous. Joanie and Shelly were driving to the grocery store. If you're going to worry for a living, worry about something you can control, for Pete's sake. I'm going to shower. *I* can't even stand the way I smell."

While the shower ran, she thought about those two things. One, he could get killed in a fire. Two, if she were paid for worrying, she'd be a millionaire.

"Tell me about Aunt Flo," he said, standing in the

bathroom doorway with a towel wrapped around his lower body, using another to dry his hair.

"I invited her to dinner. Is that okay?"

"Here?"

"Would you rather not?"

"No, it's okay. But—"

"She is not going to relax until she looks you over, Mike. She simply can't believe I'm planning to stay here for a while. And I thought we'd all be a lot more comfortable here than in a restaurant or something. I'm cooking."

"I'm getting into bed," he said, moving to close the bedroom door and then tossing the towel to the floor. "When did you tell her you'd go back to Chicago?"

"I didn't say when."

"What did you say?"

"Want to know how I sold you, huh? Well, I told her you were this big, handsome brute who—"

"Actually," he said, pulling back the covers to climb in beside her, "I want to know how you sold her on not dragging you off to Chicago."

"I said we were getting healthy here," she replied, her voice soft, her words serious. "All four of us. Is that true?"

He thought about it for a minute. "Yeah, I think that's true. Yeah, that's okay." He pulled up the covers. His eyes looked bright, but dark circles hung under them. Fires. His eyes, scorched but excited, tired but revved up. She wondered how long a man could do this work before it took its toll. "But you never told her that you love me."

"She thinks I'm crazy as it is."

"Well, in that case, I hope this is a long illness," he said.

"How long do you think you'd like it to be, Mike?"

"Oh, thirty, forty years. I want to keep you."

"Forever?"

"If I can."

"I can't make that kind of commitment. You know that. It's way too soon."

"Well, it's an open invitation."

"How can *you* do that—ask us to stay here permanently? You mean, you want to marry us after knowing us such a short time?"

"Are you going to hold that against me?"

"No. But I'm not rushing into anything."

"Just so you're not rushing *out* of anything."

"You haven't even met my family. My 'family' will blow in here at about six-thirty tonight with twenty-two servants carrying her train and polishing her crown. I think the term *formidable woman* was invented to describe Flo. Then you might add some conditions to this not-very-romantic proposal."

His hands went under her T-shirt, which was his T-shirt, and he squirmed closer. "You want romance, Chrissie? I'll give you romance."

"Mike, why would you bring up marriage so soon? Really, why?"

"It's what I want. I think it's what you want. I think you want to be a real family. I want to take care of you."

"If I wanted taking care of, I could call the Red Lion. Flo would be thrilled."

He squeezed her breasts and moved against her thigh. "Oh?"

"That's not enough, wanting to take care of someone."

He shrugged. "We can think about it for a long time, or a short time. But, Chrissie, life is short. You just never know how short. And I love you. I haven't loved anyone like this in a long, long time."

"What if you don't feel that way in another month?"

"Look, if you're not sure how *you* feel, that's one thing. You had a hard time of it, I know, so take your time and decide how you feel, okay? But I know how *I* feel, and I know that this kind of feeling doesn't come and go that fast. They trip around a little from time to time—every marriage on record has ups and downs. But love is love, and I'd rather live it than give it lip service."

"And you didn't feel this way about the other women you've been with?"

"Nope. I wanted to, but I didn't. Boy, when it hits you, it about knocks you over." He smiled. It was a feeling he liked.

"I'm afraid of being in love," she whispered.

"Really? Afraid of being in love? Or afraid of loving someone who's going to hurt you?"

"Isn't that the same thing?"

"Depends," he said, shrugging, his eyes getting that tired, drained look. He was going to nod off. "Are you afraid of me?"

"You know I'm not."

"Then it's not the same thing." He put his head on her shoulder, holding her close, snuggling up tight.

"Actually," she said almost to herself, "what I'm really afraid of is depending on someone too much. Really needing, *counting* on, someone. Giving in so totally.

Because the next stage seems to be taking it all for granted, expecting it will stay safe and satisfying forever until the only thing about yourself you're sure of is who you are in relation to the person you feel you belong to. Whether he's a great guy or a jerk, it could—whoosh—disappear, leaving you suddenly on your own. Do you know what I'm talking about, Mike? Mike?"

He had fallen asleep.

"Marriage!" Flo said, in a combination of shock and distrust. Chris sat in the beautician's chair, Florence stood behind. The kids were with a sitter, a *bonded* sitter at the hotel. "Are you even close to seeing how ridiculous this is becoming? Marriage! Layer it," she instructed, pointing a long, polished fingernail at the back of Chris's head. "But leave some of the length. No bangs. Brush it *back,* so."

"I can tell her how to cut my hair, Florence."

"Tell her then," Flo said, hands on hips.

"Well, I'd like you to cut it shorter around the top and take only about an inch off the length so that it still touches my shoulders, and—"

Flo smiled. "That's what I thought."

"I wish you wouldn't tell me what I want to do all the time." Especially when you're right, she almost added.

"Marriage, huh? He suggested marriage this soon? You certainly didn't accept?"

"Not because I wasn't tempted."

"Chris, you're going to have to be sensible at some point in your life, and now would be a good time. A little shorter on top, here," she instructed the stylist. "You're on the rebound, you can't enter into another marriage."

"Rebound? I've been alone for nearly four years!"

"Yes, but you haven't really recovered from that yet. In fact, you don't know for sure if you're divorced, widowed or still married." The stylist stopped, eyes widening. Flo dismissed her curiosity with a hard stare. The comb moved again. "There," Flo told the technician, "that looks good. Real good."

They shopped for clothes and accessories. Makeup, nail polish, files, perfume, bath oils, shampoos and rinses. Chris turned before a full-length mirror in the department store. She looked very different in tailored dress slacks, a loose angora sweater, heels and hose, makeup, a sculptured hairstyle and even a necklace. A thick, curving gold collar. Very chic.

"I'm not on the rebound. I've been on my own for four years. I haven't had any kind of serious relationship, but that doesn't mean that I didn't meet and know men. I've worked several different jobs in the past few years. I even had a couple of dates. And Mike hasn't met anyone he wanted to marry, but that doesn't mean he doesn't know women. You've got this all wrong."

"What kind of a guy offers his house for the night because a woman is burned out, and then, lickety-split, asks her to marry him?"

"Oh, you're right, only a real pervert would do a thing like that!"

"What if this has something to do with your money?"

"I don't have any money, Flo."

"*I* have money. And what's mine is yours."

"No, it's not, Flo. We aren't the same person, remember? All my money, which was Daddy's money, hit the trail."

They walked between the shops in the downtown

Sacramento open mall. As they were passing a window, arms laden with shopping bags, Flo drew Chris up short. "Look," she said, standing behind Chris and taking her parcels, giving her a full view of herself. "Do you feel any different? You look great."

Chris looked at herself in the shop window. She fingered the necklace that cuffed her neck—not solid gold, but a very nice piece of jewelry nonetheless. Classy, like Flo. "Yes, Flo," she said, meeting her aunt's eyes in the glass. "I feel different. I look more like your version of me than mine. And your version looks better." She turned around, staring into her aunt's eyes. "I don't quite know what to make of that."

"Why don't you simply enjoy it?"

But Chris had had plenty of time to think about what she needed to be happy, and it wasn't fancy clothes. She needed family. She needed to be connected to people she loved, people who cared for her and counted on her. She also liked to sit behind a computer and imagine. She imagined best in a sweat suit or jeans or a man's T-shirt. Grubbies. It might be nice, she thought, to dress up after a grueling day at the keys, but it wasn't necessary in order to become whom she was becoming. What she needed a lot more than a nice pair of slacks and a necklace was someone to talk to about the book she was working on—and for that it didn't matter what she was wearing.

Who wouldn't enjoy nice things? Oh, boy, there it was again. It was difficult to maintain an idea of what you could do on your own when you were being taken care of. That she would enjoy nice things so much more if she could get them for herself and also give them was difficult for people like Flo to understand. And there was no way to refuse Flo's generosity, for Flo spending on Chris was part of their history. But it was already starting to feel loaded. She kept waiting to hear the bait line: "After all I've done…"

You suffer too much, Chrissie, he had said. *It's almost like you want to.* No, that wasn't it. Chris hated to suffer. She wanted balance. Give-and-take. Take *and* give.

"Why haven't you ever married, Flo?" she asked.

"I never saw the need."

"Need? Is that what marriage is? Something you need?"

"You tell me. You're obviously thinking about doing it for the second time."

"I'm not really ready to make any long-term commitments; I only said I was tempted. And Steve…I mean, Fred…doesn't count. I was a victim of temporary insanity."

"Nothing counts *more* than Steve, or Fred, or whoever the heck he was, because you should have learned something from that—something about how impetuous you are when it comes to this kind of emotion. Lord, running back into a thunderstorm again before you're even dried off."

"I think you mean jumping from the frying pan into the fire," Chris supplied, laughing. "Almost literally. Don't worry, Florence. I learned far more than I bargained for." What she did not add was that she was finally *un*learning some of the suspicion, distrust and paranoia Steve had left her with.

"In fact, I know a lot of women who marry regularly. And dreadfully. Like a bad habit. I don't know what moved you to marry the first one any more than this second one, whom you've known for less than—"

"Don't change the subject, Flo. We both know you have a low opinion of my choices. I want to know about *you*. Do you have any kind of personal life these days? You look like success personified—wealth, beauty, intelligence, et cetera. I met some of the men you dated, or rather 'attended functions with,' but that was years ago. What's the deal, Flo? Are you a lesbian?"

Flo gasped and stopped walking. "Christine!"

It made Chris laugh to have shocked her aunt, but this was more of their history. Chris would be daring and in need of discipline, and Flo would be sensible and ready to give it. Big and little girl. Teacher and student. Yet as much as Chris admired Flo's composure, her command, her savoir faire, Chris neither envied nor wished to become Flo.

"Are you lonely?" she asked her aunt.

"No," she said. "Certainly not. I've missed *you*."

"But when you're not either fighting me in court or hunting for me, what is your life like?"

"You may wish to remember, dear, that my older brother died and left me a horrendous business when I was only thirty-four. The next several years were a tad busy with very demanding work and trying to figure out what to do about you."

"It might have been better for you if you'd written me off as a loss."

"Ha! The only family I have—a young woman who is in perpetual trouble, my brother's child, once my dearest friend. Why would I write you off? I knew we'd be together again someday."

"But who do you spend Christmas with?"

"Usually with friends."

"Ah. Do you have a lover?"

"Chris, believe me, if I thought it were any of your business, I would—"

"Come on, Flo, you know all *my* dirt. Come on, what do you do when you snake out of all that eelskin? Do you have anyone special and dear? Has your whole personal life been on hold so you could manage Palmercraft and Palmer House and the Perils of Pauline?"

Flo sighed. "I have the same friends I've always had. I've been seeing the same man for years. Literally years. We're both very busy, but we do quite a lot together. We're very good friends. We travel together sometimes."

"Who?" Kate said.

"Kenneth Waite."

"Kenneth Waite? Isn't he the president of some big advertising agency? What is it? Multimega—"

"He's the owner now. Waite Commercial Resources, Inc."

"How long?"

"Oh, I think he's been the owner for—"

"No." She laughed. "How long have you been seeing him?"

"Forever. I don't know. Fifteen years."

"But isn't he married? Wasn't his wife a friend of Mother's? Wait a minute...."

"As I said," Flo went on, "we are two busy people with a great many commitments. There's not a lot of room in either of our lives for romance. There never has been, although Ken has been divorced for years— seven or eight, I think. We're simply very good friends."

"You were having an affair with a married man!"

"His marriage left a good deal of room for that.

And my responsibilities have never left room for much more."

"How well organized, Florence," Chris said, shaking her head. "Are you going to get married? Ever?"

"It doesn't seem necessary, even since Ken has been divorced. We're pretty independent people."

"It sounds so distant. So…uninvolved."

"Not everyone has an overactive libido."

"Come on, don't make any cracks about my poor old neglected sex drive. Stever might have awakened it, but he certainly left it in a coma. I couldn't even fathom an interest in sex for years. Have you any idea what it's like to be absolutely insane with passion and then find out the lousy creep probably didn't even *like* you? Talk about impotence! Or frigidity, or whatever. It comes as a real blow. Here you are, willing to do anything short of crawling through cut glass for one more kiss, only to learn he was just using you. Honestly, I bet Steve, or whoever, didn't even *like* me. Whew."

"Well, I tried to tell you, but you —"

"But what about you?" she asked as they reached Flo's rented Cadillac. Chris leaned on the roof, looking across at Flo. "What's your excuse? How come you never fell in love? Dumb, embarrassing love?"

Flo tossed her bags into the backseat and put her elbows on top of the car. She rested her chin on her forearms and looked at Chris. "What is it, huh? What do they offer you that I don't understand? No kidding, what does this big, dumb fireman have that has made you gunky with devotion? A schwanz as long as a fire hose?"

Chris erupted with laughter, covering her mouth.

"This big?" Flo asked, putting up her hands, indicating something of inhuman proportions. "Or is it their vulnerability, the things they need from you? Old Stever needed a few bucks, and this guy needs to play house for a while. Or is it really just some primitive man-woman thing, some bonding that I didn't get the gene for? Come on, tell old Aunt Flo, you little slut."

How she loved her! There weren't many people who knew this Flo. The people who read the society pages expected a Princess Diana sort. But Flo operated a huge furniture business. That meant she could speak many languages; she could communicate as well with the governor's wife as with an upholsterer with an eighth-grade education. She was tough, slick, sassy. No way Mike was ready for this dame.

"Regardless of how utterly stupid I was to have married Steve," Chris said, "it's important to remember that it was a simple mistake. It's important to remember that I was young, vulnerable, and he wasn't just a bad choice—he was a criminal. Mike is a decent man.

"It's risk," Chris said. "Not the kind of risk you take to sneak to a hotel behind your husband's back, or the kind of risk required to put your money in his account, for that matter. It's the risk of your emotional self. It's exposing yourself to a person who will accept you as you are, embrace you as you are. It is the risk, Flo, of being naked in an emotional way, and betting that you won't get cold." She was quiet for a second. "I feel nice and warm," she said softly, "all the time now."

After meeting her aunt's eyes over the roof of the car, Chris opened the door and slid into the passenger side. Flo stayed above for a few moments before getting into the driver's seat.

"Christine," Flo began seriously, "would it not be just as good to buy a nice, thick parka? Mink, perhaps?"

Mike had napped and then gone to his folks' house. When he walked into the kitchen through the garage door, Chris was stirring something at the stove. He looked her over and smiled. "Wow. You look different. Gorgeous."

She turned her lips toward him for a kiss. "I let Florence have me 'done.'"

"She didn't change anything on the inside, did she? When's she coming?"

"Anytime now. And, Mike, listen… Oh, forget it, there's no point in trying to prepare you. Just try to roll with it, okay?"

He took a beer from the refrigerator and walked into the dining room. He looked at the table. "What's this?"

She followed him. "I hope you don't mind," she said
He lifted a new plate. "Flo gave me a bunch of money after she shopped me to death and told me to get something I wanted, something frivolous. It's no big deal for Flo, and it made her feel good to give me the money. And this was how I wanted to spend it. On you, sort of."

His table wore a new linen tablecloth. New ceramic plates in lavender, royal blue and beige sat between new flatware and linen napkins in china rings. There was a new lavender vase filled with fresh flowers. Wineglasses. Mike felt funny inside, a little dizzy maybe. New dishes—because she was staying and wanted a nicer set? Or was his slightly imperfect, chipped set of ironstone too flawed for this event? But he said, "Looks nice."

The kids called his name and ran to him, and his

dizziness went away. He picked them up, both of them, and went into the living room where they had things to show him—toys, books and gadgets. He was relieved to see that they wore the clothes *he* had bought them. Cheeks wandered over, tail wagging, and nudged him for a scratch. I got to *him,* Mike thought. If I can impress this mutt, I can handle Flo. Can't I?

And the doorbell rang. He remembered something. He remembered Joanie's dad saying hello but looking at him with that if-you-touch-my-daughter-I'll-kill-you look. Mike had been a mere boy. He had gulped down his nerves. He wanted to kick Cheeks in the ribs for not growling at Florence.

"So, this is the fireman," Flo said, smiling very beautifully. "Well, there's hardly anything I can do to repay you for saving my family."

Yes, you can. Leave. Go away and turn into a surly old woman. I'm good with cranky old ladies. They love me. "Just doing my job," he said, taking the proffered hand.

"And thank God you were," she added, gliding past him into the living room. She had packages. She probably didn't go anywhere without presents. She was dressed casually—gray wool fitted slacks, a fuzzy red sweater, gray pumps out of some kind of skin and a rich leather blazer. Rings and things. She smelled heavenly, expensive. But she did crouch to receive the children. "There are my angels. I have presents. It must be your birthdays."

"It isn't our birthdays." Carrie giggled, reaching for a bag. "And you know it isn't our birthdays."

"Is it Christmas?" Flo asked.

"No." They laughed.

"Then somebody must love you. No, no, you have to give a kiss and hug first."

Mike ached. He wanted to be happy for them, for them all. What was wrong with him? Where was his heart, his convictions about family? Where, for gosh sakes, was his courage?

"Here you are," Chris said, coming from the kitchen. "And you've met Mike?"

Chris kissed the cheek Flo turned toward her. They looked alike, suddenly. None of their features, for Chris was small and fair, while Flo was big and bronze. It was their style. Chris, in expensive clothes and pumps, was very different than she had been in a T-shirt and jeans, hair pulled back, no makeup. She was now more like her rich aunt.

The kids were being fed something simple in the kitchen, after which they would be excused to play or watch television, while the adults sat at the newly appointed dining-room table. Mike sat with the kids while they ate, playing with them, talking to them, watching Flo and Chris in the kitchen together. They were like his sisters and sisters-in-law when they got together around the pots. They lifted lids, gossiped, laughed, helped each other—like good friends, like family. Flo and Chris recited a litany of names he had never heard before—old family acquaintances, friends from high school and college. They were still catching up. But he felt like an outsider, something he had never felt when the women in his family played this companionable game around the food.

For the first time he wondered if he should have

gotten himself into this. He was scared of this woman. He was afraid he was going to lose Chris and Carrie and Kyle....

"Wine?" Chris asked him when they were all seated.

"Sure. Thanks."

"Well, Mike, Chris tells me you had a dangerous fire last night. No one was hurt, I hope."

"No, no injuries."

"But it must be very dangerous, this work."

"We're trained for it," he said. He saw that he wasn't helping. Here she was, trying, and he was so suspicious, he was going to hurt his own case. You couldn't come between family. Chris had tried to blend into his; until now he hadn't known how hard she might have had to try.

He had to concentrate not to shovel food into his mouth too fast. Firefighters know the minute they sit down to a meal, the alarm will sound. He was going to try to be more refined. He would eat like an accountant. "Fire is dangerous and unpredictable, but our training, which is ongoing, prepares us to make intelligent decisions. We don't take risks foolishly is what I'm saying. But still, there are times..."

"Like in saving people, I suppose. Rushing into a burning building to rescue someone. Don't you ever stand there, looking at the fire, and think 'Wait a minute, here'?"

"That's the thing we don't do, as a matter of fact. Number-one priority is protecting life. Number-two is saving the structure. But we don't go in looking for people unless there's a reason to believe someone needs to be pulled out. Usually the person who calls in the alarm informs us on the scene."

"And you wear gear? Like oxygen masks?"

"Air packs," he said, "if there's time."

"And if there isn't time?"

"Look, that's the job." He shrugged. "Time is the only advantage there is, and we don't waste it thinking things over a lot. Firefighters don't rush into a wall of flame because it's fun. We all have our jobs at the fire, we take informed risks. We've been trained to recognize possible and impossible situations. We only get into trouble when something unforeseen happens—part of the structure collapses, or an on-site explosion occurs. That's the danger."

"So," Flo said, lifting her fork, "you pretty much rush into things, huh?"

Chris gulped. "Mike's been a firefighter for twelve years," she said. "He's very experienced." She took another sip of wine. "More wine?" she asked. They shook their heads.

"It's always an informed decision. Rapid but experienced."

"Have you ever been wrong?"

Mike stared at Flo for a long moment, using his heavy, brooding brows in that frightening look of his. But Flo met his eyes as if to say she was every bit as tough as he was. Tougher. This lady had played ball in the major leagues.

Chris drained her glass and refilled it.

"Everyone has been wrong, made mistakes. But if you fold your hand after your first mistake, you fail to learn anything, how to do it right the next time."

"You should meet Mike's family, his brothers and sisters," Chris attempted. "They—"

"So," Flo continued, ignoring Chris, "tell me, Mike, does this job require…um…a college education?"

Mike's cheeks took on a stain. "No," he said. "At least half of the firefighters in our company have degrees, but I don't."

"And if you had some disability? If you couldn't fight fires anymore?"

His mouth became grim. "I'm sure I'd manage."

"Really, Flo…" Chris said.

"Hmm," hummed Flo. "I suppose it must be the big-city firefighters who have the most precarious careers. Out here in the suburbs, it can't be as bad."

"Not as many bells as in, say, Chicago. But—"

"But this matter of doing dangerous work and the disability situation must be a major factor when you consider, for example, taking on a family."

"That would certainly be a consideration, Flo," he said evenly. "But usually not the first one."

Flo leaned an elbow on the table. "And what would the first consideration be?"

"Whether or not I could stand to be under the same roof with the other person, I guess."

Chris could tell he was trying, answering Flo's most prying, unreasonable questions with patience and honesty as if this were his steady girl's father. She wanted to tell Mike that he didn't have to prove anything to Flo. She wanted Flo to shut up, to let Mike off the hook. But it was bedtime for Carrie and Kyle, so she excused herself to take them upstairs and tuck them in, reluctantly leaving Mike and Flo at the dining-room table.

She heard snatches of their conversation: intelligent

decisions...danger is danger.... There are challenges that won't get you killed....

She returned to the table to find it was Mike's turn. He had been trying, but now he was getting mad. He asked about furniture.

"The Palmers began selling furniture more than forty years ago. We started manufacturing a specialized line of indoor/outdoor furniture only twenty years ago—Palmercraft. It's been very successful."

"That's what I hear. Lots of money. That must make life pretty easy."

Chris grimaced. "My grandfather didn't have much when he started. He built the business from his garage and—"

"I don't dislike success, if that's what you mean. But it is hard work. Chris herself has a vested interest in the business."

"Oh? She never mentioned that."

"Because I don't!" Chris said, but she might as well have told Cheeks. These two were not listening to her.

"Well, you already know that business about the will, but there's more to it than that. The will was written before Chris was of age, and it provided for her. The family business was given to me because it was understood that I would always take care of Chris's needs should anything happen to her parents."

"Take care of her needs," he repeated. "Her needs before she became an adult, I trust."

"My thinking is that the furniture company is half hers."

"Really? I suppose she'd have to go to Chicago for that."

"Chicago is her home, of course."

"Oh. I thought her home burned down."

"More wine?" Chris asked in frustration. They ignored her. She filled her own glass and stared into it.

She wanted to stop them. Flo knew Chris was not interested in the furniture business. Flo would happily take care of Chris forever; in fact, if Chris showed up at the factory one morning to take an executive position, her aunt would probably give her a title, plenty of money, and have her emptying wastebaskets to keep her out of trouble. Flo controlled everything. But it was moot; Chris would never even consider it. After all, she had run through almost four million dollars indulging a naive passion for a thief. She didn't want to be responsible for any more family money. The only money she wanted was money that belonged to her.

If these two stubborn people would stop sparring over her for a few minutes, she could probably explain her position better than either of them could. She would return to Chicago at some point soon—maybe not permanently; time would tell—but she did want the kids to see where she had grown up, and she wanted to reacquaint herself with some of her past. But she didn't want to move in with Aunt Flo and have her life managed. She also didn't want to live with Mike if he was going to insist on telling her what her priorities should be. What she wanted was simply their love, as they had hers, while she reconstructed a life that belonged to her. You couldn't share your life with anyone unless you had one of your own.

"There is a lot of unfinished business in Chicago that—"

"—could probably be handled by a good accountant," Mike interrupted.

"There's nothing wrong with a lucrative business, but I was talking about home, family—"

"Home is where the heart is."

Chris refilled her glass as their conversation grew more competitive. Thank God for the wine.

"I think you're suggesting, Mike, that Chris ignore who she is and where she came from to stay here with you, when you hardly know her and can hardly provide for her in the manner she is accustomed to."

"Oh, *that* manner—a crummy little firetrap in a rotten neighborhood, struggling to make ends meet because she's too proud or too scared to call her rich aunt? I can probably compete with that lifestyle. Yeah, I'm suggesting—"

"Stop it," Chris said, but she slurred it. They looked at her as if she had just arrived on the scene. Their images swirled before her eyes, but she got up from her chair with as much dignity as was possible, given the fact that she was completely sloshed. "When I make up my mind what I want, I'm sure the two of you will let me know."

She walked a crooked line from the dining room. "I'm going to bed. I accidentally got drunk trying to ignore the two of you. G'night."

Chapter 10

When Chris awoke she had the headache she deserved. On the bedside table was a note under a bottle of aspirin. The fireman had gone off to fight fires. The note said, "I'm sorry. I had no right. Love, M."

After two aspirin and two cups of coffee she called Flo. "Shame on you," she said to her aunt.

"Chris, I'm sorry. I didn't realize we were talking about you as if you weren't even there."

"Yes, and it was awfully familiar. I felt like I was in the middle of a custody battle. I'm not going to do this with the two of you. I'm furious."

"Come and have breakfast with me. I want to work this out."

"Well, as long as you're ashamed and sorry, let me dress the kids. Give me an hour."

"An hour?"

"I have a headache."

"I can imagine."

No, you can't, she wanted to say. She didn't know how she had managed to delude herself that there was any possible way Mike and Flo would hit it off. It wasn't that they were so terribly different—in fact, they had much in common. But in their strength, possessiveness and competitiveness, each seemed to have what the other wanted. Her.

And what did she want? The thought of giving up either Mike or Flo was excruciating, but...

Chris drew herself a bath, the water as hot as she could stand it. She hadn't been in the tub long before Carrie woke up and wandered in. "Morning, sweetie. Want to have breakfast with Auntie Flo?" Carrie nodded, rubbing her eyes, and positioned herself on the closed toilet seat to take waking up slowly. Chris leaned back in the hot water and closed her eyes.

When Chris was six years old she had wanted to be a singing ballerina. A star. She'd had wonderful fantasies about wowing her friends with performances—Shirley Temple fantasies with full production sets.

At twelve she had wanted to be a chemist. She saw herself in a lab coat and glasses—and when she took the glasses off she was beautiful, a gorgeous intellectual smarter than all the handsome young scientists around her. Soon she discovered that chemistry involved math. *C'est la vie.*

At sixteen she hungered for travel and decided to be a flight attendant. Flo took whole summers off two years in a row to accompany her around the world, to help her fill that need for expansion, appalled by the prospect of Chris's serving drinks on an air carrier.

At eighteen she was in college, reading her heart out. Flo bought every book that Chris wanted to discuss. They talked on the phone for hours each week. Flo traveled to New York often to take Chris and her friends to plays, museums, art galleries and on plentiful shopping trips. All Chris's friends idolized Flo. Chris was not interested in business, but she wanted desperately to be like her Aunt Flo.

Carrie wandered over to the tub and started playing with her bath toys. "Carrie, I'm taking a bath."

Carrie was now pushing an empty shampoo container under the water, filling it and pouring it out. "I won't get you wet, Mommy."

Chris laughed. "Move down by my feet then," she said, wondering how she'd come to have such a headache over the people she loved.

At twenty Chris wanted to be the woman behind the man, as her mother had been. She would raise a beautiful family for this sharp young lawyer who had not even given his real name. But all she wanted was to be *his*.

She touched Carrie's curls.

"Mommy, you'll get me wet." Carrie looked up and smiled. "Should I get in?"

"You can have your own bath in a few minutes."

At twenty-five she had to start thinking differently. A divorced mother, short of cash and deep in debt, she couldn't remember who she was or what she wanted. More than to simply survive, though. She began writing, not masterpieces but simple stories for young adults. She wanted to give back some of the fantasies she had used through the years to sustain her impossible, illusive fancies. She knew she was fanciful. Hopeful and idealistic. She had almost lost that because of Steve, and it was what she liked best about herself. Hopeful idealists changed the world. They could also be perfect victims.

Chris was unlike Flo, who had been born to control, and unlike Mike, who addressed life expediently as a series of "informed risks." Chris made up stories for kids who, like her at six and twelve and sixteen, were dreamy, desirous and always wondering the same two things she wondered. One, what was going to happen next? And two, would it all work out?

It didn't take long for her to realize that she loved the way she felt when she was writing, and soon she knew she was fulfilling some kind of inner need and being alone was so much less lonely. Suddenly she found herself working harder than ever to learn how to do it, to make it right, to make it more than right. She took night classes whenever possible, she read how-to-write-and-market-your-book books and articles every Sunday in the library while the kids paged through picture books beside her. She read, studied, typed, tore her work apart, typed some more, scrapped it again. She *had* to get it right, because if she succeeded, she could be happy, she could make money to support her little family, and she could do it in a way important to *her* and the woman she was becoming.

Carrie scampered out of the bathroom, dripping water from her wet sleeves, and scooted back in with more bathtub toys. Chris watched and smiled as Carrie splashed and sang off-key. She decided then and there, looking at her older child, that she would never again call her marriage a mistake. Carrie and Kyle were healthy, smart and her greatest accomplishments. If she had to do it all over again, would she pay almost four million dollars for them? In a heartbeat.

"Mommy?"

"Hmm?"

"Mommy, where is my daddy?"

Chris felt her cheeks grow hot. "Well, Carrie, remember I told you that he went away when you were a baby? I don't know where he is. I haven't seen him or talked to him since he went away."

"Does he miss us, then?"

"I...I don't know, honey. But he should miss you, because you're wonderful."

"Mommy? Where is Mike?"

"He's working. We won't see him until tomorrow morning."

"Do I remember my daddy?"

"Well, I don't think so. Do you think you do?"

She shook her head. "Is my daddy the same as Kyle's daddy?"

"Yes," Chris said, appalled. "Of course."

"Is Mike supposed to be our daddy now?"

"Mike...Mike is our very special friend, Carrie, but I'm not married to him."

"He likes us to use his house," she said, smiling at her mother.

"Yes. He does."

"Will he go away from us, then?"

"No, Carrie. No, we will always know where Mike is, and he will always know where we are. Always. Even if we don't use his house forever. Even if we get a house of our own. Do you understand?"

"No."

"Well..." She'd better get used to answering difficult questions, because the older the kids became, the more serious the questions would be. "Well, even if we get our own house again, we will be good friends with Mike. We'll visit him, talk to him on the phone, see him sometimes. I'm sure of that. Do you understand?"

"No. I like Mike's house, and he likes us to use his house."

"Yes, but—"

"Can I watch cartoons until I have my own bath?"

"Yes. If you want to."

Of course she doesn't understand, Chris thought. Neither do I. She worked the drain release with her toe. So, twenty-seven years old, soaking out a headache, what did Chris want? Not a lot, actually. She wanted to keep the rain off her kids' heads, first. She wanted to reconcile with Flo so she could be rooted once more with the people, events and emotions that had shaped her. She wanted a man like Mike—the Mike who loved so deeply and with such involvement that loss made veldt-sores in him—to love *her*. To love them all. And she wanted a few hours a day to become the person she was destined to be—a creative, caring, independent woman. There should be room for all of that without any crowding. It wasn't much to ask. It was not a tiny bit more than those people she loved could afford.

Flo, though sometimes brassy, flashy and bossy, was not really a snob. Chris had been surprised at Flo's treatment of Mike, intimidating him, making it appear that he wasn't good enough. None of the Palmers, though well-to-do, had ever behaved uncharitably toward another human being; they had never taken their privilege for granted or placed themselves above others. Mike, too, had surprised her with his reverse snobbery—jabbing at Flo for having so much, insinuating that bounty made life too easy, accomplishments too effortless.

Grabbing at her was what they'd both done, and it made her very nervous, claustrophobic. Well, in another half hour she'd have it out with Flo.

"I don't know what to say," Flo said at breakfast. "I regret making you unhappy by pressuring Mike that way, but I honestly don't think I'm wrong. He doesn't have much to offer you, and I think you should be more practical."

Chris swallowed coffee as if swallowing fury. "Because he doesn't have a college education? You ought to be ashamed of doing that to him."

"I wasn't doing anything to him. Good Lord, Chris, if anything should happen to him…"

"No, that isn't it. If anything should happen to Mike, I'd have *you*. You're more afraid nothing will happen to him, that I'll stay with him forever. Just as he was afraid you were going to win and take me away. Well, I've got news for the two of you. This is a no-win situation."

"Chris, I'm not in a contest with this man. I feel responsible for you—I simply want you to reappraise the situation."

"Responsible? I'm not twelve, though you treat me as though I am. You keep forgetting that I've managed to keep my children and myself without state aid and without calling you. I did it myself. I didn't do it in designer labels, but I did do it. And reappraise what?"

"Your future plans. There are a lot of things I'd like you to consider. Your education, for instance. If you want to complete college, I think you should. Or if you'd like to consider business, I would be delighted. Whatever."

"Whatever? Or one of those two things?" she responded drily. Chris reached for Kyle's plate, automatically cutting his room-service pancakes for him. "Flo, I have future plans of my own that don't include either of those two things. Besides, I don't want to decide my whole future in the next week, so I wish you'd stop listing my options for me."

Carrie tipped her milk and it sloshed onto the table, flowing toward Flo. Flo jerked into action, mopping, her movements almost as natural as Chris's. Flo didn't seem to worry about her expensive slacks; she merely acted, as if she had been mopping up Carrie's spills since birth. Flo had only known her children for three days, Chris reflected, yet they seemed bonded. Connected by blood. Chris shook her head absently. Flo didn't scold Carrie; she simply took care of her. The way she wanted to take care of Chris. The scolding hadn't started until Chris began trying to take care of herself.

"I'm only trying to help," Flo said. "I have no ulterior motives."

"Not consciously. You just want to do for me, show me your generosity and love. So does Mike. He wants to give and have me receive. Here I am being offered so much, from two people I care deeply about, and last night was a nightmare. When I saw the two of you together, I felt as though I didn't know either one of you."

"Well. Are we *both* sorry?"

"Yes," she said, swiveling in her chair to begin cutting Carrie's pancakes. "I haven't spoken to Mike yet, but he wrote an apologetic note before he left for work. I won't see him till tomorrow morning."

"Do you have any idea what you want, Chris?"

"Oh, yes," she said, laughing humorlessly. "I want to see if I can recapture the little bit of sanity I felt between the fire and the *Missing Heiress*. I felt…I felt alive, full of feelings that for once didn't conflict or frighten me. I had a sense of family—there was Mike and his people drawing me in. And even though I was too proud or stubborn to call you yet, I was getting closer. I had safety, pleasure, hope and desire. I felt protected but independent. And then it all changed."

"Come now, let's not get melodramatic, Chris. Did I make our reconciliation difficult? I may not have cozied up to the fireman too well, but—"

"Difficult? Heavens, no, it was just the opposite. Our reunion was so ideal I was spinning from it. You forgave me for all the trouble I've caused you when I'd half expected you to refuse to speak to me. I felt like a baby you'd waited seven years to give birth to."

Flo sighed. "I suppose I've failed again somehow," she said.

"When have you ever failed at anything? The fact is, you offer me so much that it's impossible for me to live up to it."

"Christine, let's not—"

"But it's true! You want so much for me that I find it hard to want anything for myself! You can dress me, style my hair, discuss my future, spoil my kids. We've barely talked in seven years. Do you even know me, Flo? Or are you trying to create me?" She felt her eyes well with tears. "I'm sorry. I didn't mean to cry about it."

"You're overwrought. You need—" She stopped herself.

Chris wiped her eyes. "You see? If you keep doing that, I'll have to keep fighting you. I want to have our friendship back, Flo, but with give *and* take. As it stands, the only thing I can give you is obedience, and I'm too old to be happy with that."

Flo pursed her lips, and when she spoke, her voice was scratchy. It was the closest Chris had ever seen her come to crying. "I just don't want you to be hurt. I don't want to lose you. Again."

"I'm going to carve a little niche out of this world that's all mine. Not a big chunk—just a little niche. I don't want to buy the world a Coke or conquer outer space, I just want to take care of my kids and work on becoming the best of who I really am. There's more to me than being your child, Stever's latest con or Mike's charity case. That's what I was working on, Flo, when the house burned down."

"This has something to do with this idea of writing?" she asked. "Because if all you want is to be independent, to be able to write—"

"No. Yes. I mean, I was writing, and I plan to keep writing—I'm even crazy enough to think I'm going to succeed at it. What I have to do is make sure the decisions I make belong to me. I want to pay for my own mistakes. I want to take credit for my accomplishments. I don't want to be taken care of anymore."

"What I'd like to know," Flo said slowly, "is why it is reasonable for you to live in the fireman's house and eat his food and take his presents, but it's wrong for you to—"

Chris shook her head. "You don't get it, do you? I'm not going to give my life to him the way I did with Steve, and I'm not going to keep taking from him, either. I'm willing to share my life, my space, all that I am, but *share,* Flo. With you, with him and, hopefully, with others, because I've been alone way too long."

"And you can't come with me and share your life with him, only the other way around, is that it? He sounded as determined about what you need as I did, you know."

"If that turns out to be true, then it won't work."

"Why would you take that chance? Why not—"

"Because I love him." There. She'd said it. Shouldn't lightning strike or fireworks go off?

"That's ridiculous," said Flo.

"But it's true, just the same," she replied, exasperated.

"You're setting yourself up for some real trouble, Chris," Flo solemnly predicted. "You're going to get yourself hurt all over again. You hardly know this—"

"No, I'm not. I'm not setting myself up for anything at all. When I give up and let other people take over, then I'm in for it. I may be a lot of things—impetuous, idealistic, maybe even foolish, but dammit, I'm going to see if this is what I think it is. And if it isn't, I'll cry and be done with it. I won't lose four million dollars, I won't get pregnant, and I won't forget what I want from life. I'll cry. There are worse things."

"What about the kids? What about what they'll—"

"The kids," she said, "already love both of you." Carrie looked up. Her eyes were round and large; she knew there was something serious going on, but she didn't know what. "They shouldn't have to give up Mike to have you, or vice versa."

"He's awfully possessive."

"Said the pot," Chris quipped.

"We've never had any kind of family life together,

Chris. Within a year of Randy's and Arlene's death you were gone. With that—"

"I got married. Maybe you didn't approve, but the reality is that I grew up and got married. And get this— I'm *glad* I did, because I have Carrie and Kyle. I'm a grown-up now, Flo. I can't go back to being the child you can spoil and discipline. We have to get together a new set of rules for our family life. I don't want to be all you have. I don't want you to be all I have. Go home, Flo," she softly advised. "It's the only way I can come home to you, which is all you really want, anyway."

"When is that going to happen, Chris? I don't want us to be estranged forever."

"It's never going to happen the way you think it should. When I go back to Chicago, I'll be a visitor or finding my own place. Flo, let go of me. Love me for myself, not for what you can do for me. Please."

They reached a tense compromise. Flo set up a checking account for Chris with a tidy sum deposited; she simply couldn't leave any other way. Flo took Chris's word that if the worst happened and the fireman turned out to be a big lout, Chris and the kids would rent something *decent*—with smoke alarms and everything. And they decided that if Chris remained in California through Christmas, Flo would have her tongue removed or her lips sutured shut and would return in time to celebrate with them all. She would be nice to Mike or else. Chris promised to call Flo frequently to reassure her they really were reunited.

And she still cried at the airport.

Mr. Blakely's address was in the phone book. Chris took the kids out for a hamburger and then pulled up to the landlord's house at just about the dinner hour. She was not in the least surprised to find he and his family occupied a substantial piece of real estate while they rented out hovels in poor repair. Still, she felt tension grating like sandpaper against her backbone—the backbone she was only just remembering she had. She wanted to do this exactly once.

"Hello, Mrs. Blakely. I'm Christine Palmer. Is your husband at home, please?"

"I don't believe we have any business with you. You can have your lawyer—"

Chris unfolded the tabloid so that her picture flashed in the woman's chubby, ruddy face. Mrs. Blakely looked like a mean, unhappy person; she had frown lines and downcast eyes that could flare wide in surprise, like now. She was about four weeks behind on her strawberry-blond dye job; her gray roots moored her frazzled mop. The house they lived in had been custom-built and appeared both well cared for and expensive. Mrs. Blakely, a fiftyish woman, looked out of place in the doorway. She was heavy, sloppily attired in a floral cotton housedress, and held a smoldering cigarette between her yellowed fingers.

"I'm the 'missing heiress,' Mrs. Blakely, and if you let me see your husband, we can complete this transaction in a few minutes. Then I will leave you alone. If you force me to call my attorney about this, it will cost you, because I am angry."

The woman stood still for a second, stunned. Then she slowly turned like a rotating statue. "Henry," she called.

He, too, looked out of place in such a decorous environment. He wore a white undershirt, slippers, baggy pants with his belly hanging obtrusively over his belt, and he had a nasty cigar in his mouth. The slumlord.

Mrs. Blakely passed the tabloid to her husband, who looked at the picture and then Chris, taking the cigar from his mouth. She gave him a minute to get the headline, but no more. "We can settle this in five minutes, Mr. Blakely. Your faulty furnace not only destroyed my every worldly possession, it nearly killed us all. In fact, I was rescued from the burning house. Now, I am not a difficult person, only fair. I would like some refunds and some restitution. There is the matter of the deposit—the first and last months' rent—the rent I paid for the month of November, and lost valuables." She reached into her purse. She unfolded an itemized list and held it out to him. Her children stood stoically on each side of her. "I take responsibility for fifty percent of the possessions lost in the fire because I did not have renter's insurance, which I should have had. I will take five thousand dollars now, or I will take you to court and sue for pain and suffering, as well. And I can get the best lawyer in the country."

"Um…maybe you'd better come in."

"No, that won't be necessary. I'll wait right here. It won't take you that long to write a check."

A teenager shrieked from inside the big house. "Mother! Where is my—"

"Shut up, Ellen! Just a minute!" Mrs. Blakely barked.

"I oughta check with my lawyer before I—" the landlord began.

"That won't take long, either. Here's what he'll tell you—if you have been approached with an itemized list of damages and you have made restitution in that exact amount, she really won't have a leg to stand on in court if she comes after you for more. Unless, of course, there are injuries, which there were not. Now, let's get this over with, shall we?"

Mrs. Blakely glared at Chris from behind her husband. She crossed her arms over her ample chest while Henry Blakely shuffled away with the list in his hand. The worst of it, Chris believed, was the fact that they had no remorse for the danger they had allowed in renting poorly maintained property. That the rent had been low did not absolve them. The malfunctioning furnace was Henry Blakely's fault, and he had never even called to see if Chris and her children were all right. Mrs. Blakely, who should be flushing in shame at her husband's callous evasion of responsibility, stood like a sentry in the doorway while the unrepentant man went in pursuit of a phone call or a check or a better idea.

These people were poor and didn't know it, Chris decided.

"Here," he said, handing her a check in less than ten minutes. "I don't want to hear from you again."

"Oh, you won't, believe me." And she walked away from them, pity for their selfishness leaving a sour taste in her mouth.

She was up, dressed and had the coffee brewed when Mike came home from the station early in the morning, beginning his four days off.

"We're on our own for a while?" Mike asked when Chris told him Flo had gone. "What does that mean?"

"I've convinced Flo to back off and give me some room. She acted like an ass. I'm really sorry."

"Not that I was any Prince Charming. I don't usually act that way around anyone."

"Neither does she."

"She, uh, spoke with some experience," he said.

"Oh, she's a born fighter, don't get me wrong. But she's not the snob she appeared to be. She wants me back, wants me home. It's been a long separation."

"But you didn't go."

Chris sighed. "Not because I don't love her. I need Flo in my life. She can be a real pain, but we have a lot of good history, too. The Flo you met was not my generous and strong friend, but a terrified mother lion afraid of losing her cub. I apologize for her."

Mike nodded, then changed the subject. "I had this idea about Christmas," he said. "The kids like the cabin so much, I thought we might go there, have a real Christmas, chop our own tree—"

"What about your family?" she asked.

"They could spare my presence for one year. What about yours?"

"She'll come back, Mike, if this is where I am through the holidays. You don't have to accept Flo, but I can't reject my family any more than you can reject yours. Flo has never been with the kids for the holidays."

"Maybe I should call up to Pembroke Pines and see if the caterer is busy. Or will she bring her own staff?"

She flinched.

"Sorry. It's just that she made me feel so damned inadequate. Middle-class. I've never felt that way before. I guess I wanted to be the one to give you a chance to rebuild your life."

Chris bit her lip. "Maybe we should talk about this. Maybe you found me easy to care about when you thought I was helpless, destitute. Is it harder for you because I'm not? Just how far do you want to go to see if this crazy thing is real?"

He didn't hesitate to think it over. "I want to go all the way to the end. Wherever that is."

Chapter 11

"Mrs. Cavanaugh is cooking an Irish stew," Hal said, placing the plates around the table.

Mike turned from the pot he was stirring and grinned at Hal. "It's spaghetti," he said.

"Everything you cook tastes like Irish stew."

"Hey, lay off," Stu said. "I love Mrs. Cavanaugh's Irish spaghetti."

"I'd put my cooking against yours any day of the week," Mike challenged Hal. "My red beans and rice against your chili."

"Against my potato soup, and you have a deal."

"Name the day and put some green on it."

"Hey, how are things with the heiress?"

Mike stirred the pot again. "Don't call her that, okay?"

"Uh-oh. What's the matter, Little Mike? Chris go home to Auntie Flo?"

"I'd go for the aunt," Stu said. "In a minute, I'd go for the aunt. My wife would write me a note."

"My wife asked me to make a play for the aunt, and then send money."

"The auntie has gone away, for now, while Little Mike thinks about the furniture business."

Mike dumped the spaghetti into a colander. "You wanna eat, dog-breath?"

"No kidding, what's going on? You getting married?"

"Married?" he asked, as though amazed. Was he that transparent? "I've only known her a few weeks."

"What's taking you so long?" Hal asked.

"I'd have her in front of the priest," Stu said. "She's loaded, right? She's cute, too—I saw that much. Stupid me, I shoulda gotten into that house ahead of him."

"You're married already, Stuart. Although I know you tend to forget that from time to time."

"I have these blackouts. Spells."

"Yeah. You keep getting engaged."

"Naw. I go steady sometimes. A little."

There was laughter. Mike rinsed the spaghetti. He had a hard time with Stu sometimes—didn't like the way he handled personal business. Otherwise he liked him. Good firefighter. A little green about life, but good in a fire. If Stu knew what it was like to lose a family, he wouldn't waste precious time away from his; he wouldn't fool around on his wife. Hal, young like Stu, still less than thirty, got a big kick out of Stu's antics, but Hal didn't fool around. He was serious about his young family. Mike liked that. Hal was a good cook, too. He had a little business on the side when he wasn't fighting fires, which was typical of firemen.

Jim Eble was Mike's closest friend besides family. They were nearly the same age and had worked the same rig for five years. They were alike in personal values as well as sharing many favorite pastimes. But Jim couldn't go fishing with Mike too often because he drove an ambulance part-time when he wasn't on duty; he'd be paying for college educations before long.

Mike was the only one, in fact, who didn't work at something else when he wasn't here. His income was plentiful for a single man, and with all the other kids in the family married and off doing their family things, he used his days off to make sure his mom and dad had everything they needed. And he liked to go to the cabin. Maybe he didn't have another business, but things like hunting, fishing, camping and riding took time. There was no work he liked more than this work. The furniture business? In a pig's eye.

"Don't let 'em get to you, Little Mike," Jim said while they did the dishes.

"They don't get to me. They're having fun. That's okay."

"Things are okay with Chris, then?"

"Yeah, I guess. I mean, she's the same person I pulled out of the house, right?"

"Well, is she?"

"Yeah, sure."

"Hey, Little Mike, don't let the bull from these guys get in your way, huh? You know what you want, right?"

No, he didn't know what he wanted. He thought he knew, but now he wasn't sure. Sure that he loved her a lot, yes. But all that other stuff, money, was getting to him. Getting him down.

How good he had felt when he carried bags and bags of groceries into the house to fill them up—to fill them up because they were empty. He had felt like a man, a dad, a provider. Maybe it wasn't his right, but he had. He liked to put himself to use that way.

That was what firefighters did; they helped people who needed help. It didn't stop after the fire was out or the victim saved. They had their charities, individually and as a group. They were called upon to teach kids, help little old ladies, organize benefits. Brave men and women. Firefighters helped people much more gracefully than they accepted help.

Then Chris didn't need so much anymore, and things changed. It wasn't his feelings for Chris and the kids and that stupid dog that had changed; it was this terrible discomfort he felt in his gut because he wasn't in charge anymore. Because without him they could survive just fine. He wanted to be the one they needed the most. He wouldn't have thought this would be so hard. This was a side of himself he didn't like.

Packages in Christmas wrap had arrived from Aunt Flo, in case Chris and the kids were still with him by then. Without opening them, he knew they were expensive presents. When he took his jacket out of the hall closet to go to work this morning, he had looked at Chris's jackets. More than one now. He had spent a lot on the jackets he bought for Chris and Carrie and Kyle so they could go up to the snowy hills. Now, in the front closet, was a new suede coat. Auntie Flo had probably paid ten times as much. He felt reduced.

Chris looked different now. Even though she looked

better than ever, he wanted it all to have come from him. It was unfair, and he knew it, but it was still fighting inside him. He thought about his family and knew money shouldn't bother him so much. His brother Chris had a lot of money. Orthodontics was a good-paying profession, and Chris was a clever investor. Money could be loads of fun. He thought about his sister Mo who made way more money than her husband, and how stupid he thought it was that they should ever argue about it. What was the difference how much or whose or where it came from if it put food on the table and provided for the future? So why, he asked himself, was he feeling the opposite of his own beliefs?

On the first night he stayed with her in his own house he had opened up a secret part of himself and told her about his deepest pain. The shamelessness of it didn't humiliate him; he was ready to be as frank about his weakness as he had been obvious in his strength. But now, when he had this little injury inside over her money and her aunt, he didn't talk to her about it. He didn't say, "I'm in pain because you're buying new sheets when I want to buy them for you. I hurt because I feel not good enough. I'm afraid I can't give you anything." He said, "Looks nice." Then he sulked. And his pain popped out somewhere else. He yelled at the dog for chewing his socks, when he would have gladly fed Cheeks a thousand pairs for a feeling of security.

Jealous and stupid, he chided himself silently. He hoped he would get over it, because he was afraid to expose himself to Chris as the selfish jerk he really was. If she found out how tough this was for him, how much he hated that witch, Florence, how much he prayed Florence would somehow hit rock bottom, leaving Chris poor and needy again, she would leave him. She would have to. How could she stay with a man like that?

He tried to think of what he had instead of what he wanted, because he still had Chris in his bed at night, and through their intimacy an important part of his identity had returned to him. Sex with her was better than any sex he'd ever had because he loved her so deeply and wanted her so completely. Sometimes he felt surly and unaroused because of self-pity, but once it got rolling, it was fabulous. He tried not to imagine how good it would be if they had years to perfect it. They had already developed fun, lush games....

"Come on, smoky, put out this fire."

"In a minute, in a minute."

"Why do you wait so long?"

"I thought I was making *you* wait."

"I already didn't wait—twice."

And...

"Hug me for a while. Just hug me like you're not interested in sex."

"Hug you until you beg me to move, huh?"

And...

"I'm not even going to take off my shirt until you tell me what you want. No, until you *show* me..."

Well, actually, those things had happened before Flo and the money. Since then he had felt inadequate, insecure. But if Flo and the money disappeared, he would be all right again. Virile. Even with his troubles, bed was still one of their best places these days. Because of the way their bodies worked together like an efficient factory that ran on its own energy. Once it got going and he forgot his anger, she didn't ask him what was wrong and he didn't sulk or worry. He wanted it to go on forever.

He was terrified. He thought he caught a glimpse of the end.

"Flo is coming in on the twenty-third, Mike. She promises to be good. Shall we do Christmas here? Should we take her to your mom and dad's?" Chris had asked.

You can't turn family away at Christmas. You can't. Even if they're awful family. But Flo at his mom and dad's? "Let's do it here. My folks can spare me one year."

He didn't ask her if she was going away after the holiday. He didn't ask her if she was staying. She didn't mention her plans. She didn't ask him if his invitation remained open. Everything seemed to be moving out of reach. Except the money.

Chris had decided she had better not let her ex-husband get away with anything, for Carrie and Kyle's sake. It had been their grandfather's money. Flo could handle it. Chris didn't need it, didn't want it, but it could be put in trust for the kids, and some kind of dividend could be paid while they were growing up to help provide for them. They would never be poor again.

Mike had actually hoped he would be forced to take a second job to finance their college education. Like he had done for Tommy. Stupid thing to wish for, huh?

Chris didn't need that money because she was going to sell books. She loved writing, she was going to start selling, and she had big plans. A career. A good, satisfying one.

One way or the other, Chris was going to be well-off. With or without him.

"Why don't you and Chris and the kids come over for dinner?" Jim asked as they washed and dried the last pot.

"Yeah, maybe. There's a lot to do with Christmas, though."

"Yeah, I suppose. Is her aunt coming out here?"

He was slow to answer. "Yeah. Not till the twenty-third, though."

"Little Mike, take it easy. You're not going to marry the aunt, you know."

"Who said I was going to marry anyone?"

"Uh, Mike? Joanie wasn't Catholic when you asked her to marry you, was she?"

"No. Why?"

"Did you tell her that was part of the deal, if you got married?"

"No. I wouldn't do that. I just told her it would make things a lot easier if she would think about it."

"Was it hard to ask her?"

He chuckled. "Yeah. Until I did. I guess I thought she'd get mad."

"What'd she say?"

"You know what she said. She did it, right? She said that wasn't too much to ask."

"Try and remember that, huh?"

Remember what? To ask for what I need? If Chris finds out how much I need, it'll scare her to death. Hell, it scares me to death. I cover up all my needs by filling the needs of others. I give a lot better than I receive.

Remember what? That people make changes in themselves in order to make a couple? I'm trying. I'm try-

ing to change what I feel, but it hammers away inside me that I can't give her as much as Aunt Flo can—as much as she already has, for that matter.

Remember what? That when you lose the one you love, the one you counted on, you lose a part of yourself? Believe me, I remember. That was why I stayed alone.

I remember.

The bell came in. Truck and engine and chief. Mike's heart got a shot of adrenaline. He would only think about fire for a while now. Thank goodness.

Chris was scared to death of Christmas. Tomorrow Mike started his four days off over the holidays—quite a coup for a firefighter, to have so much time. In a couple of days Flo would return. If they could get through this, amicably, maybe they could get through the rest. She hoped. But Mike was so distant and quiet that she feared Flo's presence combined with Mike's cautiously suppressed anger was going to drive the last nail into the coffin.

The tree was up in the living room. It was bulging with presents, more presents than she had ever seen in her life. Every time the UPS truck pulled up with another load from Aunt Flo, Mike went out and bought more. There was no telling who would win this contest. Meanwhile the kids were having a time like they had never had. Mike, fortunately, did not seem to discriminate against them because they had wealth and Aunt Flo. His lap received them as dearly as ever.

She had asked Mattie if she could drop by their house. She wasn't sure what she was looking for exactly, but maybe some Cavanaugh wisdom would teach her something about Mike that would make things work. She was willing to do anything—short of changing who she was. Since she felt she had only just discovered the real Chris Palmer, and since she had only just discovered she liked her, she would not abandon herself again. It wouldn't be worth it. Becoming who you thought people wanted you to be made a mockery of real love. Henceforth she would only settle for the real thing.

"Chrissie, you look so different. You're doing your hair different now, huh?" Mattie asked, after she greeted Chris and the children that evening.

"I just got it cut."

"You brought us presents. Oh, Chrissie, you shouldn't have done that. Really. We have so much. Bring everyone in. Come in, come in. I have a bundt cake."

"We brought the dog—I hope you don't mind. Carrie wanted Big Mike to see the dog."

"You brought that dog?" Big Mike asked, walking toward the front door with his newspaper in his hand, hiking up his low-riding pants. "You brought that Creeps to my house?"

Carrie and Kyle giggled happily, looking up at him. How did the children know he was funny, when he never smiled? How did they know he was making jokes? Cheeks stood just behind them, right inside the door, his tail wagging while he growled.

"I don't know why you bring him here. He hates me."

"He doesn't really hate anybody, but he's very crabby."

Big Mike hunched down and reached between the children to scratch under Cheeks's chin. Cheeks growled louder; his tail wagged. "This dog is a mess," Big Mike said. "Look at him. He wants to be petted, but he makes all this noise. What a terrible dog he is. I think somebody hit this dog in the head, huh?"

"We think somebody was mean to him when he was a puppy," Carrie said. "We think it was a *man*. He's always crabby to men, but not to girls."

"You're so tough, aren't you, Creeps. Come on, then. Come on, Creeps," Big Mike said, straightening and walking into the living room, the wagging, growling dog following, the children giggling.

"Come in and have coffee, Chrissie. It's so cold. We might even get a little snow."

Chris took off her coat and tossed it over a chair. The kids were already sitting at Big Mike's feet, laughing as he said the dog's name wrong and made him look stupid, growling while he was being stroked.

Chrissie carried the presents into the kitchen. Mattie, who had waddled ahead of her, already had a coffee cup filled. "These are for the whole family, Mattie, but they're mostly for you. We picked them out together, and I want you to open them early."

"You shouldn't have, really. We have so much already."

"Go ahead. It isn't much."

It only took Mattie a minute to get inside the first box. Chris had tried to get exactly the right thing. A Christmas platter, a decorated lazy Susan, red napkins in green holly rings—enough for the whole clan, plus extras.

"I thought maybe you would like something like this. You have everyone here at Christmas, right?"

"Perfect, perfect. How nice you are to do this, Chrissie. How nice. Everyone will love it. Yes, they all come here, though I don't know why. Chris and Stacy have a big place with lots more room. They could have Christmas there, but they don't." Mattie lowered her voice to a whisper. "I think they don't like Big Mike to drive so much. At night, and all." She resumed in her normal voice. "Everyone comes here to this tiny house where we can't even move, but they come. I don't know why."

How they care for one another, Chris thought. As if they had secrets from one another, which they didn't. "I know why," she said, smiling. "This is where they belong. I love watching your family together. You're right, Mattie. You have so much."

"We've been blessed, me and Big Mike. Oh, we had our troubles like everyone else. Broken bones, for instance." She laughed. "You don't have four boys without broken bones. And the like. But we do okay, I think. Kids. They put you through it, huh?"

"You know, you've probably seen all that stuff in the paper about me, and Mike might have mentioned—"

"He told us a little bit about your aunt coming, but we don't ask him, Chrissie. It isn't our business, this with your aunt and all."

"Well, still, I'd like to explain some of that." Big Mike came into the kitchen to fill his coffee mug. "I want to tell you both," she amended, "that I haven't been taking advantage or—"

"You never mind about that, Chrissie," Big Mike said. "You don't need to tell us anything."

"It must seem so bizarre, all this 'missing heiress' nonsense. That's not really what I am at all. I was out of touch with my aunt because I was sure she would be too angry to even speak to me. I didn't know I was 'missing.' And I'm not an heiress. My aunt still runs the family business, which was half my dad's, but, well, it's not Exxon or anything. It's worth a lot, I guess, but that doesn't mean I'm really rich."

They looked at her, Big Mike by the coffeepot with his mug in his hand, Mattie at the kitchen table with her.

"I'm really not as different as I must seem."

"You don't seem different to us, Chrissie. We don't care about that story."

"But Mike…" Her voice drifted off for a moment. "I think Mike might have some trouble with it. I'm looking for a way to make him believe that I'm the same person who checked groceries at Iverson's. It's too bad it all came out so fast, and in such a bizarre way."

"Little Mike is a pretty smart boy," Mike said. "He doesn't do things he doesn't want to do. And he doesn't believe a lot of stories."

"Well, the stories are pretty much true," she said. "It just seems that Mike liked having us with him a lot more before he found out where I came from."

"You don't have to tell us about this," Mattie said, almost entreating Chris to shut up.

Chris was afraid she might cry. I love him, she wanted to say. I love him and I want him to love me the way I am, whether dead broke or monied.

"The boy likes to take care of everyone," Big Mike grumbled. "He does that with us, too. He's always taking care of us. He built that storage shed out back. He comes over, says he bought this storage shed. I say I don't need a storage shed, but he wants me to have it. So fine, I tell him. I have it. Thank you very much. But he can't let it go at that. He has to build it, too. Then he can go home, right? No. Then he has to put my lawn mower and things in it. Now he can be done with it, huh? No. He comes over to use the things he put in it. Sometimes he has to clean it out. And fix the roof. And trim the trees around the house. And paint this and that. Whew," he said, waving a hand. "He just likes to be useful."

Chris smiled in spite of herself. "How do you handle him when he gets like that. How do you act?"

"I act like I always act. 'What do I need some damned storage shed for?' I say. He builds it anyway."

"That's Little Mike," Mattie said, laughing. "We should slice up this cake."

"You just tell Little Mike you don't need it—he'll force it on you anyway."

"But," Chris said, "I can't do that."

"No, I guess not. Then you tell him to stick it in his ear if he doesn't like it."

"Don't tell her what to say, Mike," Mattie said. "Never mind him, Chrissie. He doesn't know what he's talking about. He's an old man who gets himself into all the kids' business. He gives them marriage counseling. If they listened to him, they'd all be getting divorces. Never mind him. We just want Little Mike to be happy, is all."

"Me, too," she said.

"Then everything works itself out, huh?"

"You want to make him happy, huh?" Big Mike scoffed. "Tell him, 'Stick it in your ear, I don't want a damned storage shed,' or whatever. He'll be happy." Big Mike went out of the kitchen.

Mattie got out plates and started slicing pieces of cake. You couldn't come to this house and not eat, Chris decided. They fill you up in any way they can.

"What's hard for Mike," she told Mattie, "is that he wants very much to do for us, give to us. It makes him feel good."

"Yes, he's that way. He does for everyone."

"I think he's afraid there isn't anything I need anymore. With this business about my aunt, about money."

"Well, I didn't raise the boy that way, Chrissie. Little Mike knows the important things money can't buy. I made sure my kids knew that, growing up. We didn't have too much then, when they were little, but I was real careful that they knew what's important. And I was real careful they knew people learned that two ways. One way was if they didn't have a lot of money but they had a good life. The other way was if they had a lot of money and that wasn't all they needed."

Mattie put a plate and fork in front of Chris. "He's a bullheaded boy, Little Mike, but he's pretty sharp. Don't listen to the old man, just give Little Mike some time to remember about that. A little time. He had some trouble in the third grade. In the seventh grade, too, if I remember. Maybe remembering things takes him a little time."

It might serve just as well, Chris thought, to tell him to stick it in his ear. "A little time," she repeated.

"He'll catch on eventually." Mattie laughed. "Will the kids eat the cake?"

"They'd love it," she said. And then the sirens came. Time stood still. The shrill noise mounted. They lived near the firehouse. Mattie continued slicing cake and an odd staticlike sound came from the living room.

"What's that?" Chris asked.

"We turn on the scanner sometimes when we hear the sirens. We worry a little bit, but we don't tell him. He knows it, but we don't tell him. He likes to think he's on his own."

Mattie's hand went into her apron pocket, and something in there rattled softly. Chris knew without asking that they were rosary beads. "Bring your cake," Mattie said. "We'll listen."

Big Mike said it was a house fire. At first it didn't sound too serious. She heard Mike's voice on the radio. The engine, Big Mike explained. Then the truck with the hydraulics. Another engine—maybe it was getting a little hot. Then another alarm. Police and ambulances. Chris started getting nervous following the fire by radio calls like this. She would never have one of those things, never! Then she wondered if she could get to Radio Shack before they closed to get her own.

Next the hazardous materials squad was called in. There had been an explosion. Mike's company was initiating rescue, though it was not Mike's voice they heard. And then, with eerie screeching through the little living room, came the news that there were firefighters down.

"God!" Chris said, straightening. "What do we do now?"

"Shh. We listen, that's all."

"Will they say the names?"

"No, they don't."

"Oh, God, why can't he be a house painter? This is horrible. Horrible!"

"No, they know what they're doing. They know."

"I don't know if I can take this."

"What would you change?" Big Mike asked. "What one thing would you change?"

"I would have sent him to law school," Chris said.

"Oh? He's been a firefighter twelve years now," Big Mike said. "If I had had the money to send him to law school, maybe about twenty-seven people would be dead. He takes chances, yes. About twenty-seven people, alive right now because he didn't go to law school, should thank me because I didn't have the money."

Because, Chris thought, he goes into fires to pull people out whenever he has to, no matter how scary and dangerous. And he can't think in terms of luck or miracles, because how often can you expect your luck to hold or a miracle to happen? He can't think about being heroic; he's just doing the job he was trained to do. An informed risk. Like love. Please, God.

Mattie rattled her beads.

Chapter 12

Engine 56 was the first on the scene, followed by the truck with hydraulics in close pursuit and another engine on its way. Two engines and a truck were standard equipment response for a house fire. There were no cops yet. The firefighters could count on an automatic response of two squad cars; they could also count on beating the cops to the fire. Mike's company's average response time was three minutes.

A civilian stood on the curb. He would have called in the alarm. The neighborhood was old but high-rent. The houses were all two-story, Victorian styles, around sixty to seventy years old but usually in excellent repair. The biggest problem with the houses here would be basement fires that could spread to the attic because of the absence of fire-stops. A maze of kindling.

This particular house had a nice big circular drive and an attached garage, from which smoke poured.

"I don't like 'em," Jim said, speaking of garage fires. Garages could be full of surprises; people stored paints, thinners, gas cans and such there. Not to mention cars.

As men sprang off the truck and engine, the neighbor jogged over. He was a little breathless, nervous. "There was a bunch of kids around here earlier—might've been a party. They have a lot of traffic around this place."

"Do you think there's anybody inside?" Mike asked the man.

He shrugged. "Could be. People coming and going all the time—parties and stuff. Could be a bunch of drunk teenagers in there."

Jim returned to the engine with a gas can in his gloved hand. He had gotten it from the driveway. He shook his head and set it down. This one might have been set; people didn't often leave empty gas cans in their driveways. Mike talked to the man briefly to determine when he had noticed the smoke, whether he'd seen anybody around—standard questions. He called for the peanut line to fog the site of the fire, while the ladder-company men approached the place with axes and pike poles. The truck men would cut the utilities and open it up; engine men would set up hoses and water. They pulled out tarps that would be used to protect the contents of the house from water, mud and other internal damage.

But the number-one priority was life. Structural consideration was always number-two. Jim was moving quickly, despite a hundred pounds of turnouts and equipment on his body, to the front door, next to the garage. He applied a firm shoulder to the door, pushed it open and went in.

Judging from a big bay window that faced the street and smaller windows above, the house might have a living room or dining room on the ground-level front, kitchen in the back. The front door and garage were to the right, bedrooms upstairs. Maybe as much as three thousand square feet, and a basement and attic. And this one just might have been torched.

The chief's car pulled up, and he relieved Mike with the civilian. Mike was moving to join Jim in the house when it blew. The garage door cracked down the middle, and debris flew down the drive. Two firemen en route to the site fell like dominoes. There was a medley of curses around the truck and engine while two firefighters ran to the felled men to pull them away. But they were rolling over to stand up on their own steam.

Mike crouched away from the explosion for a second, but he couldn't take his eyes off the front door. It was no longer accessible, but blocked by debris and rolling gray smoke. Flames were licking out of the place where his best friend had gone in.

Then the chief was there beside him. "We have a man in the building," Mike told the chief. "Number 56 will initiate rescue; tell engine 60 to take over incident command. I'm going after Eble. Jim."

The chief called in a code 2 for the hazardous-materials squad. They didn't know yet what they had to deal with. They didn't know yet what had exploded or whether there was more. They'd use as little water on it as possible until they knew more about it.

Mike couldn't get in the front door, but the flames from the garage had not yet reached the living room window. A shovel lay in a flower bed at his feet, and he picked it up and smashed the big bay window. He hurriedly cleared the glass and climbed in, covering his mouth with the air pack mouthpiece. This meant, unfortunately, that he couldn't call out to Jim.

These old Victorian monsters were built like mazes with lots of rooms clustered amid stairwells and hallways. Jim would probably have gone through the downstairs quickly, looking for people, and then headed for the upstairs bedrooms.

The first thing that struck Mike as odd was the total absence of furniture. What kind of place was this? People coming and going, but no furniture? To have a lot of company, you had to have a couch to sit on. He got a sick feeling in the pit of his stomach. He was guessing what was wrong.

Typical of these old houses, there was a front staircase, now blocked by debris from the explosion and with flames climbing in through the damaged wall that separated house and garage. But there proved to be another set of stairs behind the kitchen. Mike took them quickly. At the top he looked down a hallway, with bedroom doors on each side, to the landing of the front stairwell. There he saw him, lying twisted, half on his side, half on his back, maybe dead, maybe unconscious.

Jim's blackened and bleeding forehead was either injured from flying debris or hurt by his fall but not burned. And he was alive, thank God. His red, watering eyes stared up into Mike's face. A wooden chest of some kind lay on top of his leg, a board across his ribs. His arm was stretched out toward his leg, as if he'd attempted to free himself. He was wearing his air pack, but his eyes were filled with agony.

Mike tossed off the trunk as though it weighed two pounds rather than fifty and threw off the board. He couldn't let Jim lie there or take the time to immobilize the leg. He grabbed Jim's collar and dragged him backward a little way before bending down to lift him. He heard the awful growl of his friend's pain. More than 260 pounds of Jim Eble in his arms made Mike's heart pound, his muscles strain and bulge, but this was his best friend. There was no lighter load.

He started back the way he had come, toward the rear stairwell, but upon passing a bedroom door that was ajar, he looked in. There he saw what it was about. The room was filled with tables, glassware, sacks, tanks, tubing. A drug lab.

He grabbed the doorknob with the hand under Jim's knees and pulled it closed. And then he got the hell out of there.

He exited the building from the back door and carried Jim around the house to the front, where the equipment was parked. The chief met them. Mike couldn't talk until he laid Jim gently on the ground and pulled away his mask.

"Got a drug lab on the second floor, front bedroom. Maybe propane gas tanks in there. Do we have a code 2? They on their way?"

"Yep. I'll tell 'em when they get here. And a second alarm. How's Eble?"

"Jim?" Mike said to his friend.

"Goddamn trunk," he groaned. "Came flying at me, hit me in the back of the knees." He coughed. "Crunch," he said, tears pouring down his cheeks.

Mike heard the chief telling the police to empty out the neighborhood for a half-mile circumference, and the ambulances started arriving. There were three fire-fighters down, but Jim had the worst injury. His leg was almost certainly broken, his head was cut and scraped and his jaw was already starting to swell. He had arm and shoulder pain as well, maybe a dislocation of the shoulder. The paramedics began cutting off his turn-outs, trying to start an IV, applying bandages to his face.

Mike stayed nearby for a few minutes, looking on. He thought briefly about what Mattie and Big Mike were hearing on the scanner. On-site explosion. Code 2. Firefighters down, ambulances dispatched. Injuries. Second alarm. Arson-investigation team called in. Additional police backup. Evacuation of neighborhood.

Mike guessed what had happened. A home drug lab, doing a big business in the area, especially for kids, and somebody got ticked off—maybe wanting a bigger piece of the action, or maybe unhappy they weren't being extended any credit. Someone had decided to set a little fire, burn them out. The do-it-yourself chemists were using propane gas and had extra tanks stored in the garage.

If the firefighters couldn't contain the blaze in the garage, keep it on the lower level, it might reach the lab. It could turn this area into a gas chamber. Hydrogen cyanide, probably.

The Firebird—hazardous-materials men—came around the drive.

When the paramedics moved away from Jim for a few moments, Mike crouched beside him and asked, "You okay?"

"Damn. No. Got an aspirin?"

Mike smiled in spite of himself. "I gotta get back into the fire."

"Yeah," Jim panted. "Get the SOB. Please."

"You bet, bud."

Not a good fire. Oh, it would have been okay if there hadn't been chemicals that might blow, or injuries. Mike had tackled fires in old Victorians like this one, with hallways and rooms like mazes, twisting and turning and ending up blocked. Once inside you didn't know how you'd gotten in or where you might get out. It was a challenge. But this one was no good and it had to be stabilized before the heat got to the lab. Otherwise...

They managed to get the hose in the front door, over the debris, and hit the garage from all sides, while above, the men opened up the roof with pike poles to let the smoke and steam escape.

Mike fought it like fighting time. With vengeance and anger. The Hazmat squad in their rubber splash suits wandered through the upstairs, isolating the bad stuff, moving some of it out. Mike rallied to the race. It was a race to beat the fire before the fire beat them. And he wouldn't take a break, wouldn't call for relief.

He had not felt this good, or this bad, in a long time.

Dawn was dirty. The truck company would be left along with the Drug Enforcement Administration when engine 56 roared out. They smelled pretty bad. The structure was mostly intact; a lot of damage to the ground level, but the flames had never licked up against all those chemicals and gases. The DEA pulled orange tape across the site. A couple of lanky teenage boys were being cuffed and put in the back of a squad car. Arrests. For arson? Or for home chemistry? Mike hated to see anybody get away with either one. Especially since it had hurt a firefighter.

Different kinds of fires led to different kinds of feelings, especially about injuries. When you had a man injured saving a life in a legitimate, accidental fire, that was one thing. You felt proud, somehow, that one of you could be there, doing that. But when a good firefighter was downed in a torch job, or something like this, a vendetta among underworld slime that poisoned society with their drugs, it was like there was no justice. Putting out the fire just wasn't enough.

Mike noticed that Stu, dragging along in his filthy turnouts on his way to the engine, paused at the squad car. He took off his helmet and his gloves and stared into the backseat of the police car. He spit on the ground, then moved on.

It took a while for the talk to start after a bad fire. At first it seemed there was nothing to say. Then there was so much to say, you couldn't shut anybody up. But it was shift change. Not very many men would shower at the station; most of them wanted to get home, get out of there, before the next shift had time to think of a lot of questions.

There was one question, though, that no one would leave before having answered. And so Mike reported. "Jim's got scrapes, a broken collarbone, broken femur," he said, tapping his thigh. "But he's all straightened out, no surgery, casted up, and higher than a kite on morphine. He'll be in a while, and it's too soon to know if there's any disability, but the doctor doesn't think so. Nice clean break."

Then he told everyone what a good job they had done. Then he thanked God for that little bit of luck that had Jim Eble all the way upstairs instead of on the steps when that propane blew. Five seconds, either way, would have cost them all dearly.

Chapter 13

Mike went to the hospital when his shift was relieved. It could have been much worse than it was, but he was not surprised that Jim's wife, Alice, fell against him, releasing some of those pent-up tears. Hearing your husband was down in a fire was the dreaded news. Finding out he was alive was a huge relief, but temporary, because next you had to know how alive he was.

"It's only a couple of broken bones," Mike said. "How's he doing?"

"He's doing great," she said, sniffing, "but I thought I would have a breakdown. Thank God he's all right."

The newspapers sometimes ran stories about downed firefighters—basically they covered the fire, part of which was a firefighter hurt and hospitalized—but they didn't often follow up with stories about the ex–firefighter locksmith or shoe salesman. The stuff they didn't print was the terrifying stuff. Like the early-retirement injuries. Firefighters paralyzed by a fall. There were sprains, breaks and smoke inhalation—and then there were horrific injuries that made you wonder if life was the best deal for the poor guy. Like the firefighter, some years back, who had been rendered brain damaged by carbon monoxide gas from a leaking air pack. Freak things.

Then there were the heart attacks. It wasn't only from breathing smoke or straining the muscles; it was from the alarms. The stress, not from the fire—but from the constant shots of adrenaline that presented the flight-or-fight conflict to the body. Like getting an electric shock on a regular basis. Young men, sometimes, fell because of this.

"You doing okay?" Mike asked Jim.

"No, I'm not doing okay," he said, trying to smile but giving a lopsided grimace through bandages that covered his right eye and chin. His arm cast was elevated, his casted leg hefted off the bed by weights and pulleys. "This had to happen right before my time off. Some luck, huh?"

"You're not going to be in here over Christmas, are you?"

"Hell, no. I refuse to be. Everybody else okay?"

"Yeah. You left early, so you don't know. They're still out there, but it's down to cleanup now. You were the big injury of the night."

"What some people won't do for attention."

"For once you didn't puke."

"Didn't have time. Never saw it coming, in fact. Boy, that sucker blew, huh?"

"Not a good fire. There were arrests before the sun

came up, though. Nobody's getting away with anything."

"Yeah. Sure."

The response was cynical. They both knew that the
little guys with the lab might get arrested, but the big
guys who financed or set up or sold the stuff would
probably never be discovered. Street drugs. Chemicals.
Ether. Et cetera. Who would have believed they'd come
up with something more volatile, more unpredictable,
than a paint-store fire? Home drug labs.

"I owe you, bud," Jim said.

"You owe me nothing."

"I owe you big-time. In fact, you oughta get a medal."

"Don't you dare. I hate those damn things. Medals
are for cops. They eat that stuff up."

"Go on," Jim said. "Get out of here. I want the nurse."

"What for?"

"Do I need a reason? She's gorgeous, that's what for."

"I think he's going to be fine," Alice said with a sniff.

"Yeah, he'll be all right. A minute, huh, Alice?" She
nodded and stepped outside the room. Mike paused.
He thought.

"Don't," Jim said.

Mike looked down. They were good at living dan-
gerously, living on the edge of life and laying it all on
the line. They were bad at being vulnerable, because in
this they were unpracticed. You couldn't admit vulnerability and act completely in control at the same time.
Those gears did not mesh. This was why Mike was in
trouble with Chris, and he suddenly knew it. He didn't
know what to do about it or why it had to be that way,
but he knew what it was. It was one thing to tell her
about weakness and pain that was ten years old; it was

quite another to look her right in the eye and admit the fear and shame of the moment.

He looked at his best friend who had suffered severe bodily harm. He was about to try out emotion on him. Scary thing. What if you admitted your fallibility when you were most apt to be fallible? Could you run into the burning building then? That's why they never talked about it. They were all afraid of the same thing—that if they thought about it too much, they'd come apart like a cheap watch.

"Don't start," Jim said.

"I have to. There are so many things I couldn't have faced without you. You know that."

"You face whatever you have to. You have before. You will again. Just don't start this."

"You're my best friend," he said, almost choking on the sentiment. He wanted to talk about the fear he had, a fear even worse than the fear that Jim had been killed. The fear of being all alone again. And the relief that he wasn't.

"You need more friends," Jim said.

"They can't take me. You can."

"Just take the thank-you and don't get sloppy. I'm in pain. I don't want to play with you now."

"Okay, then. But you're coming back."

"Sure. Of course. It's what I do. Anyway, lightning never strikes in the same place twice."

"Yeah." Mike laughed, remembering the old joke. "Because the place isn't there anymore after the first time."

"I'm here," Jim said, solemn.

Mike touched the fingers that stuck out of the cast. He wanted to do more, maybe hug him. But he had done all that he could reasonably do. *You're here, old buddy. Thank God.*

"See ya," he said.

"Don't bother me over Christmas. I'll be busy."

Mike knew what that meant. It meant that Jim didn't want him to feel obligated in any way; he should feel free to pursue his holiday plans without feeling obligated to visit the injured firefighter, his best friend.

He stopped for coffee with Big Mike before going home. He felt grubby even though he had cleaned up. And tired, but too wired to want to sleep. And angry— about the fire, about near calamity, about the difficulty of life sometimes. And about Aunt Flo coming tomorrow…two days before Christmas. It had been building in him. He even wondered if his worry had been distracting him when they got to the fire. Otherwise, he might have been in the house and Jim might have visited *him* in the hospital. He was usually the first one in when there were people inside.

By the time Mike got to his house, it was nearly 11:00 a.m. Chris was pacing. She gave a gasp and ran to him, putting her arms around his neck and hugging him.

"Hey," he said, laughing. "Hey."

When she released him, there was fury in her eyes. "Why the hell didn't you call me?"

"Call you? What for?"

"I was worried sick! I told you I can't sleep through the sirens! You know I can't."

"Well, gee whiz, I was busy."

"You weren't too busy to call Mattie!"

"So? Did Mattie call you, tell you everything was okay?"

"Yes, but you could have called. Where have you been?"

"Look, Chris, don't get like this on me, huh? I'm wiped out, I'm mad, and I don't need this."

She ran a hand down her neck. "Okay. Sorry. I was worried. I was scared."

"Well, who knew you'd be worried? I figured you'd be polishing the goddamn silver."

He stared at her for a minute, then he turned to go through the kitchen and to the stairs. He wasn't going to his room to sleep; he thought he'd better get out of sight. He was already sorry, but he wasn't sure he could stop it. He should have known it would start oozing out of him sooner or later.

He passed a pair of chewed-up socks on the stairs and picked them up with a curse. He slammed his bedroom door. *Oh, please,* he thought, *not now. Don't let me do this. Not like this.*

But there was a new comforter on his bed. He gritted his teeth. Pillow shams. He wanted to shoot the place up. He went to his closet to change his shoes. Hanging on a hanger was a new shirt with a sweater hanging over it. He touched it. There were new pants. A new set of clothes. To wear while they entertained the aunt over Christmas?

He opened the bedroom door and called her. Loud. Angry. *"Chris!"* Then he closed the door, waited and seethed.

Chris opened the bedroom door and stepped in. "What?"

"She didn't really leave, did she. She just stepped behind her big ugly checkbook for a while, that's all. She might have seemed to leave, but she really just left you a big pot of money as a reminder of where it's at, huh?"

"She left me some money, but—"

"So you could decorate the place and make it good enough for royalty, is that it? You know, Chris, it's getting on my nerves to come home and find new towels, new sheets, new dishes—like my stuff isn't good enough for you. It's starting to really burn me up! If you want to buy a few things for my place, why don't you try asking me if I want any of this crap? Huh?"

"Look, I wasn't trying to—"

"And don't buy me clothes!" He was shouting now. He took the two hangers out of the closet and threw the things on the floor. "I'll dress myself! I'm sure it won't meet the standards of Her Majesty, Florence, but it meets *my* standards. If you want to buy me clothes, buy me some damn socks. I think the damn dog has eaten the last pair."

"I didn't buy you that because of Flo!" she shouted back. "I bought it because of *me!* I liked it. I wanted to do something nice. I'll buy socks, okay? Two thousand pair!"

"Like I don't have anything nice?"

"You have wonderful things! I don't have any problem with your house, or the way you dress, or— Jeez, I just wanted to give you something!"

"Well, I don't want anything from you, because anything you give me is coming out of Flo's pocketbook. And I've had it up to here with her!"

"What has she done to you that you didn't do right back to her?"

"Besides rub my nose in my middle-class existence? Besides outfitting you and the kids for your next appearance at court? Besides laying all these little traps for you, like your lost money? Not a damn thing, really!"

"I'm not spending Flo's money, you big dope. I'm—"

"Don't you *ever* call me a dope! Don't ever, ever—" He stopped. He knew without looking in a mirror that his face was red, his fists clenched. He took a deep breath.

"I didn't mean you were a dope in general, you dope. I meant you're acting stupid over this situation, which could be a good situation if you'd let it, but you're too stubborn and bossy to bend a little."

"Oh, man," he said, letting a mean laugh erupt. "I was a dope to think you could ever fit into a regular kind of life."

"Just because I came from a wealthy family doesn't make me *ir*regular. You didn't even know my family; you only met Flo when she was feeling threatened. You don't back a Palmer into a—"

"I didn't back her into anything. I sat there and took her abuse. *You* sure didn't stand up for me. I guess I know where *you* stand!"

"You, apparently, don't know anything about me! Did you hear me standing up for Flo when you went after her? You two were the ones determined to do battle."

"I don't want to feel this way," he said, his teeth clenched. "I don't want to feel shoddy. I don't want to care, but I do care that I'm a firefighter and she has a damn empire waiting for you. I don't like the whole damn hoity-toity, highfalutin show we have to put on! Like I can't take her to Ma and Big Mike's because they're not good enough!"

"But they *are*. They're better than good enough!"

"I don't want you to be able to buy and sell me ten times over. Even if you wouldn't, I don't want you to be *able* to!"

"You're doing this to yourself! Nobody is doing this to you! You're being a snob. It's you. Not me. Not even Flo!"

"It was good before there were all these *things*. Before I came home every day and found new *things*."

"I can't do this. Stop it, Mike!"

"Is that how it would be?" he asked her. "There's something wrong and you can't deal with it? You can't fight it out? Chris, if there's a problem, *we* have a problem. What do you think? Think it'll go away? Huh?"

"You want to give it to me? Is that it? Yell at me for a while because you're mad? It was okay when I needed everything from you, huh? When I had nothing at all. Destitute, needy, sad little divorcée—you could tell me then, 'Go work on your book,' 'Be who you want to be,' 'Be where you want to be.' But you can't live with the real me, huh? Because my aunt's money makes you feel like less of a man? Maybe because you feel like a man only when someone's hanging on you, thinking of you as a hero, but you don't have any interest in someone who can stand on her own two feet."

The room was silent.

"Yeah," he said. "I don't want to feel that way, but I do."

"You feel different? Now?" she asked softly, tears coming to her eyes.

"I wanted—" He felt his throat closing up on him. "I wanted to hold on to a family that needed to be held. Not—" He stopped again to swallow before going on. "Not one that didn't need me."

"I don't have everything I need," she whispered.

"Then do something," he entreated. "Change it back."

"I can't. Don't you see? You loved the Chris who didn't have anything. I don't want to be that Chris. If you don't love me as I am, you were loving a fantasy, a hard-luck story."

"I did *not* love a hard-luck story! It was this feisty little babe making it through tough stuff that a lot of stronger people couldn't. But it wasn't true. You weren't gutsy—you were *rich*. You always have been—you just didn't have it *on* you!"

"Oh, God," she said, shaking her head, "I should have known. I never should have stayed here. You think I've changed, but you're the one who's changed. I'm the same person, and you don't like me as much."

"No, you don't like it when it doesn't go your way. You gotta have it smooth as glass every second. That's it."

"Oh, yeah? I've been real spoiled, all right, the past few years of—"

"Oh, don't give me that bull! You never starved. You could always have called *her!*"

"Maybe I should call her now!"

"Well, maybe you should!"

They both looked stricken by what had been said. But it was too late to take it back.

Mike suddenly didn't know what to do. He yanked open the door. "I gotta have air. Gotta cool down." Reluctantly, helplessly, he left the bedroom and the house.

Mike drove around for a while but ended up at his mom and dad's. He'd pretty much known he would. It was years since he had sought his father's advice. Years since he had talked about his troubles. Years since he had admitted he had any.

"You oughta see what's under the Christmas tree," he told Big Mike. "I've never seen anything like it. And it's my fault as much as Aunt Flo's. But it'll never stop."

"It'll stop," Big Mike said. "You'll run out of money pretty quick."

"Do you know what she's got? I mean, like millions of dollars!"

"Did you stop playing the Lotto? I thought you went for an idea like millions of dollars."

"That's different. It would have been *mine*."

"'Mine,'" Mattie said quietly, half pretending not to get into this. "Kids say that when they're two. Usually they get over it."

"Ma, it isn't like you think. I thought a lot of money didn't mean that much to Chris, but she flaunts it now. I mean, she's buying things for my house all the time. Like when Flo was coming for dinner, she bought this whole new set of dishes, new tablecloth—the works. Flo can't sit down at a regular table? God forbid there should be a chipped dish. Can you imagine what it would be like if she came here? With the rest of us?"

Mattie shrugged. "She would sit down and eat or not. Makes no difference to me."

"Oh, you think that, but it isn't that way. It feels different to be surrounded by money. If I stay with Chrissie now, she'll build us a mansion."

"How terrible a thing, Mikie my boy. Just think of it—the pain of living with some money. Terrible break for you."

"Come on."

"So what would you change? What one thing?"

"The money. And the aunt."

"How would you do that?"

Okay, he thought. I can't make those changes. "Maybe I wouldn't have offered my house in the first place."

"Okay, if that makes it all better, okay. But for a minute there I thought you liked it. Maybe I was mistaken."

"I think you were." Big Mike *was* mistaken: it had been more than a minute, and he had more than liked it. He had felt restored, alive—before this whole issue of who had what and who was in charge got in his way. He'd already let it out, though, and if Chris couldn't face it any better than he could, then it couldn't be resolved. If you didn't know where the fire was, you couldn't put water on it.

He complained for a while longer, but he didn't tell them that the big problem was him. Probably they already knew. Stubborn and bossy. He liked to control things. On the other hand, *he* didn't want anything to do with a woman who would be controlled. The prospect for reconciliation didn't look good.

His parents said things like, "So what do you want? That she give the money away so you don't have to worry about it?"

"No, not that, but—"

"Maybe she should give it to you. Then it would be *yours.*"

"No, but—"

I only want to feel good again, he thought. *In control. Useful. Helpful. Needed.*

At four o'clock he was ready, he thought, to go back

to his house. His mother slapped his cheek affectionately. "Try not to be too stupid about this, Mikie."

"That will be hard for him, Mattie," Big Mike said.

"Don't do that. Don't say that. Chrissie called me a
big dope."

Mattie kissed his cheek. "Did you see Jim? He's all
right?"

"I saw him. He's doing fine, considering."

"Terrible thing," Mattie said. "Life is too short.
Sometimes when you come that close to losing someone, sometimes it makes you want to shake everything
up so you can fix it, huh?"

He thought for a minute. Was that why? He'd thought
about losing Jim and then become afraid of losing Chris
and the kids. Knowing that having them the way he
did wasn't feeling too good, he'd wanted to shake it up.
Maybe then they could put the pieces together right.
But, no. He'd just made a big mess of things.

"Yeah, Ma," he said.

When he left the house Big Mike settled, shook the
paper and hid behind it. "So?" Mattie asked her husband.

"That Chrissie. Good judge of character, that girl.
He's a big dope, your son."

"He's always my son when he does something stupid."

"Was he the one who put Matthew in the clothes
chute?"

"It was Chris in the clothes chute, and he put himself there after making Tommy go first."

"Was it? You're sure?"

"You think he's going to be all right?" she asked.

"I don't know. I'm betting on that terrible dog. I bet

you anything that if she leaves, she doesn't take that terrible dog."

"I think you hope," she said.

The house was filled with the good smells of cooking. Chris was standing at the stove. This was not what he had expected. He had come in through the garage, and now he stood just inside the door and looked at her. "I don't know how to say I'm sorry about what I said."

"You said what you felt. You can't be sorry for that."

"I'm sorry I said anything. I don't want to feel that way. I wanted to work on feeling different before I said anything."

"But you were telling the truth?"

He nodded.

"Then I'm the one who's sorry," she said. "I cooked dinner, a special one. Do you think we can bury it for one night?"

"One night?"

"I think we should have an early Christmas. You, me, the kids. Flo is planning to get in at two tomorrow. If I can't reach her and get her to cancel—I've been trying—the three of us will meet her and go back with her. You two are incompatible. This isn't good for anybody anymore. I wanted it to work, Mike. And I'll never stop loving you."

"Is it because we're too different?"

"No. Because the differences are tearing us apart. And I don't think I can fix this."

"Try. Please. I'm willing to try."

"I don't think you can, Mike, and the past ten days— maybe the next ten years—you against Flo, against where I've come from, what I can provide…"

"But you don't have to provide. You—"

"I *do* have to. I have to give, too. And not just hot food and grateful sex. I have been working, working hard, so that I could make it on my own. That effort is as much a part of who I am as any other part of me. I don't have to live in a big fancy house or be like Flo or be able to afford the finest of everything, but I do have to be able to earn money, spend it, save it as I choose. I want this whole business about the amount to be irrelevant, like at Mattie and Big Mike's. Where whoever has gives, and whoever needs takes. Not just money, but all of it. I can't live with a man who will put restrictions on what I, too, could provide."

"You could give me a chance to try to—"

She shook her head, then walked toward him. Her arms went around his neck. "You mean struggle with this until it either works or crashes down around us? You wanted to be the one, you said, to give me what I need to build my life. Oh, Mike, you can't. Neither can Flo. I've got to do that for myself. Being loved because you're helpless is not very different from being loved because you're rich."

"You're comparing me to *him?* Chrissie, your husband didn't love you—he *used* you. He didn't say he'd try to change. You're just running away."

"Not exactly. I'm going to spend Christmas with Flo, but I'm not going to move in with her. I have some money from the landlord, and if I don't sell a book soon, I'll get a job. I've done it before. I want to do it on my own. I can share my life, Mike, but I don't want to be owned. I don't want to be kept down. This situation is hurting both of us too much."

"Chrissie, I have a bad temper. I'm bossy and stubborn, like you said. I got jealous. But maybe I can change some of that. Let's—"

"Look, I'm leaving, not dying. Maybe some of this can be worked out—a lot of it works already. But not while I'm in your house. I don't know which was harder, having you try so hard to be perfect and patient, or having you blow up like you did. Let's let the dust settle. We'll email, talk on the phone. Maybe after a while…"

"Don't leave. Don't."

"I have to. I think the kids and I have been through enough for now. For now, let's not put ourselves through any more fighting. Maybe later, when things have calmed down, when this business with the 'lost money' is settled, when my book is published, you know… maybe we can work it out. It's been wonderful, and I love you. Let's try to part friends. I'm not going to disappear. If it's meant to last longer, it'll survive a separation while we both decide what we need. Let's not put ourselves through a rough Christmas."

"Is it what you want?" he asked. "Would you love me better if I had some house plans drawn up…if I wanted to help you spend your money?"

"Mike, it isn't either love me for my money or love me because I'm broke. It isn't either-or. This is who I am. I am sometimes broke, and sometimes it looks like I have a lot of money. I want to be okay either way. I think it's the only way. We did what we set out to do, huh?"

"What if I beg?"

"Then that would mean you weren't telling the truth when you asked me to stay just long enough so I could get back on my feet and you could remember what you wanted again."

He shrugged. "I never asked you to promise anything, it's true. I said open invitation."

"But you made that offer to someone else. I'm not who you thought I was. That book. My stupid ex-husband. Will you be all right?"

"In a while."

"No veldt-sores?"

Open, bleeding wound. But he was one tough guy. "Those are taken care of now. But I think I drove you away when all I wanted was for you to stay."

"Maybe you couldn't help it, what with wanting one thing but being stuck with another. It's my fault, too. I should have told you that first night you asked me to stay. At least I should have told you before we…" She held back tears, looking away briefly. "It's been pretty rugged around here since Flo came and my past became my present and we forgot we only had one small, simple goal: I needed a roof, and you needed to get in touch with what you really wanted. We got a little carried away. I don't want them to hear that kind of fight again," she said, her head nodding in the direction of the living room.

"I suppose."

"Kiss me, Mike. Kiss me so I'll never forget how wonderful it feels."

Carrie's chin quivered. "Mommy says that we're going to our Auntie Flo's for Christmas."

Mike picked her up. "Does that make you sad?"

"No. Cheeks makes me sad."

"Why?"

"He's going in a kennel for Christmas. Because he can't go on the airplane. He doesn't have a box."

"Oh, no, he's not. He'll stay with me. He can come to the cabin with me for Christmas. Okay?"

"You don't have to do that, Mike. Cheeks is pretty hard on your socks."

"I like him. I'll buy him a bunch of socks for Christmas. How's that, Carrie? Can I keep him for you while you're away?"

"Yes." She smiled. "And then you can bring him when you visit us. When are you going to visit us?"

"Oh, I don't know. Pretty soon, maybe. When are you going to visit me."

"Pretty soon, too. Mommy says we will *always* know where you are. We bought you Christmas presents, and we're going to open them tonight. It is a 'practice Christmas.'"

Let it be, he thought. *Don't let me tempt fate by showing either too much joy in their presence or too much pain in their departure. Let them be happy, leave happy, as they were happy within my arms. All of them. And then, in my memories, I will be less lost.*

Dinner was ham and things. Christmas ham. And a fire in the fireplace. And eggnog, cookies and an Irish whiskey, neat, for the grown-ups, which would either untense some tight nerves or loosen their tongues or start the tears flowing.

They only opened presents from one another; Flo's were put back in the boxes they had been shipped in to be carried back to Chicago. Chris had already made plane reservations. It was a miracle she was able to book them this time of year, but she called a travel agent and paid top dollar for first-class. It was all set.

And the opened presents would also be packed and carried away because, as Mike knew, they wouldn't be back soon. The kids were thrilled with their bounty. And Mike was surprised to be given things he had not thought they knew how to buy. A gun-cleaning set. Riding chaps. A rod and reel. And a big packet of socks. "We'll go fishing when you visit, huh, Kyle?"

"Fishing!"

"Our mother doesn't like guns very much," Carrie said. "But she said you are very careful with them."

"I am. When you're very careful and you know what you're doing with guns, as with fires, they're not so scary." Why then, he wondered, had they been so reckless with what they so briefly, so blissfully had? Had they never considered love volatile?

"Will I ride the horses some more?"

"Yes. Yes, you will. And I'll take pictures for you and email them to you. And pictures of all the Cavanaugh kids. And Big Mike and Gram. And I'll call you at your Auntie Flo's. Okay?"

"Okay!"

"Should we read a story? One of our favorites?"

"No, the new one. Read a new one."

"Okay, a new one, then." Which he did. A long, long one. But when they fell asleep, both of them, he did something he had never before done. He woke them. "Carrie. Kyle. Wake up a little bit. I'm going to take you to bed. It's my turn to tuck you in. There we go." And he hefted them up in his big arms and took them, together, to the beds upstairs.

There was an ache in his chest, but he would not give in. "I love you very much, Carrie," he told her. "And you can visit me whenever your mommy wants to." And then, "I love you very much, Kyle, and I promise to take you fishing if your mommy will let you go." And he held each one tight, kissed each one on forehead, cheeks, lips, chin. They were too tired to notice how desperately he behaved, and for this he was grateful.

He returned to Chris. She handed him another Irish. "I wish I had done better," he said. "Maybe you'll change your mind. Maybe when things are a little settled, you'll come back and work on this with me. I'm a big dope, but I'm not hopeless."

"Maybe. The timing has been all wrong. I'm not the coward I appear to be, Mike. And I'm not choosing between you and Flo—I'm only getting some distance from both of you while I think things through."

He lifted his glass to her. "That's probably good. Me and Flo, we've been lousy to you. You okay about the dog?"

"Carrie feels a lot better about it now. Do you think we'll have something to talk about on the phone? Do you think we'll keep whatever it was we had—"

"*Is,* Chris. Whatever it *is.* We haven't lost it. We just got sidetracked. Me. I got pigheaded. Our family's famous for it."

"But you're letting me go. Not arguing about it."

"I said I'd try. I don't know if I can change, I can only try. I became a different person when I started to compete with your big bucks. I didn't like the person I was becoming, but I couldn't get rid of the feelings. I want you to be where you ought to be. Here, there—it's all the same. I'll love you no matter what."

"I think if it's the real thing, we'll come back together."

"Yeah, well, you hit the nail on the head. I'm afraid if you go, you'll never be able to come back."

"Why?"

"I don't know. Because you'll find out what I've known all along: you're tougher than you think, and you have the moxie to make it on your own."

"You might find out something, too. You might find out you don't need all these complications."

"No, that's your line. I said I'll go all the way to the end. I just didn't know it would be such a short trip." He sighed deeply, fighting the feeling that the last shovelful of dirt was being tossed on the grave. "Like you said, we did what we set out to do. If you can stay, stay. If you can't…well, you're the one who thinks. I rush into things."

"Well, I could have gone earlier. I could have called Flo; then you wouldn't be feeling like you've lost something now."

"I feel fear, Chrissie, not loss. Afraid you'll decide leaving was the smartest thing you did. I want you to regret leaving, then decide it's worth it to come back. I just can't promise that I'll ever be easy to live with. And I might never like Flo. I can't make myself even *want* to like Flo. Just like Cheeks might never stop eating socks. Such is life. I'm sorry. My best isn't much sometimes."

"But I love you so," she whispered.

"Then show me. Here. In front of the fire. Show me where to touch you. Let me put out the fire one more time…."

Much later he whispered to her, "I can't say goodbye, Chrissie. Not to the kids. Don't make me do that."

"Okay. Whatever you want."

"Then I want you to sleep in my arms. And when you wake up, be smiling. It wasn't long enough, but it was good."

Chapter 14

When Chris awoke Mike and Cheeks were gone. She didn't have the time for the luxury of lying still and contemplating the past month and the decision she had made to end it; there was a great deal to be done before going to the airport. She hadn't made contact with Flo—where *was* her aunt these days?

As she hurried around the house gathering up their belongings, scraping their presence from his house, she could not still her mind. What was going to prove the most difficult to live without? The way he was with the kids? Like he should have a dozen. Natural and decisive, he never made hesitant or wrong choices for them. He spoke their language, found the right pastimes, the right jokes, and practiced affirmative discipline that showed them how good they were, how smart.

Or would it be even harder to live without the way

he was with Chris's body? As though he had known it for twenty years and was, at the same time, just working up a sweat in the first round. How could you feel wild and nurtured at the same time? Frenzied yet companionable? Out of your mind with out-of-control passion but perfectly safe? You could feel this way with a man who trusted easily and gave everything he had.

Or would the hardest thing be giving up that fanciful, foolish, idealistic notion that one could have a unit of people bonded by love, fraught with ups and downs, fronts and backs, joy and pain, a circle that actually closed around them and was tied with the knot of trust? The belief that it could be settled, ironed out, renewed. Yes, that might be hardest. Had she really fantasized fighting and then making up? Sure. Before she had lived it. Before his temper had erupted and the first punch he threw hit her square in the only identity she had.

She had not, after all, asked him to become different from the man with whom she had fallen in love. Had she?

When she went into the kitchen she found his note.

"I did all the things I have to say. Love, M."

That was Mike. Mike was better with actions than with words. When he was forced to confront his feelings, they were pretty hectic. What he wanted, she guessed, would be for them to forsake Aunt Flo, the money, the past. She almost wished she could.

There was quite a lot to pack, plus Christmas presents, opened and unopened. Then there was the car, which she took to a used-car lot. She did not strike a bargain, but she did get a ride to the airport with all their things.

* * *

"You're doing *what?*" Flo nearly shrieked. The airport was a mess. Hundreds of frustrated travelers fighting for space on overcrowded planes, airlines offering money for people who would give up their tickets. Chris held four first-class seats. Nonstop, Chicago.

"We're going back to Chicago. Today. It'll be a long wait—we don't leave until five-thirty, but—"

"Christine, what in the world are you talking about?"

"Don't start on me, Flo. It didn't work out. I made a last-minute decision. I tried calling you, but—"

"You were so damned hell-bent to stay with this big, dumb fireman."

"Don't call him dumb. He isn't dumb. He's the smartest man I've ever known in my life."

"Well, then, why in the world are you doing this? Did something terrible happen? Did he hurt you?"

"Of course not. Of course he wouldn't hurt me. He's the gentlest man I've ever known."

Flo rubbed her forehead with her fingers, exasperated. "I'm sure I'll understand all this eventually." Chris shook her head, struggling with tears she had been alternately fighting and giving in to all day long. "Me," Flo said. "It's me. He can't take me. What a wimp. I knew he was a wimp all along."

"No, no, it isn't that. I mean, he is intimidated by you and your money, but it isn't anything personal. Not really."

"Well, then, so what? I'm not crazy about him, either. So what else is new? That's the way it goes, right? You don't like your aunt-in-law. Big deal."

"And the money."

"What about the money? Does the money matter?

What matters is how people feel about each other, not how much they can spend. What happened? *When* did this happen?"

"Florence, *please*. Don't interrogate me. Please."

"All right. All right. Let's get my bags and go get a drink. We're going to be here for hours. Chris, when you go off the deep end, do you absolutely have to take everyone with you? Where is that stupid dog?"

"He kept the dog," she said.

"He *what?* He kept the kids' dog?"

"No, no, nothing like that. The dog was going to have to go to a kennel, and Carrie was upset, so Mike said he'd take care of Cheeks. He can ship him later or something—I don't know."

"He kept the dog so Carrie wouldn't be upset?" Flo asked.

"Yes, something like that. And I think he secretly liked the dog."

It took an hour to collect Flo's baggage and recheck it on the next flight. Then they found a corner table in an airport bar. The kids sipped soda. Flo had a Bloody Mary, but Chris couldn't drink; her stomach was still jumping. The kids, fortunately, were very resilient. They were excited about the plane ride, about Aunt Flo's house, and they were sure they would see Mike again soon. Chris was less sure, but she didn't tell them that.

"Now," Flo said, "let me see if I have this right. You are leaving because now that you have money of your own, he is intimidated by your ability to be completely independent of him? Is that it?"

"Yes," she said, blowing her nose. "It's just like with Steve—I mean Fred. Oh, damn, I'll never be able to think of him as Fred. It's just another way of using a person. I met Mike's needs by being needy."

"And you felt used?"

"No. Yes. I mean, I didn't feel *used,* but he was angry about the money. Angry—can you imagine? He came right out and said it, too. He resented my money. He didn't want me to buy things for him anymore. He said he'd like it better if I couldn't."

"I know men who like having fat wives. It's testosterone poisoning. They're all defective."

Chris blew her nose again. Now that she was with Flo, the tears kept coming. "Well, everything was fine until he thought about going through life competing with my big bucks. It hurt his pride, I guess. It made him feel middle-class, less of a man. I wasn't prepared for that. Here was a man, I believed, who understood for better, for worse. I certainly can't change who and what I am. I *want* to contribute. I've worked hard at being able to contribute. If he can't take my inheritance, would he be any better at coping with a successful writer? It's all the same thing."

"Too bad he wasn't willing to work on that. I don't happen to think having money is the worst crime a person can commit."

"Well, he wanted to try, but I could tell he wouldn't be able to do it."

Flo was fairly slow to respond. "There were undoubtedly many other things."

"No. Everything else was wonderful."

"There is, obviously, some reason you *knew* he wouldn't be able to change?"

"It's part of his nature to want to do for people. When

he doesn't feel needed, he doesn't feel loved. There would be a lot of trouble. I don't have the stamina for it."

"I see." Flo leisurely sipped her drink. "Well, you did the right thing, Chris," she said coyly. "He wasn't good enough for you."

"Yes, he was! For a while he was the best thing that ever happened to me. You were right—I should have learned more from my mistake with my ex-husband."

"And I'm relieved you did. Just in time, too. You'll be much happier on your own. You don't need that crap."

Tears spilled over. "Oh, I don't know about that. I've been on my own for a long time. It's been pretty lonely. For a while, having you and Mike—my old family, my new love—it was so hopeful, so— Well, I just don't see that I have any choice. Regardless of what I think I want, I don't want to raise my children in a home where there's so much conflict, so much restriction on who can do what."

"Lord knows you don't need conflict and restriction after all you've been through. If anyone deserves a happily-ever-after life, it's you. You'll be much better off. Besides, I'm sure he wouldn't change."

"I won't know that, of course, because I— Well, I just couldn't risk it, Flo. I'm tired of fighting."

"He's probably relieved that you're gone. In fact, I wouldn't doubt that he's actually pleased. After all, his life was the way he liked it before you came along."

"He was lonely. I don't think he realized how lonely—"

"But these complications with money are too much for a man like Mike," Flo said. "He likes everything simple. He wants to be the big man, water down the big fire, bring home the bacon…"

"He doesn't like to think about things for too long," Chris said.

"No, and solving this problem would take a while. He wouldn't like that."

"He likes to face things straightforwardly—"

"Can't talk about his feelings," Flo said. "Come on, let's go down to the gate. This place is a madhouse. I don't want us to get bumped because of overbooking."

They began to gather up their things. They walked, a row of four, holding hands with the kids. "But he does talk about his feelings," Chris said. "He doesn't think he's very good at it, but really he is. I honestly don't know what was worse, when he was trying so hard not to say how he felt, or when he came right out and—"

"Oh, well, water over the dam," Flo said. "I'm so glad you've finally come to your senses. You'll never regret coming home. Not for one tiny second."

"I'm not going to move in with you, Flo. I'll stay until I can get my own place, and then—"

"You can stay as long as you like, of course, but I think you ought to know, I've made a few changes myself. Remember your little philosophy about betting you won't get cold? Ken and I have decided to get married."

Chris stopped dead in her tracks. "Really?"

"Uh-huh. Ken has always wanted to get married. I was the one who was too busy or too independent or, really, too scared. It's a big step. That's where I've been the past couple of days—with Ken…working this out." Flo nearly blushed.

"I'm happy for you, Flo. If you don't know him after all these years, you never will."

"I will never be accused of being impetuous, that's for sure. You're the one with that trait. I may be slow at deciding what I want, but you, darling, leap before you look. You couldn't possibly have known Mike very well."

"Oh-ho." Chris laughed. "Within a week I knew almost everything about him."

"He was holding back some vital information, though. Like not being able to accept you the way you are. It's a good thing you saw that in time."

"I had no idea he was holding back. In fact, he always seemed to give everything that was inside of him."

"You must have been pretty shocked, then, by the way he laid it on you about the money thing. After thinking he was so stable, so transparent, hiding that little tidbit..." Flo stopped at the gate. "Look at this place. An hour and a half until our flight, and it's mobbed."

"He didn't hold back for long. He put it on the line. He said what was the matter with him and wanted to fight it out."

"You don't need that, Chris. Life is tough enough."

"I wouldn't have lasted long. I hate to fight."

"No self-respecting Palmer wants to fight. Fighting lacks decorum."

"You're a born fighter," Chris disagreed.

"I'm a born *winner*. I don't like laying everything on the line. Never have. Probably why I never married. Look at that—they're *already* offering to buy back tickets. Good thing you booked us first-class. We are checked in, aren't we?"

"He wanted to face it. He wanted to try to work on it. He didn't want to feel the way he felt. What can I do about what he feels? I can't change his feelings. I can't—"

"I think maybe we'd better get our seat assignments,"

Flo said, "or we might have a problem. Oh, I'm so relieved, Chris. You would have been simply miserable through the holidays."

"I didn't want to argue through Christmas...."

"Last night must have been hell for you," Flo said. "The big jerk."

"Last night was..." Chris stopped. Tears spilled down her cheeks again.

"I could just kill him for hurting you this way. Here I thought he was a generous, strong man who wasn't afraid of anything, but when it came down to the wire, he just couldn't—"

"He *did* give me everything he had. Even the bad stuff."

"Well, honey, don't defend the big jerk. I think you got out just in time. And I'm certainly relieved that we don't have to deal with that dog."

"The kids are really going to miss the—"

"I wondered what I was going to do about that dog. That is not the most agreeable animal. Growly thing."

"Oh, he's noisy, but inside he's—"

"Where there's smoke there's fire. That dog had a hidden agenda, like the fireman. You *think* he's just growling, you *think* he's perfectly safe, then wham. He'll bite someone someday."

Chris's eyes widened, and she slowly turned toward Flo. She stared at her aunt's profile for a minute. Then Flo turned, and Chris met her eyes. "That dog will not bite if he's not abused."

"If you say so. But we're not going to find out at the expense of my carpet."

"I never had a fight with Steve," Chris said.

"Why would he risk fighting with you?" Flo asked.

"If you didn't get along, you might have taken your money and gone home. I imagine he was very amiable. But don't think about that now, Chris. You're coming home. That's all that matters, right?"

Chris looked closely at Flo's eyes. "What are you doing to me?" she asked.

Flo put an arm around Chris's shoulders. "I'm agreeing with you, Christine. Don't you recognize it?"

"Flo…"

"If you're very careful, perhaps you can manage a life as tidy and enviable as mine. And maybe you'll be ready to take a few chances, again, when you're, say, about forty-one. What do you say, kiddo? Shall we get our seat assignments? Go home?"

It had been dawn when Mike arrived at his cabin with Cheeks. He had cried a little, then decided self-pity should be against the law. He wished he could have been stronger—strong enough to help them pack, take them to the airport, all of that. But he couldn't do it. His disappointment was overwhelming, and he would have broken down in front of them. There were certain things that children should be spared.

So he and Cheeks put on the coffee and built a fire to warm up the cabin. Later, they went for a hike. Then visited the horses. Cleaned up the cabin a little, shoveled some snow, cooked a steak on the grill, even though it was freezing out.

"Here," he said to the dog, giving him half the steak. "I'll give you a pair of socks later. For dessert."

What the hell, he thought. It had been a crazy, lunatic thing to do from the start—bringing her home like that, telling her to stay a while because it felt good. Who did stupid things like that?

Still, it might have worked. If she hadn't had money? No. It might have worked if he had not been bothered by her money. Or it might still have worked if she could stand that he was bothered. He might have gotten over that. If he had kept his mouth shut about it.

But he couldn't really live like that. It was about those changes, about that one thing that you would change to make things turn out differently. What if you got mad about the way someone squeezed the toothpaste but you could never say so? And if you said so, a whole major fight erupted and it tore you apart?

His whole family argued. At the Cavanaugh house you had better be able to hold your own during an argument, or keep your mouth shut. When something was wrong, you had better be able to either say what it was, fix it, or learn to live with it. You didn't grow up in a household crammed full of people and everyone politely tiptoed around saying, "Pardon me," "Oh, excuse me, did I do that?"

And in the firehouse, where the men were bonded by hard work, cooperation, danger, things were resolved quickly, too. You couldn't let bad feelings fester; it was critical to solve problems or learn to accept the fact that people had both virtues and flaws. Big ones and little annoying ones.

But Chris hadn't lived that way. Hadn't she told him that? There were only four of them—her parents and Flo. She was either struggling to be independent or giving in to let someone take care of her. Or she ran away. So it was just as well, then, that she left when she did. She would have gone eventually, at the first sign of trouble....

It wasn't just the money that made them different. It was the regard they had for risk. She could risk her life trying to save a dumb laptop, but she couldn't risk the discomfort of an argument, a fight. What did she think? That husbands and wives didn't fight? He had thought she *was* a fighter. Turned out it was only sometimes.

"So, what one thing would you change?" he asked the dog. "What one thing that *you* could do would make everything different?" He nudged the dog with his toe. Cheeks growled. "That's what I thought you said. Nothing. Not a damn thing. Because it wouldn't have been better if I hadn't carried her out of the fire. I would have missed out on a lot of good things if I hadn't fallen in love with her, and if I *had* kept my mouth shut, I would have opened it eventually anyway. It all would have turned out the same. Like she said, you have to be accepted just the way you are. And that's the way I am. And that's the way she is."

And I hurt, he thought, because I feel loss. But I am better for what I had. I had my arms full again; I had love that was deep and rich. And because of that, maybe it will come back to me. Maybe I can have it again someday. Just maybe. My amnesia is over. *We did what we set out to do, huh?* When I'm stronger I'll send her an e-mail and tell her…thank you. Despite the problems, because of you I am better than I was. I had been in hiding too long, and I needed to learn what a mistake that was.

He heard the sound of a four-wheel-drive vehicle coming up the road. He suspected it might be someone from the Christiansons' house. Probably they saw the light and pitied him, alone. Or maybe they thought he was with Chris and the kids and were stopping by for a friendly chat. He wished they wouldn't. He couldn't refuse to answer the door. You don't do that in the mountains. He opened the door and watched the car come up the road. It wasn't the Christiansons' car. It was a big new Suburban. Oh, hell, he thought, recognizing his brother Chris's car. Why'd they do that? He had said he wanted to be alone.

Cheeks growled and wagged his tail. The Suburban stopped, but the headlights stayed on. The door on the driver's side opened, and she got out. He could barely make her out with the headlights shining in his eyes. She walked toward him slowly, until she stood in front of him.

He tried to keep from feeling that he'd won the Lotto. "Have you come back?" he asked her.

"I was wrong. So were you. I think that means we're not finished yet."

"Is that Chris's car?"

"Well—" she shrugged "—no matter how hard I try to be independent, I just keep asking for help, don't I?" Her smile faded, and she looked up at him, tears in her eyes.

He opened his arms to her, and she filled his embrace. "I love you," he said. "I don't care how hard it is, I love you."

She cried and laughed but would not let him go. He lifted her clear off the ground. "I'm going to keep you happy for a long time," she said, her voice breaking, "because there is so much I need from you."

They stood in their rocking embrace for such a long time that soon the children were beside them, greeting the dog, plowing past them into the house, but they didn't let go of each other. Mike's face was buried in her jacket collar. Until the door to the Suburban slammed and someone said, "Ugh. Oh, *Gawd.*"

He looked over Chris's shoulder to see Aunt Flo ruining her fashionable pumps in snow up to her ankles. She couldn't move, of course, with her heels jammed into the packed snow. He laughed. It was tough for him to admit to himself, but he was even a little glad to see Flo. It meant they were going to face it, head-on, and work it all out together. That included family. And he felt strongly about family.

He let go of Chris—it figured that the first reason he would have for letting her go would be Flo. This time, though, he felt firm in his faith that he would hold her again and again, and he went to Flo. He looked her up and down with his hands on his hips. Then he scooped her up in his arms and carried her to the house. She complained the whole way, about her shoes, the snow, the cold, the long drive. He put her down inside. And once inside she looked around in silence, probably awed by the rustic sparseness of it.

Mike put his arm around Chris's shoulders. They watched the activity, the welcome fullness of it all. Cheeks was running in circles, barking. The kids were already looking in the cupboards for treats before even taking off their coats, and Flo was removing her wet shoes in front of the fire, grumbling.

"Did you bring the twenty-two servants?" he asked Chris.

"Nope. She's going to do this without the caterer. Cold turkey."

"This ought to be good."

And it was.

* * * * *

Dear Reader,

I admit to a certain weakness for dark, damaged heroes who don't know how much they need the right woman's love. Such a man is Sinclair "Sin" Riker, who lost everything as a child and clawed his way out of poverty to great financial success.

The woman he needs more than he knows? Her name is Sophie Jones. Sophie seems sweet and innocent, but she's a lot tougher than she looks and she is nobody's fool.

Sin wants something from Sophie. And he's willing to do whatever it takes to get it. Sin has a lot to learn about what matters in life—and about love. Luckily for him, Sophie Jones is more than up to the job of helping him to see the light.

I do hope you enjoy this story of Sin's redemption. And I'm so thrilled that *A Hero for Sophie Jones* is on the stands again in this two-in-one volume with a great book by the fabulous Robyn Carr.

Happy reading everyone,

Christine Rimmer

A HERO FOR SOPHIE JONES

USA TODAY Bestselling Author

Christine Rimmer

What is it about those Joneses?
Every time I think I've written the last Jones Gang story,
another Jones pops up and says, "But what about me?"
This one's for all of you who have written me letters
asking for more.

Chapter 1

The raven-haired stranger in the fifth row had eyes as black as his hair. Eyes that mesmerized. Eyes that managed to be both lazy looking and bold at the same time. Those eyes were locked right on her as Sophie B. Jones began introducing the evening's feature presentation.

"Welcome to the Mountain Star." Sophie smiled, a smile intended to include each and every one of the eighty-five people who sat in the ten rows of battered seats before her.

Though most of her guests smiled back, the dark-haired stranger did not. And he certainly seemed to be making himself at home, sitting there in an idle sprawl, an elbow braced on the seat arm and one long, graceful hand across his mouth. Thoughtfully, he brushed his index finger over his lips, an action that Sophie found extremely distracting.

Sophie made herself look past him. Smiling wider, she spread her arms in a gesture that embraced all of her guests at once. "I'm so glad you could make it, and I hope you enjoy this weekend's installment in what I like to think of as our Randi Wilding Film Retrospective."

From overhead, in the rafters of the old stone barn that housed Sophie's makeshift movie theater, came a soft cooing sound. Sophie glanced upward, then back out over the rows of expectant faces. "Pardon that pigeon." She lifted a shoulder in a what-can-I-tell-you shrug. "I thought I shooed him out of here this afternoon."

A low chuckle passed through the crowd. Sophie scanned the rows again, making eye contact, watching the little quirks of smiles come and go on the faces.

But not that one face.

Or, wait a minute—Maybe he *had* smiled. She couldn't be sure, but it had seemed for a split second as if that sinfully sexy mouth of his had lifted at one corner.

And those bedroom eyes certainly did look interested—in a lot more than the evening's feature presentation at the Mountain Star. Those eyes seemed to speak to Sophie. They said they planned to get to know her. Intimately.

Up in the rafters, that pesky pigeon cooed once more.

And Sophie told herself that she'd better get real. The man had an…aura about him. He might be wearing chinos and a Polo shirt right now, but she just knew he had a closet full of Armani at home—wherever that was, some big city, she was sure.

It took no effort to picture him cruising around in a limousine, behind windows tinted black. He was the kind of man who could cause a hush by simply entering a room. The kind of man who made women wonder: Who is he? What's he after? And is there any way I might have a chance with him?

Tall. Dark. Delectably menacing. Lord Byron and the vampire Lestat. Definitely not someone likely to be driven mad with desire by a woman who bought her dress at a yard sale and always cut her own hair.

Sophie ought to be suspicious of such obvious interest from a man like that, and she knew it.

And maybe she was suspicious. A little.

But at the same time, her hopelessly romantic soul couldn't help but respond, couldn't help feeling what those eyes said *he* felt: attraction, plain and simple.

Sophie realized right then that the barn was way too silent. How long had she been standing there, pondering the possible agendas of Tall, Dark, Et Cetera, while her audience waited to hear about the show?

Something warm and fuzzy was making figure eights around her ankles. Grateful for an excuse to look away from all those staring eyes, she glanced down. "Eddie."

The gray tabby lifted his head. Yellow-green kitty eyes met hers. *"Rrreow?"*

She bent and scooped him up. He purred and nuzzled her neck. "You're a sweetheart, you are." Petting the cat, she dared to look out at the faces again—taking extreme care this time not to allow her gaze to linger on *him*.

"Let's see. Where was I? Oh, yes. Randi Wilding. As you all probably remember, she started out as just another gorgeous blonde—on the hit TV show *Eden Beach*. She broke into movies a couple of years later. And now, at barely thirty years of age, she's become a megastar. Some still think of her as nothing more than a sex symbol, but those in the know are already calling her one of the great all-time actresses. She makes exciting, fast-paced movies that everyone wants to see, and she also makes each character she plays come alive on the screen.

"Tonight, you'll be seeing *Sagebrush and Desire*. It was Randi's second feature film. In it, she got to wear chaps and shoot a pair of pearl-handled Colts—not to mention deal with a passel of rustlers out to steal her herd. The word is that she did her own stunts, which I think you'll all agree is pretty amazing once you see the scene where she slides off the roof of a barn, turns a somersault in midair and lands square in the saddle on the back of her mustang mare—which bolts off at a dead run.

"Unfortunately—" Sophie smoothed Eddie's wiry fur "—that wasn't a big year for Westerns. *Sagebrush and Desire* remains Randi's only box-office flop. And you all know how I feel about box-office flops." Sophie paused, grinned and scratched Eddie behind an ear. "I love them on principle. So tonight at the Mountain Star, I'm proud to present...Randi Wilding in *Sagebrush and Desire*."

Friendly applause followed Sophie up the aisle. A shiver went through her as she passed the fifth row, but she didn't allow herself to turn and look into those dark eyes again.

Sin Riker watched the Jones woman as she strolled by with the gray cat in her arms. Her waterfall of honey-brown hair shone gold in the glare from the fluorescent lights that hung from the rafters overhead. She looked sweet as a milkmaid in some sentimental old print.

He shifted a little, so he could watch her as she moved beyond him up the aisle. Beneath the hem of her worn flowered dress trailed about three inches of white cotton lace. On any other woman, it would have looked as if her slip was showing. But not on the Jones woman. On her, that border of lace looked just right.

At the top of the aisle, she let the cat down and climbed a ladder to what once must have been a hay-loft, but now clearly did duty as a projection booth. Sin watched that innocent white lace until it disappeared overhead, then he turned and faced the screen again.

She wasn't his type at all, of course. He preferred a more complex woman, one who could hold her own in the boardroom as well as the bedroom, one with a little darkness in her soul—to match his own.

In the rafters, the rogue pigeon fluttered his wings. The gray cat strolled down the center aisle, striped tail held high.

"I'm so glad we came," the elderly woman to Sin's right whispered to the gray-haired gent on her other side. The man took the woman's age-spotted hand. They shared a smile. "The Mountain Star is a special place," the woman said.

Sin had to agree. This impossible theater in a barn charmed him. He had no idea why. The awful, rick-ety seats must have been stolen from some condemned movie palace and the screen had a hole in the upper left-hand corner.

He should have found the place ridiculous. Yet he didn't. Not at all. It captivated him.

As did the Jones woman herself, with those big eyes

and that sunny smile, all that bronze hair—and white lace showing beneath the hem of her skirt.

Not that this sudden, absurd fascination mattered one bit. Sin had no intention of allowing himself to be distracted by a pair of wide brown eyes. He had other, much more crucial business to transact with Sophie B. Jones.

The fluorescents overhead dimmed. Sin heard the rolling click of a projector starting up. He shifted in his seat again, trying to get reasonably comfortable, as the show began.

When intermission came, Sophie set her ancient projector to rewind the first reel. Then she climbed down the ladder to handle the concession stand.

Though Sophie had two full-time employees and a part-time maid to help her at the Mountain Star Resort, she ran the theater herself. Her guests—both the ones who took rooms in the main house and the folks who drove in from town just to see the show—loved it that way. They bought their tickets from her, she served them their refreshments, and before they saw the show, they got to hear her opinion of it.

That night the dark stranger bought a bowl of popcorn. Myra Bailey, the Mountain Star's cook, popped the corn up fresh before the show. Sophie served it in plastic bowls.

The stranger also bought a bottle of spring water.

"That's three, four, five—and five makes ten." Sophie counted change into that elegant hand. She made the mistake of glancing up, of meeting those deep dark eyes. Instantly all rational thought sailed right out of her mind. She could only stare. They just didn't make men like this anymore—if they ever really had.

He tucked the change into a pocket, his mouth barely lifting at the corner the way it had earlier, in the slightest insinuation of a smile. "I suppose you're going to want this bowl back."

She watched his lips move, and wondered vaguely what he was talking about. He prompted in a teasing whisper, "The bowl—do you want it back?"

She had to cough to make her throat open enough for words to come out. "Oh, yes. The bowl. Yes, I would. Like it back. It's recyclable. I wash them and use them all over again."

He waited, not smiling, just looking, a look that made her feel warm and weak and positively wonderful. She had no idea what he was waiting for, but it didn't seem to matter much.

Then he asked, "Where should I put it?"

She gestured way too wildly, almost whacking him one on his sculpted jaw. "Over there. On that little table by the double doors…"

He nodded. "Good enough." And then he smiled. Really smiled.

It was nine-fifteen at night and outside an August moon was shining down, but to Sophie the sun came up at that moment. Even when he turned, carrying his popcorn and water, and headed for the curtains that separated her concession area from the rest of the barn, she still felt as if she'd been blinded by the bright light of a new day.

It was ludicrous. And she knew it. Hopeless romantic or not, she had to get a grip here.

"How about a pear nectar?" the next fellow in line asked.

Sophie gave him a brisk, very professional smile. "Pear nectar it is."

Through the final reel, as Randi Wilding relentlessly hunted down and disposed of all the rustlers who'd dared to do their dirty work on her ranch, Sophie B. Jones gave herself a good talking-to.

Life, after all, was not a movie. In real life, handing a man his change should not be a transcendent experience. And it *hadn't* been a transcendent experience— except in her own suddenly hyperactive imagination, which she was squelching as of now.

By the time the final credits rolled, Sophie felt she had herself under reasonable control. She climbed down the ladder from the booth-hayloft, pulled back the curtains that masked her concession stand and opened the big barn doors wide.

Then, by the light of that almost full August moon, with another of her cats in her arms, she stood in the open doors and said goodbye to all of her guests personally, just as she always did.

Among those guests was Oggie Jones. At least once a month, he drove down from the tiny nearby town of North Magdalene for an evening at the movies.

"Quite a shoot-'em-up tonight, gal," Oggie declared when his turn came to say goodbye.

Sophie let the cat slide to the ground and held out her arms. The old sweetheart allowed her to hug him. He smelled of those awful cigars he was always smoking, but Sophie didn't really mind. She simply adored him. The first time he'd come to the Mountain Star, he'd told her to call him Uncle Oggie. And she had from then on, because it seemed so natural. Three years ago, he'd invited her to North Magdalene, a half hour's drive from the Mountain Star, northeast on old Highway Forty-Nine. She'd met his whole family, his four sons and his daughter, their spouses and their children. They'd welcomed her as if she were one of them. Since then, she'd returned to visit often.

She wasn't sure what it was about Oggie, but whenever she saw him, she always experienced the loveliest rising of affection in her heart—as if he really *were* her uncle, instead of just a sweet old character who shared her last name and her fondness for offbeat movies.

"Oh, Uncle Oggie, I hope you enjoyed yourself."

"I always enjoy myself. It's the only way to live." He leaned in closer, lowered his raspy voice and wiggled his grizzled eyebrows in the direction of Tall, Dark and Dangerous—who just happened to be standing near the concession counter showing no inclination to leave. "Someone's watching you."

Sophie shrugged—casually she hoped. "I haven't a clue why."

Oggie's small wise eyes seemed to bore holes right through her. Then he grinned. "Somethin' tells me that you ain't gonna be clueless for long."

And Oggie was right. After all the other guests had gone, Sophie's brooding stranger remained—which, Sophie told herself, didn't matter one bit.

She had work to do. Turning to the small table in the corner, she scooped up two stacks of used popcorn bowls. Then she started toward the man at the counter, who just kept on leaning there, watching her approach.

When she got about a foot from him, she paused.

"Show's over." She tried to sound breezy and unconcerned.

"I know." He didn't move. He looked completely relaxed, as if he hung around after the show all the time—waiting for her.

"Everyone's gone," she said, trying again. "Except you."

"I noticed."

She decided she was going to have to be more direct. "Now *you* have to go—and I have to clean up."

He only went on looking at her, an assessing kind of look, a look that made her skin feel warm and her heart beat way too fast.

She told her heart to settle down—and held out the used popcorn bowls. "Well, fine. If you're going to hang around, you might as well make yourself useful."

He gave her another of those almost smiles of his. Then he shrugged and accepted the bowls.

She pointed at the curtain behind the counter. "Take those right through there."

Her stranger was standing by the double metal sink, still holding his share of the bowls, when she joined him in the small alcove behind the curtain.

"Just drop them in the sink."

He did as she instructed, then stood out of the way as she piled the rest of the bowls on top, squirted in a stream of dish soap and started the water running. With a swiftness born of long practice, she began washing bowls and dropping them into the empty half of the sink.

Her stranger caught on fast. He flipped the faucet to the right, turned on the water and reached for a soapy bowl. When he had it rinsed, he held it up and quirked an eyebrow.

"Just set them right there. They'll dry by themselves."

He put the bowl on the grooved steel drainboard and picked up the next one, and then the next. From the corner of her eye, she could see those beautiful hands, working as efficiently as her own. *The Prince of Darkness does the dishes,* she thought, and had to stifle a burst of foolish laughter. His watch winked at her, platinum and gold, a watch that must have cost more than the Dodge Caravan she was still making payments on.

A few minutes later, Sophie dried her hands and then passed him the towel.

"What else?" He hung the towel back on its peg.

"Sweeping the aisles and taking out the trash."

"Hand me the broom."

She leaned back against the sink and slid him a sideways glance, "You really would, wouldn't you?"

"Sweep the floor? Why not?" He waited. When she didn't move, he added, "But I'll need a broom to do it."

She shuffled her feet and crossed her arms. "Well, I guess I just can't."

"Can't what?"

"Ask a total stranger to do my scut work."

He looked amused. "You didn't ask, I volunteered."

"No. I handed you those bowls. I told you to make yourself useful."

He laughed. It was a deep, very masculine sound. It sent lovely warm shivers racing right beneath the surface of her skin.

She said, "Look. Never mind. I can do it in the morning."

He shrugged, leaned on the other side of the sink and crossed his arms over his chest in a mirror of her own pose.

She looked down at her sandaled feet. When she dared to glance his way again, those dark eyes were waiting for her.

She had to know. "All right. Who *are* you?"

He answered without hesitation. "My name is Sinclair. Sinclair Riker."

It took Sophie a minute to believe what she'd heard. Then she barely managed to stifle a gasp.

The man beside her chuckled. "From the look on your face, I'd say the locals have been filling your ears with old gossip."

Sophie struggled to compose herself. "I...of course, I've heard of you—that is, if you're the same Sinclair Riker whose family once owned this ranch."

"That's me."

Sophie looked down at her sandals again. The old story was such a sad one. And from the way she'd heard it, he had been a vulnerable child of six when the grim events took place.

Not sure if he'd welcome a direct mention of the tragedy, Sophie ventured, "I think I heard that your mother took you away from here—to Southern California, wasn't it?"

"That's right, but my mother's been dead for a few years now."

Sophie murmured an expression of sympathy.

He shrugged. "It was all a long time ago."

What did he mean by that? A long time since his mother had died? A long time since his father had lost the ranch—and then hung himself in despair? His eyes told her nothing, though she wanted to know everything.

He turned away and stared off toward the curtain that led back to the main part of the barn.

Sophie reminded herself—again—that they'd only just met. She had no right at all to expect him to tell her things he probably didn't even like thinking about.

She asked carefully, "Are you…all right?"

He faced her again. His eyes had a strange, hot light in them.

Sophie thought she understood what he felt. "You've wondered about your family home, haven't you? You wanted to come and see for yourself what happened to it."

He didn't answer, only went on staring at her with those burning dark eyes.

She began to feel uncomfortable. "What is it? Have I got it all wrong?"

He shook his head. "No, not at all. The truth is, you've figured me out."

It was a lie.

Sin Riker knew exactly what had happened to his family home.

He owned it. The sale had been finalized two weeks before.

And now, he intended to claim what was his, to buy out this innocent and eliminate the peculiar enterprise she called the Mountain Star.

Chapter 2

Sin stared into those gorgeous brown eyes—eyes utterly lacking in guile. Eyes that said she simply wanted to know about him.

What the hell was it about her?

She wasn't his type at all.

He found himself thinking of Willa, with her black hair like a swatch of silk and her brittle, knowing laugh. Willa Tweed was his kind of woman: clever, ambitious—and sexy as hell. A talented interior designer, Willa had handled the decorating of several office buildings for him. She'd kept his interest for over a year, both in and out of bed. She'd seemed the perfect match for him, so he had asked her to marry him.

And yet, when she'd called the whole thing off, he hadn't found it difficult at all to let her go. Which, he supposed, was just more proof of his total lack of character.

As if he needed more proof.

The Jones woman's generous mouth bloomed in an artless smile. "I understand completely," she assured him. "I love this place. If I ever had to leave it, I know I'd be drawn back again—just to see it, to know that it's still here."

Watching her smile, listening to her sympathize when no sympathy was called for, Sin knew he should call a halt right then. She betrayed herself so easily. Those eyes of hers didn't know how to lie. And she was warming to him, starting to *like* him. She had a sunny, trusting nature. In no time at all, she would be telling him all about herself—all the facts of her life that he already knew.

There was no point at all in indulging in this flirtation with her.

Except that he couldn't seem to stop himself.

"Hello, are you in there?" Sophie teased. To her, it seemed as if Sinclair had been standing there, regarding her intently, saying nothing, for about half a century.

He gave her a rueful smile. "I'm here, all right."

"Good."

They shared a warm glance, standing there side by side against the steel sink. Sophie recalled how she'd lectured herself about him, up in the hayloft during the second reel.

But now that all seemed so silly. She wanted to get to know him, and she could think of no reason why she shouldn't.

Especially now that she knew his name.

Sinclair Riker. She still couldn't quite believe it.

Since the first time she'd heard the sad story of the Rikers, Sophie had wondered about them, *felt* for them really, to have owned this beautiful piece of land and then to have lost it. For the boy, Sinclair, her sympathy had gone even deeper. He'd been so young to lose so much. Her heart went out to him.

"Your name is Sophie—isn't it?" His tone chided, but very gently.

And Sophie felt a little ashamed. Here she'd been so suspicious of him, and yet she was the one who hadn't even provided her name. "Yes. Sophie. Sophie B. Jones. Most folks just call me Sophie B."

"*B* for?"

"Bernadette."

He made a low noise in his throat. "Don't tell me. It was your grandmother's name, right?"

She shook her head. "Why would you think that?"

"Because it was *my* grandmother's name."

"You're kidding."

"No." His gaze swept over her from head to toe. "So if it wasn't your grandmother's name, then whose?"

"My mother chose it. From an old movie, *The Song of Bernadette,* starring Jennifer Jones. Ever heard of it?"

He shook his head.

"Bernadette was a nun, I believe. In the movie."

"A nun," he murmured. "I should have known."

For that, she made a face at him. "I remind you of a nun?"

"Did I say that?"

"You didn't have to."

He leaned her way then, and lowered his voice. "I have to admit, I asked around a little."

She wasn't surprised. "About the ranch?"

He nodded. "Everyone I talked to seemed to know all about Ms. Sophie B. Jones and the Mountain Star Resort."

She wrinkled up her nose. "I hope they only said nice things."

"Only terrific things." He reached out and took her hand. His touch sent tiny, lovely tingles all through her. With great care, he wrapped her fingers in the crook of his arm. It felt absolutely wonderful to have him do that—as well as absolutely right. "Come on. Show me what you've done with my father's ranch."

Beyond the barn doors, the August moon shone down through the pines. A gentle breeze stirred the branches, creating haunting plays of shadow and silvery light. Somewhere off by the small creek that wound over the property, they could hear the night songs of crickets and frogs.

"It *is* a beautiful place," Sinclair said.

In lieu of a reply, Sophie squeezed his arm, then suggested, "How about the stables first?"

Before he could answer, two figures materialized out of the shadows not far from the barn doors.

"Sophie B.," a male voice said.

Sophie felt Sinclair's lean arm stiffen under her hand. She gave that arm another squeeze. "It's all right. These are friends."

The two came into the light: a man and a woman—well, a boy and a girl, really. Neither could have been much out of their teens. Sophie felt pretty sure of their names. "Hello, Ben. And Melody." Each carried a bedroll and a backpack. Even in the kind light of the moon, their jeans and T-shirts looked worn.

Melody laughed. "We scared you, huh?"

"Never," Sophie replied.

"We meant to get here for the show, but we were too late."

More likely, they didn't have the money for the tickets. Sophie would have let them in anyway, but they were proud kids, kids who didn't like taking charity—especially not for non-necessities like movies.

Sophie shrugged. "Maybe next time."

"Yeah. Next time. Cool."

Sophie knew what they wanted. "Campground's open, as far as I'm concerned."

Ben looked relieved. "Thanks. We're really beat. Come on, Mel."

They hoisted their packs and started off in the opposite direction from the main house. Sophie called after them. "Stop in and say hi to Myra tomorrow, why don't you?"

Melody called back, "Thanks, Sophie B. You're the best."

Sinclair spoke. "The 'campground' is open?" His tone seemed to mock her.

Sophie turned to look at him. But the moon was behind him. His face lay in shadow. She couldn't see his expression. "I call it a campground," she said, "but it's really just a nice, grassy spot with trees all around. On a mild night like this one, it's a great place to spread a sleeping bag." She pointed. "It's just over that rise there."

"Those two have nowhere else to go, is that it?" There was a definite chill in his voice, she was sure of that now.

She answered gently. "I don't know if they have anywhere else to go. All I know is that they need a place to stay for tonight and I can provide that easily."

"If you let people move in on you, you're just asking for trouble."

She didn't believe that and she never would. "They'll be on their way in the morning."

"How can you be sure?"

"It always works out that way. The street people who come here know how to behave."

"You've been lucky."

"I suppose I have," she admitted. "But it's not only that."

"Oh, no? What else, then?"

She shot him a grin. "I have to tell you, I never let skeptics like you get to me."

"All right, then." His voice had changed again, lost its cold edge. "Why won't you share your secret—if it's more than plain luck?"

"Because you'll only laugh if I tell you."

"No." He put his hand over hers. "I won't laugh. I swear."

His touch sent those shivers zinging through her all over again. She couldn't help relenting. "All right. In my experience, people tend to fulfill my expectations of them. So I always make it a point to keep my expectations good and high."

He said nothing for a moment. Then he let out a breath. "As I said, you've been lucky."

"Call it luck if you want to. But it works for me." She tugged on his arm. "Now, come on. The stables are waiting."

They went down a slate path, beneath the leafy shelter of a double row of maples, until they came to a rambling woodsided building from which a series of linked corrals branched off. Inside the stables, Sophie turned on the lights and they walked between the rows of stalls.

Sophie said, "I know your father used to raise horses here. Morgans, mostly, weren't they?"

"Yes. We lost them all, though. They took them away when they kicked us out of the house."

Another wave of sympathy washed through her. How could he have borne all those losses at such a young age? "It must have been awful for you."

He studied her face for a moment. "As I said…"

"I know. It was a long time ago."

Sophie paused to stroke the forehead of a friendly roan gelding and explained that none of the horses belonged to the Mountain Star. "We run a boarding service for people who don't have the space to keep their own horses. Some of the owners allow guests at the main house to ride their animals, under certain conditions—and for a fee, of course."

"Certain conditions?"

"Caleb Taggart, who runs the stables for me, has to check them out first, see if they know how to ride and how to treat a horse."

Right then, Caleb, who was six foot five and broad as an oak, appeared from the apartment he'd fixed up for himself off the tack room. He loomed huge and imposing before them. "Everything okay, Sophie B.?" He looked at her guest with stolid wariness.

"Everything is fine." She performed the introductions and the two men shook hands.

"Caleb helps me keep the grounds in order, as well as running the stables," she explained a few minutes later, when they were on their way to the main house. "He's a genius with horses."

"A *large* genius," Sin added. "And he seems very protective of you."

"He is." She grinned. "Both large *and* protective. He's worked for me from the beginning, which was five years ago."

They stopped at the edge of the wide, sloping lawn in front of the main house. Sophie told him more about the Mountain Star. "I have a fifteen-year lease on five acres—the crucial five acres we're standing on, which includes the main house, the barn, the stables and corrals, and the guest house, too, where I live. The local teachers' association owns it all—or at least they did."

His shadowy gaze was on her. "They *did?* Past tense?"

Something in his tone bothered her, though she couldn't have said what, and a small tremor of alarm skittered through her—a sudden sense that all was not as it should be.

But then she told herself not to overreact. She felt apprehensive about this particular subject, that was all. It had nothing to do with Sinclair.

She'd received the notice from the San Francisco bank just a week before, and since then she'd been trying not to stew over what it might mean to the Mountain Star. She'd asked around, but the sale had been accomplished through intermediaries, and no one seemed to know much about the new owner.

She explained, "Some corporation owns the ranch now. In San Francisco, I think. I got a letter about it just last week. It said to send the lease payments to a

Bay Area bank, and make the checks out to something called Inkerris, Incorporated."

"*Inkerris,* Incorporated?"

"Yes. Have you heard of it?"

He shrugged, which she took to mean "no."

She sighed. "I have to admit, I wasn't surprised to hear about a new owner."

"Why not?"

"The teachers' association has been wanting to sell for a long time. They bought the ranch because they had a plan to build tract homes here. But somehow the plan never got off the ground. That's when I came in. They wanted some kind of return on their investment. I made them an offer."

Two serpentine boulders flanked the base of the walk that led up to the main house. Sophie perched on one, smoothed her skirt and wrapped her hands around her knees. "It's worked out great for me. I have the run of the rest of the place—all nine hundred and ninety-five acres. A lot of the guests like to hike. And the folks who board their horses with us appreciate the convenience of being able to just come in, saddle up and ride for miles without seeing any houses or highways."

Sinclair stood over her, his hands in his pockets. "It does sound like a good deal for you."

"It has been. Too bad the teachers' association didn't feel the same way."

"You couldn't expect them to hold on to a losing investment forever."

"Of course not." She looked up at him, and they shared a smile. "I only *wished* that they would."

In a sleek, easy motion, he dropped to a crouch before her, so he was the one looking up. "You love it here, don't you?"

She nodded, thinking again how unbelievably good-looking he was, a dark angel, so lean and fine. "I've been fortunate," she said, "to have all this, though I know it isn't really mine. I would have bought it myself—if I could have afforded it. But I'm never likely to get that kind of money together." She smoothed her skirt again. "Oh, well. Maybe in ten years, when my lease is up, whatever corporation owns it then will let me renew."

Thinking about the tenuous nature of her hold on the Mountain Star always bothered Sophie. And lately, since the letter from the San Francisco bank, it disturbed her more than ever.

She looked off, beyond Sinclair's shoulder. In the center of the lawn, she could see the fountain. Caleb had put in a good deal of work on that fountain, cleaning out rusted pipes so it would work again. At its center stood a statue of a little girl, holding out her skirt to capture the shimmering streams of water as they cascaded down. The little girl was laughing—even by moonlight, her delight came across. Sophie loved that statue, and the sight of it cheered her.

Pointless to worry, needless to fret, her aunt Sophie always used to say....

"Hey." The man before her reached out. His fingers whispered along the line of her cheek. She forgot her worries—she even forgot the laughing little girl—as she met his eyes again.

Incredible, she thought, how good it felt, to have him touch her. As if it were the most natural thing in the world.

So strange. She felt so close to him. As if they'd known each other forever, as if they had a history of shared experience, as if she'd long ago grown accustomed to his touch.

Accustomed, but never weary of it.

Oh, no. She could never grow weary of his touch. Featherlight, it was. And at the same time, like a brand. Burning...

Gentle as a breath, he touched her hair. Right then, his eyes seemed full of timeless mystery as the Sierra night around them. "Do you really think that's likely?"

What were they talking about? She couldn't for the life of her remember. "Do I think what's likely?"

"That you'll convince some faceless corporation to renew your lease when your time here runs out?"

She knew it wasn't. Only a combination of good fortune and good timing had made the Mountain Star a reality. She shook her head. "But I have what I want now. And as for the future—a girl can dream, can't she?"

"Absolutely." Once more, his fingers touched her cheek. And then they fell away. He rose above her again, with the same seamless ease of movement as before. She felt regret, as if some precious impossible intimacy had been lost.

And then she stood as well, smoothing the back of her skirt as she did. "Shall we go in?"

He frowned.

She knew immediately what that frown meant: he didn't want to go in.

And no wonder. There were probably hard memories for him in that house. The old story went that the boy, Sinclair, had been the one who found his father's body—in one of the two attic rooms, dangling from a rafter beam.

"Would you rather just skip the house?" she suggested gingerly.

"Of course not." His voice had turned cold as a night in midwinter. "Let's go." He held out his arm for her again. After a moment's hesitation, she took it. They started up the walk, past the bubbling fountain with its laughing little girl, toward the house where the man beside her had spent the first six years of his life.

Riker Cottage, as the house had always been called, was a steep-roofed structure built of natural stone, with redbrick trim in the dormers and around the window casements. Sinclair said nothing as they went under the brick-lined arch that framed the front door.

Sophie had learned already that he was a man prone to silences. But his silence now had a strange edge to it, an edge she didn't like at all. She almost suggested for the second time that they not go in. But she knew from his response a moment ago that it would do no good.

There was nothing else for it. She reached for the iron latch on the heavy oak door.

The door opened on a large central foyer. From there, a switch-back staircase led up to the guest rooms. Twin parlors branched off to either side.

Sophie showed Sinclair the ground floor first. In the east parlor, they found two guests playing chess. Sinclair nodded when she introduced him to the chess players—a brief, aloof nod. Her guests seemed to take no offense to his coldness. They bent over their game again right away. But it did bother Sophie—because she sensed his chilly manner was only a cover-up for distress.

He did not want to be here, she knew it. She could feel it in her bones. He said nothing when she showed him the library, where his father's books still stood in the tall, glass-fronted cases.

In an effort to fill the ominous silence that seemed to emanate from him, Sophie talked about the small changes she'd made. "I couldn't bear to tear out the wainscotting," she said of the shoulder-high paneling that lined the walls of most of the rooms. "But the old wallpaper had to go. Cabbage roses on a black background, if you remember. It was just way too dark. I chose only light colors for the ceilings and upper walls. I think it helps."

"Yes," he said flatly. "It helps."

In the kitchen, he seemed to relax a little—enough to point out deficiencies of which she was already fully aware. "How old is that stove?"

"Too old," she confessed. "Myra, the cook, is always saying rude things about it."

"Myra is right." He looked in the too-small refrigerator and ran a hand over the chipped counter tiles. "You could use a serious upgrade here."

"Tell me about it."

"So why haven't you done something?"

She had. She'd gotten some estimates. Even without the chef-style range and refrigerator Myra wanted, a remodel of the kitchen would cost at least fifteen thousand dollars. It was fifteen thousand more than she had.

But that wasn't his problem, so she only said, "I'll get around to it. Eventually."

He looked at her then, one of those looks she couldn't read at all. "You're sure about that?"

"I like to think positive."

"I noticed." It sounded like a criticism, but she let it pass.

She led him up the narrow, dark back stairs next. "I can't show you much of the other two floors," she explained as they climbed. "This is my peak season and all of the rooms are occupied. But we can at least take a quick look around."

He followed behind her, saying nothing. She didn't like his silence. It spoke to her of a deep unease. He did not want to be here, and yet he was forcing himself to stay, to carry on with this unnecessary tour.

Finally she couldn't stand it. She stopped midway and turned to him in the confined space.

"Are you sure you wouldn't rather forget about this?"

He just looked at her, his face a blank.

"Sinclair? Can you hear me?"

Sin did hear. And he wanted to reply. He wanted to tell her that he was fine, to order her to get going, get it over with, show him the rest of the damn place and be done with it.

But somehow, he couldn't make any words come out. Too many memories swirled around him: smells and sights and sounds. Fleeting impressions of the life he'd once lived here.

The smell of his mother's cinnamon cookies baking. Even in their last days here, when money got so tight they rarely had meat, she still baked those cookies. For him. Because he loved them.

Cinnamon cookies. And roses.

His mother had loved roses. She would pick them

from the poorly tended garden, where they grew in a wild tangle, and put them in vases all over the house.

And stories.

His father used to tell him stories. About Great-grandfather Riker, who had labored in the gold mines, deep in the earth, alongside the Cornishmen who came all the way from England to work the mother lode. Great-Grandfather Riker had died in a cave-in, but not before he'd borne a son, Sinclair—for whom Sin had later been named. The first Sinclair Riker had grown up smart and lucky and used every penny he could scrape together to buy land, to create the Riker Ranch.

Which Anthony had lost barely a decade after the first Sinclair's death.

Yes, his father's voice. He could hear it now. Telling the old stories.

And his father's laughter, deep and rich, he could hear that, as well.

And his mother, he could hear her, too, singing to him.

She used to sing all the time, when he was little. She would move through the dark rooms of the cottage, filling them with roses, making them seem light with her smiles and her songs. But then had come the bad day, the day they had to leave their home forever, the day when he stumbled down from the attic, unable to speak.

His mother had been standing at the window in the west parlor, staring out at the sunshine and the overgrown lawn. He had run to her, buried his face against her skirt.

Her soft arms went around him. She knelt down. "Sinclair. Darling. What's happened? You look as if you've seen a ghost." He backed from her embrace, grabbed for her pretty white hand. Ridiculous squawking noises were coming from his mouth.

"Sweetheart, slow down. What is it? What's wrong?"

He gave up on trying to talk and started yanking on her hand.

"All right, I'm coming. I'm coming. Settle down."

He ran then, through the hall to the kitchen, up the back stairs—these very stairs he stood on now—pulling his mother along behind, all the way, up and up, to what used to be the maid's room, long ago when they could afford a maid.

When she saw it, she screamed. A terrible, never-ending scream of despair.

And after that day, she never sang again.

A cool hand touched his face. "Sinclair?"

He realized he was clammy under the arms and across his chest. He lifted a hand to swipe at his brow. It came away dripping with his own sweat.

"Let's go outside," the Jones woman said. She stood so close to him. God, the scent of her. Like sunshine and flowers, like something so clean and fresh. The reality of her, the *life* in her, seemed to reach out to him....

He put out both hands and took her around the waist. She gasped. He felt her stiffen under his touch, but he couldn't help himself. He yanked her tight against him and buried his face in the thick, sweet tangle of her hair.

Chapter 3

Sophie's first instinct was to push him away.

Her second was to gather him close.

She never acted on the first. It passed as swiftly as her own sharply indrawn gasp of dismay. She was already wrapping her arms around him as they fell together against the wall of the stairwell. His lean body shook under her hands.

"It's okay," she murmured, so low the words were barely audible, even to herself. "Shh. It's all right."

He held on, tight enough to squeeze the breath from her lungs. His heart beat fast and furious, in time with her own. His face pressed first against her hair, then lower, into the curve of her neck. She felt his mouth on her skin in a caress that wasn't so much a kiss as a hungry demand for shelter from the chaos inside his own mind and heart.

He needed to touch someone. He needed someone to hold him.

She understood that. She let him touch. And she held him tight, his body branding all along hers, hot and needful, pleading without words.

How long they stood like that, pressed against the wall, she couldn't have said. Gradually, though, his heartbeat calmed and his breathing slowed. His hard grip loosened. She found she could breathe again.

He lifted a hand and stroked her hair. She felt his lips move at her neck in a tender kiss, sweet with gratitude.

And then at last he pulled away, grasping her shoulders and stepping back in the cramped space. His baffled gaze found hers. "God. I'm sorry." A dark curse escaped him. "I don't know what—"

She reached across the distance he'd made, put a finger on his mouth. It felt so soft. Tender. Bruised. "Let's just go. Outside."

He stared at her for an endless moment—and then he captured her hand. "Yes. Now."

He turned and headed down the stairs, into the kitchen, through the pantry, and out the door there— fleeing that house, and pulling her after him.

They ran across the rear lawn and into the grove of oaks that grew just beyond the edge of the grass. There, at last, he stopped. He threw himself back against one thick twisted trunk. He still held her hand. He gave a tug.

She fell against him. And she dared to laugh, a nervous sound, breathless and vivid at the same time. "Sinclair?"

He took her face in his hands and tipped it up so the

dappling of moonlight through the branches showed her to him.

He felt so angry suddenly. Angry, exposed—and aroused, as well.

He pressed himself against her, wanting her to feel his desire—half hoping she would jerk away in outrage, close herself off from him—and thus allow him to close himself off from her.

But she didn't jerk away. Her body seemed to melt into his.

"I don't know you," he said, each word careful, determined.

Her soft, full mouth invited him. She said his name again—his grandfather's name, the name she knew him by. "Sinclair..."

"I don't know you." He said it through clenched teeth that time.

She smiled, the softest, most beautiful smile. "You know me."

"No..."

"Yes."

He lowered his mouth to hers, to stop her from saying that—and discovered his error immediately. Her mouth was as soft as it looked. And as incredibly sweet. He moaned, the sound echoing inside his own head, as he plunged his tongue into that sweetness.

He was out of control, gone. Finished. Not himself. Not himself at all.

He took her by the arms, hard—and pushed her away. She let out one soft, bewildered cry—and then she just looked at him through those eyes that reproached him at the same time as they seemed to say that they understood.

She flinched. He realized he was holding her arms too tightly, hurting her. He let go. She stumbled a little, righted herself, and then gave him more distance, stepping backward until she could lean against another tree, not far from him.

For a time, all he knew were her eyes through the night—watching. Waiting. And the night sounds—crickets and plaintive birdsongs, some small creature moving about, rustling in the dried late-summer grass nearby.

Slowly he came back to himself. More or less. "I'm sorry," he told her again, knowing as the pitiful words passed his lips that they weren't nearly enough. "I don't know what happened in there. Or just now, either."

She waved away his apologies. "It doesn't matter."

"Damn it, it does matter." The words came out low, but hard with leashed fury.

She only leaned against that tree, looking at him. He wanted to cover the short distance between them, grab her again, and shake her until she admitted what a bastard he was. But somehow he contained himself.

She just went on staring, those wide eyes so sweet, full of understanding and patience.

"Don't," he commanded.

She winced at his harshness. "Don't what?"

"Don't look at me like that."

And she immediately turned her head and looked away.

There was silence, but for the sounds of the night.

After a few moments, she turned her face to him again. "Would you like to see my favorite spot?"

Impossible though it was, he knew immediately the spot she meant: a certain place along the nearby creek.

Past the oak grove, around the bend—a tiny grotto, green and magical, with willows growing all around and yellow-green moss like a blanket on the ground. He had found the place himself as a child. And loved it. And thought of it as his.

Anger arrowed through him again. Who the hell was she to choose his spot as hers?

"Sinclair." Her knowing eyes seemed to see right through him. "It's all right. All of it. Really."

He shook his head and locked away from her, because it wasn't all right. It was crazy. This whole thing—the wide-eyed woman and the August night, what had happened in that damn house and what was happening inside him now. Never in a million years would he have imagined that tonight would go like this.

No. Tonight was supposed to have been nothing more than a scouting expedition, a chance to check out his adversary in person before she even knew that he planned to reclaim what was his at any cost.

Sin slumped against the oak tree. Short seconds ago, he had been furious. Now his fury had fizzled to nothing. In its place remained a raw awareness of his own idiocy.

He'd grabbed the woman, in the house and here— and forced himself on her, completely out of nowhere. And what point could there possibly be in becoming irate because she favored the same section of creek he had liked as a child? It was ridiculous.

Ten to one, he'd learn it wasn't the same spot he remembered anyway. After all, decades had passed. The creekbed would have shifted in high-water years. The place he remembered wouldn't even exist anymore.

"Please." She came away from her tree trunk and

took two hesitant steps toward him. "Come with me." She extended her hand.

He took it. He *was* an idiot. No doubt about it. A shiver went through him—from the sudden breeze that had come up, he told himself, a breeze that chilled him as it dried the sweat of his preposterous anguish from his skin.

"This way." She was already turning toward the creek.

He stumbled along behind her, dazed—spellbound in spite of himself. Out of the oak grove and into an open field of tall, dry grass that made her calf-length skirt whisper sweetly as she ran. He looked up. A million stars winked back at him, jewels of light strewn across a midnight ground of sky.

As a child, he had run like this. Under this same Sierra sky in high summer, with the moon benign and shining white, smiling down on him.

The field sloped away and they came to the creek. It sparkled in the moonlight, its dark surface glistening as it fled over the rocky bed beneath.

She turned to him, granted him one brief, conspiratorial glance. "Not far now." And then she was off again, along the bank, pulling him after.

Within moments, they came to the spot. And it was the same. Exactly the same as he remembered it.

She pulled him up onto the big black rock at the very edge of the stream, the rock he used to sit on for hours as little boy. "Here," she said. "Right here. Sit down." He obeyed her command, dropping down beside her as she gathered her legs up, smoothed her skirt and wrapped her slender arms around her knees.

They sat there saying nothing for the longest time,

close enough that their shoulders brushed whenever either of them shifted so much as an inch. As the silent moments passed, Sin found that an answering stillness was growing inside him. He welcomed that stillness. After what had happened in the house and in the oak grove, that stillness felt cool and clean as the creek water sliding past at their feet.

Finally she said softly, "This spot appeared two years ago."

He looked at her, wondering what exactly she meant.

She told him. "We had a wet winter. The creek changed course. In the spring, this beautiful little glen was here."

He almost said, *No, it was here before. Right here. When I was little.* But he held the words back. Clearly the spot he'd loved as a child had been washed out years ago. This one was a new one, in just about the same place. No big mystery. Just an eerie coincidence.

She nudged him lightly with her shoulder, then asked in a shy voice that thoroughly captivated him, "Do you like it?" He looked at her directly as he had not dared to do since he'd forced his kiss and the knowledge of his desire on her, back in the shadowy grove of oaks.

She asked again, "Do you like it?"

"Yes. I do. Very much."

She let out a breath, a sigh that seemed to come not only from her, but from all around them—from the whispering willows, the gleaming creek and the tall pines, as well. "I knew that you would. I'll bet when you were little, you had a spot of your own, along this creek." A lock of that honey-colored hair lay curled on her shoulder. He couldn't resist touching it, smoothing it into the mass of thick waves that flowed down her back.

"Sinclair?" she prompted, her eyes bright as twin Sierra stars.

"Hmm?"

"Did you have a spot you called your own along this creek?"

"I might have."

She faked an injured look. "You're not going to tell me."

He touched her face, rubbed his thumb across her full lower lip. "No. I'm not." His body stirred again as her smile bloomed under his caressing thumb.

"It's all right. Keep your secrets."

"Thank you. I will."

Beneath his brushing thumb, her mouth felt like some ripe, ready fruit. He went on stroking it, back and forth, images flashing through his mind—the two of them, moving, naked, on the soft blanket of moss nearby; a big bed, with both of them in it, her skin like cream against snowy sheets.

Her eyes went lazy—with a desire that answered his own. And she canted toward him, closer, in a clear invitation to a kiss.

Sin wanted that kiss, the way a starving man wants bread.

And because he wanted it so badly, he refused to take it.

Inside his veins the blood pounded in hard, heavy bursts. And still, he pulled his hand away and sat back a fraction.

She remained absolutely still for a moment. Then she made a little show of rearranging her skirts. He knew she was gathering herself back from the brink of the intimacy they hadn't quite shared.

He watched her compose herself, wondering why everything about her enchanted him, why he wanted to touch her so, when touching her should have been the last thing on his mind.

There *was* something about her. Something he couldn't turn away from, couldn't stop reaching toward—an innocence that beckoned. A goodness that lured.

Fool that he was, he did reach out again. He touched her white hem of cotton lace. "Your slip is showing."

She sat a little straighter. And then she stretched— an indolent movement that would have looked brazen on any woman but her.

Sin rubbed the soft, lacy fabric of her slip between his thumb and forefinger as she lifted her heavy hair with both hands and tipped her face toward the moon and the trees overhead. She smiled. Her throat gleamed, pale and perfect in the darkness, and her breasts pushed insolently against the supple fabric of her dress.

Watching her, Sin could feel his own natural restraint slipping inexorably away, like the water in the creek before them, so steadily and smoothly he could almost have told himself he didn't know that he would end up in her bed tonight.

But he did know. And in terms of his real goal, it was a mistake. In terms of his real goal, it would gain him nothing. Chances were, it would only make things all the messier later.

Sin Riker was a ruthless man. But even a ruthless man had his standards. It was one thing to check out his adversary, another altogether to climb into bed with her. For a man of his fastidious nature, having sex with people he intended to get rid of showed no discernment at all. It was simply a line he'd never crossed and never intended to cross.

But you will cross it now, a voice in his head taunted. *You will spend the night in her bed—and she will hate you later when she learns exactly what secrets you've kept from her tonight.*

He released her hem as she let her hair drop, the bronze mass cascading in a curling tangle down her back. "It's not a slip, it's a petticoat," she informed him. "And it's supposed to show."

"A petticoat." The old-fashioned word charmed him. "Yes."

"Women don't wear *petticoats* anymore."

"This woman does." As she spoke, she took his arm and laid it across her shoulders. She slid him a mischievous grin. "All right?"

"Fine with me."

She leaned closer to him, fitting herself against him as if she belonged there. It felt very good. Soothing. To have her body touching his from shoulder to hip.

They were quiet once more, until she let out a sigh, and he whispered, "What?"

"Nothing. Life." She found his free hand and twined her fingers with his. "And you. I feel so close to you. Is that crazy?"

"Definitely."

"I don't care."

"You should care."

Sophie registered the warning in his voice. She lifted her head from his shoulder and looked at him again.

Something had happened to her back in the house and then among the dark oaks. Some...*sureness* had come over her, that nothing that occurred between her and this man would ever be wrong. That a bond existed between them, never-ending and unbreakable: he who'd lost this place so young and she who was entrusted with the care of it now.

Yes, it was corny. And outrageously, impossibly romantic. And to Sophie B. Jones, that was just fine.

She lifted his hand and pressed it to her lips. "You feel it, too." He started to speak. She shook her head. "Don't."

"What?"

"Don't say you don't feel it. Don't tell a lie like that."

He said nothing. He was thinking of his other lies, though she couldn't know that.

She whispered, "And we *do* know each other." Now she guided their twined hands to her heart. "Here. Where it counts."

Sin could feel her heartbeat, feel the firm slope of her breast.

And her face was turned up to him, once more offering a kiss.

This time he couldn't resist. He moved closer. And so did she. Their lips touched so lightly.

It wasn't enough.

Not near enough.

He wanted more. He would *have* more.

With a low, hungry moan, Sin settled his mouth over hers.

Chapter 4

Warmth and life and breath made flesh, she melted into him. The scent of her surrounded him. Her soft lips gave beneath his, opening like some night-blooming flower to let him inside.

He took what she so freely offered, pressing her back against the dark rock they sat on, pulling her up even closer to him, so he could feel her slim body all along his as he plundered the sweetness beyond her parted lips.

But the rock was no good as a lovers' bed. Finally he had to end the kiss before they rolled off into the creek below. With a low groan of regret, he pulled away and looked down at her.

Her brown-and-gold hair spilled across the rough rock and her face, in the darkness, glowed like some rare pale flower. Her eyelids fluttered open and she stared back at him, giving him a mirror of his own yearning—as well as her absolute trust.

Trust he would ultimately demolish.

"I live in the guest house, did I tell you?"

He nodded.

"Come there with me now."

His body ached for the pleasure and release she would bring him. Yet, somewhere, far back in his mind, a stern voice commanded, *Stop now, walk away. Or give her the truth.*

"Sinclair. Come with me." She lifted a hand and laid it on the side of his face. He turned toward that hand. She sighed when he kissed the tender heart of her palm. "Come with me," she murmured again.

He opened his mouth, put his tongue out, tasted her flesh. She whispered his name on a moan.

He clasped her waist, and then higher, until he encompassed the soft globe of her breast.

"Now, Sinclair." She grasped his shoulder, the touch urgent and needful. "Let's go now."

He lowered his mouth to hers once more, stopping just short of the kiss they both craved.

"Sinclair." She used his name as a plea.

"Yes," he said against her parted lips. "Yes. Let's go. Now."

She led him along the creek again, and through the open field and the grove of oaks, then across the back lawn, through a rose arbor gate, to the small woodframe house a hundred yards from Riker Cottage.

He recalled that house vaguely. For a while, when he was very small, his grandmother Bernadette had lived there. It held only good memories for him. With no feel-

ings of uneasiness at all, he stepped over the threshold
into the small living room.

"I'll turn on some lights," she told him breathlessly.

She left him standing near the door as she went to
flick on a Tiffany-style standing lamp in a corner. The
warm light spread over the room, showing him fat,
comfortable chairs, a sofa upholstered with twining
vines and flowers, and tables that looked like antiques,
though none of them matched. Before the lace-curtained
front window stood a big Boston fern in a Chinese pot
painted with rearing dragons.

On the walls were a number of pictures she must
have picked up from estate sales or at flea markets,
charming old-fashioned country scenes and a series of
Victorian-looking prints. In one print, a turn-of-the-
century lady sat at a writing desk, staring off into the
middle distance as she composed her next line. In another, a man and a woman sat across from each other on
twin love seats, sharing a coy look. And in a third, three
golden-haired children picked flowers in a lush garden.

All the individual pieces were different than the ones
his grandmother had owned. But it still felt exactly the
same. Inviting. Comforting. Cozy. Warm.

"Hopelessly quaint, I know," Sophie said softly, still
standing there by that Tiffany lamp.

He let himself look at her again. "I like it." And he
did. Which was just more insanity. His house in the
Hollywood Hills was all clean lines, light woods and
floor-to-ceiling windows. Thoroughly modernist, with
no clutter at all. A monk's mansion, Willa had called
it. And maybe it was. As a grown man, there had been
no appeal for him in Victorian prints and overstuffed
furniture.

Until tonight…

"Well." Sophie brushed her hands nervously against the front of her skirt. "I'm glad. That you like it." Though a smile tilted the corners of her mouth, he could see the apprehension in her eyes.

He understood. Out there by the creek, under the spell of the night, making love with a stranger had seemed like just the right thing to do. But this wasn't a woman who gave her body to strangers. And now that they were actually here in her private space, her real nature had resurfaced. She couldn't keep the doubts at bay.

Which was good, Sin told himself. Looked at logically, it was the best thing that could have happened— so why did he feel this sharp pang of regret?

Hesitantly she moved toward him, stopping a few feet away, on the other side of that huge Boston fern. "I…my bedroom's that way." She gave a quick, awkward toss of one hand, toward the arch beyond her shoulder. He let his gaze follow the gesture, then looked at her once more.

She gulped. "Well. Shall we…?"

Slowly he shook his head.

Bewilderment clouded her beautiful eyes. "No?"

"Sophie. You're not ready for this." *And neither am I, for that matter.*

She took in a breath and let it out slowly. "Yes. I am. I…"

"Listen."

"What?"

"Just be a little practical. Think about safety. Think about…pregnancy."

Her face went red to the roots of her shining hair. "Pregnancy." She whispered the word.

Bluntness would be the kindest course. He took it. "Do you have contraception? Because I sure as hell don't."

"Oh." She gulped again. "I'm not… I didn't even think…"

"I know. Neither did I. Until right now."

She pressed her lips together, embarrassed, confused. She looked absolutely gorgeous to him in her indecision. He found he was becoming aroused all over again.

Best to get out. Now. "Look. It's been…beautiful." He allowed himself a grin. "And awful."

She actually smiled back. And then her eyes turned sad. "You're going."

"Yes."

"But…*where?*" Her honest face was so easy to read. She'd just realized she knew next to nothing about him. Nothing but his name, his distant past—the feel of his mouth on hers. "Um…where are you staying?"

He named his hotel in nearby Grass Valley.

"How…how long are you staying there?"

He shrugged. "I can't say for sure. I have some business to take care of. I'll be here till it's handled." *Which will be as soon as I can send you on your way.*

"I see." She dragged in another long breath and squared her slim shoulders. "Will you come back? Please? Tomorrow night. I'm free, same time as tonight, after the movie's over."

He nodded. He would come back, all right. And he would have himself thoroughly under control. He'd get things straight with her. Explain that he was her new landlord—and he wanted her out. He'd make her his offer. She would take it or not.

And that would be that. She would leave—or he would be forced to move to plan two.

Either way, this thing between them would be finished, which was good. It never should have gotten started in the first place.

"Around ten?" she asked so hopefully. "The show ends around ten."

His conscience, rusty and rarely used, prodded at him: Why put it off? Why not tell her right now?

He opened his mouth to do it. But all that came out was, "Fine. I'll see you at ten tomorrow night."

Sophie barely slept a wink that night. What had happened between herself and Sinclair almost didn't seem real, now he was gone and she lay all alone in her bed.

Really, she hardly knew a thing about him. He hadn't mentioned what he did for a living. Or how long he'd be staying in Grass Valley, or where he would go when he returned to wherever he now called home.

If he didn't come back tomorrow night as he'd promised, the only way she could find him would be to visit that hotel he'd mentioned. And if he'd checked out, she might never see him again.

But then, it was silly for her to think that way.

Of course, he'd come back. He'd said that he would. And tomorrow night, she vowed to herself, when they were alone again, she'd learn more about him.

She'd also make sure she was better prepared to go where her heart led her. True, she had a full day tomorrow. At this time of year, there was always more work to do than hours in the day. But inevitably, Myra would send her to pick up a few things. She could buy what she needed while she was out.

* * *

He didn't come to the movie.

Sophie sold the tickets from the small booth Caleb had made for her, right outside the barn doors. As each of her guests appeared out of the trees, coming from the small graveled area she'd designated as a parking lot, her heart rose—only to fall when she saw it wasn't him. By the time she'd closed the doors, shut the curtain from the entrance and concession area, and moved down in front to begin her introduction, she felt utterly bereft.

Which was so silly.

She'd told him to come *after* the movie—which he *had* seen just last night. There was no reason in the world for him to show up before ten.

Except that she *wanted* him to. And though she knew it was totally irrational, she kept feeling in her heart that he should know and respond to the longing she felt, that he should feel it, too, and be incapable of staying away.

Since he hadn't appeared before the show, she started hoping that he might come during intermission. She knew just how it should go: he would walk in, and she would hand him a bowl of popcorn and a bottle of spring water. She would look in his eyes and see a yearning so powerful—a longing every bit as overwhelming as her own.

"I saved a seat for you," she would say, her voice low and intimate, only for him.

He would give her one of those looks of his, a look that meant to be distant—yet couldn't help being tender. "Thanks for the popcorn," he would murmur teasingly.

"You can help me wash the bowl later."

He would chuckle and head for the seat she'd saved him in the fifth row.

Through the whole of intermission, she kept expecting to look up and find him there, waiting to be handed his water and popcorn. But it never happened because he didn't come.

The show ended at ten o'clock. When she pushed open the doors, she just knew he'd be waiting on the other side, with the pines and the moon, the night breeze and the stars.

He wasn't.

She forced goodbye smiles for her guests. By ten-fifteen they had all disappeared back through the trees toward the parking lot, except for the few who needed a place to spread their sleeping bags for the night. She sent them off to the campground.

And then, all alone, she trudged back inside.

He wasn't coming. She was certain of it now. Tomorrow, she'd have to reach some sort of decision. Should she risk making a complete fool of herself trying to track him down? Or just set her mind to forgetting him?

Overhead, in the rafters, that pigeon she could never quite shoo out of there set to cooing. Sophie thought she'd never heard such a sad, lonely sound.

She looked at the stacks of empty popcorn bowls and thought of how Sinclair should have been here, offering, as he had last night, to help with the cleaning up. She kept remembering the way it had been last night, the two of them, in the little space in back, leaning against the sink, flirting, getting to know each other a little.

She couldn't face those bowls right now. It was just too depressing.

She cleaned up behind the concession counter, then moved on to the rows of seats, gathering up the few empty drink containers that the occasional thoughtless guest inevitably dropped on the floor. She got the broom and swept up, and finally carried the trash out to the big industrial-size bin around back.

By then, it was nearly eleven. And the popcorn bowls were still waiting.

With a sigh, Sophie scooped up half of them and carried them through the curtain to the sink. She had squirted in the dish soap and started the water running when that low velvety voice spoke from behind her.

"Let me make myself useful."

A warm shiver passed through her and her heart rose up. Suddenly she felt light as a white cloud in a clear summer sky.

But she didn't turn. Oh, no. After what he'd put her through, he didn't deserve to know he had her full attention—not yet, anyway. He came up on her left side, carrying the rest of the bowls. She edged to the right. The bowls in his hands tumbled into the sink. She watched the soap bubbles rising up beneath the stream of water.

She started washing, still not looking at him. "You're late."

He moved around her, to the other side of the sink. "No, I'm not." Turning the faucet his way, he started to rinse.

"I said ten o'clock."

"But I've been here since before the show started."

She dared a quick glance at him. Tonight, he wore a blue shirt and dark slacks. And he was every bit as fine as she remembered. He stole her breath and made her heart do flip-flops. "Here? At the Mountain Star?"

He nodded. "Down by the creek." *Thinking of your eyes. Wanting only to see you.* Dreading *what I have to say to you.*

Sophie picked up another bowl, swirled it in the soap suds and passed it to him. She felt as if she might laugh out loud—or burst into tears. Yet she strove for lightness, and somehow found it. "Afraid to face me, huh?"

You don't know the half of it. "Could be." He rinsed the bowl, set it to dry. "Caleb finally found me there."

"By the creek, in *our* spot?"

He looked at her then, a look of heat and longing, a look that made a day of agonized waiting worth it, after all. He turned off the water. Without that soft, rushing sound, the small space seemed to echo.

Into that echo, he asked, "You think of it as *our* spot now?"

"I do."

He lifted his wet hand and put his finger beneath her chin. She felt that touch all the way down to the absolute center of her being.

"What…were you doing there?"

"Nothing. Just sitting." He tipped up her chin. "Eventually Caleb found me there. He wanted to know what I was up to. I told him I was only sitting. Enjoying the creek and the trees. He let out a grunt, as if he didn't believe a word I'd said. And then he walked off and left me alone."

"You said it yourself. He's protective of me."

Sinclair moved his hand upward, so he cradled the side of her face. Sophie felt all quivery and warm—full of hope. And delicious desire. She did what he had done the night before, turning her face just enough that she could touch the soft inner pad at the base of his thumb with her lips. Water still clung there. She put out her tongue and licked it away.

He said her name, low and rough. "Sophie." It sounded like a warning as well as a plea.

Though only a few of the bowls had been washed, she reached for a towel, dried her hands and passed the towel to him. He used it, then hung it back on its peg.

Before he could lower his hand, she caught it, cradled it, then smoothed the fingers open, so she could stroke his palm. "I thought you weren't coming. It was awful. Never do that to me. Please. Never again."

"Sophie…"

She looked up into his eyes.

He muttered roughly, "We can't…"

She did not waver. She kept looking right into his eyes. "Yes. We can. And we will."

"You don't know…" He let the words trail off.

"What?"

Now, he wouldn't meet her eyes.

She touched his jaw and guided his face around so he had to look at her again. "Tell me. You can say anything to me. Anything at all."

But he said nothing.

Somewhere nearby, just beyond the curtain to the concession area, that pigeon started cooing again. They both turned toward the sound, and then back to each other.

He said her name again, low and rough, the same as before, "Sophie."

She only said, "Yes."

And then he reached out.

She went into his arms, joyous, eager, offering up her mouth.

And he didn't refuse her. He didn't try to argue with her anymore.

He only put his lips on hers and wrapped his arms around her, pulling her close and hard against him.

Heat and need shot through her, swirled around, moved out to the surface of her skin and then flowed back in again. And he went on kissing her, endlessly, only stopping once—to lift his mouth and slant it the other way.

Finally, with a joyous, breathless laugh, she pulled away. He made a sound, a needful moan deep in his throat, and tried to pull her back.

She resisted, moving away another step. "Come on. Let's go."

"Go where?" he demanded hoarsely.

"The guest house."

He stared. He looked stricken. Almost guilty. So strange.

"Sinclair? What is it?"

And then he was reaching for her, yanking her close again, kissing her some more. She sighed in delicious surrender, wrapping her arms around him, letting him have what he demanded of her, pressing herself close.

That time, he was the one who broke the kiss. He tucked her head beneath his chin and held her so cherishingly, rocking from side to side a little, leaning back against the sink.

"You're too trusting," he whispered into her hair.

"No. This is right. You and me. This is…meant to be."

"Too damn trusting…" he muttered again.

She looked up, sought his eyes. "Is there someone else? Is that it?"

His brows drew together. "Someone else?"

"Another woman. A wife? A fiancée? A…live-in lover? Whatever."

He shook his head. "No one. Not anymore."

"Not…anymore?"

"There was someone," he admitted. "It didn't work out."

"What was her name?"

"Willa."

"Are you…still in love with her?"

"Love?" He was frowning.

"Yes. Love. Are you still in love with her?" Breath held, she waited for his answer, feared it wouldn't come.

But it did, at last.

"No. No, I'm not in love with her."

The surge of relief Sophie felt made her realize how afraid she'd been to ask those particular questions. "I'm so glad," she whispered. "So very, very glad."

He dragged in a breath. "Sophie—"

She didn't let him get any further. "I just want to *be* with you. Maybe it's not logical. Maybe it's not even wise. But it is right. I know it. It's the rightest thing in the world."

He only said her name again. She could see how much he wanted her, it was shining in those black eyes. So she lifted on tiptoe and pressed a quick kiss on his beautiful mouth. "Come with me. Now."

"Sophie, I—"

She stepped back. "I'm going to the guest house. And this time, I am *prepared*." By some miracle, when she said that, she managed not to blush. "Are you coming?"

He neither moved nor spoke. For an awful minute, she was sure he would say no.

But then, at last, he nodded.

She let herself breathe again. And she held out her hand.

Chapter 5

Her bedroom was like her living room: charming and old-fashioned. She had a big high bed with a carved headboard. A three-mirrored vanity. A heavy, bow-fronted bureau. Lacy curtains. Ferns.

Sin looked around him, wondering how the hell he'd gotten there, thinking that there was no excuse, by his own hard and cold rules of who he was and how he operated, for him to be there.

Yet he made no move to leave. Because he wanted her, a desperate kind of wanting that made no logical sense at all. And because she wanted him in return.

Last night her doubts had saved them both.

But not tonight. Tonight, the light of certainty shone in her eyes. Tonight, there would be no one saved. Tonight, she was ready. The conviction in her eyes held him. It beckoned him.

Goodness that lured.

She had the box of contraceptives waiting, right there by the bed. She gave him a sweet, rueful smile. "See?" she whispered. *"Prepared..."*

He grabbed her then, and started kissing her again— hard, hungry kisses. She sighed and kissed him right back, turning cruelty to sweetness.

Baffled, bewildered, aching with want, he fell across that big old bed with her in his arms.

And then it was all awkwardness, all rolling and sighing and pulling at buttons, tugging at sleeves. Within moments, they were both naked, their clothes strewn beneath them, more softness on that soft bed.

Her sweet hands caressed him, her body called to his, a call he could neither deny nor refute.

They fumbled together with the box on the side of the bed. He rose above her. And then he was in her.

They both sighed. She looked up at him through those shining, trusting eyes.

Fast, it was. And needful. Without wariness. Or fore-play. Like no sex he'd ever known.

He kissed her on her white throat, latching on, suck-ing, and then moving lower to her full waiting breasts. She held him close against her heart, a heart that beat so strong and steady and sure.

By then, somehow time had slowed. Everything. Slowed. They moved together, rising and falling, con-nected, sharing pleasure. Sharing breath.

He remembered the stars last night. Running with her beneath the moon. The bed of green moss. The creek flowing on, forever, in that place that had been his. That place that shouldn't even exist anymore.

Yet it did exist. And it had become *theirs*. She had said so.

She said his name. His whole name. "Sinclair…"

He lifted his head and looked down into her stunned, sweet face as her pleasure crested. Her body contracted around him, beckoning, urging.

He surrendered and joined her, pressing hard. Holding. Forever. Throwing his head back in a silent cry as his release finally took him down.

She moved in his arms, her gentle hand straying up to touch his brow. "Are you okay?"

He made a sound in the affirmative.

She sighed. "I'm glad."

He stroked her arm. "How about you?"

"I'm okay, too. Very much okay."

"Good."

She brought her sweet mouth closer. And he couldn't resist kissing her. She sighed some more, every smooth, supple inch of her eager and warm, soft. So fine and good.

"Oh!" she said into his mouth. She could feel him against her, wanting her. "Oh…"

He combed his fingers through the warm silk of her hair as the miracle began all over again.

All through that night, he kept thinking—whenever he *could* think—that this would be all of it, that he would somehow get enough of her. That after this, it would end.

But it didn't seem to be happening the way he kept thinking. Each touch only served to make the hunger stronger. Each release became a prologue to a kiss.

The smooth terrain of her body beguiled him. His

hands and his mouth wandered everywhere. And she welcomed each separate, yearning caress.

Sometime near dawn, they finally slept.

He woke before her. It couldn't have been that much later than when they'd dropped off. His mind felt clear and sharp as a cloudless winter sky.

He thought, I will wake her now. And somehow, I'll tell her— But then she stirred. "Sinclair?" The word in his ear on a sweet exhaled breath.

And he was lost. He told her nothing. Only reached out and put his hand on her smooth belly.

She let out a small cry—of surprise and delight.

He moved his hand down.

"What do you do?" Her head rested on his arm and her legs were twined with his. "For a living?"

Carefully he told her, "I'm in property acquisition."

She moved beneath the sheet, untangling her legs from his, lifting up on an elbow. "Real estate? You buy and sell property?"

"Yes. For development mostly. Shopping malls. Office complexes."

"You said the other night that you had business to take care of. Are you planning to buy property here in Nevada County."

"Possibly. I'm…looking into the situation."

A coiling lock of hair fell over her eye. She blew it away. "Where do you come from?"

He stalled, saying nothing, trying to decide just how much to reveal.

She leaned in closer and pitched her voice to a teasingly conspiratorial level. "I'm asking you where you live."

He gave her the truth. "Los Angeles."

She grinned, flipped to her stomach and punched at her pillow. "There. That wasn't so hard, was it?" She turned to her back, laced her hands behind her head and beamed at the antique light fixture overhead.

The fine bow of her collarbone tempted him. He indulged himself, moving close enough that he could run a finger from one shoulder to the other across the ridge of that bow.

She rolled her head to look at him. "Was it?"

"What?"

"Was it so hard?"

"No," he lied. "Not at all."

"You don't like to talk about yourself." Her tone had grown serious.

Again, he thought of what he should tell her—at the same time as he finally admitted to himself that he was not going to tell her. Not for a while yet.

He felt like a man under some sort of spell. A spell destined to end badly.

And soon.

But he would take what he could get while it lasted.

She said, "It's all right. I'll get the truth out of you." Now she looked mischievous. "One little bit at a time." She sat up. "How about a ride? Before breakfast."

"A ride?"

"You know. On a horse." She tipped her head. "Or maybe you don't ride."

"I ride. When I get the chance." It was part of his plan, to raise horses here. As his father had done and his grandfather before him.

She gave a small laugh. "How well? Can I vouch for you with Caleb?"

"You can vouch for me."

The sheet she held at her breast slid down, exposing the upper edge of one pink aureole. If she didn't get moving soon, he wouldn't let her go at all.

She must have seen the heat in his eyes. Her mouth went soft and her own eyes went dreamy. "I'm the general jane-of-all-work around here."

"So?"

"So, if we don't go for that ride now, we won't have time to go at all."

He reached for her, and the sheet fell away.

She sighed as he kissed her. "Maybe tomorrow morning…"

He lifted his mouth from hers, just enough to whisper, "Maybe tomorrow morning, what?"

"Maybe tomorrow morning, we'll go riding…." Smiling that dreamy smile, she pulled him down.

"Sinclair Riker," Myra said, as she set a roast beef sandwich and a big glass of milk in front of Sophie. "I can hardly believe it. And he's come back to see what became of his home?"

"Yep. And to look into doing business here, I think." Sophie picked up the sandwich. "This looks great. I am starving." She took a hefty bite. "Umm."

Myra watched her chew for a moment, then pulled out the chair opposite her and sat in it. Sophie cast her a questioning glance. The older woman poked a loose strand of graying red hair back into the net she wore when she worked, then moved the salt and pepper shakers closer together in the middle of the table.

Sophie swallowed the bite of sandwich. "Okay. What's up?"

They were alone in the kitchen, but still the cook leaned forward and lowered her voice. "He spent the night, didn't he?"

Sophie swallowed. "Myra," she said gently. "You are not my mother."

Myra sat back in her chair and crossed her freckled arms over her middle. "Well, of course, I'm not."

"And anyway, how would you know if he spent the night?"

Myra uncrossed her arms and looked at the table. She must have spied a few crumbs, because she began blotting the table with her fingers. "Caleb ran into him down by the creek last night—and then saw him leave this morning."

"And naturally Caleb reported right to you."

"You know how he is." The cook rubbed her fingers together over her other hand, then blotted the table some more. "He just wants to protect you."

"I don't need protecting. Honestly."

"But…" Myra seemed unable to find the right words. She stood, went to the sink and brushed away the crumbs she'd blotted up. Then she turned back to Sophie. "It's only…you just met him, right?"

Sophie set down her sandwich. She pushed back her chair and went to stand beside the older woman. Myra had come to the Mountain Star in response to Sophie's ad for a live-in cook. She'd been the first applicant for the job. Myra had worked in restaurants, both at the stove and as a waitress. Her references had been impeccable. But more important to Sophie, Myra had kind eyes. Sophie had just known that they would be great friends. And she had been right.

"Myra, remember how you used to worry, when we

first started out? When we opened the campground and people who needed somewhere to spend the night began showing up?"

Myra made an obstinate noise in her throat. "That was different."

"No. I don't think so. You were worried that one of them might cause us harm. But none of them have. It's all worked out fine."

"They're good kids, most of them. I see that now."

"Myra, you give them food. To take with them when they go."

"Only leftovers, you know that. In order not to waste them. And you did tell me to use my judgment about it."

"That's right. Because I trust your judgment."

"Well," Myra muttered grudgingly. "Thank you."

"And now, I would like for you to trust mine."

Myra's gaze skittered away. "Of course, I trust your judgment."

"Good."

"But…this is so unlike you."

"No." Sophie touched her friend, very lightly, on the shoulder. "It's exactly like me. Myra, I…" She couldn't quite say the word *love* at that point, though that was what she felt inside. Still, her relationship with Sinclair was all too new, too overwhelming, to go putting labels on it. She finished rather lamely, "I trust him. I do."

"But how do you know if he's a man worthy of trust? You don't even go *out* with men."

Sophie laughed then. "When would I have time? You know how it is around here. I barely manage to fit in a few hours' sleep at night." And last night, not even that much, she thought, and had to hide a goofy smile.

"Yes," Myra jumped in, "and that's what I mean.

You're not…experienced. You're not careful. You're a perfect target for some fast-talking fortune hunter."

Sophie made a show of rolling her eyes. "Some fortune. We run this place on a shoestring, and you know it perfectly well. Sinclair knows it, too."

"How does he know?"

"Because he has eyes. Because I gave him a tour of this kitchen. All he had to do was glance around. He could see I don't have the money to fix it up right."

"Is that what he said?"

"Honestly, Myra. He's not after my *fortune*. I promise you."

"Then what is he after?"

Sophie pretended to be hurt. "What? You find it impossible to believe he might just be after *me?*"

"No." Myra's ruddy face lost its obdurate expression. "I don't find that impossible. You know I don't."

"Good. And I'm not a total innocent. I've been around a little—back before the Mountain Star, when I had a Saturday night to myself now and then."

"You've…been around?" The cook frowned.

Sophie immediately regretted her choice of words. "Oh, Myra. You know what I mean. There was a time when I actually dated. And I was engaged once, before I came here."

"That's right, I'd forgotten. That lawyer from San Francisco…"

"The point is, I'm not a complete fool when it comes to the opposite sex."

"Oh, I do hope you're right." The cook glanced at the rest of Sophie's sandwich, which still waited on the table. "You'd better eat that before the bread gets dry.

And drink all that milk. The way you work, you need a good lunch."

"Myra, are you all right about this now?"

Myra sniffed. "I don't approve of what you're doing." And then she couldn't help smiling. "But I do approve of *you*." She sighed. "I suppose it's your life."

"Thank you. For caring."

"Eat your lunch, then."

"I will."

After she finished her sandwich and drank all of her milk, Sophie went looking for Caleb. She found him in the stables, wearing those high rubber boots of his, swamping out stalls.

He looked up when he saw her, then went back to work.

"Caleb, I think we'd better talk."

He went on pushing his broom. "Maybe later. I want to get this job done now."

"Caleb."

He stopped, glanced at her narrowly, then set the broom against the wall. "What?"

She found she didn't know how to begin. "Look. Let's go out to the big pasture." The big pasture was several hundred yards from the stables, to one side of the series of working corrals. The horses whose owners hadn't come to claim them for the day would all be there now.

"Sophie B., I got my work to do."

"It won't take long. I promise."

Reluctantly he followed after her, out into the sunlight. They leaned on the fence of the pasture and watched the horses. The big spotted gelding Pretty Boy came over, lipped Sophie's empty palm, then ambled away.

Sophie watched him go. "Sinclair is welcome here, Caleb," she said softly. "I...care for him."

Beside her, Caleb grunted, a disapproving sound.

"Caleb, I know what I'm doing."

Caleb grunted again.

"Give him a chance." She reached out, put a hand on his huge forearm. "For my sake."

He actually looked at her then. "You think you know what you're doing?"

She nodded. "I *do* know what I'm doing. I'm sure. In my heart, where it counts."

"It's happened pretty sudden."

"Things that happen suddenly aren't necessarily bad."

He actually smiled then, something he did rarely, because his teeth were crooked and that embarrassed him. "I guess you got a point. I like things slow, myself. But that's maybe just me."

"Sometimes you simply have to be ready. Or the best things in life will pass you by."

Caleb turned back to the horses again. "The vet said Black Angel's doing fine." The Arabian mare had come up lame a few weeks ago. A bad sprain, but not a break, thank heaven. The owner had had a fit, though both Sophie and Caleb knew the limp had started right after the woman had taken the mare out for a long ride on the twisting trails of Riker Ranch. Caleb had suffered the owner's abuse, then wrapped the injured pastern joint, stalled the horse and called in the vet.

"She looks good as new," Sophie said.

Caleb turned his pale blue eyes on her again. "I guess

if you think this Sinclair Riker's okay, it's good enough for me."

Sophie touched his arm again. "That's what I hoped you'd say."

"He just better treat you right, that's all."

"Oh, Caleb. He's a fine man."

"If you say so."

"I do."

That night, Sinclair arrived at intermission. Sophie looked up and saw him. He smiled. She almost dropped a can of grape soda on a guest's sandaled foot.

"Careful, Sophie B.," the guest warned.

She apologized, handed the guest his change and waited on the next person in line—a true exercise in concentration since every atom in her body seemed to be bouncing around in pure joy.

Finally everyone had been served. Sinclair straightened from the little table by the door, where he'd been leaning, watching her. In three long strides he stood before her.

She looked up at him, feeling stunned and glorious. Out of her depth, over her head—and thrilled to be that way. "Hi."

"Hello."

"Popcorn? Bottled water?"

He shook his head. "Not tonight."

"Oh." She felt at a loss, all at once, like an actress who had forgotten her next line. "Will you…watch the rest of the show?"

"I think I'll pass. Those poor evil rustlers. I can't stand to see them all die a second time." He was teasing her.

By some minor miracle, she found she could tease back. "They deserved to die. They crossed Randi Wilding."

"Who looks damn good in a tight plaid shirt."

She put on a reproachful expression. "Randi Wilding is more than a sex symbol. She is a genius on film."

"I still think I'll pass up the second half."

"And do what?"

"Go for a walk—if that's all right."

"You know it is."

His mouth twisted wryly. "Maybe you should give me a grounds pass. Something that says it's all right if I'm here—in case I run into Caleb."

"Caleb won't bother you. He knows you're okay now."

His eyes gleamed. "And how does he know that?"

"Because I told him."

"And how do *you* know that?"

"I have my ways." She glanced toward the curtain that led to the rows of seats. All her guests were waiting to see the second half. "And I also have to get that projector going."

"I know."

Neither of them moved.

"Sinclair, I really have to go."

He reached out and slid his hand under her hair, cupping the back of her neck and pulling her close. "I know," he said again. And then he kissed her.

Oh, had there ever been such kisses as his? They seared her synapses. Sent her eyeballs spinning...

When he let her go and stepped back, she swayed toward him, like a green tree in a high wind. He laughed then. "Just so you won't forget me."

"As if I ever could."

"Go on. Your audience wants to see the rest of the show."

Somehow she made her feet turn toward the hayloft.

Afterward he was waiting. He helped her wash the bowls and sweep the floor. Then they went to the guest house together.

They were barely through the front door before he was grabbing her, pulling her close, kissing her as if he might die if he didn't. She kissed him back. She felt just the same way—as if she must kiss him, or she wouldn't survive.

They took off all their clothes and lay down on the couch.

The things they did there should have made her blush for shame.

But she didn't blush. And she felt no shame. She felt only rightness.

And pure ecstasy.

Those beautiful hands moved over her, revealing all her secrets, making her cry out. Making her moan. She lifted herself up to him, offering herself, welcoming whatever glorious anguish his next caress might bring.

Finally he said, "The bedroom. Now."

He got up and took her hand and tugged her along, totally naked, dazed, yearning, fulfilled and yet still hungry, into the other room. He let go of her hand just inside the door and she stood there, watching him, as he moved toward the bed. His body glowed in the darkness, lean and hard, the muscles spare and tightly sculpted. So beautifully formed. So perfectly male.

As she looked at him, she wondered at herself.

"This isn't like you," Myra had said.

And it wasn't.

Or rather, it hadn't been, Until Sinclair

And now she couldn't get enough of this. Of him. Of his body. Her body. The two of them. Joined.

He found the box of contraceptives, took one out, rolled it down over himself. And then he turned. "Come here."

The yearning inside her rose up, hotter than ever, to meet the command in his voice. In his burning dark eyes. There was a thrumming all through her, a rhythm of pure need.

She moved toward him. He sat on the edge of the bed, held out his hand. She took it. He pulled her onto his lap, there on the edge of the bed.

She settled over him, gasping a little at the torrent of pure feeling as he filled her. He guided her legs around his hips and his mouth found her throat in a long, hungry kiss. She closed her eyes, let her head fall back.

Heaven. A forbidden heaven, it was. She soared through it, her whole body shimmering. Joyous. Free.

Finally, near the end, she made herself open her eyes and look at him.

He stared back at her, a look as deep and powerful as the uproar in her blood.

She whispered, "I love you. Love you, love you…"

The fulfillment came. Hard and fast. Her head fell back again. She left all conscious thought behind as sensation had its way with her.

Chapter 6

Right at daylight, she shook him and called his name.

He put an arm over his eyes and groaned.

"Sinclair, I want you to go riding with me."

He sneaked a glance out from under his arm. Her hair hung over her bare shoulders, glorious and tangled. She looked like some sleepy angel—a frowning angel.

"What's the matter?" He lowered his arm.

"I just realized that you don't have riding clothes."

He grinned at her. "I do. In the car."

"You do?" Now she was beaming, happy as a good child on Christmas Eve.

"You said you wanted to ride this morning, so I brought some jeans and boots."

She yanked back the sheet. "Well, don't just lie there. Get up. We have to get going. Come on…"

* * *

The hulking stableman didn't seem much friendlier, but he stayed out of the way as Sin and Sophie saddled up a pair of horses and got ready to go.

The sun was just sliding over the edge of the mountains when they started on the trail that wound off into the trees not far from the main house. She led the way through the pines and then out into a sunny, rolling pasture overgrown with tangled wild rosebushes. Soon enough, they went back into the trees again and then upward, switching back and forth toward the rocky crest of a high hill.

When they reached the top, they stopped and looked out over the blanket of evergreen below, broken up here and there by small meadows and the shining ribbons of mountain streams. Sin leaned on the saddle horn, thinking that the damn pines were choking out everything. They encroached on all the meadows now, saplings and even midsize pines dotting what had once been open land. Something would have to be done about them, or the ranch would be nothing but forest.

"Is it the same as you remember it?" she asked.

He let out a low laugh. "Sophie. I was only six." Yet he did remember. His father had brought him up here once, about a year before the end. To look out over the land, just as he and Sophie were doing now.

"All that you can see is ours," his father had said. "Riker land. Your grandfather scraped and saved and wheeled and dealed for every square foot of it. It's what makes us who we are."

Even now, over thirty years later, Sin felt his blood

stir as he remembered his father's words. Anthony Riker had always been a hell of a talker. He could bring tears to the eyes of the coldest heart when he quoted poetry or told the old family tales.

Unfortunately he'd hated work and never planned ahead. Busy telling stories and quoting Browning and Shelley, he'd let the land that "made them who they were" slip right through his fingers. And then he'd killed himself, a final dramatic statement that also allowed him to escape a future in which he'd no longer be Anthony Riker of the Riker Ranch, but just another nobody trying to scrape by day-to-day.

Beside him, Sophie spoke. "It gives me such a feeling of…peace, just to look at it. To know that even with all the ugliness in the world, a place like this exists."

The brown gelding Sin rode snorted and tossed his head, eager to be moving again. Sin patted his neck to settle him down a little and set his mind on practical matters. "It's overgrown. A little clear-cutting would help." He used the logger's term for the removal of every last tree from any given area. Sophie sent him a sharp, disapproving glance. He laughed. "Come on. Clear-cutting has its uses, in spite of what your average rabid conservationist would like you to believe. Give it another twenty years, and those pines down there will choke out everything."

She looked out over the land, her angel's face wistful. "I suppose. But still, it's so beautiful and wild-looking."

"Overgrown," he reiterated grimly. Then he couldn't resist adding, "I'm surprised that teachers' association you mentioned didn't bring in some logging crews. The lumber would have brought them a little return on that 'bad investment' of theirs."

She made a face at him. "You'll be pleased to know that they did get some crews in here at first."

"But lately?"

"The past few years, the laws have become so much stricter. It's hard to get permits to cut trees, even on private land."

"Hard, but not impossible."

She smiled at him, a rather sad smile. "Maybe Inkerris, Incorporated, will put some loggers to work."

He only shrugged, though he knew damn well that Inkerris, Incorporated, planned to do exactly that.

She clucked her tongue at the mare she rode. "Come on. I have to get back."

He didn't argue, just turned his horse for the trail.

"Stay for Sunday brunch," she urged once they'd handed their horses over to Caleb. "It's buffet style. We put it out from ten to one. You could go back to the guest house and relax for a while, then wander on over and get something to eat."

The offer held definite appeal—except for the idea of entering that house again.

It was as if she read his mind. "You're uncomfortable about visiting the cottage again. I understand. Listen, I could load you up a plate and bring it back to the guest house and we could—"

He cut her off with a flat lie. "I'm not uncomfortable about that damn house."

She looked down at the pine needles under their feet. "Fine."

He dragged in a breath. "Look. I'm sorry. I spoke too harshly."

She shot him a glance. "So stay for brunch."

"No, I can't. I've got some work to do back at the hotel." Another lie. His only job here was getting rid of her—a job that had not progressed at all as he'd planned.

She met his gaze again. And smiled. God, she could finish a man off with that smile. "You could go work for a few hours—and come back for brunch. I'd fix us each a plate and take it to the guest house."

The word *yes,* was out of his mouth before it even took form in his brain.

At the hotel, he showered, checked his messages and called Rob Taylor, his personal assistant in L.A., at home. Rob had a number of issues to report on. Sin listened with half an ear, made a few suggestions, then said he had to go.

By then, it was nine-thirty. Too soon for a man who had "work" to do to be showing up again at the Mountain Star. He checked at the front desk and got the name of a local health club that took drop-ins on Sunday, then he got in his rental car and drove over there.

He worked out for an hour, pushing his body until the sweat was streaming off of him and his muscles felt like limp spaghetti. When he couldn't press another pound, he showered for the second time that day.

He was on his way back to the Mountain Star when he noticed the gray sedan behind him. A late-model Plymouth or Dodge. So nondescript as to be almost invisible. But now that he thought about it, it seemed he'd seen more than a few late-model gray sedans in his rearview mirror the past day or two.

Right then, he was just leaving the part of Grass Valley known as the Brunswick Basin, a busy shopping area packed with strip malls, fast-food restaurants and gas stations. He swung into the next parking lot: home to a bank, a title company and a beauty parlor. The gray sedan sped on by. When Sin pulled back onto the road again, the car was nowhere in sight.

Through the remainder of the short drive to the ranch, he tried to think which of his current competitors or business associates might want him followed. No one came immediately to mind. But that didn't mean anything. He had a reputation for sealing up prime pieces of property before his potential rivals even realized that the property could be bought.

He'd left L.A. in the middle of last week. No doubt by now, the word would be out that he was gone. It was entirely possible that someone had had him followed just to see what fabulous deal he might have in the works.

Sin smiled to himself. If someone had had him followed, they should have done some spying a little closer to home first. Sin paid his people well and expected their discretion, but information could always be obtained at a price. An effective rival could have learned that the property in question already belonged to him— and that this was a purely private matter anyway.

Sin signaled, slowed down, and turned into the long driveway that led to the Mountain Star. He wasn't overly concerned—but nonetheless, he would remember to keep an eye out for nondescript sedans.

Sin and Sophie had their private brunch in the bedroom of the little house.

Afterward she couldn't linger. She had to get right back to work. Reluctant to return to his hotel where he would only sit and contemplate the sheer idiocy of his own behavior, Sin wandered out to the stables. There he found Caleb, the surly stableman, helping an angry-looking blonde onto the back of a coal-black Arabian mare. The woman, who might have been anywhere from thirty to forty, wore English riding gear—jodhpurs, a neat little hat and knee-high boots. Once she found her seat, she sawed on the reins, forcing the mare to prance.

"Easy," Caleb warned.

The woman cast him an icy glance, yanked on the reins some more, and rode out into the sun as if she owned the world.

Shaking his head, Caleb watched her go. Then he turned and saw Sin standing there.

"That's a fine mare," Sin said.

"And that woman's set on ruining her," Caleb replied. He turned to leave.

Sin should have let him go, but instead he heard himself say, "Wait."

The big man turned. "Yeah?"

"How did you meet Sophie?"

Caleb broadened his stance a little—a pose that Sin read as wariness. "Why do you need to know?"

"I don't. I'm just curious."

A gray cat came strolling toward them across the red dirt in front of the stables. It looked like the same one Sophie had held in her arms that first night, while she gave her cute little introductory speech before the Randi Wilding Western. The cat ran up to Caleb, let out a meow and then sat back in a sinuous movement on its hind legs.

The stableman bent, scooped it up and began petting it in long strokes. The cat closed its eyes and purred in ecstasy. Caleb said, "She found me here."

"Sophie?"

Caleb nodded, his big head bent down, his gaze on the purring cat. "She came here by accident. She was living in the city then."

"The city? You mean San Francisco?"

"Yeah. She came up here for a weekend with a boyfriend."

Sin felt a completely irrational surge of jealousy. "A boyfriend."

"That's right. She was going to marry him."

"Why didn't she?"

Caleb looked up. "You'll have to ask her about that." He looked down at the cat again, went on stroking the gray fur. "She was alone when she came here, though."

"You mean to the ranch itself?"

"Uh-huh. Just drove up the driveway one day, curious, wanting to look around at the old Riker place. She found me in the barn. I was...camped out there. I had nowhere else to go." He raised his head, his pale eyes proud, defiant of any judgments Sin might make.

"You were homeless."

"That's what they call it." His gaze was on the cat again, stroking, rubbing. "She wasn't even scared of me. She's like that. She trusts. Everybody gets the benefit of the doubt with her." He shot another quick glance up at Sin. Sin caught the meaning of that glance: *Everybody gets the benefit of the doubt with her, even some who probably shouldn't, even you....*

The cat rolled over in the groom's huge arms. He scratched its belly. "Anyway, she found me here. We started talking. I told her I loved horses, could fix just about anything with a motor and knew what to do to bring the grounds back under control—everything was grown pretty wild by then. She always says she got the idea for the Mountain Star that day, with just her and me. Talking in the barn."

Sin decided to go for the throat. "You're in love with her."

Caleb crouched and let the cat down. It strolled away, tail high. Then slowly Caleb stood. He assumed that wide, guarded stance again. "I love her. But not the kind of love you think. I'd do anything for her. She's the sister I never had." He paused, looked at Sin sideways. "You ever had a sister?"

"No."

"A man feels protective of a sister. I suppose what I'm tellin' you is, I would do bad damage to a man who hurt her."

"I see."

"Good. And I got work to do."

Sin watched him walk away.

That night, as they lay in bed, Sin kept thinking of that other man, the one she had almost married.

And Sophie knew, the way she always did, that something was bothering him. "Okay, what is it?"

He went ahead and told her. "I spoke with Caleb today."

"He was civil—I hope?"

"Civil enough. He told me you were almost married once."

"That's true."

"What happened?"

Sophie thought, *he wasn't you,* but didn't say it. She'd gone and cried out her love just last night, and he'd said nothing. She didn't want to push him with constant declarations of her feelings. To her, it seemed she'd been waiting all her life for him to come and find her. But in reality, this was only the fourth night since he'd walked into her movie theater and stole her heart. She wanted him to feel free to open up to her in his own time and in his own way.

"Sophie?" His warm breath caressed her shoulder. "Tell me about him."

She didn't hesitate. She wanted him to know all about her own life, just as she hoped he would soon tell her more about his. "His name was David. He was a lawyer. Family law. He handled my aunt Sophie's estate— she was the one who raised me, really. My parents were killed in a car crash when I was only five.

"I met David when Aunt Sophie died. That was six years ago. I was twenty-one, with a degree from a business school and a job in an insurance office. I felt very grown-up. After we'd been dating for about six months, he asked me to marry him. He was a good man and I was…lonely. With Aunt Sophie gone, I had no family left. I said yes."

"And?"

"And then we came here. For a weekend. I went off by myself one day, exploring. I stopped at this coffee shop in Grass Valley and got talking to some of the old fellows at the counter. They told me a few stories. About the town."

He added for her, "And about the Rikers, who carved an empire here—and then lost it, all in the space of two generations?"

"Yes." She turned toward him, cuddled closer. "I asked where the Riker Ranch was. They gave me directions and I found my way here. I drove up the entrance road and…fell in love."

"With this place." It wasn't a question. He understood.

"Yes. I wanted to move here. To spend the money my aunt had left me to create the Mountain Star."

"And David didn't share your dream."

"He had his life in San Francisco and he didn't want to move." Sinclair's black hair had fallen over his forehead. Tenderly, Sophie combed it back with her fingers.

"Do you still think of him?"

"Sometimes. But not with regret. It just…wasn't meant to be."

He reached for her, cupped the back of her neck. "Lucky for me."

"Oh, Sinclair…"

"Kiss me."

She did.

For a good while, they didn't speak. The only sounds in the lace-curtained room were soft moans and sighs.

Later she gathered all her courage, and asked, "When did your mother die?"

He hesitated, but then he did answer. "About three years ago."

"Of what?"

"Complications from diabetes, the doctors said."

"You don't believe that?"

He moved away from her a little, and sat up against the carved headboard. "I believe she wanted to die. Diabetes can be managed, but she refused to take care of herself. She was never happy, in all those years after my father killed himself."

She pulled the sheet against her breasts and sat up beside him. "It must have been hard for you growing up, if she was unhappy."

"We got by." The three words were like a wall with a sign on it: *Keep Out.*

Still, she pressed on. "What did she do...for a living?"

He gave her a long, deep look. "You don't want to know."

She felt for his hand, twined her fingers with his. "No, that's not true. I do want to know."

"All right." He paused. She thought for a moment that he had changed his mind and wouldn't go on, but then he said, "She lived off of men."

Sophie hoped she hadn't heard right. "Excuse me?"

Sinclair chuckled, a cold sound.

"You ought to see your face. You shouldn't have asked."

She scooted over even closer to him, brought their twined hands to her heart. "But I want to know, I do. Whatever you're willing to tell me."

He looked at their clasped hands, then pulled his away. "All right, Sophie. I'll tell you. She was a whore."

"A...?" She gulped, her throat closing over the ugly word.

"You heard me. A whore."

"But I don't understand. You're saying she became a...prostitute? Just like that?"

He made a low, impatient sound. "No. Not *just like that.* She drifted into it. She was a pretty woman and men were attracted to her. Like my father, she had little ambition to get out and make things happen. At first, I remember she had a job in an office. We lived in east Hollywood then, a tiny 'garden' apartment in a neighborhood that had gone downhill. The job didn't pay much. She was always late with the rent and always worried about how we would get by. And then she met someone at that office. I suppose you could say she was his mistress for a while. Then he dumped her and she lost the job. She met someone else. And someone else. Eventually, she stopped having affairs. She went out with men and went to bed with them and they paid her for it.

"She went on like that until I got old enough to do something about it. I bought her a little house in the San Fernando Valley and I took over paying her bills for her. She lived quietly after that, but she drank. Drinking and diabetes don't mix." He was looking at the far wall. "Three years ago, she died."

At last, he turned his gaze her way again. "Heard enough?"

She kept picturing him as a little boy, in that tiny apartment he'd mentioned—all alone, while his mother went out with strange men. "How did you stand it? How did you live?"

"Let's say I was determined."

"Determined to do what?"

Sin wondered what the hell was the matter with him, to have revealed so much.

"Sinclair."

"Umm?"

"What were you so determined to do?"

He backpedaled—smoothly, he hoped. "To…better myself, I guess you could say." He settled down onto the pillows and pulled her close. "You ought to get some sleep."

She wrapped one arm around him, twined those long, smooth legs with his. "Sinclair?"

"What?"

"I'm so sorry for her. And for you."

"Don't be," he commanded. "She's gone now. And I've got what I wanted."

She snuggled up closer. "You mean money, right?"

"Right," he lied in a whisper, "that's what I mean." He smoothed her shining hair back from her temple and placed a kiss there. "Now, go to sleep."

"Sinclair?"

"Sophie. Go to sleep."

She sighed. She had a thousand more questions, and he knew it. But he wasn't going to answer them. He'd already told her way too much.

She must have realized that he was through talking, because she said no more.

The next morning, right as the sun rose, she dragged him over to the cottage to eat breakfast in the kitchen with her and the help—which included Caleb, the cook named Myra and a skinny little part-time maid called Midge.

Sin still didn't care much for spending time in that house. One of the first things he intended to do once he took over was to tear the damn thing down and build again.

But that morning, with Sophie next to him, the old demons stayed away.

Midge was a talker. She had a boyfriend who kept leaving and then coming back, a mother who wouldn't quit giving her advice—and she'd flunked her last semester at Sierra Junior College.

"Oh, I dunno," Midge informed them all between big bites of scrambled egg, "I just dunno what to do. Maybe I should get a full-time job. Get my own place, not have to listen to Mother anymore. But then, higher education has always been my dream. Without a college degree, how will I ever really make something of myself?" She gulped down more egg and fluttered her skimpy lashes at Sin. "What do you think, Mr. Riker?"

He said something neutral.

She started babbling again.

The red-haired cook spoke up the next time Midge paused to shovel in more food. "So, how long will you be staying in town, Mr. Riker?"

Beside him, he felt Sophie go very still. She'd asked him that question herself once, the first night he came here. He had evaded. And she hadn't asked again.

"Mr. Riker?" the cook prompted, reminding him of a disapproving schoolmarm who'd waited too long for a response from a student she didn't much like anyway.

"I'll be here another week. Maybe two." Idiocy. Pure and simple. Things couldn't go on this way for another two weeks.

But even as he admitted the impossibility of the situation, he knew he planned to carry on with it—and with Sophie—for as long as the lie lasted.

"Sophie says you're here on business."

"Yes."

"And what kind of business is that?"

Sin caught the warning glance Sophie sent Myra's way, but Myra kept her sharp green eyes right on him.

"I'm in real-estate acquisition."

"You're buying property here, in Nevada County?"

"I'm...checking out the situation."

Caleb joined the interrogation then. "What does that mean?"

"Caleb, please." Sophie jumped to the rescue. "Sinclair is our guest."

Sin put his hand over hers. "It's all right." He looked at Caleb—and began dishing out more half truths. "What I mean is, before I would buy property here for potential development, I would have to thoroughly investigate the climate for such a project."

"The climate?"

"Would the community be open to it? Would local government stymie us at every turn—or make the thousand and one permits we'd need easy to acquire?"

"We don't want another shopping mall around here anyway," Caleb said sourly.

Now it was Myra's turn to shoot the big man a quelling look, after which she started in on Sin again. "So, you're here to find out if you want to do business in Nevada County. Is that it?"

"You could say that, yes." Though it wouldn't be true.

"And that could take two more weeks?"

"It could."

Right then, someone tapped on the door that led out to a small back porch. All heads turned that way. Sin knew a shameful moment of total relief, to have the inquisition over—at least for the moment.

Myra pushed back her chair. "That'll be the campers." She went to the door.

Two thin, shabbily dressed older men stood there, bedrolls and packs slung over their shoulders. "Good morning, Myra." One of them tipped the sweat-stained felt hat he wore.

"You just hold it right there." The cook bustled off toward the pantry.

The man in the felt hat caught sight of the rest of

them and tipped his hat a second time. "Howdy, folks—
Sophie B."

Sophie gave him one of those smiles of hers, a smile
bright enough to light up the whole room. "Hello, Edgar.
And Silas, how are you?"

"Just fine, ma'am. Beautiful day."

"Yes. It certainly is."

"Come on in," Sophie said.

"No," the one called Edgar shook his head. "We got
to be going."

Myra emerged from the pantry carrying two small
brown paper sacks. "Just a little something. It'll be
lunchtime before you know it."

"We surely do thank you, Myra."

"That we do. A bite always comes in handy."

"You boys take care of yourselves now."

"You know we will…." They went off down the walk
and Myra closed the door. She returned to the table.

Sin looked at Sophie. "Bag lunches for the homeless?"

Midge piped up again. "Edgar and Silas aren't homeless. Well, not exactly, anyway. They're prospectors.
They dredge the South Fork. But they never made a
big strike. So they kind of ended up living day-to-day."

Sin held back a chuckle over that one. His grandfather had worked in the mines, after all. And his father
had been an expert on the history of the area.

Silas and Edgar had chosen the wrong business.
Though some hard-rock mining concerns still operated in the gold country with reasonable success, no
dredger he'd ever heard of had made a big strike in the
past hundred years or so.

Midge went on. "But they do drink, I heard—Edgar

and Silas, I mean. They both got a liquor problem, like a lot of miners. It's sad. It comes from busted dreams, the way I see it. If you got no dreams left, you got to soothe yourself with something."

Sin hardly heard her. He was looking at Sophie, remembering how it had irritated him the other night when she'd sent those kids out to sleep on his land.

Today he felt differently. Today he felt… admiration. Yes, *admiration* was the word. Admiration for a woman who didn't have the money to put a decent kitchen in her rundown resort, but still let her cook pass out food to every down-and-outer who knocked on the back door.

Admiration.

It wasn't like him. Not like him at all.

Sophie smiled at him, reached for her coffee cup and drained the last of it.

Midge went on, "But still, I gotta say, it might not be so bad. To live free in an old van like Silas and Edgar. And in the summertime, to sleep out under the stars. To have Myra give me bag lunches when I got really hungry. It might be better than *my* life, for instance.

"I mean, it's not easy, worrying every day about my GPA, listening to my mother nagging and wishing that my boyfriend would either ask me to marry him or get his sorry butt out of my life. I just—"

Myra had heard enough. "Finish up. I want some help to get the breakfast on in the dining room. And then you've got vacuuming and dusting and a freezer to defrost."

Midge let out a long, deep sigh. Then she picked up her fork and finished her second helping of scrambled eggs.

Chapter 7

Sin left as soon as he'd finished his breakfast. After all, he had to keep up the fiction that he had lots of work to do, checking out the local business climate, courting the county politicos.

Sophie walked him to his car. They stopped on the path before they reached the parking area under the pines.

"The theater's closed tonight." She swayed a little closer to him, turning her face up, so her sweet mouth was only inches from his. "And tomorrow night. And the next night, too. I only run it Thursday through Sunday. Did I tell you that before?"

He looked at her slim nose and her wide mouth and those beautiful eyes. He was like some adolescent with his first crush—he just couldn't get enough of looking at her.

"Sinclair, did I tell you?"

"You might have."

"Well, anyway, now you know. That's three nights a week I have to myself."

He knew what she was hinting at, and gladly played right along. "I hope you're planning on spending those nights with me."

She went on tiptoe and kissed him, a little peck of a kiss. "I would not spend those nights with *anyone* but you."

A quick kiss was never enough. "Kiss me like you mean it."

She cast a glance around. "Well, I don't *think* anyone's looking."

"I don't give a damn if they are." He pulled her close and took the kiss he wanted—a long, slow, achingly sweet one.

Finally he had to take her by the waist and put her away from him. "I'd better go. I know you have to get to work."

She let out a rueful little sigh. "And you, too."

The conscience he wasn't supposed to have jabbed at him. "Right." He kissed the end of her nose, not daring to kiss anything else or he would scoop her up and carry her back to the guest house and keep her there all day long. "Tonight." He backed away, knowing he had to go, but jealous of losing sight of her.

"Tonight." She stood there in the shadow of the pines until he drove away.

That day went much like the day before. Sin returned to his hotel. He checked in with Rob. Then he went to that fitness club again to swim and lift weights.

A gray sedan pulled out into traffic behind him when he left the health club's parking lot. Sin drove slowly, signaling clearly at every turn, making it easy for whoever it was to trail right along. Glances in his rearview and side mirrors told him little. The driver was male, of medium build. He wore a tan shirt, had a crew cut. Dark glasses hid his eyes. He might have been twenty or forty or anywhere in between.

Finally, about two blocks from his hotel, Sin put on his blinker and carefully pulled to the shoulder of the road. The sedan drove on by. Sin looked over just as the car passed him. The eyes behind those dark glasses were looking right at him. Sin waved.

The gray car sped off.

Sin sat there for a moment before pulling out again. Whoever lurked behind those dark glasses understood now that Sin had spotted him.

And why in hell was he being followed in the first place? What was there to discover about his visit here—beyond the fact that he was having an affair with Ms. Sophie B. Jones?

Could that information be of use to someone in some way? Offhand, Sin didn't see how.

Sin had lunch at the hotel restaurant, then placed a call to his second in command at Inkerris, Incorporated. His associate said just what he expected him to say. The two projects they had in the works were running smoothly and he couldn't think of any reason someone might put a detective on Sin.

"But I'll be happy to check into it more thoroughly."

Sin told him not to bother. "If it becomes necessary, I'll handle it at this end."

When he hung up, he found himself wondering about Sophie, remembering all the questions he saw in her eyes—questions he knew she was careful not to ask for fear she might chase him away.

Could she have decided to get some answers another way?

No. He couldn't believe that. Not Sophie. She didn't have a devious bone in her body.

Sin chose an orange from the fruit basket on the coffee table. Staring through a sliding glass door at the small garden patio outside his suite, he slowly began removing the peel.

He'd learned early that it didn't pay to trust anybody. People did what they had to do to get what they wanted. If you put your trust in them, they would only betray you, one way or another. He'd seen it time and time again. It was how the world worked.

Yet, in spite of his very real and practical cynicism, Sin trusted Sophie Jones. He could find no deceit when he looked in her eyes. Though it went against all he'd trained himself to believe, he simply could not picture her hiring somebody to follow him around.

Besides, he thought wryly as he separated off a slice of orange, Sophie couldn't *afford* to have him followed. She spent every cent she had trying to keep her precious Mountain Star in the black—and feeding every stray creature, human or otherwise, that wandered into her life.

No, whoever had decided to find out his business in Northern California, it wasn't Sophie B. Jones.

Sin ate his orange. He made a few more calls.

And then he waited.

Until he could see her again.

* * *

That night went by like the ones before it—too swiftly, even though Sin and Sophie had more time with that impossible theater of hers closed. They walked down to the spot by the creek and sat there for an hour. Then they wandered back to her little house, where they stayed until daylight.

In the morning, as the sun rose, they rode out, taking a different series of trails than the time before, though they did cross the pretty little pasture where so many roses grew wild. He left her around eight and returned to his hotel to pass the day somehow.

Until he could see her again.

The day seemed to drag on forever. He didn't see a single late-model gray sedan. His shadow had either given up—or become a lot more careful.

That night Sophie asked him if he had any family left at all.

"No. There's no one."

She was lying on her stomach, her chin propped on her hands. She rolled to the side and sat up, tugging on the sheet so it would cover those high, full breasts. "I used to be the same way."

Since he had most of his mind on that sheet—and the tempting prospect of peeling it back—it took Sin a few seconds to really hear her words. Then he frowned. *"Used to be?"*

"Yep." She wiggled around a little, pulling the damn sheet even higher.

"Sophie. That makes no sense. You either have a family or you don't."

"I don't." She was smiling way too smugly. "But I do."

He thought he took her meaning then. "I understand. Caleb's like a brother. And Myra thinks of you as a daughter."

She wiggled around some more. The sheet slipped a little. She caught it, pulled it back up. "I do think of them as family—but I wasn't referring to them a minute ago."

"Damn it, you're driving me crazy with that sheet."

She went wide-eyed. "I am?"

"You know you are."

Her lashes fluttered down. "I do?" She let the sheet fall. And she looked right at him.

He swore low with feeling. And then he reached for her.

Sometime later, she lay beneath him, the sheet all tangled around their feet. She sighed and stroked his back. "What I meant was…"

He made a sleepy noise of complete contentment.

She poked him in the shoulder. "Sinclair. I'm trying to talk to you." She nudged him again. "Come on. Listen. Please."

He let out a few grouchy groans, but then she whispered, so sweetly, "Please."

He slid to the side and propped his head on his hand. "All right. What?"

She reached down for the sheet, found it and pulled it over them. "Remember, before you distracted me—"

"*I* distracted *you?*"

She giggled. "Well, all right. Before we distracted

each other, I was talking about how I used to think I had no family, but I do, after all?"

"I remember." Though it made no sense at all. He had paid well to learn all the facts about her. Those facts included parents long deceased and a beloved aunt who'd died when she was twenty-one—and that was it, as far as relatives went.

"Sophie, what are you driving at?"

"Well, I have an *honorary* family."

"This is getting more incomprehensible by the moment."

She smoothed the sheet, flipped her hair back over her shoulder. "If you'll just listen, I'll explain."

"I'm listening."

"Good. I suppose you never heard of the family they call the Jones Gang."

"Is this a joke?"

"No. I promise. This is for real."

"The Jones *Gang?*"

"Well, that's just what people call them. Most of them live in North Magdalene, up Highway Forty-Nine, between Nevada City and—"

"I've heard of North Magdalene."

"Well, okay. Did you know that there are a lot of Joneses there?"

"No, I have to admit I didn't know that."

"Well, there are. A *lot* of Joneses. And they've kind of adopted me. Because I'm a Jones, too, though I'm not a real blood relation."

He thought that over. "You've been adopted. By the *Jones Gang.*"

"Yes. That's exactly right. I have been adopted… informally, of course."

"Of course. Why the Jones Gang?"

"Why did they adopt me?"

"No, why are they called the Jones Gang?"

"Because they're a pretty wild bunch—or they were, until they all found love and settled down."

"Wild?"

"Yes. Bad actors. Hooligans. One step away from being outlaws. You know?"

"I suppose."

"I want to take you there."

"You do?" The idea of driving up Highway Forty-Nine to meet a family of hooligans didn't particularly excite him.

She must have seen his reluctance in his face, because she nudged him with her elbow. "Come with me. Tomorrow, in the afternoon. I think I can swing a few hours away from here, if I work like crazy all morning—how about you? Do you think you can manage to get away?"

From waiting all day until he could see her again? It shouldn't be too difficult.

"Please?"

He couldn't resist the appeal in those eyes. "I think I can find the time."

Her smile took his breath away. "I'm so glad—oh, and maybe we could swim. In the river." The Yuba River wound its way in and out of the canyons along the highway. "It's the best time of year for it."

"I'll bring something to swim in."

"Oh, I just know you're going to love the Joneses."

"We'll see."

"Sinclair. You're so cautious."

"Sophie. You love everybody."

"Maybe so. But the Jones family is special. Just you wait and see."

At two the next afternoon, they walked into a bar called the Hole in the Wall, which stood in the middle of Main Street in the tiny mountain town of North Magdalene.

Sophie had already explained to Sin that the bar—and the restaurant next door—were Jones-owned businesses. As were the gift shop across the street, the service station a few doors down, the one motel and the gold sales store up near the end of town—which was easily visible from the beginning of town, as North Magdalene wasn't much more than a bend in the road. The sign at the foot of Main Street read, Welcome To North Magdalene, Population 229. Smokey Says Fire Danger Is High.

Inside the Hole in the Wall, Sophie bounced right up to the bar, towing Sin along behind her. "Hello, Jared," she said to the tall, rangy character with the steel-gray eyes who stood behind the beer taps.

Those steely eyes softened. "Sophie B. Jones. How've you been?"

"Just terrific. This is Sinclair. Sinclair Riker." The bartender nodded and Sin nodded back. "Where's Oggie?" All during the short drive up there, she had babbled away about the wonderful Oggie Jones, patriarch of the Jones Gang, the sweetest, wisest, most delightfully eccentric old man in the whole world.

Jared twitched a thumb in the direction of a green curtain strung along the back wall. "The old man's playing poker. Not to be disturbed—for a while, anyway. Why don't you two grab a couple of stools and have a beer on the house?"

Sophie considered, then shook her head. "Thanks, but I think I'll show Sinclair around town now and then take him swimming. We'll come back later." Just then a tall, pretty woman with strawberry-blond hair emerged through the door behind the bar. "Eden!" Sophie smiled wide in greeting.

"Hello, Sophie B. It's good to see you."

Sophie made the introductions. Eden was Jared's wife and helped him run the bar and the restaurant next door. She shook hands with Sin, and then asked, "So, can you two hang around for dinner?"

Sophie looked at Sin. He gave her a fine-with-me shrug.

"Around seven? We'll throw some steaks on the grill and open a bottle of wine."

"We'd love it."

"I'll invite the old man, too," Jared said. "As soon as he gets through cheating at poker."

"That would be terrific."

"Do you remember how to get to our place?"

Sophie said she did, then she grabbed Sin's hand again and dragged him out into the sunlight.

They trooped up and down Main Street. They went in Fletcher Gold Sales, where Sophie introduced him to Sam Fletcher, who was married to the remarkable Oggie's only daughter, Delilah. They stopped at Wishbook, the gift and sundries shop, which was run by Evie Jones Riggins, Oggie's niece. They even peeked in at the counter of the garage and exchanged greetings with Patrick Jones, Oggie's third son—the others being Jack

Roper, the sheriff's deputy, who was illegitimate, but still very much a part of the family, Jared, the bartender, and Brendan, who drove a big rig for a living. Each of them was married, and most of them had children.

Sophie rattled off names and relationships as if she'd known every one of them for her whole life. Sin smiled and shook people's hands and tried to keep the names straight. He also wondered why the hell he was enjoying himself so much, wandering around this tiny town, meeting strangers he was never likely to see again.

But then all he had to do was glance at the woman beside him and it all came clear. Her pleasure was infectious. She adored these people and he couldn't help liking them, too.

They used the rest rooms at the garage to change into their swimsuits. Then they got back in his rental car. She directed him down a street called Bullfinch Lane, across a bridge to the other side of the river.

"This is Sweetbriar Park. Just pull in there."

He parked the car and then she led him along a path that finally opened up to a sandy beach at the river's edge. There, in the shade of the oaks that grew near the sand, two women sat in fold-up lawn chairs. Out in the bright sunlight, a number of children of varying ages made castles of sand and splashed in the shallows. Across the gleaming water, several older kids sunned themselves on the rocks.

Sin felt a sharp stab of disappointment. He'd imagined they might actually manage a little time alone.

No such luck. Right away, one of the women looked their way and waved. "Sophie B.! Hello!"

Sophie dragged him over and introduced him to Regina Jones, Patrick's wife, and also to Amy Jones, who was married to Brendan, the truck driver. The older kids on the other side of the river dived in and swam across, to be introduced, as well.

Finally, after he'd met Regina's stepdaughters and their teenage girlfriends, admired several life-jacketed toddlers and said hello to two boys named Pete and Mark, who were also related to Joneses in some way he didn't quite catch, he was allowed to spread his towel in the warm sand.

Sophie yanked off the big beach shirt she'd worn over her cute blue suit and tossed it to the ground. "Last one in's a claim jumper!" She raced for the water's edge and dived in so quickly, he'd lost the game before he even realized he was playing it.

He took off and hit the water fast. Damn, he'd forgotten how cold the Yuba could be! She was halfway to the big rocks on the opposite bank, swimming in strong, even strokes across the current, before he caught up with her. He seized her ankle and gave it a tug.

She went under. Five seconds later, she came up sputtering. "No fair!" She tried to splash him.

He caught her arm and reeled her in closer—though not as close as he'd have liked to. After all, there were those two Jones women and all those little Joneses sitting back there in the sand.

"Sinclair!" She faked outrage, wriggling and squirming—and laughing in spite of herself.

He'd lost hold of her ankle, but he kept a firm grip on her arm. "So I'm a claim jumper, am I?"

She batted her water-soaked eyelashes. "If the shoe fits—"

"You cheated."

"No, you just weren't fast enough."

"You have to say 'go,' or it doesn't count."

She stuck out her tongue at him as the current tugged at them, trying to pull them along.

"That does it." He put his other hand on her head and pushed. She went under—and reached out and pulled him down along with her. They wrestled in the cold water, air bubbles bouncing all around them, her long hair snaking and swirling, caressing his shoulder, floating against his cheek.

Finally they both shot to the surface, gulping in air— and laughing. His hand held her waist, hers was pressed against his heart.

"Oh, Sinclair..." Her eyes went tender.

Like a bright light popping on in a dark room, the knowledge came to him: he was happy. Happy. Splashing in the icy water of the Yuba with Sophie, acting like a silly kid, while all those Joneses watched from the bank.

He moved forward, treading water, holding them both in place though the current kept trying to carry them down. "Sophie." Their lips met, cold and wet on the surface, so warm underneath. He pulled back.

She said, "I can't help it. I *have* to say it—I love you, Sinclair."

He kept treading water, thinking of all the lies he'd told, of the kind of man she thought he was and the man he really was. Of how this could never last. The truth would find them soon.

"Sophie, I—"

And then Regina Jones started screaming.

"Anthea, my God! Anthea!"

Sin turned just in time to see the orange life jacket and the small dark head of one of the toddlers, bouncing along toward the rapids a hundred yards downstream.

Chapter 8

Sin and Sophie struck out as one, swimming fast down the center of the stream. Sin was vaguely aware of the others on the bank, but they didn't have the chance he and Sophie did, with the strong power of the current beneath them, pushing them along. The others in the shallows would have to swim out to get the river's aid.

Within twenty feet, they left the depths behind. The river flattened out and the streambed came up to meet them. They ran with their feet and swam with their hands until the water level dropped so low there was nothing they could do but stumble along, falling on the slippery rocks beneath their feet, gaining an unstable purchase and then surging forward once more.

Ahead of them, the life jacket bobbed, the little head going facedown, popping upright again, then floating back, so the tiny nose pointed at the blue sky above. Sin could hear the crying now—and the choking each time the small head went down and came up again.

Sin shoved at the rocks with his legs, pushing himself onward, leaving Sophie behind.

Luck shined on him in the form of two boulders sticking out above the surface with several dead branches wedged between them. The orange life jacket got stuck in the eddy created by the rocks and the debris. For several blessed seconds, the child swirled in a circle, the life jacket almost catching on a tree branch, the child sputtering and choking, gone past crying now.

But it couldn't last. Too soon, the relentless current had its way. The little body spun on out of the eddy and went tumbling downstream once more.

By then, though, Sin had come within a few feet. He shoved again with his legs, lunging forward. By some miracle, he caught a strap that trailed off the back of the life jacket. He gave a yank and then he had the child around the waist.

He got the little body onto his shoulder just as he lost his footing—his legs went straight out in front of him and he rolled along on his rear end for several more yards, his feet scrambling for purchase again as he struggled to keep his burden above the water.

And then he felt Sophie's hand, grabbing his swim trunks from behind. He stopped rushing downstream and immediately wedged his feet in behind a couple of rocks to hold him there. He looked back. She had herself braced firmly against the rocks, as well.

"Give me Anthea," she instructed. "You're stronger than me. You can pull us all back to the bank."

He handed the child over. Sophie hoisted her to one shoulder and then held out her hand. They didn't get three steps before the others met them in the middle of the stream with the water rushing fast all around. They made a chain and passed the little girl, who'd started choking and coughing again, back to the safety of her mother's arms.

On the beach, one of Regina's stepdaughters—the younger one, Marnie—was crying. "I turned around. It was just for a minute. And then she was gone. Oh, Anthy..." She spoke to the toddler, who sat on her mother's shoulder by then, looking soggy but otherwise all right, sucking furiously on her thumb. "Anthy, I'm so sorry...."

In answer, Anthea pulled her thumb from her mouth and offered it to Marnie.

"No, thanks," Marnie said, smiling through her tears—and then she was reaching out for her stepmother, "Gina, I know I said I'd watch her. It's all my fault. I'm so sorry...."

Somehow Regina managed to embrace her stepdaughter with one arm while she held the smaller child cradled in the other. "It's all right," Regina soothed the older girl. "She's safe. She's all right." She looked up, caught Sin's eye. "Thanks to you."

A grateful chorus of agreement went up, from all those other Joneses. Sophie still held his hand. She gave it a squeeze. He glanced into her shining eyes—and for one, brief, impossible moment, he saw the man she thought he was reflected there.

That night, Regina and Patrick and their daughters joined them for steaks at Jared and Eden's house. The story of Anthea's rescue was recounted more than once—by Marnie first, and then by Regina when old Oggie Jones arrived and demanded to hear it, too.

Later, after dinner, feeling a little uncomfortable with all the praise and gratitude the Joneses kept showering on him, Sin wandered outside alone. He found a place at the railing of Jared's deck and stood staring out at the pines, thinking that soon he'd go in and find Sophie so they could be on their way.

"I guess you showed up in town just when we needed you." The rough voice of Oggie Jones came from beside him. Odd. The old man walked with a cane that announced his appearance wherever he went—yet Sin hadn't heard him approach.

Sin turned his head and met the old man's strange small eyes. "It was mostly luck."

"Luck don't mean squat if a man doesn't act fast." Those too-wise eyes seemed to bore right down into him. "You acted fast. And this family thanks you for it."

"Anyone else would have done the same thing."

"But *could* anyone else have done the same thing?"

What was that supposed to mean? Sin didn't think he needed to know. "It worked out all right." He felt ready and willing to drop the subject for good. "That's what matters."

The old man let out a low, amused cackle of a laugh. "Good point. And how about for you?"

"What?"

"How's it working out for you?"

Sin faced him squarely. "Are you getting at something here?"

"What do you think, Mr. *Sin*clair Riker?"

Sin noted the emphasis on the first half of his name

and felt the skin along his shoulder blades tighten. No one here knew him as Sin.

He recalled that gray sedan. Someone had decided to have him followed. Could this strange character who thought of himself as Sophie's uncle be that someone? Coldly he suggested, "I think if there's something you want to say to me, you had better say it outright."

The old man pondered that suggestion, then grunted. "Son, you don't know me at all." He pulled a cigar from his shirt pocket and began peeling the cellophane wrapper off. Sin watched those gnarled hands rumple the wrapper and tuck it away in another pocket. "Sophie B. tells me that you are the Sinclair Riker whose family once owned the ranch where she lives now."

"That's right."

Oggie bit the end off the cigar and spat it over his shoulder, beyond the deck. "And how long you stayin' in our beautiful county?"

"I'm not sure."

"Where *you* livin' now, anyway?"

"Los Angeles."

"And you're here to buy property, Sophie B. says. Is that so?"

"Possibly."

The old man cackled some more. Out in the trees, an owl hooted. Sin looked toward the sound—and away from whatever those wise eyes thought they knew. He heard the hiss of a match striking, saw the quick flare of light in his side vision. And then the smell of smoke wafted his way.

The rough voice spoke again. "When a man falls in love, it changes everything. Changes *him.* You know what I mean?"

Sin faced Sophie's "uncle" once more, but said nothing. Wherever the old man was headed with this gambit, Sin felt certain he could get there all on his own.

Oggie studied the burning end of his cigar. "Let me tell you a little story."

"If I said no, would it matter?"

"Hell, no." He flicked his ash. "You listenin'?"

Sin shrugged.

"I'll take that as a yes." Oggie leaned against the railing, sucked in smoke and blew it out. "I come here, to North Magdalene, when I was thirty-five, a footloose gamblin' man. I saw my wife-to-be the first day I walked into town. I knew she would be mine the minute I laid eyes on her. What I didn't realize until later was that I would be hers, as well.

"Beautiful Bathsheba…" Oggie gestured grandly. The red end of the cigar made bright trails through the darkness. "…the empress of my heart." He shook his head. "She's been gone for nigh on thirty years now. But in here—" He tapped his chest with the heel of his hand. "In here, she lives on. Because of her, I am the man you see before you now. Because of her, I put down roots. And those roots go deep, deep as if I had been born in these parts. Because of her, I got…commitments." He said the word with reverence. Then he turned from the night to look at Sin again. "And because of her, I just might go on forever—meddlin' where people wish to hell I'd get lost." He let out another of those low cackles, and leaned in closer to Sin. "That is what you're thinkin', ain't it? That you wish to hell I'd mind my own business."

Sin couldn't help smiling. "You don't strike me as a man likely to be affected by what other people think."

The old man thought that was funny. He cackled again, louder this time.

Sin added, "And love may have changed you. But I am not you."

The old man thought that was *really* funny. He threw back his head and brayed at the moon.

Watching him, Sin felt the tension that had coiled inside him fade away to nothing at all. Oggie Jones was just a sentimental old character who liked to hear himself talk. He knew no more about Sin than anyone else did. And the odds were very small that he'd hired some P.I. to follow Sin around.

And even if he had, what could he have found out? The name of Sin's hotel, the health club he visited— and that he'd been spending his nights in the slim, soft arms of Sophie B. Jones.

The hotel and the health club meant nothing. And anyone who saw him with Sophie could have figured out the rest.

The old man puffed on his cigar awhile longer. The smoke trailed toward the moon. At last, he said, "It's after ten. I'll bet you want to get goin'."

"Yes. We should probably be on our way."

"Well, come on, then. Let's go inside and find that woman of yours."

"Did you like my adopted family?" Sophie asked as they drove the twisting road back to the Mountain Star.

"Yes," he said honestly. "I liked them."

"I'm glad." She leaned across the console and rested her head on his shoulder. "What did you think of Oggie?"

He recalled those wise eyes, that cackling laugh. "He's one of a kind."

She lifted her head, brushed a hand against his shoulder. "I just love him."

"I gathered."

She sighed. "I know he rubs some people the wrong way. But I think he really *cares*. I think he would do anything for the people he loves."

Sin felt for her hand, brought it to his lips, then had to let go to negotiate the next sharp turn. "I think you're right."

"You do?"

He nodded, keeping his eyes front to watch the road. She settled her head on his shoulder again.

They drove the rest of the way in silence.

By the time he pulled into the drive that led up to the Mountain Star, she had dropped off to sleep. She didn't stir as he parked the car, or when he turned the key and the engine went quiet.

"Sophie…" he whispered.

She moved a little, made a small, sleepy sound of protest, then snuggled against his shoulder as if it were her pillow for the night.

"Sophie, we're here."

She said something unintelligible, and finally lifted her head. "I went to sleep."

"No kidding."

She yawned and stretched.

He said, "You're still half-asleep."

She gave him a look that had nothing to do with sleeping. "Let's go to bed."

Once they got inside, she wanted a shower. They took one together. He lathered her hair twice for her, the sweet-smelling bubbles running down his arms. Then, when they stepped out onto the bathroom tiles, they dried each other.

Soon enough they were kissing, and laughing, the towels dropping at their feet.

He carried her to the bedroom and laid her on the bed. She looked up at him, lifting her arms, her still-wet hair snaking on the pillow, reminding him...

Of the two of them, wrestling underwater, the bubbles rising all around them, her hair floating against his chest.

Happy.

He was happy.

Living a lie with Sophie B. Jones.

"Sinclair..." she beckoned him.

He sank down upon her, burying his face in the wet, coiling strands of her hair. She pulled him close, sighing.

And when her fulfillment shuddered through her, she said it again.

"I love you, love you, love you, I do...."

In the morning, they went riding. And he stayed for breakfast after.

She kissed him goodbye before he left, in the grove of pines near his car, her sweet body pressing close, her hair smelling of sunshine and last night's shampoo.

"It's a new movie tonight," she told him, pulling back just enough that she could look up at him.

"I know, I saw the ad in the *Union*. The next installment in—"

"Our Randi Wilding Film Retrospective." She looked exceedingly pleased with herself. "Tonight, it's *Kerri-*

gan's Honor. Randi plays an FBI agent whose mother and sister are raped and murdered by a gang of thugs. Naturally, she has to kill them all…in very imaginative ways."

"Naturally."

"You're going to love this one, I just know it. And next week, we'll have—"

"Stop. Let's take it one week at a time."

Something happened in her eyes then. Their brightness dimmed a little. She looked down at where her hands rested against his chest, and then back up at him. "Sinclair?"

"What?"

And she dared to ask, "Is there going to *be* a next week for us?"

What could he say to that? How the hell did he know?

She fiddled with a button on his shirt. "I don't want to push you. I honestly don't, but…" And it all came pouring out. "Oh, Sinclair, I have to tell you, sometimes, when you leave, all I can think is how much I *don't* know about you. I don't even know where you live— well, L.A., I know that. But L.A. is so big. What part of L.A.? And what is your house like? Do you know your neighbors? Are they nice? And where do you work? What do you really *do* there? And your friends. What are your friends like? Will I ever meet them? Will they hate me or like me?"

"Sophie. No one could hate you."

"Sinclair, do you understand what I'm asking you?"

He knew then that he could put off telling her no longer.

But where to begin?

"Sinclair, can you understand?"

"Yes. Of course, I can."

"Could we talk? Really talk? About the two of us. About…what will happen next? Could we talk…tonight?"

"Sophie…"

She put up a hand between them, for silence. "Tonight. All right?"

He thought of the long day of work she had ahead of her. At least, if he waited till tonight, she'd have a few hours to herself after everything had been said. Maybe that was the best way. If there was such a thing in this situation.

Or maybe he was just putting off the inevitable again….

"Please, Sinclair."

"All right, Sophie. Tonight."

"Thank you." She moved close again to brush a kiss against his lips. It wasn't enough for him—when it came to her, nothing was ever enough. He grabbed her close and kissed her hard.

Then, as she had other mornings, she stood beneath the pines to watch him go.

Sin drove back to his hotel by rote, hardly seeing where he was going, thinking of the obsession that had got hold of him the day he'd learned his family's ranch could be his again. The timing had seemed perfect. He had the money and the time to build himself a big new house, fill the stables with thoroughbred horses and live the life of the gentleman rancher. His second in command at Inkerris, Incorporated, would be taking over from him. Within a year he'd hardly have to travel to L.A. at all. Within a year, no matter what kind of fight

she had tried to put up, he would have been able to remove the one obstacle to his plans: Ms. Sophie B. Jones
and her five-acre lease.

He'd intended only to get rid of her.

But now he couldn't bear to lose her.

Love changes a man, old Oggie Jones had said.

But Sin was a realist. No one changed that much in
five days. He still wanted his land back, wanted his
heritage back.

And love? It was a word people batted around a lot.
His father had talked about love all the time—the love
of family, the love of the land. And then he'd lost the
land and opted out by hanging himself. And his mother
had *loved;* she'd loved him and his father—and she'd
claimed to love the first ten or so of the string of men
who'd put food on her table.

By the time he was nine years old, Sin had learned
that love was something it didn't pay to believe in,
something he simply did not have time for if he planned
to crawl out of the hole his father and mother had put
him in. He got his first paper route when he was ten, and
he was working as a busboy by the time he was sixteen.

He'd been careful to stay on the right side of the law.
He'd given a wide berth to the drug dealers in his neighborhood—and not out of any nobility of spirit. There
was fast money in drugs, and money of any kind interested him. But unfortunately drug money was fast
money he could lose if he got caught. And he couldn't
afford a prison record following him around. After all,
he wanted to rebuild for himself the fortune his father
had lost. So he kept his nose clean.

He bought his first house, a run-down rental duplex
in San Pedro when he was twenty-one. He forced the

tenants out over their constant—and sincere—protests that they had nowhere to go. Then he fixed the place up himself, reselling it a year after he bought it for three times what he'd paid for it.

By eight years ago, when he was thirty, Inkerris, Incorporated, was going strong. He'd come a long way. In the next eight years, he went even further. And *love* had played no part at all in his success.

No, Sin Riker didn't believe in love and he didn't have time for it. And he certainly didn't deserve it—a fact that Sophie was going to have to face tonight when he told her the truth.

Three times, she had told him she loved him. After tonight, he doubted she'd be telling him again.

Sin parked his car in the hotel's lot and went in the main entrance, where he stopped at the front desk.

"Sinclair Riker, room 103," he told the clerk. "Any messages?"

The clerk pointed toward the small sitting area opposite the desk. "Someone to see you."

Sin turned just as his former fiancée stood from a damask-covered wing chair. "Sin, darling. Where *have* you been? I've been waiting for over an hour."

Chapter 9

"Willa. I had no idea you were coming."

"Oh, I'm sure you didn't." After pausing to brush lightly at the few wrinkles that had dared to crease the front of her pencil-thin silk skirt, Willa strolled up to him and slid a proprietary arm through his. "We have to talk." She scrunched up her perfect nose. "What's that I smell? Horse, I do believe."

He looked down into her exotically slanted blue eyes. "I've been riding."

"Riding?" She squeezed his arm, raised a black eyebrow. "Oh, I have no doubt at all about that."

The light dawned. "You hired a detective service to have me followed."

"I certainly did." She made a tsking sound with her tongue. "And it cost me a serious chunk of change, too.

I was assured you'd never know. But then you spotted him anyway—on Monday, wasn't it?"

"Sunday, actually. Monday was the day I let him know that I knew."

She ran a long, red, beautifully manicured fingernail down his arm. "I should probably demand at least half of my money back."

"What do you want, Willa?"

She lifted a shoulder in a delicate shrug. "I told you. We have to talk."

"All right." He started to move toward the sitting area just a few feet away.

She hung back, casting a glance at the desk clerk. "Privately, please—how about your room?"

He dragged in a long breath and let it out slowly. "Fine. Let's go."

In his suite, Willa tossed her envelope bag on an end table, kicked off her Italian pumps and dropped to the sofa, stretching her long, silk-clad legs out along its length. Once she'd made herself comfortable, she got right to the point. "You've been having an affair, Sin. With that sweet little nobody who's living at that ranch of yours."

Sin leaned against the closed door and folded his arms over his chest. "*Sweet,* Willa? Was that how your detective described her?"

"I have pictures."

He shook his head in disgust. "God, Willa."

Willa recrossed her legs, ran a smoothing hand up her already smooth stockings, then looked up to make sure he saw the provocative gesture. "She's not your type at all. So *nice.* Big innocent eyes. Acres of long, badly cut hair. And those outré calf-length dresses that look as if they were made from Laura Ashley window treatments. Honestly, Sin. I'm disappointed in you."

Sin straightened from the door. "Is that all you got me up here to tell me?"

Willa sighed and cast a glance heavenward. "Isn't it enough?"

"You're completely off base here, and you know it. How I spend my time—and who I spend it with—are no longer any of your concern."

She swung her legs to the floor and rose, catlike, to her feet. "Of course what you do is my concern. I'm your fiancée."

"What the hell are you talking about?"

"Sin, please. Let's not play games. You know I'm going to marry you."

"I am not the one who's playing games."

"Oh, Sin." She dipped her chin and looked up at him archly from under her lashes. "You know I only play the games you like." She sauntered toward him.

"Stop."

She paused, put a hand on her hip and pretended to look confused. "What, darling?"

"Let me refresh your memory."

"My memory is fresh enough."

"*You* called it off, Willa. You said, and I quote, 'I have no intention of moving to the middle of nowhere to raise horses in the pine trees. If that's what you think you want, then you and I are through.'"

Willa sighed. "I was just trying to get you to come to your senses."

"You failed."

"I can see that. And I'm willing to...reevaluate my position on this issue."

"It's too late."

She shook her smooth cap of black hair. "No, it's not." And then, in a stunningly swift move, she reached behind her. He heard the zipper of that clinging silk dress as it started to slide.

"No, Willa."

"Yes, Sin."

The zipper parted all the way. The dress slid off her shoulders. She pushed it down, over her boyish hips and her perfect legs. Within seconds, she stepped free of it. Now she wore only a black garter belt and silk stockings. Her small, perfect breasts pointed right at him.

She was a beautiful woman. And she left him absolutely cold. He wondered abstractly what he'd ever seen in her. "Put your dress back on, Willa."

"After I'm done here."

"You are done. Believe me."

She started toward him again.

"Willa. Don't do this."

She didn't stop until she was against him, her impudent breasts pressed into his shirtfront, her grasping hand finding him through the fabric of his slacks.

Flaccid. She felt that. And the confident gleam in her eyes faded a little.

"It's no good, Willa." He had a powerful urge to shove her away, but he controlled it. She expected the old games to work on him. He couldn't really blame her for that. They'd always worked before.

Her hand moved, stroking, squeezing, trying to inspire some response. But there was none. At last, she let go and stepped back. "Your little *sweetheart* must be very...demanding."

"Leave Sophie out of this." He kept his tone gentle, but she couldn't have mistaken the underlying thread of steel in it. "And put your dress back on."

A tight, feral sound escaped her red mouth. Sin thought for a moment she might make some remark about Sophie that he wouldn't be able to let pass. But no words came. Finally she turned and stalked back to where she'd left her dress. She bent down, shook it out and stepped into it. She reached behind her. He heard the zipper close. Then she ran her hands down her waist and hips, straightening, smoothing.

She went to the sofa, collected her shoes, slid them on and grabbed up her bag. It was only a few steps to the door. She stopped with her hand on the knob to grant him one final caustic glare.

"You will regret this," she said.

All he felt was sadness, for both of them. Two hard, acquisitive people. They'd struck sparks off each other once, sparks that had ignited to a white-hot blaze. But there had been no warmth to it. Only heat without comfort, like the heartless fires of hell.

"Do you hear me, Sin Riker? You will be sorry."

"Willa, I swear to you, I already am."

"Not sorry enough, I'm afraid." She went out the door, slamming it smartly behind her.

She'd been gone a good ten minutes before Sin admitted to himself how very simple it would be for Willa to make him sorrier still.

About an hour after Sinclair had left for the day, Sophie sat on a stool in the hayloft, checking the sprockets on her aging projector, trying to figure out which one might be sticking. Last Sunday, the old monster had nearly burned a hole in the first reel. Naturally though, right now, it seemed to be working all right.

"Hello? Is anyone up there?" It was a woman's voice, one Sophie didn't recognize. The voice came from the foot of the ladder that led up to the loft.

Sophie rose from the stool and went to the top of the ladder. A tall, black-haired fashion plate of a woman stood below. "Sophie B. Jones?"

"That's me."

"The big man at the stables said I might find you here. I wonder, could I steal a few minutes of your time?"

"Sure. Be right down." Sophie returned to the projector, swiftly rewound the short bit of test reel and turned the thing off.

The woman watched from the foot of the ladder as Sophie climbed down. "You actually run a movie theater in here?"

Sophie jumped from the last rung, brushed off her hands and shook out her long skirt. "You bet."

The woman looked up toward the rafters and then right at Sophie. "Charming." Her inflection said she found the barn—and Sophie herself—anything but.

Sophie moved back a step. "You didn't say your name."

"Willa. Willa Tweed."

The name rang a bell somewhere far back in her mind, but Sophie couldn't quite remember why. She gestured at the rows of theater seats that marched away from them, down toward the screen. "Have a chair."

Willa Tweed licked her lips—nervously, it seemed to

Sophie. "No. I think it's better if I stand." She took in a long breath and let it out slowly. "I have to admit, now that I'm here, I simply do not know how to begin…." She let the words trail off. A long, significant pause ensued, a pause in which Sophie's own uneasiness increased. Finally the woman spoke again. "I've come about Sin."

Sophie felt more confused by the moment. Was the woman a representative of some religious group? "About sin? I'm afraid I don't—"

"Sin," Willa Tweed said again, impatiently. "Sin Riker."

"You mean…Sinclair?"

The woman's mouth tightened. "Yes. Sinclair Riker. My fiancé. That's exactly who I mean."

Right then, Sophie remembered where she'd heard the woman's name before:

"There was someone," Sinclair had said. *"It didn't work out."*

And Sophie had asked, *"What was her name?"*

He had answered, *"Willa."*

Sophie said very carefully, "I don't understand. Sinclair told me it was over between you and him."

The woman laughed, a brittle angry sound. "Oh, I'm sure he did. I'm sure he told you whatever he thought you wanted to hear."

Sophie fell back a step. "No. I don't believe that. I don't believe he would—"

Willa threw up a hand. "You have no idea what Sin is capable of." She made a low, derisive sound. "Honestly. Your own situation says it all."

Sophie's heart was pounding way too fast. She put

a hand against it, in a pointless effort to make it slow down. "My own situation?"

"The problem that Sin came here to handle in the first place—you."

"Me?" Sophie shook her head. "He came here to handle *me?*"

"Yes. You and your inconvenient five-acre lease on his precious ranch. Of course, he would have offered you a good price for it. Did you take it? If you haven't, I suppose he must think you will. I suppose right now he thinks he can talk you into just about anything. And I also imagine he's right...don't you?"

Sophie tried to comprehend what the woman was babbling about. "No. It's not his ranch. Not anymore. Not for years and years. You don't understand, he—"

The woman laughed again. "*I'm* not the one who doesn't understand. Sin owns this ranch now. And if you don't know that, you're a bigger fool than I ever imagined. My God, you must be making lease payments—to Inkerris, Incorporated. Don't you get it? It's an anagram. For his name."

"His name," Sophie echoed numbly.

"Exactly. Sin Riker. Inkerris. Switch the letters around a little and you can have either one."

Sophie felt weak in the knees. A rickety folding chair stood not far away. She backed up quickly and dropped into it.

Willa Tweed watched her through glittering ice blue eyes. "So, I can see that the anagram got past you. And it appears that Sin has told you virtually nothing."

"I don't—"

"Let me fully enlighten you."

"No, I—"

The woman ignored Sophie's weak protest and continued right on. "About six months ago, Sin saw some notice—in the *San Francisco Chronicle,* I believe it was, though I can't be sure. He takes a lot of newspapers. He finds potential properties in them."

Right then Tom, the black cat, poked his head through the split in the curtains that led to the outside doors. He let out a small, curious *"Mnneow?"*

Willa glanced back briefly, saw it was only a cat, and then turned on Sophie once more. "But I'm getting off the point, which is that Sin found a for-sale notice about the *former* Riker Ranch in that paper. And from then on, he was a man obsessed. He wanted that land back."

Sophie's mind seemed to be working way too slowly. She asked idiotically, "He...wanted it back?"

The woman let out a delicate little grunt. "That's what I said. He wanted it back. So he got his people on it."

"His people?"

"Oh, come on. You understand. He has people who work for him, people whose job it is to investigate any property that catches his interest. In the case of this ranch, his people found that the only problem was you. Somehow you had managed to get yourself a lease on five acres of this place. Sin didn't like that at all. He wanted to know more about you—about how you were going to take it when he told you he wanted to terminate that lease. So he investigated further. He had a detective service following you around for six weeks."

The idea made Sophie's stomach roil: someone, some total stranger, had watched her go about her life for a month and a half. How could that have been? "No..."

"Yes. He learned that you were very...attached to the

little enterprise you've created here. And that it would probably be difficult to get rid of you until your lease was up. Which would be another ten years. But Sin didn't care. He bought the property anyway, a very low-key acquisition through intermediaries. He used a San Francisco bank to handle the whole transaction so that, until he was ready to approach you with his offer, you'd know next to nothing about the new owner."

Tom strolled up to Willa and began rubbing at her ankles. She delicately kicked him away. The cat moved on to Sophie, jumping onto her lap. Sophie absently stroked his warm fur. The purring started, a warm, friendly sound—in direct contrast to the frosty blue of Willa Tweed's eyes.

Willa went on. "Sin finds that works quite well—to come in with the deed in his hand and all the leverage he can muster lined up behind him. Then he makes his offer. And the smart ones take what he offers."

Sophie held Tom tighter. The cat purred louder.

Willa asked, "Shall I tell you what happens if they *don't* take his offer?"

Right then, the curtain to the concession area stirred again. Sinclair stepped through it.

Sophie's hold on Tom loosened. The cat slipped lightly to the floor and sauntered off toward the rows of seats. Sophie watched him go. So much easier to watch the cat than to look at Willa Tweed—or to meet the dark burning eyes of the man by the curtain.

Willa must have turned and seen Sinclair. Sophie heard her hard laugh. "Sin, darling. Come join us. I was just explaining the facts of life to your sweet little girlfriend here."

When Sinclair didn't reply, Willa laughed again.

"Well, it may be the middle of August, but I do believe I detect a certain chill in the air."

Tom disappeared down a row of seats. Sophie made herself look at Willa again. The dark-haired woman faced away, toward the man by the curtains to the concession stand. Her back was very straight and proud.

"I suppose it's time I was leaving," Willa said.

Sinclair moved clear of the curtains as Willa started his way. Just before she went through, she turned once more to Sinclair. "I do believe you're sorry enough—now."

Sinclair said flatly, "Goodbye, Willa."

"Yes," Willa replied. "I would say that's exactly the word for it." She pushed the curtain aside and stepped through.

Chapter 10

Once Willa was gone, Sophie stayed in her chair, not moving, for a very long time. And Sinclair just stood there, near the last row of seats, as silent as she was.

Finally she made herself look at him, made herself ask in a voice that came out all weak and whispery, "Are you engaged to her?"

He met her gaze, unwavering. "I was."

"Until when?"

"She broke it off a couple of weeks ago."

"She said otherwise. She said you were still her fiancé."

"Then she lied."

Hope kindled in Sophie then, a hot, hungry little flame. Maybe it was *all* a lie, all those awful things the woman had said....

But, no. How could Willa have known the name of

the faceless corporation that owned the ranch now—unless Inkerris and Sin Riker were one and the same? Beyond that, there were all the details of his life that he hadn't told her. And most damning of all was Sinclair himself, standing there, looking so bleak, his expression telling Sophie better than words ever could that at least some of what Willa had said was true.

Sophie straightened in the chair, ordered some volume into her voice. "She also said that *you* are Inkerris, Incorporated. That you own the Riker Ranch now, that you came here with the intention of manipulating me into giving up my lease."

Tom appeared again, sidling up to Sinclair. Sinclair bent and lifted him into those strong arms. The cat immediately started purring. Sophie could hear it clearly from all the way over in her chair.

"Is it true, Sinclair? Is that really why you came here?"

He let the cat down. "Yes."

The single word pierced her like a blade to the heart. "Oh, Sin…" She heard herself call him by that name for the first time. And realized that it fit him. "Five days. Five whole days. We've been together every moment we could. You never told me. You never said a word."

She waited for him to explain. For him to simply say that he didn't tell her of his schemes because he couldn't figure out how to do it without running the risk of losing her.

Which was nothing but the truth.

However, the truth, at that point, wasn't good enough for Sin.

He stood at the top of the aisle in Sophie's barn theater, looking into her wide, wounded eyes and he knew that the time for explanations had passed. At that moment, Sin Riker hated being inside his own skin.

"Please," she said in a broken voice. "Tell me. Explain to me why you—"

He put up a hand. "Sophie, it's no good."

"What?" Those innocent eyes pleaded with his. "No good? What's no good?"

"You know."

"No. I…I want to understand. I want you to tell me—"

"There's nothing to tell. Nothing that will make any difference. We're…night and day, you and me. And everything we had was based on lies. *My* lies."

"No. Don't say that. In your heart, you—"

"Sophie. Face it. It's just no good. Look at you. You pass out bag lunches to the homeless."

"So?"

"Sophie, I have never given anything away in my life."

"But.. you had to fight, I understand that. You had nothing. And you had to make a place for yourself in the world."

He shook his head. "Look at you. Sitting there defending me. I don't deserve defending, Sophie."

She raised her chin, did her best to look defiant. "I believe you do."

"You *want* to believe. But believing won't change the facts. Maybe it's time you heard the truth. Maybe it's time I made it clear what I had in mind for you."

He could see the denial in her eyes, he could read her so well by then. Not if it's ugly, she was thinking. Not if it's cruel.

He goaded her. "Are you ready for the truth, Sophie?"

She pressed her lips together, looked away. Then she drew in a breath and faced him once more. "Yes. All right. Tell me the truth."

And he did, in a voice without expression. "The truth is, I was going to destroy you if I had to." He began walking toward her. "If you had refused my offer, you were going to find yourself in a world of woe trying to run this place."

She watched him advance, shaking her head. "No, you couldn't have. You *wouldn't* have."

He kept coming until he stood right in front of her, looking down. "Oh, yes, I would. I've done it before. And I've done it often."

She swallowed, eyes wide as saucers now, staring up at him as if he frightened her. "Driven people out, you mean?"

He nodded. "I've become quite…skilled at it, over the years."

Her sweet mouth was trembling. "You sound like you're proud of it."

He shrugged. "It's just the way the world works."

"No. Not always. Sometimes—"

He didn't let her finish. "Sophie, you're an innocent." He touched her cheek. It was soft and warm as a peach in the sun. She held very still. She *endured* his caress. He dropped his hand away, stepped back just a fraction. "It's the way *my* world works."

"But not mine."

"My point exactly. Your world and my world. Night and day. Shadow and light. They don't exist in the same space. They never have and they never will."

"People *can* change, Sinclair."

"Please. Call me Sin. Everyone does—and do you want to hear the rest or not?"

She drew her shoulders back again. "Yes. All right. Tell me the rest."

He began where he'd left off. "Here, it would have started with a fence."

She frowned. "A fence?"

"Around the five acres you're leasing, to keep you and all your guests off the rest of my land. You see, I know you depend on the use of the whole ranch, to make sure those horses you board get the exercise their owners pay you for.

"Second, I would have built another house. Right on the other side of that fence I just mentioned. Construction can be so *loud,* Sophie. Your guests wouldn't have liked it at all.

"And then, there's this 'theater' of yours. I believe certain zoning regulations are being stretched here. I would have made sure those regulations were strictly enforced—" he gestured at the battered seats, the torn theater screen "—which would have shut this part of your operation down, I'm afraid.

"And do you know what it's like to have the health department after you? To have inspectors paying you regular visits, harassing Myra in her run-down kitchen, just on the off chance that your facilities aren't as *clean* as they ought to be? And what about that damn campground? I know that some of the kids you let stay there have to be runaways. And who knows what they're carrying in those dirty bedrolls. I would have had the police on them, shaking them down. You would have taken some heat, I'm afraid, if any of them were underage or carrying drugs."

She fidgeted, making the folding chair creak. And once again, she couldn't stop herself from defending him. "But, Sin, you didn't do any of those things. You didn't do anything at all, except share five perfect nights with me."

"Sophie. The point is, I have done all those things before. And I would do them to you. If you refused my offer. Because that's who I am, Sophie. That's how I operate. It's all strictly legal. It's all aboveboard. It's what I have every right to do. But what someone like *you* would never do. Because you've got too damn much heart."

"But...you've changed. If you *were* like that, you're not like that anymore."

"Sophie. You are impossible. Not only an innocent, but a romantic, as well. I'm the same man I always was. And whatever this thing is between us, it couldn't last. Frankly, as a general rule, innocence bores me. And romance, as far as I'm concerned, is for starry-eyed fools."

Sophie stared up at him. She yearned to keep arguing with him, keep on defending him.

But it was painfully clear he didn't want to be defended.

And her doubts kept crowding in, reminding her that he had never once said he loved her, though she'd declared her own love repeatedly. That he really had lied to her from the very first.

Five whole days. That was the simple truth. Five whole days in which he had constantly misled her, in which he hadn't uttered a single word about his real aim in coming to the Mountain Star.

Sin could see those doubts in her eyes. He understood that he had lost her—and knew that it was no more than he deserved. "Listen," he heard himself say. "I have a deal for you."

Sophie closed her eyes. He could see it was all too much for her. She needed time to absorb what he'd told her, time to figure out what to do.

He gave her no time. "Sophie, look at me."

She opened her eyes. He had never seen her look so weary. "What deal?"

"You stay current on your lease and things will go on here just as they have been. You can pass out free lunches for the next decade- -and more. I'll see to it." The words came out of his mouth without him even knowing he would say them. But once they were out, he knew he would abide by them. "Goodbye, Sophie."

He turned on his heel and headed for the door. Behind him, he heard her cry out softly, "Wait…"

He paused, fool that he was, and turned around again. She had risen to her feet.

She took a step toward him. "Tonight. We were going to talk tonight. Would you have told me all this then?"

The fool inside him sang out, Yes! Everything. I meant to tell it all.

Sin ordered the fool to silence, and asked coldly, "What does it matter?"

"I…it would be something."

"Innocent," he said, infusing the word with all the considerable cynicism at his command. "That's what you are."

"Please. I just want to know. Did you plan to tell me tonight?"

He hesitated on the verge of the truth, but finally answered, "No." Another lie. The kindest one, really.

After all, he had planned to get rid of her. And then,

once he'd met her, over and over he had planned to tell her the truth. He had never done either. So what did his intentions really mean in the end?

Nothing. Nothing at all.

She caught her lower lip between her teeth. "Oh." Her whole sweet body seemed to droop. "I see."

He turned again. And went through the curtain, the desperate fool inside him hoping against hope that she'd call him back once more.

But she said nothing. And so he kept on walking, across the plank floor of her makeshift lobby and out the open barn doors.

Back where he'd left her, Sophie stood listening. She heard Sin's footsteps retreating. And then she heard nothing except the birds singing outside, and that pigeon she could never get rid of, suddenly taking flight up there in the rafters over her head.

She remembered the projector.

She'd been trying to fix it.

She turned and went to the ladder, started to climb. Halfway up, she stopped. She wanted to be outside. She *needed* to be outside. The projector would just have to wait.

Carefully, she descended. She felt so...slow suddenly. Like someone trying to walk through deep water. Or someone very old and frail.

Outside, the sun shone down and a gentle breeze stirred the pines, making them whisper and sigh to each other, a sound she'd always loved, a sound that had always created a sensation of lightness inside her.

Now she didn't feel light. She felt heavy. Numb.

She walked under the rows of maples, past the stables. Skirting the lawns of the main house, she moved into the shadows of the oak grove, passing through it and then out—across the open pasture, and down to the creek. To the special place. *Their* special place, hers and Sinclair's.

Sin.

He had told her to call him Sin.

"I don't know you," he'd said that first night.

"You know me," she had replied. And he had. He had known so much about her. He had *paid* to learn about her; he'd had her followed for six weeks. Someone had been watching her. Some detective, keeping tabs on her, recording all the details of her life.

Sophie shivered at the thought. She sat on that big dark rock that stuck out into the stream—the rock on which he had kissed her, where she had pleaded with him to come to her bed—and she shivered through her numbness.

"You know me," she had told him.

And he had.

It was she who had not known him.

And that woman. That awful, cold woman: Willa Tweed.

Sin had said he didn't love that woman. Yet he had once meant to marry her. They must have shared something together—desire, perhaps. No doubt Sin must have wanted Willa Tweed once.

Just as he had wanted Sophie.

Sophie rubbed her hands down her shivery arms. Romantic, he had called her. As if it were an insult. And an innocent.

Well, maybe she was. An innocent romantic.

But surely, after what had happened today, she'd never be quite so naive or sentimental again.

She'd been right to let him go, she was sure of it. Because *he'd* been right. In the end, they were much too different from each other. It couldn't have lasted.

She understood that now.

He had said she could keep the Mountain Star.

Could she really believe that?

Time would tell. She'd go on as she always had. And if he came back with his offer to buy out her lease, well, she'd deal with that when the time came. At least now she understood completely what would happen if she refused.

Sophie lay back on the rock. It was a hard bed, but she didn't expect comfort right then. She closed her eyes, listened to the water rushing, the birds singing their midday songs, and wished she could just stay numb forever.

Because she had a terrible feeling that when the numbness passed, the pain of her heart breaking would be impossible to bear.

Chapter 11

Her arms full of last night's sheets, Sophie descended the back stairs. She went straight to the pantry area, which also did duty as a laundry room. She set the sheets on the dryer, put detergent in the washer, and then loaded the sheets in on top. She started the cycle and closed the lid.

Upstairs, Midge was supposed to be making up the last of the beds. Sophie knew she ought to trudge back up there and make certain that Midge kept on task. So far that morning, the maid had been utterly useless.

It was a matter of love over duty. Last night, Midge's boyfriend had finally proposed and Midge had accepted. So today, the maid had her mind on wedding announcements and not on getting the beds made.

Sophie started for the stairs again, then stopped when

she got to the base of them. She looked up the narrow, dim stairwell—and remembered.

That first night. Sinclair so grim and distracted as she showed him the lower floor. And then, on those very stairs, grabbing for her, burying his face in her hair. And herself, holding on, promising him that it would be all right....

Sophie closed her eyes in a vain attempt to block out the memory. She turned from the stairwell. Midge was happy. Happiness was rare enough in life. If the beds at the Mountain Star didn't get made until later than usual today, it wouldn't be the end of the world.

Really, Sophie knew she ought to go back over to her office in the spare room of the guest house. She ought to boot up her trusty old Macintosh and balance the accounts.

She ought to. And she would. In a few minutes.

She wandered toward the kitchen. Myra was making her famous blackberry jam today. The smell of the cooking berries hung sweet and heavy in the air. Sophie followed that late-summer scent.

When she reached the doorway, she saw Myra over at the stove, stirring a big, steaming kettle. Caleb stood beside her.

"What's wrong with her?" Caleb spoke quietly—a man who didn't want to be overheard. "She hasn't been herself for three or four days now."

Myra went on stirring. "Since *he* stopped coming round—have you noticed?"

"I noticed." Now Caleb sounded grim. "He's run out on her, hasn't he?"

"She's not talking."

"I'd like to talk to *him*."

Sophie spoke up then, her tone falsely bright. "Please, don't even think about it."

Both of her employees whipped around. "Sophie B.," they muttered in unison. She would have smiled at their guilty expressions—if she'd been in a smiling mood.

"We were just..." Myra hesitated, then finished rather lamely, "...worried about you."

"Don't be. I'm fine."

Caleb jumped in. "That's not true. We all know it's not. You drag around here lookin' miserable. We just want to help."

Sophie waved a hand in front of her face. "There's nothing you can do. Honestly. I will be fine. In a while."

Caleb fisted both big hands. "Just give me that bastard's phone number. It's all I want."

"Caleb, stop it."

"You let me at him."

"Caleb. Listen. It's nothing you can do anything about. Leave it alone."

Myra laid her freckled hand on Caleb's arm. "She's right. It's not for you to settle."

Caleb muttered something truculent, pulled out from under Myra's steadying grip and stalked out. Myra turned back to her cooking blackberries. Sophie dared to come forward, into the room.

"Caleb only wants to make things right," Myra said carefully.

"I know. But there really is nothing he can do."

"He knows that, too. But he doesn't like it one bit." The cook tapped the spoon on the edge of the pot. "And neither do I."

"I will be all right." Sophie uttered the words way too grimly.

"Sure you will." Myra shot her a determined smile, then gestured toward the big table in the center of the room. "Now, bring me that tray of sterilized Mason jars."

The days passed. Sophie went through all the motions that equaled her life. But the joy, the pleasure, seemed leached from it all. Her world had a dullness to it now. It wasn't the way she'd expected to feel. She kept waiting for the real pain of loss to begin, for her heart to break—or else to feel better. Neither seemed to happen. One bleak day passed like the one before it.

Sinclair never tried to contact her. She mailed off the lease payment. And by the time Labor Day had come and gone, she started to believe he must have meant what he said: if she paid her lease on time, she could keep the Mountain Star.

That realization should have helped, shouldn't it? But somehow, it didn't. Except to make her feel angry beneath the dullness.

As if he had bested her somehow. Outdone her in goodness, when he was the one who was supposed to be bad.

Sometimes, at night, she would wake from sensual dreams of him. She would look out the window at the star-thick Sierra sky, wishing he was there beside her, to caress and kiss her, to ease the ache of wanting him.

She almost hated him then, for the way her own body betrayed her. She wanted to forget him, to stop remembering, stop yearning.

To reclaim her life again, the way it used to be, before she had ever laid eyes on him. To return to the time of her own innocence—yes, that was it. To the time when she trusted without question, when she gave without thought of the price it might cost her somewhere down the line.

Going through the motions. Yes, that was her life now. She still did the things she believed in: the campground remained open; Myra continued to give away food they probably should have saved for the paying customers. Midge quit and Sophie immediately hired someone even more hopeless, a four-months' pregnant, unmarried nineteen-year-old named Bethy, whose boyfriend had recently taken off for parts unknown.

Bethy was plagued by continuing morning sickness, which seemed to strike about an hour into her shift. Then she'd have to sit down and chew soda crackers— or simply head home to the house she shared with an older sister and the sister's family. That would leave Sophie making beds, washing sheets, sweeping floors— and resenting it mightily.

Sophie knew that she ought to let Bethy go. And that depressed her further. The girl did need the job. But even Sophie couldn't justify having someone on her limited payroll who never managed to get any work done.

Worst of all, to Sophie's mind, her theater had stopped giving her pleasure. By the weekend after Labor Day, she was showing the fifth installment in her Randi Wilding Retrospective. It was one of Randi's very best films, *Shadowed Heart*. The actress played a woman with mental disabilities who managed to show a whole town the real meaning of love and sacrifice. Sophie had been preparing her introduction to that one for a long time. And then, on Wednesday, September third, Randi Wilding died in a plane crash. The news was all over the papers. It was something Sophie would have cried over once: all that talent and beauty, snuffed out forever. Yet when she heard the news, she felt nothing at all.

She stayed up late into the night, reworking her introductory speech, trying to put into it all the emotions she couldn't make herself feel.

When Thursday night came, the theater was packed. Sophie had to use all of her old folding chairs to seat everyone.

And then, when she got up there in front of them all, her much-rehearsed speech came out sounding utterly flat, totally empty of warmth and compassion. Her audience watched her politely. Some, the ones who visited often, stared with puzzled, slightly worried expressions. In the end, grasping at straws, she threw in a few jokes about the pigeon in the rafters. No one so much as chuckled. She felt only relief when she finally headed for the hayloft to get the darn thing rolling.

Oggie Jones, whom she hadn't seen since she and Sin visited North Magdalene together, showed up on Friday night. When she sold him his ticket, he asked her how she was doing. She pasted on a smile, and chirped out, "Just fine."

He leaned toward her, narrowing his eyes. "You don't look so fine. How's that man of yours?"

A tiny flame of anger licked up inside her. She was getting so tired of having people tell her she didn't look fine, and she didn't need old Oggie Jones asking her about Sin. She did not need that at all.

"I have no *man,* thank you." She shoved his change at him. "And, for your information, I meant what I said. I really am *fine.*"

"Well, pardon me for givin' a damn," the old man growled.

Tears of confusion and shame stung the back of Sophie's throat. Oh, what was *wrong* with her, to speak so sharply to dear Uncle Oggie? She wanted to tell him she was sorry, ask him to please forgive her for behaving so badly. But he was already gone, toddling on that manzanita cane of his toward the open barn doors. She turned a quivery smile on her next customer, promising herself that she would smooth things over after the show.

But then, all through her lifeless introduction, she kept feeling the watchful weight of that beady dark gaze on her. It was nearly as unsettling—though in a totally different way—as the first night Sin had sat in her audience and listened to her opening speech. She had the very unpleasant feeling that Oggie would not let her simply apologize for her rude behavior and be done with it. He was going to bring up the subject of Sin again, she just knew it. And she didn't want to deal with that, not tonight. Not at all.

At intermission, he made things worse. He hobbled up to the concession stand and ordered exactly what Sin had ordered that first night.

"Gimme a bowl of popcorn—and maybe some bottled spring water. Yeah, that sounds refreshin', don't you think, gal?"

She gaped at him. Oggie *never* bought anything at intermission but coffee, light and sweet.

He let out one of those cackling laughs of his. She'd always thought that laugh charming and folksy. Tonight, it just set her nerves jangling like loose pennies in a rolling jar.

"Come on, popcorn and bottled water. Snap it up, now."

She shoveled the popcorn into a bowl and gave him the water. He made a big show of counting out exact change. Then he said, "You know, gal, with this cane and all, I don't believe I can carry both the bowl and the bottle. I think you're gonna have to help me back to my seat."

There were five other customers waiting behind him. Sophie cast them a rueful glance, half hoping that one of them would either complain—or volunteer to help dear old Uncle Oggie themselves. But this was the Mountain Star, so they all smiled in tolerant understanding.

One of them spoke up. "You go ahead, Sophie B. We can wait."

Oggie chortled away. "Yeah, they can wait." He flung out a hand, indicating the water and popcorn. "Let's move." He turned and started for the open curtains to the main theater, looking way too happy with himself.

Sophie was forced to pick up his refreshments and follow in his wake.

At his seat—on the aisle, thank heaven—he had to make a big event out of laying his cane down just so and settling himself in. Then he winked at her. "Hand 'em over, gal." She passed him the bowl and the bottle of water. "Thank you," he said, nodding his grizzled head like some backwoods potentate. "I surely do appreciate your kindness to an old man." His tiny eyes twinkled merrily.

She gritted her teeth together and kept on smiling, wishing with all her heart by then that she didn't owe him an apology.

Shadowed Heart was a real ten-hankie tearfest. By

the time the final credits rolled, all the women were sobbing and the men kept surreptitiously swiping at their eyes. Sophie stood by the door as she always did, saying her farewells—farewells that had become a bit perfunctory of late.

Her guests lined up, still dabbing at stray tears. All except Oggie Jones. He stumped right over to the concession counter, where he made a major production of leaning lazily, looking like a doddery imitation of Sin on that first night.

Sophie could easily have wrung his wrinkled neck.

Finally, when everyone else was gone, she turned on him. "What do you think you're doing?"

He grinned. "Waitin' for my chance to find out what the hell's gone wrong with you."

She glared at him, longing to confront him with his cruel behavior, especially those petty impersonations of Sin. But if she did that, she'd only be introducing the subject she refused to discuss. Finally she settled for insisting, "There is nothing wrong with me."

He snorted. "Liar."

She felt as if he'd slapped her. And she longed to slap right back.

In an effort to get control of herself, she turned and scooped up an armful of empty popcorn bowls. When she faced him again, she managed to mutter tightly, "All right. I want you to know I'm sorry for the way I snapped at you when you bought your ticket."

"Eh? Sorry, are you?"

"Yes. And now I really must ask you to leave. I have work to do."

"I'm goin' nowhere."

"Excuse me?"

"I said, I'm goin' nowhere. You and me are gonna have a little talk."

"No, we're not. You're leaving and I'm going to—"

"Put those bowls down."

"I beg your pardon?"

"You heard me. Put 'em down."

"You have no right to tell me what to do."

"Someone's gotta." He hit his cane on the floor. Hard. "Put 'em down."

They scowled at each other. Sophie wanted to scream. And say terrible things. And throw the damn bowls in his mean, wrinkled face.

And then, out of nowhere, her eyes filled up. Her throat burned. She realized she was starting to cry.

Oggie spoke more gently. "That's right. It's okay. Set the bowls down now. And you and me will talk this out."

The tears were flowing down her cheeks by then. With a ragged sigh, she turned and set the bowls back on the table.

"Good." He stumped over to her. "Come on." His voice was so soothing, so gentle and kind. He put an arm around her. "It's okay, gal. We'll go outside. We'll talk this out."

Sophie surrendered, burying her head against his bony shoulder and sobbing out her loss into his frayed white shirt.

They sat out in the middle of the lawn, in the cool darkness, on the edge of the fountain with the laughing little girl.

Oggie produced a handkerchief and Sophie blew her nose and blotted the tears. "You tell your Uncle Oggie now, gal. I've solved worse problems than you could ever dream of, believe you me."

And so, between occasional persistent sobs, blotting her eyes when she had to, Sophie told the old man everything. How she had loved Sinclair and given herself completely to him. And the awful, cruel way that he had betrayed her.

When she was done, they sat there in the darkness for a moment, Sophie and the kind old man, with the fountain gurgling behind them and the crickets singing in the grass.

At last, Oggie shook his head. "So then, I guess you don't really love him after all."

Sophie sniffed. Surely she hadn't heard him correctly. "Wh-what did you say?"

"I said, I guess you don't really love him, after all—right?"

She backed away from him an inch or two and spoke with thoroughly justified indignation. "What are you talking about? Of course I love him."

"Then why did you let him go?"

Sophie gaped. How could he even ask such a thing? "He had a detective follow me. He *lied* to me. He pretended to be what he wasn't. He planned to run me out of here if I didn't sell out to him."

Oggie coughed into his hand. "Right. I get it, now. You love him. But you don't love him *enough*."

Sophie hiccupped a final sob away. She could not believe the gall of this old man. Here she'd poured out her heart to him and he had the nerve to accuse her of not loving enough. "How can you say that?"

"Well, because it's the plain truth. Because if you loved him enough, you'd be thinking about what he actually *did,* which was to go away and let you have this place, after all."

"But…" She said the one word, and then couldn't think of what to say next. Pure outrage had rendered her speechless.

Oggie, however, had plenty to say. "And while we're on the subject, it's quite a damn deal you got here, gal, I gotta tell you. You lease a few buildings and five acres pretty damn cheap and you—"

That got her mouth working. She demanded, "How do *you* know what I pay for my lease?"

He waved a hand. "I'm Oggie Jones. I got my sources."

"But I…you…"

"Stop your sputterin'. I'm still talkin'. Where was I? Right. You lease five acres for a nice low price—and you get to use the rest of the place like it was your own."

He had it all wrong. She hastened to set him right. "The teachers' association that owned it before—"

"Gal. This ain't before. This is now. And now, Sinclair Riker owns this ranch. And except for that five acres you won't let go of, he's got the right to do whatever he damn pleases with it—within the boundaries of the law, of course. And what *does* he do? He leaves the whole shebang to you."

"He didn't *leave* it to me. He only said—"

"You told me what he said. And it amounts to letting you have this place, to run it the way you want to for as long as you want to. Hell, this Sinclair Riker's a damn hero, if you ask me. And any female worthy of the name Jones would chase him down and tell him so." He put up both hands, then. "I know, I know. You're a generous woman. You help out those in need. Everyone for miles around talks about you. They'll be callin' you *Saint* Sophie B. before too many more years. But it seems to me that you're not so generous when it comes to the man you love." He shook his head. "I am sorry to have to be the one to tell you this, gal. But someone has to. And bein' as how we're family—by name and feelin', if not by blood—it falls to me to give it to you straight. And the straight story is, you're mopin' around now, because deep in your heart, you know you have let your man down."

She gasped. "Let *him* down? No. That's not true. You didn't listen to what I told you. *He* let *me* down. He—"

"Save your excuses for someone who'll buy them. You let that man leave when you should have held on until you could figure a way to work things out. And now you know you gotta go after him. But you're scared to go after him—scared he might turn his back on you now."

"Oh, that is wrong. That is so wrong."

But Oggie was already grabbing his cane, levering himself to his feet with a grunt.

"Wh-where are you going?"

"Home."

"But…"

"But *what,* gal?"

"You can't just say all these cruel things and then leave."

He chortled quite merrily. "Watch me."

Stunned, furious—and just a little bit afraid that he might be right, Sophie stared after him as he hobbled away.

Chapter 12

The next morning, Sophie called L.A. information. She requested the phone number for a company called Inkerris, Incorporated. A recorded voice came on and gave her the number.

She wrote the number down. She didn't plan to use it, she really didn't. Last night, instead of sleeping, she'd thought a lot about what Oggie had said. Maybe the old man had a point in one sense. Sin *had* ended up letting her have the Mountain Star, after all. And she would always be grateful to him for that.

Their relationship—or whatever it had been—was over, though. They were from two different worlds. And now they'd both returned to their real lives.

However, it felt good to know for certain that she could reach Sin if she had to—just in case something important came up concerning the ranch.

Having the number did create a little problem, though. She found that as she went through the day, she just couldn't stop thinking about it. Thinking that she had it. And if she wanted to, she could just pick up the phone and— On Sunday, she gave in. She called the number. A recorded voice informed her that business hours were Monday through Friday, from nine to five. She hung up, her heart beating too fast and her face burning hot.

Monday morning, she got up early and went out for a long ride. She ended up on that ridge where she'd taken Sin the first day they rode together. She looked out over the sparse pastures and thick pine forests below and thought of what he'd said: the trees needed thinning. They would choke out every meadow if left unchecked. And they created a virtual invitation to a forest fire— especially this time of year, when the weather stayed hot and the grasses were dry and brittle as old paper.

Anger rolled through her, low and insistent, like far-away thunder. She'd always found such pleasure in the sight of those trees. And now, because of *him,* she'd started to see them as a potential problem.

The mare she'd chosen tossed her red mane, eager to be moving again. Sophie kept her in check down the hillside and then let her have her head when they found a clear spot—in the meadow of the wild roses, which also reminded her of Sin.

Everything. *Everything* reminded her of Sin.

Once she'd returned the mare to the stable, unsaddled her and brushed her down, Sophie went back to the guest house to wash up before breakfast.

In the bathroom, she splashed cold water on her face and reached for a towel. She scrubbed away the water and then looked up, catching her own eyes in the mirror. She frowned at herself.

And then, in the back of her mind, she heard Oggie's voice, from the other night.

"Now you know you gotta go after him. But you're scared to go after him—scared he might turn his back on you now...."

Sophie let out a small cry and threw down the towel.

"Oh, all right," she said to the mirror, as if the old man's face looked out at her instead of her own. "I am. I'm just terrified he won't want me anymore."

She knew what Oggie would say then, "Terrified or not, gal. You still gotta go."

She headed straight for the cottage. She needed breakfast—and to find out if Myra and Caleb could handle things by themselves for a couple of days.

Myra said cautiously, "I believe we could manage. It's after Labor Day. We've even been running with a room or two empty during the week. If Bethy will just hold up her end, I'm sure everything will be fine." Bethy wasn't there that morning; she had Monday and Tuesday off.

Caleb swallowed a bite of sausage and demanded, "What's up?"

Sophie answered patiently, "I just told you. I want to visit Los Angeles for a couple of days."

"What for?"

"It's...personal."

Caleb scowled. "So, that's where he lives."

Myra pretended to clear her throat as she slid a warning glance at Caleb. "Now, don't you worry about things here, Sophie B. We can get by. I'm sure that we can."

Caleb wouldn't be deterred. "Why the hell do you want to see *him?*"

"Because…" I love him, Sophie thought. And I can't spend the rest of my life wondering if he might have loved me, too.

"Because what?" Caleb challenged.

"Because…" she said again, then found herself finishing, "…he owns this ranch now."

Caleb's fork clattered against his plate. Myra gasped.

And Sophie felt even worse. "I know, I should have told you before. I *meant* to tell you before. But lately I've been so…"

"Confused and upset." Myra reached across and patted Sophie's hand. "We do understand."

Caleb wasn't so easily put off. "Wait a minute. You're saying that corporation that bought the ranch is owned by Mr. Sinclair Riker, is that it?"

Sophie nodded. "I'm afraid so."

"You make your lease payments to him."

"In effect, yes."

"He owned this place in August, when he was here, with you."

"Yes. That's right."

"But he sat at this table and *said* he was here to look for property deals. He never said—"

"Caleb. Please. Let me work this out my own way."

"That man is trouble. He's no one for you to be runnin' off to see."

"Please, listen. I appreciate your concern. But this is my problem and I will handle it my own way."

"Has he got plans to try to kick us out?"

"No," she answered quickly, silently adding, Or at least, I don't *think* he does, not anymore.…

Caleb made a low, disgusted noise, then stabbed another sausage. "I don't like this, Sophie B."

"But can you—*will you*—take care of things here if I leave for a day or two?"

"Of course we will," said Myra.

Caleb forked up another sausage and sawed it in half before he grudgingly answered, "All right. We'll take care of things."

Back in the guest house, Sophie tried information again, hoping she might discover Sin's home phone number. But there was no listing for a man named Sinclair Riker. So at nine on the nose, she dialed Inkerris, Incorporated. Her hand shook as she punched up the numbers and her voice sounded thin and squeaky when she asked for the address there. The woman on the other end rattled it right off. Sophie had already hung up before it occurred to her that she might simply have asked to speak to Sin.

She punched Redial—and then hung up before it rang.

She was already a nervous wreck about this. She just couldn't afford to be put off by some receptionist. No, she would go down there. All the way to L.A. And she wouldn't come back until she'd spoken with Sin face-to-face.

What exactly she would say to him, she hadn't a clue. But she would *see* him. She would *talk* with him. And by the time she came home, she'd have some kind of idea if what they'd shared had been anything more than a beautiful—and ultimately heartbreaking—summer fling.

* * *

The next morning, Sophie flew into LAX from Sacramento. She bought a map at the airport and rented a car. Then she fought her way through the awful traffic to the Century City offices of Inkerris, Incorporated.

The sight of the building completely intimidated her. It was a tall, imposing, very modern structure of black marble and glass. She drove by in her small rented car and wondered how she'd ever get up the nerve to go inside, walk up to some security guard and ask to speak to Sinclair Riker.

Oh, Uncle Oggie had been so right. She never should have let Sin leave her side until she was sure he didn't want to try again. Her original cowardice had only made things all the more difficult in the end.

A hotel, she decided. She'd find one first. And then come back and walk through those tall, gleaming glass doors. It was putting off the inevitable, she knew it; more evidence of her own cowardice. But she did it anyway.

She found a room in a small hotel about a mile away from Inkerris, Incorporated. Then she sat on the end of the bed for a while, staring at her own reflection in the mirror over the low chest of drawers and telling herself she had no more excuses now.

It was after three when she finally slipped through the doors of Sin's building. She found herself facing acres of marble floor and two banks of elevators. Over near the far wall was an information desk, with a directory on the wall behind it. She drew her shoulders back and marched over there. The man behind the desk watched her as she approached.

She tried to simply scan the directory over his head, but then he asked, "May I help you?"

She cleared her throat. "I'd like to speak to Sinclair Riker, please."

The man gave her an indifferent smile. "Your name?"

She had to cough again, in a rather futile effort to make her throat relax. "Sophie. Sophie B. Jones."

"Do you have an appointment?"

"Uh…no. No, I don't."

Right then, a phone near his elbow buzzed. He put up an index finger. "Just a minute." Then he picked up the phone. "Lobby. Yes. No. All right." He hung up and looked at Sophie again. "What is your visit concerning?"

Now how could she answer that? She stammered, "I-it's a personal matter."

He looked at her sideways, a look that she read as disapproving—or disbelieving. But then he did pick up the phone and punched a button. "This is Jerry in the lobby. I have a Ms. Jones down here. To see Mr. Riker. She says it's a personal matter." He paused, listened. "Yes. Good enough." He hung up, smiling for the second time, as indifferently as before. "Mr. Riker isn't in. Would you like to leave a number?"

Sophie's heart sank. That was it. She'd been turned away. By Sin himself, possibly. Or maybe not. How could she know? And what in the world was she going to do now? "I…"

Now the man looked impatient. "Just give me a number. I'm sure he'll get back to you."

She drew herself up. "No. Really. I'd like to speak with his…assistant, please."

"Ms. Jones…"

She tried to stand even taller. "Please."

With a shrug, the man picked up the phone again. "This is Jerry downstairs again. Ms. Sophie B. Jones would like to speak with Mr. Riker's assistant, rather than leaving a number here." Jerry listened, looking Sophie over while whoever was on the other end of the line spoke. Though the air conditioning in the building seemed to be set on high, Sophie felt the sweat break out under her arms. At last, he said into the phone, "No, I don't think so," and then, "All right." He hung up, looked at Sophie. "Take the far bank of elevators. Top floor. Penthouse."

She stared, hardly daring to believe she'd actually made progress, no matter how minimal.

"The far bank of elevators," Jerry said again, clearly uncertain whether she'd heard him or not.

She gave him a grateful smile. "Yes. All right. And thank you."

He smiled back, more warmly than before. "You're welcome."

She turned and hurried toward the elevators.

On the top floor, the elevator doors slid open onto a wide reception area. The marble floors were inlaid with diamond patterns. Fabulous Egyptian-design rugs covered parts of that floor, with leather chairs grouped around them. A long desk ran along one wall. Behind that desk sat a gorgeous brunette.

"Ms. Jones?"

"Yes."

"Have a seat. Mr. Taylor will be with you shortly."

Sophie sank into one of the leather chairs to wait. The brunette started typing. Sophie's nerves hummed in anticipation and dread. The big room seemed so quiet, except for the brunette, punching the keys: *click-click-click-click*. Sophie hoped it wouldn't be long.

Twenty minutes later, the brunette looked up. "Are you sure you wouldn't rather just leave a number?"

"No," Sophie said. "I'll wait."

And wait she did. For another hour and ten minutes, as the brunette typed away and intermittently answered the phone. Then, near five, the phone buzzed again. The brunette picked it up. "Yes?" The brunette's clear blue eyes met Sophie's—and then she quickly looked away. "No. Not yet," she said gingerly.

Sophie's heart thudded dully in her chest. She just knew it was Sin, asking if she'd given up and left yet. She wanted to jump to her feet and demand that he talk to her. At the same time, she wished she could just sink through that leather chair, down ten floors and right on through the ground all the way to China.

The brunette hung up. "Mr. Taylor will be right out."

Sophie gulped. She didn't know whether to feel relieved or more nervous. "Thank you."

A few moments later, the tall mahogany doors to the left of the brunette's desk swung open. A movie-star-handsome blond man in a suit straight out of *GQ* appeared. He saw Sophie and advanced on her, holding out his hand.

Sophie leaped to her feet.

"Ms. Jones." His hand was cool, firm and dry. Sophie's own hand felt suddenly clammy. She resisted the urge to yank it away and wipe it dry on her skirt.

He let go, granting her a smile as cool as his handshake. "I'm Rob Taylor, Mr. Riker's personal assistant. What can I do for you?"

She put on her best no-nonsense tone. "I'm here to see Mr. Riker."

A tiny frowned creased his tanned brow. "I thought Jerry downstairs told you—"

"That he isn't in. Yes. The man downstairs did tell me that. But I—"

"Ms. Jones." His tone had turned from bland to patronizing. "Really. I'm sorry you insisted on waiting to talk to me. I realize we've wasted too much of your time. But Mr. Riker honestly is not here."

She couldn't just give up now. "When will he be here?"

"Ms. Jones—"

"Tomorrow. In the morning? Is that the best time to—"

"Ms. Jones. Please. Give me your number. I will make certain that he gets it."

Beyond his shoulder, Sophie could see the beautiful brunette. Watching. Probably wondering what was the matter with her, that she had such difficulty taking a hint.

"Ms. Jones, I—"

Sophie sighed. "All right." She had a Mountain Star business card in her purse. She took it out, groped around for a pen, and then scribbled the name of her hotel on the back of it. "I don't know the phone number there offhand. But it's over on—"

Rob Taylor took the card almost before she finished writing on it. He glanced at it. "I know the Helmswood Arms." He gestured at the brunette behind the reception desk. "Tessa can look up the phone number." He took Sophie's arm and herded her toward the elevator doors. "I'll see that Mr. Riker gets your message." He pressed the button and the doors opened. "Have a nice day." He guided her into the car. The doors slid soundlessly shut on his too-handsome face.

Sophie wanted to fling herself at those doors, pound on them, order them to open again. But what good would it do? If she got out of the car, Rob Taylor would probably only shove her back inside again—or call Jerry downstairs and have her bodily removed from the building.

The elevator began going down.

As she descended, Sophie couldn't help thinking that the wisest move now would be to check out of the Helmswood Arms, head to LAX and wait on standby until she could get a flight home. Instead, she returned to her room, took a long, hot shower, put on a clean dress and visited a deli for a ham on rye.

By the time she sat down with her sandwich, she felt marginally better. She had to think positive. After all, it was entirely possible that Rob Taylor had only told the truth: Sin simply hadn't been there.

Maybe she was whistling at the moon, but she would give it—give Sin—another twenty-four hours. Her flight back was scheduled for tomorrow evening. She could keep trying until then. Maybe he would call. And if he didn't, she'd gather all her courage up and storm the gates of Inkerris, Incorporated, one more time.

Sophie consumed all of her sandwich, a large glass of milk and both of the big slices of dill pickle that came with it. As she ate, she plotted her next attack on the marble and glass bastions of Inkerris, Incorporated.

Tomorrow, if Sin hadn't called, she would try a different approach. This time, she'd go in as the owner-operator of the Mountain Star, a tenant of Inkerris,

Incorporated. She'd tell Mr. Taylor that she simply had to see Mr. Riker concerning the property she leased from him.

It might not work any better than citing "personal" reasons had. But it certainly couldn't do any worse.

By the time she got back to her room after visiting the deli, she'd almost convinced herself that the message light on the phone would be blinking. It wasn't.

She told herself she would not become discouraged.

However, she just might go nuts if she sat in that room all evening, staring at the four walls. L.A. was full of small movie theaters, the kinds of places that showed movies only someone like Sophie would enjoy.

She got a *Los Angeles Times* and chose a place that was showing *It Came from Outer Space* and *Attack of the Killer Tomatoes.* She ate bad popcorn, drank flat root beer and laughed at awful dialogue. By eleven, when the show was over and she emerged into the balmy L.A. night, she almost felt good.

But back at the hotel, the message light remained dark. She hardly slept the whole night, her nerves on a razor's edge, waiting for the phone to ring.

It never did.

The next morning she rose at six. She took a long walk down city streets that were already clogging up with cars. Around eight, she stopped for breakfast at an outdoor café. She ate croissants and poached eggs, sitting next to a potted palm beneath a Cinzano umbrella. Then she returned to her room—to find she had no messages.

She waited until nine-thirty. And then she grabbed her purse and headed for Inkerris, Incorporated, one more time.

* * *

Sin stared out the window behind his desk at the spectacular view of Century City as Rob Taylor filled him in on yesterday's messages and today's appointments.

"Oh, and I almost forgot," Rob said when the endless list had seemed to be finished. "Some young woman came to see you." Rob sighed, sounding put-upon. "She was very persistent. A Ms. Jones. Ms. Sophie B. Jones."

Sin spun his chair around. "When was she here?"

Rob blinked. "Yesterday. In the afternoon. She—"

"Did she leave a number?"

Rob fell back a step. "Well, yes. That is, she left a card, with the name of her—"

"Give it to me."

"I—"

"You do have it?"

"Yes. Of course. That is, I gave it to Tessa to look up the number."

"What number?"

"The number of her hotel."

"What hotel?"

"Helmswood Arms, I believe."

Sin grabbed the phone and buzzed the receptionist. Rob kept babbling. "Honestly. If I had known—"

He waved his assistant to silence. "Tessa, do you have the number of that hotel where Sophie Jones is staying?"

"Of course, Mr. Riker. Just a minute." Sin waited, glaring at Rob, wanting to scream at poor Tessa to snap it up. Finally she spoke again. "Here it is. Shall I call it for—"

"No. Give it to me."

"Certainly. 555-3072."

He disconnected Tessa and punched up the number, growling Sophie's name as soon as a voice said, "Helmswood Arms."

"One moment, please." He heard a line ringing. Five rings, and then the hotel operator came back on. "I'm sorry. She's not answering. Would you care to—"

"What's your address there?" He grabbed a pen and scribbled it down, then slammed the phone back in its cradle and once more turned his attention on the hapless Rob. "I'm going over there. Now."

"Yes. Of course. Whatever."

"If she comes back here, you ask her to wait and you call me on my cell. Is that clear?"

"Yes. Perfectly."

Sin was already striding for the door. He paused only to bark over his shoulder. "I mean it, Rob. Give her coffee. Give her caviar. Give her whatever the hell she wants. But if she comes here, do not let her go until I get back."

Rob was still swearing he'd handle everything as Sin slammed out the door.

Sophie entered the lobby of Inkerris, Incorporated, at nine-forty-five. This time, she had sense enough to head straight for the elevators before Jerry, behind the information desk, caught so much as a glimpse of her. The lobby was busier that time of day than it had been the afternoon before. The up light was already on. She waited with several preoccupied-looking button-down types for the mirrored doors to slide open.

When they finally did, Sin was standing inside.

Sophie's heart went racing. Her feet felt cold and her

face felt hot. Neither she nor Sin moved an inch as the button-down types bustled around them, getting on and off the elevator car.

A thousand unreconciled emotions did battle inside her. He looked so unbelievably handsome, more handsome than she remembered, if that was possible. And he was so perfectly dressed, in a dark gray silk suit and a blue shirt and a tie of some deep, rich indefinable color between blue and black.

He looked…urbane and sophisticated. And certainly not the kind of man who could be interested in her, not in a hundred thousand years.

Oh, what had possessed her to come here? They'd shared five days—or, more specifically, five magical nights.

But looking at him now, here in the marble and glass confines of his own world, she just couldn't believe that those days and nights had meant anything near as much to him as they had to her.

Just then the doors started to close.

Sin shouted, "Hold that door!"

But it was too late. The doors kept on sliding together. He commanded, "Sophie. Stay there." And then the doors shut all the way, with him inside—and her still standing there, staring at the place where he had been.

"Stay there," he had said.

She supposed he meant he would come back down on the next car. She *hoped* that was what he meant. Or maybe he had meant, stay there—and away from me.

Well, it didn't matter. Laying eyes on him again had left her feeling a little unsteady, anyway. Staying there for a while would suit her fine.

A small marble bench stood against the section of

wall between the two banks of elevators. Sophie stumbled over and dropped down onto it.

The seconds ticked by like centuries. At last Sin's elevator car descended again, the doors opened and he stepped out. Sophie stood from the bench. He turned and saw her there.

For a moment, when his eyes met hers, she thought everything would be all right after all. They would run to each other across the black marble floor. He would sweep her into his arms. All their differences would simply melt away....

For his part, at that moment, Sin felt exactly the same.

But then skepticism took over.

There might be any number of reasons she had come here to find him. He decided he'd be wise to approach her carefully until he understood better what was really going on.

As Sin decided to proceed with caution, Sophie felt the moment of hope fade away. Once again, he was simply that incredibly handsome, sophisticated stranger who couldn't possibly be interested in someone like her.

He started toward her, his stride purposeful and his eyes wary. She had no idea what he intended to do, until he reached her and held out his hand.

"How are you, Sophie?"

They shook. Like two casual acquaintances. She felt his touch all the way to her toes, at the same time as she made her lips turn up in a polite smile that pretended she didn't feel anything at all.

"I'm doing all right. How about you?"

He shrugged and, to her sincere regret, released her hand. "I'm all right, too." Behind him, the button-down types came and went from the elevator cars. "I meant what I said, Sophie." He had lowered his voice a little. "I won't take your Mountain Star."

She looked at him levelly. "Yes. I...believe that now."

"Then what brings you here?"

I love you, and I want you to come back to me! her heart cried. But how could she blurt that out here, by the elevators, with all those busy people milling around a few feet away?

"Is there a problem at the ranch?"

She hesitated, her mind all caught up in what she longed to say, what she was afraid to say. "A...problem?"

"Something you came to see me about?"

Now it seemed to her that some of the button-down types were beginning to stare. "I wonder...could we go somewhere a little more private, do you think?"

"Of course." He started to reach for her hand—she could have sworn that he did. But then he only touched her on the shoulder. "Come with me." He turned for the elevators again. She followed after him.

They got on the elevator with two young, well-dressed women. "Good morning, Mr. Riker," the women chirped, almost in unison.

"Good morning, Sarah. Danielle." He nodded, so polite, so correct. A king dispensing the favor of his attention on his subjects.

Sarah and Danielle got off on the fifth floor. Sin and Sophie rode the rest of the way up in an awkward silence that made the close space seem way too small.

It was a relief when the doors opened onto the penthouse reception area.

Tessa looked up from her keyboard. She smiled.

"We'll be in the west conference room." Sin put his hand at the small of Sophie's back, causing the skin there, even beneath the layers of clothing, to burn—making her whole body tighten and yearn. "See that we aren't disturbed."

"I'll do that," Tessa promised.

Sin looked at Sophie. "Can I have Tessa bring you anything?"

She wished he'd take his hand away—she wished he'd never let go. "Anything?" she repeated idiotically.

"Coffee? A sweet roll?"

"Coffee," she said automatically, because it seemed like something she ought to say, though she'd had two cups at breakfast and that was more than enough.

"I'll bring it right in," Tessa promised.

Sin exerted the slightest pressure on Sophie's back—guiding her forward toward the tall mahogany doors. Once through them, they went down a wood-paneled hallway to another pair of double doors. He ushered her through.

The room they entered had a huge, diamond-shaped table in the center of it, with leather chairs all around. There were three sofas along the walls, and chairs and low tables grouped around them—for more informal meetings, she supposed. One wall was solid glass. It afforded a panoramic view of the well-groomed Century City streets below.

Sin guided her to a sofa and chairs near that wall of glass. "Have a seat."

Really, she wanted to stand. She had such a strong feeling of unreality about all of this. She'd come to talk of love—and here they were about to have what felt like some sort of business meeting. Still, to remain on her feet would only make her look as apprehensive as she felt. She dropped into one of the chairs.

Just then a small door down at the other end of the room opened. Tessa came in, carrying a coffee service on a black lacquer tray. She hurried over and set it on a low table about a foot from where Sophie sat perched on her chair.

Efficiently, Tessa poured. She arched a brow at Sophie. "Sugar? Cream?"

"No, black is fine."

She passed Sophie the cup and saucer, which started rattling the moment Sophie got them in her hand. She slid them onto the table in front of her, stifling a sigh of relief when the clattering stopped.

"Mr. Riker?" Tessa held up the pot for him.

"No, thanks. That's all, Tessa."

Tessa set down the pot and left them alone.

Sin was still standing, leaning a little against a credenza not far from the sofa. Sophie felt a flash of resentment. He'd asked her to sit. And yet he remained in the superior position on his feet, looming over her.

"You're not drinking your coffee," he remarked quietly.

She reached out, plucked the cup from the saucer and took a sip that burned the back of her throat when she swallowed. Somehow she managed not to completely humiliate herself by having a choking fit right there in front of him.

She set the cup down.

He crossed his arms over his chest.

And she remembered that first night—the two of them, standing by the twin sinks in the back room of her barn-theater. He had leaned against the sink then, just exactly as he leaned against that credenza now....

"What is it, Sophie? What can I do for you?"

She thought, I love you. Do you love me?

But she couldn't say it. She didn't know *how* to say it. Not anymore. Not here, not now. Not to this urbane, sophisticated man. And not in the west conference room on the penthouse floor.

"Sophie?" He looked puzzled—and maybe a little concerned. "Please. Tell me what's on your mind."

And she heard herself announcing, "Listen, I have a deal for you."

She waited for him to laugh out loud.

But instead, he lifted a dark brow and actually looked interested. "Oh, really?"

"Yes. Really. I wonder, would you consider becoming my partner in the Mountain Star?"

Chapter 13

Sophie could not believe she had said that—but now that it was out, she decided she would just go with it. Until he turned her down, which he surely would. Then she could slink away like the complete coward she was.

He was watching her, the consummate business-man, revealing nothing, willing to let her play her whole hand. She picked up her coffee cup, took a second, much more careful sip and set it back down. "I mean, I understood you had planned to live there anyway, right? Back when you were…" How to say it diplomatically? "…hoping to convince me to give up my lease?"

"Yes," he agreed, looking reasonably serious, as if he actually were considering this outrageous "deal" she was making up as she went along. "That was my plan."

"So, that would mean that you must have your affairs pretty much in order here." At the word *affairs,* she thought of Willa Tweed and had to hold back a slightly hysterical laugh.

Sin wasn't thinking of Willa at all.

He said, "That's true."

And it was. Since he'd left Nevada County—and Sophie—Sin had been trying to figure out what the hell to do next. Inkerris, Incorporated, was now virtually run by his former second-in-command, who had plans to buy Sin out completely within the next couple of years. In the past few weeks, since his return, Sin hadn't bothered to change those plans. He had realized he was ready to move on to something different.

But a partnership with Sophie? She couldn't be serious. And *he* had to be losing his mind to even consider such a suggestion. He had wanted the ranch to himself. That had been the whole point.

She forged ahead. "What I've been thinking is, well, maybe we could work out a way that we both end up getting what we want."

He prodded her on. "And what way is that?"

"Well, as I said, I was thinking of kind of a…" She gulped, as if the next word had gotten stuck in her throat.

He helped her with it. "A partnership, you said. A partnership between you and me."

"Yes. That's what I said. Is that crazy?"

"Well…"

"You think it's crazy."

"Sophie, I didn't say that."

She went for broke. "You know how you were always saying you'd like to build yourself another house? Well, you could do that. You could. Remember that meadow, the one with the wild roses?"

He nodded.

"Well, that would be a beautiful place for a house. And it's over that little hill from the other buildings. So the construction noise shouldn't carry too badly."

The developer inside him immediately began thinking of access roads, of septic systems, of getting power out there. But none of that should be too much of a problem. It wasn't that far away from the other buildings, or from paved road. And the meadow she referred to *was* beautiful.

She was frowning. "Maybe you don't like that spot."

"No. I like it. It's a beautiful spot."

"But you don't want to do it."

"I didn't say that."

"But I—"

"Sophie, exactly what do you mean by a partnership?"

"Well, maybe you don't want a partnership."

"I didn't say that. I asked what kind of a partnership you're talking about."

It was clear from the dazed look on her face that she hadn't the faintest idea.

He heard himself suggesting for her, "You could use an investor more than a partner."

"Uh...tell me more."

"Someone who would finance the improvements you need—Myra's new kitchen, a new projector for that theater of yours...."

"You mean, I would still run things and you'd take a percentage of the profits in exchange for putting money into the Mountain Star?"

"That's the general idea."

She scrunched up her sweet face.

"What?" he demanded. "What are you thinking?"

"Well, Sin, you have to know that there aren't really enough profits to get excited about."

Yet he *was* getting excited. "There could be profits. If you added on to the main house, so that you wouldn't have to turn people away in the busy season. And if you expanded the stables and hired men to work with Caleb, so you could enlarge that boarding service of yours."

She murmured faintly, "Add on to the main house? Expand the stables?"

He backed off a little. "We wouldn't have to do everything right away. We could…take it slow. Fix the kitchen, buy that projector…"

"Yes, yes, of course we could." Now she was sitting forward on the edge of her chair, her chin tipped up and her hands folded in her lap. Sin thought he'd never seen such an enchanting sight.

But go into partnership with her? It could never work.

Then again, why in hell would she offer such a thing—unless she had hopes that the two of them might rediscover what they'd lost?

Which they couldn't, of course. They were miles apart now—if they ever really had been that close.

But still, he might be of use to her. At the very least he should be able to get her to fix up that damn kitchen and put a new roof on the main house.

Take it slow. That was the best way. "Maybe I should come up there—for a few days or a week. Nothing formal, right now."

She looked more confused than ever. "Nothing formal?"

"I mean, we won't actually form a legal partnership yet. Nothing on paper. I'll just come and stay for a while. We'll really look into what needs to be done around there. And I'll check into your idea of building a house in that meadow you mentioned."

A few days or a week, Sophie thought. It wasn't a bad idea. Surely in that time, they could begin to find their way back to each other—or she could start learning to accept that it hadn't worked out.

He was saying, "We could see how well we work together. How we…get along. What would you say to something like that?"

She hardly knew what to say. It wasn't exactly what she'd come here for. But it was a whole lot better than nothing. She put on a bright smile. "I think it's a great idea. When can you come?"

"I have a few things to wrap up here. But I could manage to get away by next Monday, say? What do you think?"

"I think that would be just fine."

"Great then. We're agreed."

"Yes. Agreed." It seemed like one of those times a person should offer to shake hands, so Sophie popped out of her chair and extended her arm. They shook, as they had down in the lobby. Her palm burned, pressed so close to his. She thought of their nights together, of the way they always slept with their legs intertwined, of waking in the morning to find herself all wrapped up with him, so close she could hardly tell where her body ended and his began.

He let go of her hand. They stared at each other.

She edged back a few steps. "Well, I know you have work to do and so I suppose I'd better—"

"How about lunch?"

"Lunch?" She said the word as if she'd never heard it before—and then felt her face grow warm.

He smiled that almost smile she remembered so well. "I'll pick you up at noon. At your hotel. How's that?"

"My hotel?" she echoed numbly.

"The Helmswood Arms, is that right?"

"Uh, yes. The Helmswood Arms."

"At noon, then?"

"Well, that would be…yes. That would be nice."

Oh, it felt lovely, just to sit across from him, to look at him, to hear his voice.

But never once during the lunch they shared did he say anything about the two of them, about all that had happened between them less than a month before. Not that she could blame him for that. She said nothing either.

And she was the one who had come to see *him*.

It just…all felt so different now, between them. Careful. Cordial. And distant.

Before, when he'd appeared at her theater and swept her off her feet, it had been so perfect, so natural. So right. The idea of hesitating to reach out, to touch him, had never even occurred to her then. He'd owned her heart that first night. And by the second night, he'd shared her bed. It had been pure magic, the instant connection between them.

Now she still felt the yearning. The need to get closer.

But she didn't know how to go about it anymore. It was as if loving him was a special skill she'd mastered once on the first try.

And now somehow she'd fallen out of practice. She'd

lost the magic touch that had brought them together so effortlessly before.

"Innocent," he had called her just before he left her.

And she had been.

Now she was wiser. More guarded. Less willing to risk her wounded heart.

Now she could sit across from him in a restaurant and talk and laugh and never once blurt out, *I love you— do you love me, too?*

They ended up arguing over the bill. She wanted to pay it, he insisted he would take care of it. Then she suggested they split it.

He looked pained. "Don't be ridiculous."

She jumped to her own defense. "I don't think it's ridiculous that I offer to pay half."

He tossed down his platinum American Express card and the waiter swiftly scooped it up. "Sophie. That's not what I meant."

"You said—"

"Sophie." He just looked at her, across the snowy white tablecloth and the little centerpiece of pink roses. "It's taken care of. Let it go."

"But I—"

"Let it go."

She sank back in her chair. He was right. She knew it. It was only lunch, after all. The real problem had more to do with all she'd yet to say to him than who picked up the check. She folded her hands on the table and looked down at them. "I guess I'm…a little nervous about all this."

"Do you want to call it off?"

She snapped her head up and searched his face—for

all the good it did. She couldn't for the life of her guess what might be going through his mind.

"I asked if you wanted to call it off."

"No! I mean…just because I'm nervous doesn't mean I've changed my mind."

"You still want me to come stay at the Mountain Star, then?"

"I do."

"You're sure?"

"Positive—but are you sure *you* want to come?"

"I wouldn't have suggested it if I didn't." The waiter returned and set the bill tray down with a flourish. Sin picked up the pen and signed the receipt. "All right," he said, once the waiter was gone again. "So we have a deal—or at least, the beginnings of one."

"Yes. We have a deal."

Sin insisted on taking her back to the Helmswood Arms. Before she got out of the car, he asked when she would be flying home.

"Tonight at six-thirty."

For a moment she could have sworn he was going to suggest she might stay longer. But he didn't. He only wished her a safe flight and promised he'd see her in five days.

She ended up standing on the sidewalk in front of her hotel, watching his long black limousine pull away and drive off.

"Well, I hope you got *that* out of your system," Caleb said when he picked her up at Sacramento International.

Sophie granted him a sour smile. "It's nice to see

you, too—and you can stop talking about Sin as if he were some kind of virus."

"*Sin?* Is that what you call him?" Caleb snorted. "It fits."

She waited until they got home and she could get both him and Myra together before she explained that Sin was considering investing in the Mountain Star and possibly building a house nearby.

"He'll be arriving Monday, to stay for a week or so. It will be a sort of…trial period. We'll decide after that if we think a partnership between us might work out."

Caleb let out a short Anglo-Saxon expletive. "I don't get it. I don't get any of it."

Sophie kept her voice low and firm. "Please treat him with courtesy, Caleb."

"Why?"

"Because he is coming here in good faith, he owns the property we're standing on and…because I asked you to."

Caleb muttered more swear words, then demanded, "Did he walk out on you or not?"

"Caleb, please…" Myra chided.

"It's all right, Myra," Sophie said. She faced Caleb. "He did leave, yes. There were…problems between us. And instead of trying to work them out, I just let him go. I shouldn't have done that. That's why I went to find him. And now, we're starting over."

"As *business* partners?"

"Yes, possibly."

"It doesn't make any sense."

"It doesn't *have* to make sense. All I'm asking is, will you treat him with courtesy?"

Caleb glowered.

And Myra spoke up again. "Caleb. This is not our choice to make. And Sophie B. is the boss."

Caleb folded his big arms over his chest.

"Caleb," Sophie murmured softly, "please..."

He grunted. "All right. I don't like it, but you *are* the boss."

Sophie spent the next five days on an emotional pendulum, swinging back and forth between euphoria and dread. She couldn't wait for Sin to come—and she couldn't help wondering what kind of awful mess she might have gotten them into.

On Sunday, remembering how uncomfortable Riker cottage made him, she moved her clothes and a few personal things there, to a small attic room next to Myra's room.

Certainly he'd enjoy the space and privacy of the guest house more. She figured she could still use her office there without inconveniencing him too much, for the original period of time he planned to stay.

After that, who could say? Anything might happen. Maybe they'd be truly together again. Maybe they'd be business partners.

And maybe he'd simply fly back to L.A. and get on with his own life, leaving her here to get on with hers.

He arrived at eleven-thirty on Monday morning, right when Sophie just happened to be making the bed in one of the rooms that looked out over the front driveway. She ran to the window when she heard the car drive up. At the sight of the shiny black Lexus below, she knew that it had to be him.

She tossed the lace pillows against the headboard and smoothed the quilt one more time. Then she flew out to the hall, raced down the front stairs, flung open the old oak door and rushed outside.

Halfway down the walk, she began to feel foolish, running at him headlong like some eager, impetuous child. She ordered her feet to move at a more sedate pace.

His door opened and he emerged from the car. And Sophie found herself hovering there, at the edge of the walk, clasping her hands together, awkward and shy as a preteen in the grip of a first crush.

"So," she said nervously. "You're here."

"Yes," he concurred. "I am."

They stood there in the late-morning sun just looking at each other—for an embarrassingly long stretch of seconds. Again, she thought it could never work out. He was too handsome, too rich, too…everything.

And they would never get past this awful uneasiness with each other.

Sin was experiencing similar emotions. Those wide eyes regarded him anxiously—as if, now he'd come, she had no idea what to do with him.

Finally he suggested, "I'll just get my suitcase and—"

"No."

What the hell did that mean? Had she changed her mind—and not bothered to call and inform him of the fact?

But then she explained, "I've put you in the guest house. I hope that's…all right."

All right?

Pure elation made Sin's heart do something impossible inside his chest, something that felt like a forward roll.

He could hardly believe it. Here he'd been telling himself for five days that he had to be crazy to come here, that what had once been was over. And all the time Sophie had intended for him to move back into the guest house with her.

He understood everything, then. Yes, she looked anxious. She was afraid he might say no.

Laughable thought. That he could ever say no to her...

"Sin?" She stared at him, adorably apprehensive. "Will that be all right?"

"That will be just fine."

"Well, then, why don't you just follow the driveway over there?"

He wanted to pull her into his arms right then and there, but he didn't. He could wait—somehow—until they were alone. He suggested, "Come with me."

"Sure." She started to turn, to cut across the lawn.

"Sophie." She stopped, whirled toward him again, her huge eyes questioning. She wore old jeans and a T-shirt with *Mountain Star* emblazoned across the front. Her glorious hair had a ragged-edged scarf tied over it. He couldn't wait to take that scarf off. He gestured at the passenger's side of the Lexus. "Get in."

She waved a hand. "Oh, that's not necessary. I'll just run across the lawn and—"

"Sophie. Get in."

She hesitated a moment more, then she shrugged and went around the front of the Lexus. They settled in next to each other and he drove the short distance to the guest house.

She had her door open again almost before he

brought the car to a complete stop. "I'll help you with your things."

"Sophie, that's not necess—"

But she was already halfway around to the back. Shaking his head, he popped the trunk latch.

She had the trunk lid up and was hauling the heavier of his two bags out when he got back there himself. He took the bag away from her and grabbed the garment bag, as well.

"Sin, I don't mind—"

He gave her a look. She stopped protesting in mid-sentence.

Inside, she led him straight to her bedroom. "Well, here we are." She gestured him through the doorway, lingering on the threshold herself.

Hiding a knowing smile, Sin tossed the garment bag across the bed and set his suitcase on the needlepoint rug. He turned to her.

She was fiddling with that ragged scarf she'd tied over her hair. "I...hope you'll be comfortable here." She threw out a hand toward the bureau. "I cleared out the drawers for you. And there's room in the closet for your other things." She smoothed the scarf, let her hands drop to her side—and then couldn't leave them there. She clasped them nervously together. "I hope you won't mind, if I go ahead and use the office room. But I'll try not to bother you, I promise."

He didn't know what she was babbling about. "Not bother me?"

She rubbed her arms as if the room were cold. "Well, I mean, as much as possible, I'll leave you your privacy."

"My *privacy*."

"Yes. I mean, I'll just use the back door, if that's all

right. And the front of the house will be completely yours."

Completely mine, he thought, somehow restraining himself from parroting her words for the third time in a row.

It had all come painfully clear.

She wasn't inviting him to share her house at all; she had moved her things elsewhere. He would be staying here alone.

And he knew why she'd done it.

Because *she* knew how he felt about the main house. She'd seen his absurd reaction to it that first night they met.

She knew his ludicrous weakness—and he hated that she knew. It was almost as bad as the other things she knew about him: all his schemes and his lies.

He asked very quietly, "Where are *you* staying?"

She shrugged, a gesture that was way too offhand. "There's a cute little room in the main house. I moved my things there."

"A cute little room that just happens to be up in the attic. Right?"

She shifted her stance. Her gaze slid away, then back. "Yes. In the attic."

"One of the two maid's rooms, right? A room nobody wants—unless you're operating at capacity and they can't get anything else."

She'd stopped shifting from one sneakered foot to the other. Her eyes looked wounded and defiant at once.

He demanded, "Which one of the maid's rooms is it? The one where my father had the bad taste to hang himself?"

She hiked up her chin. "No. Not that one."

"Oh, that's right. That would be the bigger room of the two. I suppose Myra's got that one."

"Sin, why are you—?"

"Answer me. Does Myra have the larger room?"

"Yes. But what does it matter? The two rooms share a *bath,* for heaven's sake. I just…I knew you'd be much more comfortable here."

"I'm sure you did."

"Sin, what is the matter? I thought you were pleased with the idea of staying here. And then, all of a sudden, you—"

He scooped up his garment bag and grabbed for the suitcase. "I'll take the damn attic room." He stalked toward her. She stayed right in his path. He had to halt a foot away from her or knock her down. "Get out of the way."

"No. Really. This is silly. I don't see why you—"

"I won't stay in your damn house, and that's that."

"But I only thought—"

"Don't think. If you want to know where I stand on something, ask me. It's very simple. And much more effective than reading my mind." He took another step. "Move."

She sucked in a small wounded gasp. "You're behaving totally out of proportion about this."

"Move."

She met his gaze, still defiant, for about a count of five. And then, with a tiny defeated sigh, she stepped out of his way. He brushed past her and kept going, headed for the front door.

Chapter 14

Sophie trailed after him as far as the front room. He set down his big suitcase to fling open the door, then grabbed it up again and went through without looking back. Sophie stopped where she was in the middle of the room, watching him leave, wondering how things had gotten so awful so fast. He reached the car, tossed his things in the trunk, shoved the door down and marched around to the driver's side.

He reached for the door handle. And then he stopped. He glanced up at the blue sky and down at the fine shoes on his feet. Finally he turned and looked through the open door of the guest house right at Sophie.

Cautiously she crossed the floor and went out to stand on the porch that ran the width of the house.

Sin started toward her. He stopped at the base of the three steps that led up to where she waited.

"I'm sorry," he said.

She couldn't bring herself to say it was all right; it wasn't. She forced a smile. "I guess we're both a little on edge."

"I meant what I said. I won't put you out of your house."

"Yes. All right."

"Do you still want me to stay?"

She should probably have hesitated, at least. But she didn't. "Yes. I do—and things have slowed down considerably since you were here before. I can put you in a much nicer room." She tried a rueful smile. "I could even see to it that you have your own bath."

He put a foot up on the first step and stuck his hands in his pockets. "A nicer room—with a bath—would be great. But I want it clear that you'll charge me the same as you'd charge anyone."

She hadn't planned to charge him at all. She opened her mouth to protest.

He didn't even let her start. "I swear to you. I can afford to pay for my room."

The black Lexus gleamed in the sun behind him. She looked down at those beautiful shoes of his. "I know you can. I only wanted..." She didn't quite know how to finish.

"What?"

"For you to feel welcome, I guess."

"Do you think you could look at me, instead of my shoes?"

She forced her gaze upward. He wasn't exactly smiling. But then again, he'd never been a big one for smiles. At least he looked reasonably friendly—in that broody, intense way of his.

"I promise to feel welcome," he said, humor lighting his eyes just a little.

She wanted to argue some more, to insist that she didn't feel right about having him pay. But she knew it wouldn't do any good. "All right, then," she conceded. "You'll take a nicer room, complete with its own bath. And I'll charge you for it, full price."

He took his foot off the step and his hands from his pockets. "Come on, then. Better get me checked in."

She gave him the room they called the north suite, so named because its bow window faced that direction, providing a view of the back grounds and the oak grove beyond. She wondered, as she climbed the stairs ahead of him, if he would remember it from his childhood. She was pretty sure it hadn't been his parents' room; the original master suite was in the front of the house. However, the room might hold a few memories for him, anyway.

But Sin said nothing of memories. He dropped his suitcase on the rug, tossed his garment bag over a chair and cast a baleful glance around.

"Where's the phone?"

Patiently she explained that they didn't have much of a phone system. There was a line in the kitchen, which had an extension in Myra's room. And a pay phone in the entrance hall that the guests could use. "It's part of the charm here," she added, sounding sheepish in spite of herself. "The Mountain Star is a place to get away from ringing phones."

He turned those intense black eyes on her. "Which means, in the off-season, you can't count on the executive trade."

"The *executive* trade?" She really did try not to scoff.

"We're not set up for that kind of thing, and we never planned to be. Families come here. And couples looking for a romantic hideaway—"

He dismissed her explanation with a wave of his hand. "Fine. Whatever. I have a cell phone."

"But you could use the kitchen phone. I'm sure that would—"

"No, thanks. I'll manage. I want to get this whole thing moving right away, and that means I'll need a phone to myself."

"To call contractors and get estimates, you mean?"

He gave her another of those dark looks he was such a master at. "That is what I'm here for, isn't it?"

She only stared at him, picturing a phalanx of contractors descending on the Mountain Star, coming up with estimates for extensive improvements she wasn't even sure she wanted made.

He blew out a breath. "All right. What is it?"

"Well, I just don't…"

"What? Speak up."

She squared her shoulders and spoke out loud and clear. "I thought we said we would take it slow."

"We did. I'm getting estimates, that's all. *I* thought that was what we'd agreed I'd do."

It was. And she knew it.

"Sophie, there's no law that says we have to make the improvements right away—or *ever,* for that matter."

"Right."

"We have to start somewhere."

"Of course, we do."

"I want to get an idea of what is possible and what it will cost."

"That does make sense."

He was pacing back and forth. "So what is the problem?"

I love you, and I'm a coward. "Nothing."

He stopped pacing, turned to face her. "Then you're giving me the go-ahead to get the damn estimates?"

"Yes. Certainly. It's what we agreed."

"Well, at least that's settled."

"Yes."

"And once I get all the figures together, we'll sit down with them, all right?"

She nodded.

"We'll see where we want to go from there."

"Yes. That's reasonable. I understand."

"So," Myra said an hour later. "How's our new guest settling in?"

Sophie picked up her fork and started in on the stuffed tomato salad Myra had just set in front of her. She took a bite, chewed and swallowed. "Umm. This is wonderful. What is that spice —cumin?"

"Did I ask you what you thought of lunch? I don't think I asked you that."

Sophie drank some milk and set the glass down carefully. "He seems fine."

"You use that word a lot lately. *Fine.* Have you noticed that?"

"Myra. What are you driving at?"

There was a bowl of fruit on the kitchen table. Myra turned it, moved the bananas from the left side to the right. "I thought you were giving him the guest house."

"He refused to stay there."

"Why?"

"Myra, I don't have the answers to everything."

Myra clucked her tongue. "A little on the prickly side, are we?" She fiddled with the bananas some more. "Maybe you ought to ask him."

"Ask him what?"

"Why he refused the guest house."

Sophie knew her friend was right. "There are a lot of things I ought to ask him."

"And will you?"

Sophie picked up her fork again, then set it down. "I keep meaning to."

"But when *will* you?"

"Soon."

Myra sighed. "Better eat your lunch."

Sophie hardly saw Sin the rest of the day. He spent a couple of hours in his room—no doubt putting his cell phone to use, calling every contractor in the county. And then, later, he went out. He returned in time for dinner and sat down in the dining room with the rest of the guests. Once he'd finished eating, he retreated to his room.

Sophie ate later in the kitchen with Myra and Caleb. Afterward she helped Myra wash dishes and set up for the next morning. Then she crossed the lawn to the guest house. She lay awake very late, thinking of Sin, telling herself to give the situation time—and worrying that he'd never get a moment's sleep over in the cottage, where the past haunted him so terribly.

In the north suite in Riker Cottage, Sin did lay awake. But his sleepless state had nothing to do with being in the cottage.

On that level, he had changed. He wasn't sure exactly how. But as soon as he'd stepped through the front door that morning, he'd realized that no bleak memories would torment him there now.

Perhaps, when he had walked away and left the place to Sophie the month before, he'd let go of more than his obsession to get it back.

In any case, to him Riker Cottage was just a big old house now. A structure of wood and rock that needed a new roof and probably ought to have a termite inspection ASAP.

No, the past didn't keep him awake. Sophie did.

Sophie, who might want him and might not. Who had proposed a partnership between them.

Maybe.

Who offered him her bed.

Without her in it.

He had been certain of one thing when he came here this time: that the next move would have to be hers.

But after today, Sin Riker wasn't certain of anything at all.

The next day the contractors started coming. Before noon, Sin had two men crawling on the roof and three going through the kitchen with their tape measures and their clipboards. Since it was Bethy's day off again, Sophie vacuumed and dusted the parlors, foyer, stairs and landings, cleaned the guests' rooms—and tried to stay out of their way.

After lunch, it was more of the same. Sophie made more beds and more contractors appeared. By three, when all of her maid's duties were done, Sin had gone off somewhere. Sophie headed back to the guest house to tackle the accounts.

She'd just settled in at her desk when the phone rang. It was Myra in the main house.

"Jennifer Randall's on her way," Myra said. Jennifer Randall was the owner of Black Angel, the Arabian mare who'd been injured a couple of months before. "She came banging through the back door a minute ago, looking for you."

"She's angry?"

"Steamed."

"Is her horse injured again?"

"Not that she mentioned. She's just on the warpath over something Caleb said, I think."

"Thanks for the warning."

"Good luck."

Sophie hung up just as the pounding started on the back door.

"He is rude. Rude and pushy. And I refuse to board Black Angel here for another day unless you do something about him." Jennifer Randall paced back and forth in front of Sophie's desk.

"Ms. Randall, what exactly did Caleb do?"

"What did he do? What he always does. Treating me as if I don't know how to handle my own horse. Today he actually tried to give me instructions on caring for my tack. I have had it. He is rude. And I don't like his attitude…telling me how to *ride,* for pity's sake. Giving me orders on how to take care of my equipment. I don't have to put up with that. And I won't."

"Ms. Randall, I—"

"Will you do something about him?"

Sophie mentally counted to ten. "Just what is it that you would like me to do?"

"Reprimand him. Make it clear to him that if he wants to keep his job—"

"You're asking me to threaten to fire him?"

The woman froze in midstride and planted both fists on her hips. "Yes. That's exactly what I'm asking."

Patience, Sophie thought. "Ms. Randall, I won't fire Caleb. He does the work of three men around here. All of the others who board horses here consider him an excellent groom. And he's also a dear friend."

"Well. Then I'm afraid I'll have to take Black Angel out of your care."

Sophie opened her mouth to try to dissuade her, and then shut it. She had to face facts here. The boarding fee Jennifer Randall paid every month simply wasn't worth all the trouble she caused.

The woman began pacing again. "Quite frankly, Ms. Jones, this is no way to run a business. Stable help should be just that—help."

"Ms. Randall," Sophie said. "We are sorry to lose Black Angel. But I think you're right. It's for the best."

Jennifer Randall stopped pacing. She turned. "What?"

"Of course you'll need a little time to find another place to board her."

"But I—"

"A few days, is that enough?"

"Why, I—"

Sophie rose. "I'm sorry it hasn't worked out."

The woman sucked in a gasp. "Well, I never—"

"I really don't think there's anything more to say."

"I cannot believe—" This time the woman cut herself off. "All right. I'll make other arrangements. Within the next few days."

"Thank you."

"And I have to tell you, I will *not* be recommending the Mountain Star to any of my friends or associates."

Sophie winced, but made herself say evenly, "I understand."

"And I intended to ride today. I *still* intend to ride today. I expect that man to take good care of Black Angel until I find her a new place."

"Of course. There'll be no problem, I promise you." She delivered those words to Jennifer Randall's back, since the woman had already whirled to flounce out. Sophie sank into her desk chair, wincing again as she heard the kitchen door slam.

Caleb appeared about fifteen minutes later, filling the doorway with his muscular bulk.

Sophie looked up from her computer and gave him a smile. "You okay?"

"I've been better. The Randall woman just rode off on Black Angel. She did come and talk to you, didn't she?"

"She sure did."

"What happened?"

"We agreed that she'd find another stable."

He looked down at the floor. "That's a lot of horse. Someday that woman will get herself thrown bad. Or Black Angel will come up with worse than a sprain."

"Caleb, look at it this way. It's not our problem anymore—or at least it won't be within a few days."

He took a step into the room. "I'm sorry, Sophie B."

"It's not your fault. I know that."

"We can't afford to lose any boarders."

"That one we couldn't afford to keep. Now lighten

up. You did the best you could with that woman, and we're lucky we're going to be rid of her."

"I'll always feel bad for poor Black Angel."

"In this situation, there's really nothing you can do."

"I guess I know it."

"Then will you please stop shuffling your feet and acting like the world's come to an end."

He gave her a reasonable semblance of a smile.

She said, "Go on back to the stables. And don't worry. This worked out for the best all the way around."

"I hope you're right."

"I know I am."

As soon as she finished recording the receipts for the previous week and paying a few bills that just couldn't wait another day, Sophie headed for the barn to fool around with her projector some more. The darn thing still wasn't working right.

She saw Sin, out in the driveway saying goodbye to one of his contractors. He waved at her and she almost stopped, to share a few words with him, to see how his day was going. But after yesterday, she hardly knew what to expect from him: another argument, most likely. After dealing with the Randall woman, she just didn't feel up to more conflict right then. She returned his wave and kept on walking.

The contractor got in his pickup and drove away—and seconds later, Sin fell in step with her.

"What's up now?" he asked.

It was an innocent enough question. But still, her stomach clenched like a fist. She just knew he'd find something to criticize soon enough. "I'm going to the barn to look at my projector. It's been acting up."

"Does it ever *not* act up?"

"Good question." She walked a little faster. Next he'd start in on how she needed a new projector.

And he did. "Sophie, we've got to look into replacing that thing."

She murmured something noncommittal and kept on walking.

He stayed with her—and moved on to the next order of business. "What the hell happened to that skinny maid you had?"

"Midge quit a few weeks ago. I have a new maid now. Bethy."

"I didn't see any Bethy today. I saw you cleaning the rooms by yourself."

"Bethy has Monday and Tuesday off." She had no intention of telling him that Bethy was four months pregnant and morning sickness kept her from working most of the rest of the week. He'd find out soon enough, she supposed. And then she'd get an earful on that subject, too.

They had reached the barn. He took one door and she took the other. They swung them wide and braced them open. They entered the cool, dim interior. Sophie pulled open the curtains to the main room and turned on the overhead fluorescents. She spotted an empty plastic bottle down near the screen, so she went to collect it.

Sin remained at the top of the aisle. "What happened with the bossy blonde. The one with the black Arabian mare?"

How could he know about Jennifer Randall? The man must have radar. She scooped up the bottle and started back toward him. "So. You heard about that."

"Pretty hard not to. She came stomping into the

kitchen in those tall boots of hers just when I got back from looking over that meadow where we talked about putting my house."

She reached him and went by on her way to the trash can by the concession counter.

He caught her arm. "Stand still a minute, will you?"

She knew that he'd only touched her in order to slow her down. Still, that touch loosed a chain of sensual re-actions, like little firecrackers exploding along the wait-ing surface of her skin. She clutched the empty plastic bottle tighter, hoping the action would help to still her own response.

It didn't.

His face changed, his mouth going softer, his eyes kindling with heat. Those exquisite five nights they'd shared seemed to rise and shimmer in the air between them. She knew he remembered, just as she remem-bered—the taste of his kisses, the way he used to reach for her, his hand sliding under her hair, cupping her nape, pulling her close...

Abruptly he released her.

"Tell me about the woman," he commanded, all busi-ness once more. "The blonde with the black Arabian mare. Some problem with Caleb?"

She blinked. "How did you know?"

"She mentioned the groom when she came storm-ing into the kitchen—and not in a flattering way. How did you work it out?"

"She's taking the horse elsewhere."

"When?"

"I gave her a few days to find another stable."

She waited for him to start criticizing Caleb and

mentally braced herself to remain reasonable as she took Caleb's side.

But he surprised her. "Well, the sooner she's out of your hair, the better, the way I see it."

She opened her mouth to argue—and had to switch directions in midword. "I...completely agree with you."

"There's nothing more dangerous than a bad horse-woman who refuses to admit she doesn't know what the hell she's doing."

Unless it's a bad horse*man,* she thought—but decided that since they were agreeing on something, she'd better not push her luck. "Yes. That's true."

"Which reminds me of something else. How well are you insured? Not well enough, I'll bet. We'll have to look into that. Especially since you insist on bedding down the homeless in that *campground* of yours. I went by there today, by the way. You need to get those people to pick up their trash."

She couldn't stop herself from rolling her eyes.

His eyes narrowed. "What does that mean?"

"What?"

"You just rolled your eyes at me."

"I did?"

"You know damn well you did."

"Well..."

"Well, what?"

"Well, Sin, I don't know—"

"Yes, you do."

She drew in a fortifying breath and started again. "I'm feeling a little overwhelmed, that's all. You're so *driven* about all this."

He made a low impatient sound. "There's no sense in fooling around. I have a couple more people coming tomorrow. Then I'll have all the estimates I need. I can tell you what I'm willing to invest here, you can show me your profit-and-loss statements. And we can make our decision."

She felt as if the barn's stone walls had started moving in her. "We can?"

Those black eyes never wavered. "That was the deal, wasn't it?"

"But I thought—"

"What?"

"I thought we'd have more time."

"*I* don't need any more time."

"But…"

"But what?"

"Well, this is all happening so fast. I just don't…I mean, don't you need to get some idea about that house you might build? Don't you need estimates there, too?"

"Sophie. I have plenty of money. I can hire a general contractor—or do the job myself. All that's required is that I make a decision—to do it or not."

She couldn't think of a thing to say to that except, "Oh."

"Sophie."

"Yes?"

"What is going on here?"

She backed up a step.

"I know this is probably a shock, coming from me, but I think it's time we got honest with each other."

"Honest?" She repeated the word as if unsure of its meaning.

He raised a sardonic brow. "Yes. Honest. As in you tell me your truth and I'll tell you mine."

She thought suddenly of little Anthea Jones, bobbing down the river in her orange life jacket—out of her depth and out of control. "I don't...what truth?"

He ran a hand back through his hair. "Look. I think you're going to have to decide just what the hell you want from me."

She retreated another step. "I...we...I mean..."

"Do you even *know* what you want from me?"

Her hands felt all sweaty and her throat felt so tight. "I..."

He didn't relent. "I asked you a question. Do you know what you want from me?"

She almost moved back a third step—and then somehow managed to hold her ground. "Yes. I do. I know."

"What?"

"I..."

"Say it."

And somehow she did. "I want you to come back to me. I want us to be together. The way we were before."

Oh, dear Lord, she had done it! She had gotten the words out at last....

Unfortunately Sin didn't seem very impressed. "This isn't before."

How could a man be so obtuse? "Well, I know that."

"Are you sure?"

"Well. Certainly. Yes. Of course, I'm sure."

"Listen to you." His voice was gentle, forgiving. Kind. She hated that. She was the gentle one, the kind one. Not him. "You don't sound sure. And you don't behave as if you're sure. Not by a long shot."

"I..." How could she tell him? Why did he refuse to understand? "I...came to L.A. To find you. I was hoping..."

"Hoping what?"

"That we could work things out."

"You offered me a partnership, Sophie. A business agreement."

She experienced an utterly childish urge to hurl the plastic bottle at him. "Because I didn't know how…to reach out to you. I didn't know what else to do."

"So, you never really wanted a partnership at all?"

"I…" Not another word came into her mind.

He kept pushing. "*I,* what?"

She could have cried. Just sat down on the plank floor and sobbed her heart out. "Oh, Sin, I…"

"What?"

She confessed in a small voice, "I guess I just want you."

"You *guess?*"

Oh, this was not going the way she'd imagined at all. She'd *told* him that she wanted him. Didn't that count for anything at all?

Apparently not. "All right," he said grimly. "You want me. You *guess* you want me."

Anger, frustration, longing—they were all tangled up inside her. "I *do.*" She forced some conviction into her voice. "I do want you."

"You want me. The way it was before."

"Yes." She clutched the empty bottle hard again. "And I have to know. Do you want me?"

He was shaking his head.

She wanted to scream, stomp her foot, tear her hair. "What does that mean, shaking your head like that? Does it mean you don't want me, after all?"

He made a low noise in his throat. "I don't think that's the question."

"It is too the question!" She only realized she was

shouting when the pigeon up in the rafters took flight in distress. Sophie let out a startled cry as the bird came at them, swooping past Sin and down on Sophie. She ducked. It flew on by, through the pulled-back curtains, and out the wide-open doors. Sophie stared after it, thinking of all the times she'd tried to chase it away. And now, just like that, the bird was gone.

"Sophie."

She had no choice but to face him.

"Come here."

She froze, riddled with suspicion. Torn in two with yearning. So confused. Nothing made sense anymore. Nothing at all. "Why?"

"Just come here."

She didn't want to go to him—and at the same time, she wanted nothing else.

She took one awful step forward. And then another. And then the one that brought her right up close to him.

"I'm here, aren't I?" he asked quietly. "Why the hell would I come here if I didn't want you?"

She had no answer for that. She had no answer for anything.

He raised a hand. She flinched.

He made a soothing sound. And then he traced the line of her hair where it fell along her cheek, a caress that sent heated shivers singing all through her. His hand moved down, over the curve of her jaw to her neck. It paused at the place where her pulse beat so fast—and then continued on to the little hollow at the base of her throat. He stroked that hollow lightly, gently. The tangle of emotions inside her shifted, resolving themselves into one dominant sensation: desire.

"I can't seem to forget the feel of you." Low and caressing, his voice curled around her. "It's kept me awake a lot of nights...."

All she could whisper was, "Yes..."

"You remember, too."

Again she murmured, "Yes."

He turned his hand over, brushed the side of her throat with the back of his index finger. "Those five nights we had together, do you want them again?"

She licked her lips and nodded.

He raised his other hand, cupped her face. And brought his mouth down on hers.

Chapter 15

Sophie dropped the plastic bottle. She heard it roll quietly away.

And then she forgot all about it.

Sin's mouth moved on hers, at first coaxing—then demanding her response.

She opened for him, sighing. His tongue mated with hers as he wrapped his arms around her and pulled her close against him.

He was hard. She moaned at the feel of him.

And then he put his hands on her shoulders. His fingers dug in, hurting her a little. He put her away from him.

"I'd say that answers your question." He dropped his arms, backed away another step.

All she wanted was his lips on hers. She swayed toward him. "Sin—"

He took her shoulders once more, steadying her. "Let's just get this whole thing clear."

"I don't—"

"You want me. I want you. I don't see *wanting* as the issue at all. Do you, *honestly?*"

Her body thrummed with yearning. Why wouldn't he simply sweep her into his arms again?

"Sophie. Answer me."

She shrugged off his hands, ordered her traitorous body to stop making a fool of her. "Yes. I mean, no. All right. We…want each other."

"Exactly. And we can be lovers, the way we were before. At least, for a while." His fine mouth twisted in a wry grin. "However, in my experience, that kind of thing never lasts all that long."

"But I—"

"You *did* say that you wanted it to be the way it was before."

Oh, why did he refuse to understand? "I meant that we were so close. We never argued We were… intimate, in the best kind of way."

"Sophie. It was all based on lies. Is that what you want?"

"Of course not. You're twisting what I've said."

"No, I'm making a point."

"What point?"

"That partnership you offered, that was a good idea."

What in heaven's name was he getting at now? "It was?"

He nodded. "If we're going to be together, we're going to have to share. And I think that's our problem."

He was making no sense at all. "Sharing? *Sharing* is our problem?"

"Yes. Neither of us has a clue how to do it."

She could not get her mind around the utter unfairness of that statement. She shared all she had. She helped others daily. And he knew it. Wasn't he always complaining about her campground? And what about the Mountain Star itself, forever on the verge of going under because she was such a sucker for someone in need?

She told him quite proudly, "I know how to share."

He was shaking his head again. "Uh-uh. You know how to *give*. The two are not the same." He smiled then. A real, rueful, tender sort of smile. "I think you like what you have here, and you're not sure you want to share. And I do understand that. I felt the same way. Once upon a time."

A thousand arguments scrolled through her head at once, but not one of them found its way out her mouth.

He had more to say. "Do you want a lover, Sophie? Is that all you want from me? I would be that for you. For a while. As a matter of fact, I'm kind of at loose ends now. Considering a career change, considering a *lot* of changes. I wouldn't mind a little…diversion. Something to pass the time while I figure out what to do with the rest of my life."

"A…diversion?"

He lifted one shoulder in an elegant shrug. "Why not? I find you extremely…diverting." His gaze traveled over her, searing where it touched. "Is that what you're really after here? Just a little diversion?"

"I…no, of course not."

"Well, then, I'll get my estimates together. By tomorrow evening, how's that?"

She swallowed and somehow managed a reply. "All right."

Without another word, he brushed past her. She turned and watched him vanish the same way the bird had gone—through the curtains and out the doors.

That night, Sin didn't appear for dinner at six-thirty with the rest of the guests. Instead, he showed up in the kitchen an hour later, just as Myra and Sophie were about to sit down.

"I wonder, Myra—have you got an extra plate for me?"

Myra folded her freckled arms and gave him a slow once-over. "I imagine I could dig one up."

"I would appreciate it."

Myra got down another plate, a set of flatware and a fresh napkin. She set him a place.

"Thank you," he said.

The cook cast a fretful glance toward Caleb's empty chair. "Now, where is Caleb?"

"He'll be in," said Sophie, picking up her napkin, trying not to let her gaze collide with Sin's. Since he'd left her in the barn that afternoon, she hadn't been able to stop thinking of the hungry way he'd kissed her—not to mention the hard things he'd said. The more she dwelled on his words, the more disturbing truth she found in them.

She *didn't* want to share the Mountain Star. It was hers, she had created it to be just what it was. And she feared that Sin wanted to make it into something else altogether.

She shuddered every time she thought of what it might become, with phones in every room and busy, impatient executive types running in and out. Everything new and shining and…antiseptic. A place where neither her campground nor her theater would really fit in. She didn't want that. Not on her life.

But, oh, she did want Sin. And she knew that to have him more than temporarily, some kind of compromise would have to be reached.

Tomorrow night.

Too soon.

Much too soon.

"Sophie B.," Myra said.

"Um, yes?"

"Mr. Riker just asked you to pass the rice."

"Oh. Yes. Of course." She picked up the bowl and tried not to look directly at him as she handed it to him.

"Thank you."

"You're welcome."

Sophie heard the back door open. That would be Caleb. She steeled herself for the surly attitude he'd assume as soon as he saw who had joined them for dinner.

But Caleb hardly glanced at Sin. He came and stood by his chair, where he shifted from foot to foot the way he always did when something upset him.

"Sit down," commanded Myra. "Eat."

Caleb spoke to Sophie. "That Randall woman never did come back today. And I'm gettin' real worried. It'll be dark soon."

Sophie set down her fork. "Do you know which way she went?"

Caleb nodded. "That trail that heads northeast, up into the mountains."

Sophie tucked her napkin beside her plate and stood. "Come on, then. We'd better go and find her."

Sin's chair scraped the floor. "I'm going, too."

Caleb grunted and cast Sin a dismissing look. "We can handle this ourselves."

Sin swore. "Look. That woman has gone and gotten herself lost on my land. There's no way I'm staying behind."

By ten of eight, with perhaps a half an hour of daylight left, Sin, Sophie and Caleb were mounted, armed with electric lanterns and on their way.

The wind had come up. It blew at their backs as they headed out. Caleb led them on the path he'd seen the woman take, around east of the cottage, and then to the north across the meadow of wild roses.

Once beyond the meadow, they started climbing up into the mountains. The face of the full moon grew brighter above them as the sun sank behind the western hills. The wind blew harder, making the trees rustle and sway.

It was full dark when they found Black Angel, peacefully nibbling grass in a clear spot between two huge, old cedar trees, her ebony mane swirling. Caleb dismounted and approached her. She looked up, whinnied in recognition and came right to him.

He patted her neck and murmured in her ear. Then he turned to Sin and Sophie. "The rein's broken, leather sawed clean through." He shook his head. "I warned that damn woman...."

A really strong gust of wind blew by them, stirring the horses, making them dance. Sin looked up at the moon. "We can't search much longer. It's getting too late. We should bring the sheriff in on this."

Caleb suggested, "It'll be another hour before they can get their people mobilized. Let's go on a little ways."

Sin frowned. "But not far."

"All right."

They hobbled Black Angel so she wouldn't wander off and rode on through the trees that seemed to close in around them, blocking out the pale glow of the moon. Soon enough, they had to switch on the big lantern flashlights to see the trail ahead.

Caleb spotted the little riding hat, blown against a tree trunk, about a half mile from where they'd come upon Black Angel. The groom swung down from the spotted gelding he rode and grabbed it up. "It's hers." The three shared a look.

Sin made the decision. "Let's go on."

Caleb remounted. The wind shoved at them, blowing hard, strong now even in the shelter of the trees. At last they reached a rocky stretch. The trees thinned out to nothing—and Jennifer Randall came limping at them, falling, picking herself up, staggering forward, and sobbing as she tried to run.

"Oh, thank God! Help. You have to help…." She stumbled down on them, her hands out, her face smudged and her hair wild in the whipping wind. The horses grew nervous, they pranced and tried to shy away from her, dislodging rocks that tumbled down the mountain behind them.

Sin passed his lantern to Sophie and swung out of the saddle. The Randall woman fell into his arms—and then immediately started struggling to get free. "Oh, God. Oh, we have to hurry…."

Sin tried to calm her. "Hold on. Slow down…"

"No. Listen. I…had to start a fire. I was hoping

someone would see and come rescue me. But then the wind…oh, we have to hurry! We have to hurry now!"

They all understood then what the woman meant.

"Douse the lanterns," Sin commanded.

Sophie and Caleb obeyed. The world went dark. They looked higher up the mountain. There, rising above the thick crown of trees, ribbons of smoke spiraled in an eerie, curling dance toward the silvery moon.

"Come on." Sin put an arm around the Randall woman. "We've got to move." He helped her over to the others, stopping beside Caleb's horse.

The woman's handsome face turned ugly beneath its layer of grime. "No. I will not ride with that—"

Sin spun her to face him. "We don't have time for any of your games now."

The woman looked into those hard, dark eyes, bit her lip—and nodded.

Caleb put a hand down and Sin hoisted her up in front of the groom. Then he went to his own horse, lifted the flap on the saddlebag and brought out his cell phone. The wind whistled hard around them as Sin punched up 911.

They had some degree of luck. The wind didn't turn. They found Black Angel where they'd left her and led her back with them.

They were crossing the meadow where the wild roses grew when the first helicopter sailed by overhead, laden with fire retardant to drop on the blaze.

"Most beautiful sight I ever saw," Caleb declared, watching as the copter swung away toward the mountains behind them.

"Let's just pray they're in time to contain the damn thing," Sin added bleakly.

Jennifer Randall whined, "Can we please get moving? I need a doctor. My ankle is killing me."

At the Mountain Star, the firefighters in their cross-country vehicles were already arriving. The head of the team took a few precious minutes to question the Randall woman, then suggested someone drive her to Sierra Nevada Memorial to have her ankle x-rayed. Myra volunteered for that job. Sophie cast the cook a grateful glance.

As the owner of the property, Sin was allowed to head back out with the firefighters. He suggested they also take Caleb along, to show them the smoothest way overland.

Sophie stepped up. "I'd like to go, too."

Sin focused those eyes on her. "Stay here. You have guests to worry about."

His imperious tone rankled. And she feared she might go crazy, sitting there, doing nothing, just waiting for news. But she knew he was right.

In the cottage, the guests gravitated toward the kitchen, where Sophie kept Myra's radio tuned to a local station, which provided periodic reports on the fire. They all clustered around the big table, sharing pot after pot of Myra's coffee, telling old stories of other forest fires they'd heard about or seen, falling silent whenever the radio announcer came on with more news. Overhead, through the hours, they heard the helicopters rattling by.

Myra returned at a little after ten to report that Jennifer Randall had no broken bones. "A bad sprain is all."

"Where is she now?" Sophie asked.

"I drove her home. She complained all the way—that her ankle hurt and her nerves were shot. She says she's going to sell that horse of hers. You should have heard her." Myra stuck her nose in the air and pursed her mouth. "'Black Angel has become totally unmanageable.' That's exactly what she said."

One of the guests asked, "You're talking about the woman who started the fire?"

"I'm afraid so," Sophie said.

The guest shook his head. "If the forest service had any sense, they'd stick her with the bill for this mess."

A murmur of agreement went up from the others.

Sophie stood. "How about more coffee?"

"I'll have some."

"Me, too."

Myra clucked her tongue. "I'll get it." She bustled over to the counter to get the pot.

By midnight, the wind had died down. The radio announcer said the fire was ninety-five percent contained. There would be no more reports unless it kicked up again. They heard the firefighters returning, driving past the house and out to the highway. No more beating helicopter blades disturbed the quiet of the mountain night.

The guests wandered back to their rooms, keyed up from too much coffee, but all determined to try to get some sleep. Caleb came in at twelve-thirty, to find Sophie and Myra in the kitchen alone.

"It's gonna be okay," he said. "They got to it soon

enough. It looks like Sin's lost about ten acres of trees. But he said he could afford that just fine."

"Sin?" Sophie asked gently.

Caleb shuffled his feet. "All right. He's not so bad. I could get used to him if I had to—just as long as he doesn't go breaking your heart again."

Myra demanded, "But where is he now?"

"He's comin'. He waited to ride back on the last truck. Should be here pretty soon now."

The cook pushed her bulk out of her chair. "Caleb, you didn't eat a bite of dinner. Let me—"

"Naw. I'm not hungry. I want to check on the horses and get me a little sleep." Caleb headed out the back door, leaving Sophie and Myra alone again. Sophie turned to her friend—and found those green eyes studying her.

"You'll be waiting up for him, won't you?"

They both knew who Myra meant by "him." In lieu of an answer, Sophie picked up an empty coffee cup and carried it to the sink.

"Do you love that man?" Myra said to her back.

Sophie set the cup down and turned to face her friend.

Myra asked again more gently, "Well, do you?"

Sophie told the truth. "Yes."

"Does he love you?"

"He's never said."

"Maybe you should ask him."

"Maybe." Sophie looked down at the floor, then up at Myra once again. "If he and I…worked things out, there would be some changes around here."

Myra pushed in her chair. "No sense in running from change. It always finds a person anyway."

* * *

Once Myra headed up the back stairs, Sophie sat at the table alone, waiting and listening for the sound of that last truck coming in. Eventually she got up, washed out the coffeepot and set it up for the next morning. There were a few dishes waiting in the sink. She opened the dishwasher and loaded them in.

At ten after one, she heard the sound of a vehicle outside. She froze in the act of wiping a counter. The sound faded away quickly toward the front of the cottage. Sophie still didn't move. She strained to hear the front door opening, but that sound never came.

She looked down at the sponge she'd been using to wipe up counters that were already clean—and realized that if she wanted to speak with Sin, she would have to go looking for him.

She dropped the sponge and ran out through the west parlor to the front hall, where she threw back the old door and hurried out onto the walk. She caught a glimpse of taillights disappearing toward the highway.

And that was all. The moon shone on the grass, making it gleam whitely. Somewhere off in the trees, a dove cooed. The crickets played their never-ending, chirruping song. And off to her left, the little-girl statue still laughed without sound as the water from the fountain cascaded down.

She ventured farther along the walk, out under the broad pale face of the moon. The night was still, the wind that had threatened such havoc faded away now to nothing but a hint of a breeze. On that breeze she could faintly smell wood smoke, an acrid reminder of disaster averted.

Wood smoke. Crickets. The splash of water in the

fountain and the gentle cooing of a dove. But no sign of the man she'd been waiting for.

Still, Sophie knew where to find him.

Chapter 16

He sat on the black rock, his back to her, looking out over the dark creek that flowed by a few feet away.

Sophie tiptoed across the soft bed of moss, coming up on his left side, and then hovering there, not sure how to begin.

He turned his head and his eyes met hers. He didn't look surprised to see her.

She asked too brightly, "Is there room for me on that rock?"

He said nothing—but he did scoot a little to the right, leaving a space for her beside him. Carefully she edged onto the rock and sat down.

"Clouds gathering," he said.

She followed his gaze. A grayness crept across the sky, blotting out the stars and drifting in gauzy tendrils over the broad face of the moon.

She said, "Rain would be good to finish off whatever's left of the fire."

He looked at her again. "We were lucky. This time."

She dipped her head in a brief nod. "I know."

"The land needs tending, Sophie. Whatever happens between you and me, I'm going to take steps to thin out some of those trees."

"I understand."

He stared at her for several seconds, his eyes hard, as if he didn't believe she understood at all. Then he turned his gaze to the dark waters of the creek once again.

She waited, not sure how to talk to him, doubting that he even wanted her there. The creek murmured softly as it flowed by and the leaves of the willows and oaks rustled, whispering to each other in the now-gentle wind.

Finally she drummed up enough nerve to reach out and lay her hand on his arm. The contact, as always, sent desire singing through her. She concentrated on ignoring it, on finding the right words to say. "Sin, I can't tell you how much I appreciate the way you dealt with Jennifer Randall tonight. In fact, if you hadn't been here—"

His hand closed over hers. "Don't."

"But I—"

"Don't thank me. No damn testimonials. Not now. Not tonight."

She swallowed, nodded. "All right."

Slowly he brought her hand to his mouth. His lips brushed her fingertips. She hitched in a gasp and he smiled, black eyes gleaming, both feral and knowing at once. "If you're so grateful, then show me."

She closed her own eyes, drew in a breath and let it out slowly. "How?"

His teeth scraped the pads of her fingers, so lightly. "You know."

And she did. She knew very well.

He pushed his other hand beneath her hair and clasped her nape, just the way he used to do. She shuddered in longing. The scent of him teased her: sweat— and wood smoke, from the now-vanquished fire.

"Kiss me." It was a command.

It never entered her mind to disobey. She lifted her mouth and he took it fiercely, holding her head still as he plundered the secrets beyond her lips. She felt his teeth, rasping, scraping the inner surface of her lower lip.

She had no choice but to kiss him back—and not because he demanded it, but because she hungered as he did. Because her whole body yearned.

With a lost cry, she reached for him, clutching his strong shoulders, the need in her rising, answering his. Her tongue met his, twining. She pressed herself against him, offering her body, reckless, on fire....

Then, without warning, he tore his mouth away from her.

Oh, how could he do that? She couldn't bear for it to end. Her need for him seemed to hang there, pulsing like a heart, in the charged air between them.

With another pleading cry, she tried to hold the kiss.

But he kept that from happening, his hands gripping her shoulders. He whispered roughly against her parted lips, "This damn rock's too hard."

She stared at his mouth, dazed, longing for his kiss again—and yet knowing that making love right now would fix nothing, really. Too much remained unresolved between them. Too much begged to be said.

He frowned at her. "Don't even start."

She blinked. "What?"

"Thinking."

"But, Sin—"

He rolled off his side of the rock and reached for her hand. "Come on."

"I don't… Where?"

"To that guest house of yours."

They went in through the back door. He led her to the front room from there. And then he left her in the middle of the floor and dropped into one of her two overstuffed chairs.

His dark gaze ran over her. "Take off that shirt."

She looked down at the front of herself and then back up at him.

"Take it off."

So she did, unbuttoning each button very carefully, her fingers awkward and slow. Finally she had all the buttons undone. She slipped it over her shoulders.

"Let it drop."

The shirt whispered to the floor.

"Now the bra."

She reached behind her, undid the clasp. Holding the scrap of lace against her breasts to keep it from falling, she slid the straps down.

"Sophie. Let it go."

She straightened her arms. The bra dropped away.

He rose from the chair and approached her, taking her hand, leading her to the sofa. "Lie down."

She obeyed. He knelt at her feet, pulled off her boots and her socks. Then his hands found the snap of her jeans, flicked it open, took the zipper down. She stared into his eyes as he peeled the jeans off, taking her underpants with them.

At last, she lay naked to his gaze.

He began to caress her, teasing, arousing—laying claim to every inch of her.

He parted her thighs. His dark head dipped between them. Sensation rolled over her, a wave of fire, consuming as it took her down.

"It's raining," he whispered, his hand at the heart of her again.

She listened to the soft pattering on the roof as her body lifted, opened, invited him once again. She moaned, and the rain went on, soft and insistent as her own hungry sighs.

They went to the bedroom. She helped him undress, her hands working swiftly now, undoing all the buttons, pushing the shirt back and off his hard shoulders.

She wrapped her arms around him, felt the teasing scrape of chest hair against her aching breasts. And then she was sliding down to her knees, parting the fly of those black jeans he wore, eagerly taking him into her mouth.

Sometime later, they lay across the bed.

His lips closed over her breast, drawing deep, pulling the need from inside her once again. He let go, looked into her eyes. "Do you still hear the rain?"

She nodded, her fingers combing through his silky hair, listening to the soft, insistent drumming sound. His hand strayed down, found her—tender, wet, open. Brazenly ready for him.

He arched a dark brow. "This doesn't solve anything, does it?"

She bit her lip, shook her head—and then cried out as his fingers delved in.

He reached across her, opened the drawer in the nightstand, brought out the small box. With great care, he peeled open the foil wrapper. "Help me."

They lay on their sides, facing each other. He wrapped her leg over his hip. She hitched in a breath as he filled her.

He put his hand on her nape again, held her eyes with his own—and began to move.

When the fulfillment came that time, the words rose inside her, pushing so hard, needing to get out.

She started to say them. "I lov—"

He put his hand on her mouth. "No. Don't. Not tonight...."

"But I—"

"No."

She moaned. The words retreated. All that remained was the two of them, the sweet hot point of connection.

The end came, swift and complete, shuddering outward from the center of her, blotting out everything, even the rain.

Chapter 17

Sin woke right at dawn. He opened his eyes and saw Sophie asleep beside him, the covers pulled close around her against the morning chill.

He wanted to reach for her.

But he didn't.

He shouldn't have seduced her last night. She was already confused when it came to him. What had happened last night would only serve to confuse her further.

He slid to the side and lowered his feet to the floor, careful to disturb the covers as little as possible. Once free of the bed, he gathered up his strewn clothing and crept out to the kitchen. A few minutes later he slipped outside fully dressed.

He tried the back door of the cottage. It was open. Inside, the smells of breakfast greeted him: bacon, coffee, biscuits. Myra stood at the counter by the sink, peeling the rind off half a cantaloupe.

He had a thoroughly sleazy urge to try to slink past her.

Before he could decide whether to act on that urge, she turned and spotted him. "I suppose I don't have to wonder where *you've* been." She held the half cantaloupe in one hand and brandished a paring knife with the other.

He knew that anything he said at that point would only make things worse. So he gave her a shrug.

She made a sort of *tsking* sound and waved that knife again. "Are you going to marry that girl or not?"

He shrugged again. "I doubt if she'll have me."

Myra looked at the knife and then at him. She grunted. "All right. Go on with you. Have a hot shower. It looks like you need one."

He turned and made for the stairs.

After his shower, he shaved. He put on clean clothes. By then, twenty minutes had passed since he'd mounted the stairs. He knew he'd lose his mind if he stayed in that room. So he yanked open the door and got out.

Myra was watching for him, standing at the stove this time. "Are you eating with us, then?"

"I'm not hungry." He started for the back door.

She slid her bulk sideways, just enough to block his path. "A man needs a good breakfast."

He gave her his hardest, meanest glare—the one that had never failed to send everyone at Inkerris, Incorporated, scurrying for cover.

Myra grunted and waved a freckled hand. "Fine. Be that way." Grunting a second time, she stepped aside.

He brushed past her. She called to his back as he went out the door, "You'll never know unless you ask her!"

Outside, the air was brisk and cool, everything smelling wet and fresh from last night's rain. He started walking fast. He didn't realize he was headed for the stables until he got there.

He found Caleb brushing the black Arabian mare. The groom turned and saw him, brush pausing in mid-stroke.

"One damn fine horse," Sin said, for lack of any better remark.

Caleb left the stall and latched it behind him. "Breakfast time."

"That's what Myra said."

"You coming?"

"I'm not hungry, thanks."

Caleb shook his head. "Not goin' so good, huh—with Sophie B.?"

Sin felt no desire at all to answer that one, so he kept his mouth shut.

Caleb added, "I'll send her on out here as soon as I see her." He tossed the brush.

Sin caught it. "Just because you send her doesn't mean she'll come."

The groom grinned at that. "She is a bossy one, under all that sweetness. She likes running things."

"I noticed."

"But she could be convinced to change a little. By a good man."

Sin felt a rueful smile lift the corners of his mouth. "A *good* man?"

Caleb nodded. "Some men aren't as much as they think they are. And some men are more."

"You think so?"

"I know so. I seen it for myself."

"Sin?"

No answer.

Sophie sat up, pushed back the covers and swung her feet to the floor. Outside the lace-curtained window opposite the bed, the sky was an innocent blue, the clouds all cleared away. Drops of water from the rain still clung to a rosebush that grew thick and thorny, tied to a short trellis just beyond the glass. Heavy dew silvered the lawn.

"Sin?"

Only silence.

He must have left—without waking her, without a word. She hung her head, stared down at her bare knees. They had goose bumps all over them. The room was *cold.*

She jumped up and ran to the bureau to find some clothes, pausing to glance at the clock by the bed before she put them on. It wasn't that late. Myra would be putting breakfast on the table about now.

Oh, where had Sin gone?

And why had he left her to wake up alone?

She remembered the night before, her knees going weak at the sheer erotic beauty of it. But then her need to find Sin snapped some strength into them.

She pulled on clean underwear and padded to the bathroom, where she rinsed her face and tugged a comb through her tangled hair. Then she yanked on the rest of her clothes and headed for the cottage.

She found Myra and Caleb in the kitchen, about to sit down to breakfast.

Myra was setting the plates around. She glanced up and clucked her tongue disapprovingly. "There you are. Bethy just called. She says she's feeling pretty queasy and won't be able to come in today."

Sophie closed her eyes, rubbed her temples. "I'll have to talk to her."

"You'll have to *fire* her, and you know it."

"We'll see— Listen, have you seen Sin this morning?"

Myra and Caleb shared a look. Then Myra confessed, "He came in a half an hour ago, then went out again. Without his breakfast." The words were informational, but the tone was pure mother hen. "I guess we all know where that man was all night."

Sophie blew out a breath. "Myra..."

"When are you going to settle this mess with him?"

"Just tell me. Where is he now?"

Caleb spoke up then. "He's in the stables. I left him there a few minutes ago."

She found him standing at Black Angel's stall, just looking at the horse, who wasn't paying any attention at all to him.

At the sound of Sophie's footsteps, he turned. He held a brush in his hand.

She made herself ask, though it came out all ragged-sounding, "Why...did you just leave?"

He tossed the brush onto a low stool near the rough plank wall.

"Sophie..." His voice sounded as torn as her own.

They stared at each other.

And at that moment, she knew.

He loved her, too. As much as she had ever loved him.

And probably more.

"Oh, Sin…"

He forked a hand through his hair. "I shouldn't have done that last night. I shouldn't have—"

She couldn't bear the distance between them and hurried to close it, stopping just inches away. "Don't apologize. Please."

He closed his eyes. "I can't take this. I hate this."

She reached out, put her hand on his arm. "I know…"

He looked down at where she touched him, then into her eyes once again. "You don't know. You can't know. I…don't know what I'm doing anymore. Since I met you, I don't know who the hell I am."

She clutched his arm harder. "It's all right."

He laughed then, a painful sound. "You said that the first night. Remember? When I grabbed you on the back stairs of the cottage?"

"I remember."

"And you were wrong. It wasn't all right. It was all a damn lie."

"We got past the lies."

He pulled away, stepped back. "You don't trust me anymore—not that I blame you."

She couldn't let him think that—even if it was just a little bit true. "But I do. I do trust you now."

"You don't. And I *want* you to trust me. Which is insane. I've never been the kind of man who gave a damn for a woman's trust."

She tried to make him see her side. "I just… We're so different. In what we want for this place. And I'm afraid. You're so strong. So…determined. You could make the Mountain Star successful, but then it might not really be the Mountain Star anymore."

He said it again, so sadly, "You don't trust me."

And right then, they both heard the low sound.

Sin's eye's hardened. "What's that?"

Sophie glanced down the stalls, to where she thought the sound had come from. "I don't know."

The sound came again—a groan. Someone groaning.

Sin spun on his heel and strode down the rows of stalls. Sophie followed after him.

At the last stall, one that looked empty, he stopped. "In here." He swung open the gate.

Bearded, filthy, dressed in tattered jeans and a grimy sweatshirt, a man huddled, shuddering, against the far wall.

Chapter 18

At the sight of Sin and Sophie, the fellow cried out, put his filthy hands over his face and backpedaled madly. It was as if he thought he could push his starved body through the wall—and away from the two who had found his hiding place. "No, no, don't! I'll go… I'll get out…."

Sophie moved toward him. Sin caught her arm. "Let me."

She felt a powerful urge to shake him off and rush around him. But she made herself curb it. She nodded. "All right."

Sin took one cautious step, and then another. The man drew tighter and tighter against the rough wall. Convulsive shivers rattled through him and his eyes gleamed feverishly bright. "I…went to the campground.

I heard it was all right, that a man could bed down there, find peace for a night. But the rain came. It got cold...."

Sin reached him, knelt beside him, spoke with aching gentleness. "You needed a dry place."

"Yeah. A dry place..." The thin body shook harder.

"It's okay," Sin whispered. "It's all right...." He reached in his pocket, came out with a key and tossed it to Sophie. She reacted just fast enough to snare it from the air. "Get the Lexus," he commanded. "We'll take him to the hospital."

"No!" A bony hand shot out, closed over Sin's arm. "I can't afford no hospital."

"It's all right," Sin answered softly. "I can."

The fevered eyes shone brighter—with stubborn pride. "Don't want no charity."

"Don't worry," Sin reassured him. "We don't offer charity here. We have what you need. And there'll be work to do later in exchange."

The man squinted, peered closer at Sin. "Who are you, anyway?"

"Call me Sin."

A ragged laugh escaped the man then, a laugh that turned to a racking cough. When the cough finally subsided, he muttered with some humor, "Sin, eh? I guess I know you already."

"I'm sure you do. What can I call you?"

"Jake. The name's Jake."

"Come on, Jake. Let's get you to a doctor." Sin cast a glance over his shoulder. Sophie hadn't moved.

She *couldn't* move. She could only stare at Sin, thinking of how she had loved him, right from that first night. Of how he had lied to her, how he had taken her innocence, abused her trust.

And how it didn't matter anymore. Because in the end, he had become everything she'd ever dreamed of in a man.

"The car?" Sin demanded.

She shook herself. "Yes. Right away." She turned and ran, out the east door of the stable and across the front driveway to the long garage that branched off the side of the cottage.

Sophie drove to the hospital. Sin sat in the back with Jake. When they arrived, Sin filled out all the forms, taking responsibility for the cost of the sick man's care.

"It's acute pneumonia," the doctor said an hour later. "We've pumped him full of antibiotics and we're getting fluids into him. Now, we'll just have to wait and see."

At a little before eleven, Sin and Sophie got back in the Lexus and returned to the Mountain Star. It was a silent ride. At the cottage, Myra was waiting for them.

"Where on God's earth have you been?"

Sin explained briefly about Jake.

Myra shook her head in sympathy for the poor fellow, then insisted they sit down and have a bite to eat. "And after that, Sophie B., you'd better get going on those rooms."

Sin stopped in the act of pouring himself a cup of coffee. "I thought you said you'd hired someone to replace that maid who quit."

"Sure she did," Myra scoffed. "Bethy's her name. She's got a baby on the way and she's always calling in sick."

Sophie sank to the table. "I realize I have to talk with her." She waited for Sin to start in on her.

But he only carried the cup he'd filled over to the table and set it down before her. "Have some coffee."

She looked up at him in sheer gratitude—for what he hadn't said. "Thank you."

"And you," Myra said sternly.

Sin glanced her way. "Me?"

"Yes, you. Some man called about insulation. He's coming at two."

As soon as she'd eaten, Sophie got right to work cleaning rooms. At one, Myra called her down to the kitchen and gestured at the phone. "It's Bethy."

Sophie picked it up reluctantly—only to learn that Bethy had decided to move to Fresno, where she could live with another sister and work in a florist's shop.

"I'm so sorry to let you down like this," Bethy said, sounding much more contrite than she ever had all the times she'd called in sick.

Sophie smiled at the phone in pure relief and promised Bethy that she'd manage somehow.

Myra was frowning as Sophie hung up. "What now?"

"Bethy's moving to Fresno to work in her other sister's flower shop."

One of Myra's red eyebrows inched toward her hairline. "That means we have a chance to hire someone who'll actually do the job."

"Exactly."

"No sad cases this time," Myra bargained. "Promise me. Someone who'll show up on time and stay till the work's done."

Sophie raised her right hand, palm out. "I do solemnly swear."

Myra harrumphed. "I'll believe it when I see it."

* * *

Sophie finished the rooms at a little after two. By then, Sin was busy with the insulation specialist. Sophie wandered downstairs and out the back door. She waved at Caleb, who was riding the old tractor mower across the broad lawn.

At the guest house, she showered and changed into one of her favorite dresses—the one she'd been wearing the first night she met Sin. She went back outside next and chose three red roses from the bush just beyond her bedroom window. She carried them back to the cottage, found a small crystal vase in the cupboard, and took the bouquet up the back stairs to Sin's room.

It looked lovely on the small stand by the bed. Sophie set it down and turned it, so the velvety red blooms were facing out.

"My mother loved roses." His voice came from the doorway behind her.

She turned to him, a smile trembling across her mouth. "I hope you do, too."

He didn't even glance at them. His eyes were all for her. "They're beautiful. Thank you." Then he stepped beyond the threshold and closed the door. That brooding gaze took a slow tour of her, from her head to her toes.

He said, "Your slip is showing."

She smoothed her skirt, drew her shoulders back. "It's not a slip."

"I know. It's a *petticoat*."

She felt as if she might cry. "You…remember."

"I do."

Turning away just a little, she swiped at her eyes. "Is the insulation man gone?"

He closed the distance between them, guided her chin around. "He's gone."

She moved in a fraction closer, lifted her mouth. "Will you...kiss me, please?"

Light as a rose petal, his lips brushed over hers.

"You were wonderful with poor Jake."

He kissed her again, another soft breath of a kiss. "Do you think you could learn to trust me, after all?"

She smiled against his mouth. "I don't have to learn that. I do trust you. Now."

His strong arms encircled her. "Shall I show you my estimates?"

She snuggled against him. "We'll get around to that."

"I'll try not to push too fast."

She sighed. "And some things I just don't want to change."

"That's fair. We'll work on compromise."

"Right along with sharing."

"Sounds good to me."

Cradled close against his heart, she looked up at him. "I love you. And I know now that you love me."

"Reading my mind again?"

"Am I wrong?"

"No, Ms. Sophie B. Jones. You are very, very right."

Epilogue

The next night, Oggie Jones appeared at the Mountain Star Theater.

One look at Sophie's face and he knew. "I guess I don't have to ask how things worked out with you and your man."

Before he left, he invited both of them to his eighty-first birthday party.

"We'll come," Sophie promised. "If you'll come to our wedding and give me away."

"You got yourselves a deal," the old man declared.

Three weeks later, on October ninth, Sin and Sophie attended Oggie's party at the Hole in the Wall Saloon. More than one toast was raised to the bride- and groom-to-be.

Sophie married Sin the following Saturday, the eleventh of October, in the Mountain Star Theater. A number of Joneses were there, including little Anthea, who somehow managed to wander off during the ceremony. A frantic search ensued. Jake, Caleb's new assistant, found the child at last—in the stable, unharmed, sitting on the stool beside Black Angel's stall.

Once everyone had stopped fussing over Anthea, Oggie admired the horse. Sin explained how he'd bought her for a song from a woman who'd decided owning a spirited horse wasn't for her.

The party in the cottage went on all night.

Oggie was the last guest to leave. When Sin and Sophie walked him out to his Cadillac, the sun had just raised its blinding face above the rim of the mountains to the east.

"Drive carefully," Sophie admonished him.

"I will. All the way to L.A."

Sophie and Sin exchanged a look. "What's in L.A.?" they asked in unison.

"A nephew," the old man replied. "A nephew I haven't even met yet."

Sophie frowned. "Is he expecting you?"

Oggie pulled a cigar from his pocket. "Hell, gal." He peeled off the wrapper and bit off the end. "You oughta know by now that nobody's ever expectin' old Oggie Jones."

* * * * *